"**W**HAT am I to call you now?" He meant it as a joke. "Still my Lady Abbess?"

She sipped her wine. Her mouth formed the kissing shape. "I am still the Abbess of Garnheim," she said coldly. "I do not expect my horse to call me Sweet just because I have ridden him."

Johan sat up. His voice was tight with anger. "I will not call you 'my lady.' Do you understand?"

"You are a peasant," she murmured. "I can have you whipped."

His shirt was on the floor, and he bent to pick it up.

"Surely you are not leaving, bellfounder." She was mocking him. "Come, I'll put the lamp out and you can pretend I'm someone you are not angry with."

"I need not pretend."

She shrugged. "Then I will pretend *you* are somebody else. Like last time."

He struck her across her face, pleased to see that the blow frightened her.

Their eyes met. She said, "I can have you killed."

"Well, lady," Johan said evenly, "you can have me beaten and killed. But you cannot have anybody else make your cannons for you."

THE
FATHER
OF
FIRES

Kenneth M. Cameron

FAWCETT POPULAR LIBRARY • NEW YORK

THE FATHER OF FIRES

Published by Fawcett Popular Library, a unit of CBS Publications, the Consumer Publishing Division of CBS Inc.

ISBN: 0-445-04640-6

Printed in the United States of America

First Fawcett Popular Library printing: March 1981

10   9   8   7   6   5   4   3   2   1

For my brother

CHAPTER ONE

THE GREAT BELL of Mouers trembled.

The voices of the crowd in the square below rose to the tower, and the bell trembled in sympathy; when the crowd sighed or shouted, the confusion of tones was a smothering blanket and the bell was still, but when one man spoke, his voice, tuned as if by intent to the bell's, made it shiver in accord with him, and, like an animal poised to spring and quivering in its eagerness, it vibrated.

The bell was made of bronze. It had been cast seven years before for the great church of Mouers, the masterpiece of the renowned Johan of Mouers, whose voice, rising now from the square, caused the bell to tremble. Around its rim were the words that Johan of Mouers had formed in wax and covered with clay and cast into the great instrument:

Man is the bell. God is the tongue that makes him sound.

When Johan of Mouers lifted his head he could see its lip like a blue-green arc in a dawning sky; when he lifted his head, although his conscious mind was fixed on his task, he knew the bell was there and he knew its magnificence; knew, too, those words on its wheel-sized mouth:

Man is the bell. God is the tongue that makes him sound.

Johan threw his head back. His right hand was raised and he could see the foot-long blade in it. He had forged the knife, made it especially for this day. A big man, big as the sergeant of the Emperor's men-at-arms, who gaped from the wall of their little garrison by the chapter close, he stood straight, with his hand raised, and the crowd around him stood silent, intent, watching him and watching the glittering knife.

There was a wooden block in front of him, carved from an

oak bole and painted to look like rock. Stretched across the block was his son.

The boy watched the knife. His father's big left hand rested on his chest with a weight that made breathing hard, the weight proof of his father's fierce concentration.

Johan spoke. Unseen, the bell trembled.

> "Almighty God, I am obedient,
> And know myself thy instrument.
> My son with knife I now will kill
> As Thee has asked; it is Thy will.
> Even as myself I love the boy,
> Of my life both jewel and joy
> Is he, and host of happiness.
> Father his son to slay is wickedness,
> Unless to serve Thee be his aim
> And sacrifice to make, in Jesu's name.
> Sorrow and sadness will be mine
> While I remain with humankind,
> Until, if I Thy vassal yet remain
> And come to Thee from Death's domain
> Joy will I know to see Thy face.
> My son I give to gain man grace.
> See, Lord! I hear thy dread intent;
> I hear, and am obedient!"

His fingers tightened on the knife. A woman in the crowd sucked in her breath in horror. He straightened, seemed to grow taller still, as if to gain height from which to plunge the blade with greater force.

Then, from a wagon in the square, on which was a painted canvas castle with a painted wood rainbow arching over it, stepped a man in white robes. A treaded plank led from the wagon down to the street, and he started down it.

"Stay thy hand, Abraham!" he cried. Pleased, relieved, the crowd shifted its weight; clothes rustled, voices whispered. "I am an angel, sent by God!" He paused, two feet above the paving.

> "He sees thy act, and He is good.
> No son he takes, but beast instead
> And lifts his other edict dread,
> The will accepting for the act.
> Isaac thy son will live! For pact,

> Around thee seek and find a sheep
> And with its life thy promise keep."

Johan of Mouers stepped to a painted tree six feet away and untied the ewe that was tethered to it, a young sheep that had grazed over the common lands and nibbled the Abbey grass. Docile and obedient, it followed him. His son scrambled down from the painted block, and the sheep, struggling a little now, was laid on it.

The angel turned to the crowd.

> "See what God asks, these good things three:
> Obedience, faith, and humility.
> Learn then from this, sacrifice to make,
> And beg forgiveness for *His* Son's sake
> Who died to save us these years gone,
> When God gave up *His* loved Son!"

The sheep bleated.

Johan spoke, his voice now a clarion that echoed from the buildings.

> "I thank thee, Lord, my son to spare!
> Take then this life, and find it fair!"

The blade flashed in a downward curve, and blood spurted from the severed artery, flowing over the woolly coat that had been washed that morning for this moment, welling over Johan's left hand and down the painted block. There was a butcher's in the next street where the same thing could be seen every day; there was hardly a woman in the crowd who did not kill chickens with a twist of the neck or gut fish or kill geese with her own hands. Nobody flinched; nobody gasped. They applauded and sighed with relief.

Johan raised the animal by the hind legs. Blood ran down its muzzle and puddled on the paving.

"You have done well," the angel said, "and God is pleased."

And the great bell of Mouers, moved now by the thick ropes, swayed to one side and then to the other, then back, and the great tongue struck the curved bronze and the bell spoke, louder in the square than any human voice, drowning all the others that rose in cheers.

Man is the bell. God is the tongue that makes him sound.

Johan shrugged himself out of the coarse robe in a tent behind the Abbey. The cloth was wet across his back, and he shivered, aware suddenly of his own sweat and the bitter smell of the costume. Toweling himself with the robe, he wiped the shining gloss from the hard muscles of his shoulders and arms and from the first thin layer of fat that was building over his belly. A scar like the mark of a paw puckered his right breast, the print of a splash of molten bronze from a casting twelve years before, and he touched it gently, because it still was oddly sensitive, like a new burn. Flour dusted out from his beard under his flailing fingers and made a cloud around his face, and some of it went up his nose; he sneezed and turned his head aside, batting at the dust with his right hand while one thick finger of his left pressed under his nose to stop another sneeze. Looking up, finger still to nose, he saw his son standing in the tent opening. The boy was hot and happy, breathing hard from running to show off his own costume to his friends. He ran forward and threw himself on his father, laughing at the sneeze that came then; Johan hugged him and sneezed once more.

"Did I do good?"

"Very good." He hugged the boy. "I'm proud of you."

"I wasn't afraid of the knife."

"Good. I'm glad."

"I knew you wouldn't stab me really." He hung to Johan's neck, his feet off the ground. "A father wouldn't hurt his son."

"Our Father gave His son up to be killed."

"I know! I mean—a father like you." The boy wriggled loose and pulled his robe over his head. His torso was already strongly muscled in a short, chunky body, on which soft hairs lay like new grass. He balled the robe and drew back to throw it at the corner of the tent.

"Hang it up!" his father bellowed. "St. Eloi's Guild has to pay for it, boy."

The child sighed and shook out the robe. "Would Abraham really have killed Isaac?"

"Of course. God told him to. It was part of God's order. It would have been good if He had let it happen."

"But He didn't, because it would be wrong for Abraham to kill his own son. Wouldn't it?"

Johan spoke slowly, but his impatience showed. They had

10

been through the argument before. "It would have been wrong, except that God told him to do it. God spoke to Abraham. In those days, God spoke to men."

"But he doesn't speak to men any more, I know!" The boy was wriggling into his clothes; combing back his long hair with his fingers, he said, "Can I go?"

"Yes, until mass."

"My mother said she was afraid I would get lost in the crowd."

"Go along; it's all right. Until mass!" Johan caught his son's shoulder. "You are to be in the *house* when the mass is sung, do you hear me? Are you listening to me?"

"Yes, I *am*."

Johan nodded. The boy darted away. He dusted more flour from his beard and mopped his damp, chilled chest again. His back was turned to the tent opening when he heard the fabric stir, and he looked over his shoulder and saw Brother Michael there, the monk's left hand still on the tent to hold the flap open.

"Brother?"

He was a Dominican of the Abbey, one of the few left since the plague years. He looked like an old man, tired from too many years of trying to do the work of the ones who had died. The Abbey was crumbling to ruin around him and the three others who survived; he was crumbling, too. He was forty but he looked far older; his pale skin sagged, the bone of his big nose pushing against the flesh as if it were hurrying to rid itself of it. Still, his eyes were lively, sometimes almost manic, and his voice had energy and enthusiasm still. "Johan," he said happily, "you were wonderful! I believed you were Father Abraham."

Johan shrugged, pleased. "I only spoke your words. I did the way you told me."

Brother Michael came into the tent. "You were wonderful," he murmured, his smile fixed on some point between them. He touched the discarded costume as if trying to buy time; glancing over his shoulder at Johan, he said nervously, "My Lord Bishop wants to see you."

"Me?" He pulled a shirt over his head. "What about?" The Bishop was a distant, almost an unreal, figure, hardly less awesome than the Emperor himself, who had never been in Mouers and who existed entirely in the laws he made and the symbols on his soldiers' colors and the allegiance he attracted.

11

"I don't know. Reverend Father sent me to find you. He said the Bishop wants to see you." Michael seemed as puzzled as Johan. "I think the Lady Abbess of Garnheim is there, too." He sounded as astonished as if he had been talking of the Pope.

"Well, I ain't afraid of *her*." Johan guffawed. "Is it about the play? I don't want to be pointed at like a prize pig in front of a lot of people."

But Michael might as well not have heard him. "And one of the Franciscans. They're all at dinner."

Johan pulled up the wedge of cloth over his groin and retied it, then gathered the skirts of his shirt and belted them so that the upper part billowed out over his hips and belly. Speaking Michael's words as Abraham, he had been oblivious of the crowd, but as he had paced out of the square he had seen a group on the balcony of the old Dean of Chapter's House, hardly daring to look straight at them because one, he knew, was the Bishop. Yet he remembered that there had been a Franciscan there, and there had been at least one of the Garnheim nuns and another woman, perhaps the notorious Abbess herself.

"I brought clothes for the mass. They'll be good enough, yes?"

Michael nodded.

Johan pulled the laces tight on his doublet and tied a bow in the strings. "I don't really expect trouble at the mass, do you? I wore good clothes. I thought I should be an example. Of not seeming to expect trouble, I mean." He looked at Michael's tired old face. The monk's antic eyes flicked over him, nervous and afraid.

Johan suddenly yanked down the codpiece he had just tied up. "I've got to piss." He walked around behind the tent and urinated; lacing up, he saw two women standing in the little alley that led from the square. They had discreetly turned their backs. One showed big, handsome buttocks under a clinging fabric, and he kept looking at her, slowly lacing up the codpiece again. When she looked around, as he hoped she would, he was still pulling it tight, and he slowly tied the strings as he smiled at her. When he had quite finished, his eyes still on hers, he walked toward her, aware of the aggressive bulge under the tight cloth.

"Did you like what I did?" he said. He leaned his left hand on the shadowed wall of the great church, and his arm arched above the two girls like a doorway.

They looked at each other and giggled, and the one with the big buttocks said, "Oh!" and covered her mouth and nose and giggled some more, bent forward toward him.

"Did you like the play, I meant."

"Oh! It was fair marvelous, yes, we was took so with it!"

"Come to the mass, have you?"

"Oh, coom t'watch. Coom t'see, y'know, what may happen, y'know."

"Oh? What may happen?"

"Oh, why—!" She looked at her girlfriend and giggled again, her palm over her nose as if she were trying to force the end of her nose up, though it was upturned too much already. *Silly bitch,* he thought, but he went on smiling at her. She had a wide peasant face and was no older than eighteen, and he knew how she could be managed. "Oh, they do say, trouble may coom at yon mass. They do say that."

"There'll be no trouble," he said. "And if there is, you look out for me. Maybe you and your friend would like something to eat after the mass; would you like that?"

They started to giggle again. He would have to get rid of the girlfriend; well, that could be managed.

There was a sound behind him, and Brother Michael was standing at the other end of the little alley. "I think Reverend Father meant you to come to the Bishop now, Johan."

"After the mass," he murmured to the girl, and, taking one of the strings which laced her bodice tight to flatten her breasts, he gave it a little tug. He left them giggling and went back to the tent, where he thrust his massive arms into the sleeves of a knee-length coat and then mashed a soft hat on his wiry hair.

"I pray there will be no trouble today," Michael said.

"There will be no trouble."

They crossed the sheep-cropped grass behind the church and passed along between its wall and the darker stone of the defunct chapter house, now abandoned to all but the pigeons. Beyond, the paved square opened, the old Dean of Chapter's house close against the church on the east side. There was only a nominal Dean of the Chapter now, a priest of the Bishop's household who balanced that title on the same pile with a half-dozen others and who served in the post on only those rare occasions when there was a visitation to Mouers; for the rest of the time, often for as long as three years, the house was closed and silent. Indeed, all the buildings around the church, except for the crumbling Abbey itself, were dark at night and it was not safe to walk there.

Two of the Emperor's soldiers were standing a ceremonial guard. They let the bellfounder and the Dominican pass through into the house, where they were made to wait in a musty-smelling anteroom whose meager furniture had been brought in the Bishop's train of mules. The rest of the house, except for the Bishop's bedroom and such few rooms as were needed for his servants, would be empty. Johan looked around him with dismay; his own house was a palace by comparison, the furniture the best that could be made, one of his carpets imported all the way from Trebizond, he had been told when he had bought it, his two best platters gold and his salt dish enameled silver. Brother Michael smiled sadly. He could remember when there had been six priests and the Dean living in that house.

"My Lord Bishop will see Johan the Bellfounder." The young priest did not wait for them; aristocratic, bored, he assumed they would know enough to follow. Two turnings brought them to a heavy door, where the priest knocked and then went in without waiting for answer. Johan and Brother Michael followed.

A table had been set up the long way of the room, beyond whose western end was the balcony from which the Bishop's party had watched the play. The glass in the windows, small-paned, rippled, faintly lavender and green, changed the square outside to a vision he had never seen; only here and there where the glass was broken could he see familiar sunlight and stone. This, then, was the Bishop's idea of Mouers, this tinted, uneven picture, seen once in every year or two or three.

"Leave us, Brother Michael." The Abbot looked kindly at Michael as he spoke. They were, Johan knew, old friends—novices together at Hamburg once. Brother Michael went out, and Johan felt instantly naked, stripped of comfort and support among these powerful strangers. He had lived all his life in Mouers, had never been more than forty miles away from it, and he was acutely aware of his status.

Four people sat at the long table. He knew Brother Nikolas, the Dominican Abbot; he recognized the Franciscan next to him as one who had lived in the town for a year and who preached poverty and railed against the abuses of the church, even of the Pope himself. His holiness offended Johan

14

because the man brandished it like a weapon. Too, he smelled.

At the end of the table to his right was the Abbess of Garnheim. Scandalous and handsome, a woman whose dress barely fell within the most liberal idea of convent garb, she had distant connections to the Emperor's family and ruled her convent as if it were a duchy. There were jewels on her shoulders and her hands—jewels, many said, that came from the dowries of her novices—and there had been at least one man in her bed, because she had been married and widowed before she had come to Garnheim. She met his eyes coolly. *She would have been a good-looking female*, he thought, *but too skinny for me.*

At the end of the table opposite her, with the rippled window behind him, was Karl Sigismund of Muhldorf, Bishop of Muhldorf and Mouers, thirty years old, hard-faced, glowering. He looked to Johan like a soldier, and there was a strong suggestion of the soldier in the few square inches of chain mail that showed under his open robe.

The Bishop, too, had dressed for the mass.

Johan dropped to his knees and reached forward to kiss his ring. Surprised, the Bishop flinched; then, glancing around the table and meeting the Abbess's tolerant grin, he thrust the hand forward and let the bellfounder brush his knuckles with his lips. Johan pushed himself up and bowed to the others, although he had doubts about the Franciscan, whose well-advertised humility should not have deserved his bow.

"I am Johan the Bellfounder. I was sent for." His eyes moved from the Bishop to the Abbess. If they heard pride in his voice, and a certain dryness in the words "sent for," they made no response.

The Abbess was toying with the silver-handled knife she had brought to eat with. The Bishop was flung back and to one side in his chair so that he sprawled at an angle to the table, the window light faintly coloring the right side of his face and touching an old scar that ran from his hairline down to his cheekbone. He was studying Johan, his head leaning on his left hand while the right played with the cords of his shirt, which just showed above his armor.

"Master Bellfounder," he said evenly, "what do you know about cannons?"

Johan looked at the Dominican monk as the one person in the room he knew and trusted a little, but he was looking down at the table and playing with some crumbs there. Johan was conscious of the pressure of the table on his thighs and of the bulging codpiece above it.

"Cannons, my lord?"

"Aye, cannons—great guns. You know what cannons are?"

Johan leaned forward a little, his fingertips on the table, so that his coat fell forward and masked, he hoped, his groin. "I have heard of them, my lord."

The Bishop nodded. His interest seemed now to have shifted to his own knife, with which he was breaking up a bread crust. He had a harsh voice that grated on the ear; it, too, belonged to a soldier.

"What do you know of *making* great guns, bellfounder?"

"Nothing, my lord. Nothing at all."

"It cannot be so different from founding bells, I think. Can it be so different?"

"I cannot say, my lord."

"But it cannot be *so* different!" The Bishop leaned forward, gesturing with the knife as if he were scolding Johan. "What is your great gun but a long bell with a hole for the *touche,* eh?"

Johan disliked subjects he did not understand. He disliked most of all speculation, which he thought frivolous and effeminate. "I suppose there must be a difference," he said carefully. "I have heard the soldiers talk of great guns made hooped for more strength, not just cast like a—"

"Aye, hooped! Hooped or not hooped, are they so different?" His harsh voice rose sharply and he flung the knife on the table. It rang and bounced and skidded halfway along, coming to rest near Johan's hands.

The Abbess stirred. "My Lord Bishop is a famous diplomatist," she said. When she spoke, sometimes she sucked in her cheeks like somebody sucking on a plum, the expression making her seem skeptical and wry.

"I do not like quibbles!" the Bishop shouted.

"The bellfounder is not quibbling, if I hear him right; he is giving you such experience of his craft as he has, I think. Are you not, bellfounder?" Her eyes turned to his, intelligent, superior, amused.

"I don't know what I'm doing, lady. I don't know what is being asked of me here." He looked back at the Bishop, who was massaging his forehead and exhaling fiercely like a man much put upon. "I would like to know what is being asked of me," he said.

"My Lord Bishop," the Dominican Abbot explained patiently, "is curious to know, Johan, if *you* could make great guns."

Johan was already a man of standing in Mouers—head of the Guild of St. Eloi, the next mayor of the city if he had his way. He had learned to act and speak slowly, as befitted a man of stature, neither saying servilely what was expected of him nor jumping rashly at possibilities. "Then I must ask my Lord Bishop," he said, "if he is asking me if I would make cannons, or only if I could make them."

The Bishop swung forward. "Well, well, yes, then—would, could, bellfounder, have it as you will! Would you, could you, make great guns?"

Johan touched the tips of his fingers to the table, lifted them, touched them again as if he were playing some instrument there. After some seconds, he said, "Your little tubes, yes, I think I could make those. Your little hooped firepots such as the soldiers talk of, yes, I think I could make those. But your great guns, my lord, that are said to be as long as a man is tall and round as a horse's head—my lord, they would take as much metal as a bell royal."

"And?"

"And the expense, my lord! One such gun would cost his lordship..." He began to calculate, but the Bishop interrupted.

"But could you *do* it?"

"In six months, perhaps."

"What in the name of all the saints would you need six months for?"

Johan, secure now, began to bend down a finger for each item he mentioned, touching that finger with the index finger of his right hand. "For learning of cannons, at least a month, perhaps a year; for buying of that quantity of metal and mixing it, another month; for making a mold of sufficient size, and building a special hearth and casting pit, at least a month; for—"

The Bishop groaned.

"My lord?"

"Too long." The Abbess had spoken. When he looked at her, he was surprised to see that she was sucking on a real dried fruit. She looked at him, her teeth closed over it and her cheeks sucked in, bit and pulled the fruit away and spat something on the floor. "We have but four months, bellfounder."

"I do not understand."

"In four months, the Ritter Josef Redhand will march on Garnheim and on Mouers. He has claimed them as his own already." Before he could protest, she said, "Ten days ago." She pushed out her lips as if for a kiss and smiled. "The same day that the Emperor appointed his own Pope."

"*Elected* his own Pope," the Franciscan rasped.

"If it was an election, then horse turds are sugar buns," she said sweetly.

"It was a legal and a defensible act," the Franciscan whined. His humility was overcome by his conviction. "The Emperor properly saw fit—"

"—to appoint a Franciscan as his Pope, I *know*," she drawled. The last word was drawn out as her lips made the kissing shape. "I am sure that his action will be found eminently legal and defensible by those who already agree with him, but alas, friar, we *already* have a Pope at Avignon, who, though he be a dotard and fool, is nonetheless in the saddle and well astride! It is at the least an inconvenience, you will agree, that the world must live with *two* Popes!"

"When one was too many," the Bishop growled.

"My lord!" the Abbot murmured, glancing at Johan.

The Bishop clutched the edge of the table. "It is not essential to the church to have any head but Jesus Christ!"

The Franciscan nodded vigorously. "So says the Englishman William of Occam, a friar of St. Francis." He held up a finger. "Hear what our beloved Cesena, General of the Order of St. Francis, has said: 'The body of the Church in Council is superior to any Pope, for he can be fallible and tumble into error.'"

The Dominican straightened. "Our own Jean Quidort of *my* order, he says, in his *De potestate regia*, he says that the Council rules and is superior to any Pope, king or—your pardon, my lord—bishop!"

The Abbess stared into space. "This gets us nowhere," she sang softly.

The Franciscan hunched forward to glare around the Dominican's bent figure at her. "It is important that the people understand the theological basis of our acts. Marsilius of the University of Paris says—"

"Karl Sigismund, Bishop of Muhldorf and Mouers, says," and the Bishop's hand came down with a smack on the table, "that if he does not have cannons in four months he will lose his bishopric to an invading hothead!" He looked at Johan, his voice almost appealing now. "The Pope—I mean the old Pope at Avignon—has released the Emperor's vassals from their oaths, so that this Ritter sees fit to lay claim to lands that previously were the Emperor's."

"The free city of Mouers does not *belong* to the Emperor," Johan said slowly. "We are *allied* with him."

"Allied, belong, what difference will it make if the city is invaded? The claim is sanctioned by the Pope—the old fool is even preaching a crusade against us! The Emperor is in Rome, will *be* in Rome for a year at least, meddling in politics and trying to help the helpless Visconti; the Emperor will be busy with his new toy Pope, and we will be left to defend our own poor selves. Now do you understand, bellfounder?"

Johan flexed his fingers on the tabletop. "Does this mean, my lord, that the new Pope will lift the ban of excommunication we have all suffered under?"

The Bishop leaned back and sighed heavily. His eyes rolled as if in supplication. "The ban of excommunication is a legal quibble. It was put upon us because the Pope—the old Pope, I mean, *damn* these two Popes!—would not recognize the Emperor. In my eyes—in the eyes of many lawyers of the church—there has never been a valid excommunication. Is that clear?"

"But, my lord—"

The Bishop struck the table, and the knife that he had thrown jumped and rang. "Why do you think I am saying mass today? Does an excommunicated bishop say mass for excommunicated communicants?"

"Then why is my Lord Bishop wearing mail?" the Abbess said drily.

"Because there may be trouble from some zealot! That is a secular matter!"

"And therefore," she said, "the bellfounder's concern is understandable. These common people do not understand quibbles over law, my lord. They understand obedience; they want—"

The two friars and the Abbess began to speak at the same time. They reminded Johan of nothing so much as a chapman haggling over a price. The Bishop looked at the three of them with an expression of outrage, as if, for all his own burst of temper, it was unthinkable that they should dare to get angry. Johan suddenly understood that it was this bickering, which had been going on before he had arrived, that had aroused the Bishop, and not his own caution. He studied the

19

man now and saw his fatigue and his concern, and he felt sympathy for him. Karl Sigismund, it was said, was the son of a cordwainer, a commoner without the perquisites of the wellborn. He had fought his way up through the church with brains and audacity, and it was clear that he retained the toughness and the impatience with hair-splitting of the cordwainer's boy.

"My Lord Bishop!" Johan said loudly in a lull in the argument. The Abbess looked up. The Bishop turned to stare at him, ready to be enraged.

"My Lord Bishop," Johan said more quietly, "these arguments mean nothing to me. The Abbess is right; common, free men do not waste their time with them. We don't care which quibble will justify one Pope against the other. We care for God and for the sacraments of God's church, which we've been denied since the Pope at Avignon said we were excommunicated.

"For three years, we've lived with some of us believing that our priests were proper priests and some of us believing that they were not priests and that they mocked the sacraments. Some people in Mouers have not made confession in three years; some people have buried their wives and their fathers without last rites because the priests were fakes, they said. Even in my own house..." With his head lowered, he had a sullen, bullish look that threatened them. "My daughter won't marry, she says, until a proper priest from Rome marries her; she doesn't want to be a whore, she says. Meanwhile, she's getting older, and she cries and whines.

"Now you come to Mouers to say the mass. You come in armor. You come to ordain three more priests for us. Well, I will do what I can for you—I will go to mass, though there may be trouble; I will try to make cannon, though I do not know how; I will fight against this Ritter who comes on crusade against us, though the Pope has egged him on to it. But you must get this new Pope to lift the ban of excommunication from us! Call it a quibble, but it is breaking people's hearts! Do that for us, and I will fight for you."

The Bishop's chair scraped back. Standing, he was six inches shorter than the bellfounder but almost as broad across the shoulders, his arms long and grotesque. Despite their difference in height, he put one arm over Johan's shoulder and grinned down at the others. "Go on with your debate," he said. "Win or lose, we will need arguments to justify ourselves with." He moved a little, and Johan could hear the links of mail grate against each other.

The Abbess raised her head jerkily until it was tilted back and she was looking down her equine nose at them. "May we come to practicalities, my lord?"

"Such as what, Lady Abbess?"

She sucked in her cheeks again. "Such as who will pay, my lord." The vowel was long and drawling—*p-a-a-a-y.* "I mean, who will pay for the quantities of metals and the rest? Who will make gunpowder? Who will hire men to fight? War is not fought for free, even by this free city of free men."

"If we pray to Almighty God—" the Dominican began.

The Abbess silenced him with a snort. "I will have forty virgins of all ages praying night and morning, friar; I do not, however, expect a shower of bronze cannon each midday as a result. Well, who will pay?"

The Bishop dropped his hand from Johan's shoulder and stalked to the window. "You know what my treasury is after two years of being cut off from the church."

"You, friar?" Her voice was light as she looked at the Franciscan. "Or you?" The Dominican looked down at the table. When neither spoke, she laced her fingers together and sat very straight and addressed the Bishop's chair as if he still sat in it. "The Abbess of Garnheim will guarantee ten guns and will put three hundred peasants into the field." Something turned over in Johan's chest, an excitement like the first glimmer of lust. He was thinking of the money that the making of ten great guns might bring. But the Abbess had not finished. "If—!" she said. She looked at them. "*If* the Abbey of Garnheim is defended."

The Bishop looked through the colored windows at the square, where people were moving, broken into meaningless shapes of light and dark on the rippled glass. "The Abbey of Garnheim stands by itself in open fields," he said. "Bring your nuns into Mouers."

"I will not."

"Garnheim is not defensible."

"Then make it so. That is what cannons are for. I will not abandon it, nor will my ladies."

"Your ladies will abandon it fast enough if a hundred of the Ritter's men-at-arms rampage through the Abbey with their great cods at the ready!"

"On the contrary, my lord, the very sight would cause

21

them all to fall on their backs." She smiled sweetly. "To study Heaven, I mean."

The Dominican's breath hissed in.

"Oh, come, brother; my ladies have renounced the world, but they are no more immune to temptation than you or my Lord Bishop—or me, for that matter. I mean to keep them as separate from the world's lures as I can, and to that end I will not bring them into Mouers." She smiled at Johan. "I risk my own soul by coming here as it is."

"Your self-sacrifice is famous in the neighborhood," the Bishop said sourly.

"As is your wealth and generosity, my lord."

"I was not born to my office like some, that's true!"

The Dominican cleared his throat. "We were all born to high office, in His sight."

The Abbess looked at him with curdling distaste. "You *must* tell me when next you mean to preach, brother," she said, "and I will send some hundred or so of my peasants to listen." Her eyes came again to Johan's. "Speak for me, bellfounder; tell them they will need money from me."

"It is true, my lord. The metal for the cannons, alone, will cost a great deal."

"The Ritter has sworn to march on Corpus Christi Day. Can you make these cannons by then—four months?"

"With God's help, I will."

The Bishop shrugged. "Well, then that is what I will say, too, lady—With God's help, I will defend Garnheim, if that is the price for saving my office. Will you hear me swear it, or will you have it written?"

"Oh, swearing will do, my lord." She began to pluck brooches from her dress and throw them on the table. "You have all heard him, so we will not trouble a scribbler." She skinned bracelets down her left arm and let them fall one by one on the pile of brooches. "These will pay to get you started, bellfounder. When you need more, come to Garnheim. As you are a man of business, we shall do business together." Her lips formed a kiss, and she smiled; her fingers touched the pile, moved over it, and took back one prized brooch and pinned it between her breasts. "I think it is time for mass, my lord."

22

CHAPTER TWO

THE BISHOP OF MUHLDORF and Mouers did not process to the church but went almost secretly, led by six armed men, and entered the sanctuary from the rear, with the same men moving up the side aisles to guard him. Johan, standing near the altar, kept his right hand under his coat to touch the knife there while he prayed there would not be trouble.

When the Bishop put his hands down to touch the first of the three priests he was to ordain—excommunicants made mock priests by an excommunicant bishop, some said—there was a cry from the back of the church that was taken up along the side chapels, and a knot of yelling women ran toward him through the crowd, shouting and pitching garbage that lofted above the communicants and fell on the choir screen and the steps. Johan and twenty other men ran forward; the women struggled and one threw a clay pitcher that smashed and spattered cow's blood down the choir stalls and over the Bishop's vestments.

"Murderer!" she screamed. "Antichrist!"

It seemed a mad thing for her to cry, for there had been no murders yet and the Bishop had preached Christ's message, but the woman screamed and stammered and was hysterical. Johan wrestled with another of them, shocked at the brutal hatred on her face.

"Be still, woman!" he whispered. "Shut up!"

Grasping her from behind with her wrists locked in one of his hands, he lifted her and carried her out with her weight on his chest and belly, her feet kicking uselessly in front of them, and on the steps outside he threw her down in disgust and stood over her.

"You're mad, you bitch!" he shouted. "What did you mean to do here, then?"

She spat at him and he struck her hard and she began to weep uncontrollably. She was a homely girl, worn and tired-

23

looking, her hands red and cracked from work. Blubbering, she tried to speak, but he understood only "Antichrist" again.

He sighed heavily and turned her over to one of the Bishop's guards. There was a crowd of forty or fifty across from the church, a few of them sullen, sympathetic to the women and defeated now; the others were greedy with curiosity. He saw the girl he had talked to in the alley among them, lips parted, jaw hanging stupidly.

"Peasant," he muttered, disgusted in his turn, and he went back into the church, and afterward hurried home without looking for her.

"What did they think they would do?" he said that afternoon to his wife. They were sitting in their garden near an arbor where dead apple leaves had gathered during the winter, crushed and sodden now. The earth was bare, but the sunshine had warmth in it at last. "What did they mean to do?" he said again.

"They fear for their immortal souls." Her hands flitted through the air like butterflies. Her face was sullen, like those of the defeated ones in the crowd.

"The Bishop is God's anointed priest."

"He is cast out. We are all cast out."

"Bah! That's politics! It's not good sense!"

"He is cast out; we all are cast out for our sins. Our sins are terrible in the eyes of Almighty God!" Her head shook from side to side; her eyes closed and tears ran down her cheeks. He wondered if the woman he had struck had a husband, too, who did not understand her, did not understand her fervor for sin. She seemed perversely triumphant in her sense of sinfulness, even glad to be cast out. Because he thought he might cheer her, he put his arm around her waist—his thoughts were on the girl in the alley then—and tried to pull her close. "Come, come, it ain't so bad as that."

Her body was dead, something hung up at the butcher's. "We are damned," she whispered.

"Oh, Katrin—" He tried to squeeze the soft flesh on her hip, and she was suddenly angry with him and hurried off into the gloom without a word. Johan groaned, spat and stood up, angry and ashamed in the dappled shade of his arbor. *She is like a sickness,* he thought, and was ashamed of the thought, but it was true; her vicious sense of sin had spread all through his house, making his daughter into a whining spinster, even making his young son too quiet, too guilty, for a child.

24

"You are too proud to know your sin," she had said to him once. But, in God's name, if you were human, what were you to do? He was proud—of his success, of his son, of his city that he had now agreed to try to save with cannons. *She is a sickness,* he thought again.

He had his son called and told a servant to fetch one of his horses, and with his son behind him he rode out of the walled city as far as the hill to the east, from which he could look on toward the Abbey of Garnheim, whose roof still caught the sunlight though the hill blocked it from the sand-colored walls; and he could look west, back at the city itself and its green farms, dappled now with the long shadows of afternoon. The city of Mouers was a miracle; he believed that. A hundred years before, there had been only swamp there, and dike by dike men had drained it and penned it in like a sluggish animal and turned the morass that had given the city its name into land that men could live on—free land, claimed by nobody, not even the Emperor. Here, then, was Mouers, with its ten thousand people, contained within its walls like a relic, owning its own farms in a green band around it and owing fealty to no one but God.

"It's a beautiful thing to look upon," he said to the boy. He did not understand; perhaps one day he would. One day when his mother did not spread guilt like a sickness and crazed women did not disrupt God's priest.

"Ride fast!" the boy shouted when they started back, and he galloped down to the East Gate with his son behind him, briefly delighted with the moment, loving his son and the city that made them both free.

On the Thursday after, he called a meeting of the masters of St. Eloi's Guild, goldsmiths and armorers and blacksmiths, all men who worked with metal and fire and shared his craft, and he picked their brains for what they knew of cannons. It was little enough, but they would find out more. Two, at least, had seen cannons used and could tell him something of their fearful thunder and of the stone shot that could batter down great walls, and nothing that they could tell him made him feel that he could *not* make guns. Other men had made them; what other men could do, so could he.

On Saturday, he was called to dinner at the Dean of Chapter's House, where the Bishop gave him sheets copied from a book that talked of guns, half of it sounding like romance, with fire-breathing dragons, but perhaps there would be some little information there, too. The Bishop rattled on, telling

25

him of this great siege and that, events he had heard or read about; and after an hour, Johan tired of the man's almost childish enthusiasm for huge cannon and tried to bring him a little down to earth.

"My Lord Bishop," he said quietly, "these are mighty guns you speak of, and wonders of the world, I am sure—great cannons of the army of Mahomet, and guns for hurling down the walls of Jerusalem. But we are going to protect Mouers, not lay siege to it; and we are committed to protect Garnheim, which means we must fight in open country against an army. With all respect, my lord, I do not see how a gun that is as big as Leviathan and hurls a shot that will topple a church tower is what we will need."

The Bishop drank from his cup, and a trickle of wine ran down next to his mouth; Johan thought of the blood the woman had thrown. Johan hesitated, unwilling to say more, and the Bishop drank and looked at him and finally said, "Do you think you know more of battles than I do, Bellfounder?"

"No, my lord."

"Do you think you cannot make great guns?"

"I think I can, but—"

"Then make them!" The Bishop banged his cup; he was a little drunk. "Make *something*! Make little firepots if that's all you can manage, but make *something*! I do not want to stand on some field with nothing between the Ritter and me but three hundred peasants from the Abbess's farms. The Ritter can call up fifty bowmen, they say, and six hundred men. An informant tells me he has a siege gun, but how big it is or how real it is..." He looked moodily into his empty cup. "I would like to *smash* him."

"There will be gunpowder?"

"Aha!" Laughing, his mood suddenly changed, the Bishop poured more wine for both of them. "Aha! Yes!" He tapped his nose, a jarring, peasant gesture. "There will be gunpowder." He looked around him, pretending that there might be spies or spooks or God knew what, and tapped his nose again and leaned far over the table and whispered, "My sorcerer is at work!" The Bishop guffawed. "My sorcerer is an old friend of yours. Brother Michael!"

Johan was frightened and tried not to show it. Talk of witchcraft and magic was not so funny in the best of times. "Brother Michael is not a sorcerer," he said, but it came out as a question.

"He is, he is! A man of science. He conjures; he tells me of spirits, of signs and potent marks to be drawn on the floor or the wall or I don't know what."

"What does Michael know of gunpowder?"

The Bishop's mood shifted again. He drank, and when the cup revealed his face again it was sullen. "He knows about as much of gunpowder as you know of cannons, I guess, bell-founder."

There was a disturbance in the great church again on Sunday, and in the little Church of the Holy Sepulcher down the hill, one of the newly ordained priests was struck in the head by a knife hilt, and two men held him against the altar while a third tried to stab him. He was saved by his parishioners, and there was a melee in the sanctuary.

"Nobody killed, thank God!" the Mayor said. Looking over the scene, he shook his head piously and clucked and clapped his hands softly together as if applauding silently. Outside, he said in a low voice to Johan, "Why don't they close this place? It ain't fit to keep sheep in."

"It was the first church." Johan looked over the Mayor's shoulder as three women with brooms and wooden water buckets went into the tiny structure to wash it. "It's the parish church of the fullers and weavers. Tear it down and you'd have a riot."

The two of them might have been planning a crime, they spoke so softly. "We must do something," the Mayor said. "People are angry. They're afraid. Mouers has always been a quiet town."

"We've got to get rid of the troublemakers. Drive them out before they can do more harm."

"How?" The Mayor sounded petulant when he was worried. "I don't know. I don't want to have all this worry. Four years ago, Karl Goldsmith was mayor, he said it was a year-long celebration. He sold the lead off the old town stable roof, and everybody treated it like a joke. He got fat, he was so happy being mayor. His wife got pregnant that year; she hadn't had a kid in thirteen years. Look at me—blasphemy, impieties, riots—I'll be lucky if I live out the year with my balls intact."

"You'll be all right. But act now. We've got to drive the troublemakers out before they get too strong."

The next week, he proposed an ordinance to the corporation, one to which the aldermen listened seriously because of who he was and who he would be in the town. After desultory debate, they voted the new rule in, and voted for it again the next week so that it became law:

Interruption of service in any church of Mouers presided over by any priest ordained or appointed by our loved Karl Sigismund, or remarks about our loved Bishop or his priests or his churches, or meetings together to discuss interruption of such services or to make remarks about our Bishop or his priests, or any other such impious and blasphemous acts, will be punishable by a fine of fifty kraters or a whipping of ten strokes with the good lash, or both.

And,

All guilds and companies and brotherhoods now chartered in this city will march to the great church two Sundays hence, and will confess and take Christ's body from our loved Bishop or his priests, and will reconsecrate their banners and their charters and be blessed by the Bishop and his priests; and anybody who will not march or who will not take the Eucharist or who is sick and says he cannot march or take the Eucharist or who meets with any other persons to protest the march of the taking of the Eucharist, will be fined three shillings for each offense, and one shilling for every day for each offense thereafter that he does not present himself before the Corporation and give explanation for his crimes.

And,

Every guild and company and brotherhood that is chartered in this city will present to the Corporation the list of its members and the name of its chaplain, and said chaplain must be a priest ordained or appointed by our loved Bishop, Karl Sigismund, lest such guild or company or brotherhood be stripped of its charter and declared null.

"I see only more trouble," the Mayor said when the corporation adjourned after midnight.

"Trouble burns trouble," Johan said. "Give a few of them a good whipping, they'll stop. A few fines will drive out the dissenters." They stood in the street outside the Corporation Hall; their breath went up in the clear March night like smoke.

28

"How far do you think it will go, Johan?"

"God only knows."

"I pray every night there will not be more trouble."

Johan said nothing to that. He knew there would be more trouble.

The Mayor sighed, touched Johan's shoulder. "These are terrible times." He called to his servants and disappeared around a corner, the light from their torches falling on a high, damp wall long after they were gone.

Brother Michael's laboratory was a tower room in the Abbey on the side away from the great church, with one window that looked out over the low roofs that huddled around it like newborn goslings striving to get under their mother's wings for the night; beyond the houses, it looked over the river and the long rectangles of the Mouers farms. If one leaned out a little, he could just see, over the hilltop where Johan had ridden with his son, the tawny stone and the gray roofs of the convent of Garnheim.

To Johan, the long-abandoned laboratory was like some secret vice discovered in an old friend. It did not matter to him that Brother Michael professed to be pursuing God's knowledge and not the Devil's; the laboratory was an obscenity. The Brother Michael who labored there was not the weary and innocent man who had written the play of Abraham, but a participant in a mystery that gibbered in its own language and scribbled in its own hieroglyphics. When Michael chose to, he would let Johan a half-step into this exotic world, open its door a crack, but never more than that. A smugness showed in Michael, too, and a new impatience; coming to the laboratory one day, Johan was almost knocked down by his apprentice. Behind the boy, Michael was waving an iron rod and shouting.

"He is no good, that boy, no earthly good!" Michael's pinched chest heaved as he tried to catch his breath. "Do you know what he did? Do you know what he did?"

"What, Brother?"

"He bathed the unicorn before the virgin was in flux!"

"He what?"

"He—oh, never mind! You wouldn't understand."

Michael began to work among his strangely marked jars and crocks, where signs of fish and water and death's-heads were scrawled; he seemed to have forgotten Johan entirely. Some minutes later, he looked up angrily as if surprised to find an outsider standing there, and with a slap he covered the parchment he had been poring over. "I have to be alone!" he snapped. "Can't you see I have to be alone?"

"Forgive me, Michael."

The monk nodded. Not until Johan was leaving the room did he uncover the parchment. Outside, the boy apprentice was leaning in a crumbled window, tossing pebbles from the casing down into the street below.

"Is yon monk still riled at me, master?"

Johan looked at the boy. Perhaps fifteen, he was runty, almost dwarfed. *No good* was Johan's assessment of him, yet Michael had picked him out because of some special property in the date of his birth.

"Mind your tongue," Johan said curtly.

He journeyed to Muhldorf with the Bishop, where the Muhldorfers were surly to him. They had no wish to help the smaller city defend itself; there was, after all, no claim being made on their land. He was allowed, after some pressure by the Bishop, to study the city's guns: the gigantic Black Swan, a *magnum ingenium* with a removable breech that screwed into the huge barrel and that needed, it was said, most of a morning to load; the Raven, a smaller cannon whose ball was the size of man's head and whose breech was held in with wedges, though there was a visible gap where the flagon-shaped breech met the tube; and at two ribaldekins—clusters of a dozen small barrels mounted in line on a horizontal bed and fired from a single train of powder. These little multiple guns attracted him, because they seemed portable and the barrels were simple wrought-iron tubes; but a cannoneer confided to him that they were cranky and inaccurate and the powder in the open trough that fired them too often blew away at the critical moment. None of the guns had been made in Muhldorf; the great Black Swan had been captured from the Turks, and the other guns had been made in the south. Johan studied and measured and tapped and questioned. They would not fire the guns for him, but a cannoneer, his interest whetted by two stones from the Abbess's jewels, promised to come to Mouers if Johan would pay him well.

"Are there no small guns, then?" he said to the cannoneer that evening as they huddled over a little table in the Bishop's house. "No little guns such as you could have twenty or fifty of?"

"Nay, master; where to find fifty cannoneers? This is a
30

special mystery, the firing of great guns. Not every lurker with an eye and two hands can be cannoneer."

"Then there is no use to small guns?"

The man's lips curled. "Aye, small bombards and such. The Turks, when their guns was blown, they dug holes in the ground and filled them with gunpowder and pebbles, they fired them and killed more of themselves than us. Nay, for cannons, great guns is best, for knocking over walls and frightening folk and like that."

"And bronze? Bronze guns?"

"Aye, them made of bronze is best if proper made. Don't burst, they don't, like iron guns. A good big bronze gun mounted on your wall or pulled by twenty horses, oh, aye, there's a gun!"

"Well, if I make such a gun, will you come to Mouers and teach us how to shoot it?"

"Oh, well, now, master—it is my mystery, and I got my responsibilities to it. For such a thing, master, sharing of secrets—"

"One hundred kraters and your expenses."

"That don't mean gunpowder nor ball, nor match nor fuse nor nothing else, now!"

"No, we'll provide. Will you do it?"

"Well..." The man swallowed. "I'd thought, you see—two hundred kraters, as, if I was found out, selling my secrets—"

"A hundred and fifty."

The man shrugged. There was no way he would be made happy about thus selling the only prize he owned.

Johan went back to Mouers and shut himself up in a little room above his foundry, where he put down everything he had learned and made drawings of the Muhldorf guns as he remembered them, quite accurate drawings with the dimensions and the materials they were made of, down to the lashings that held the guns to their wooden platforms.

He took his drawings out to Garnheim and showed the Abbess. Embarrassed with her at first, he became more easy as he found she could be as businesslike as any man.

"How many will you make?" she said.

"One, at the first."

"One will do nothing for us."

"I will make more when I know the first is good."

"How many?"

"Five. Six, maybe."

"Five, six—that is not enough! We must have twenty!"

31

"Lady, no king in Christendom has twenty bronze great guns."

"And no king has to defend such a place with such a feeble army, bellfounder. Make me twenty guns! You will be a very great man, if you can do such a thing."

"I will tell you after I have made the first."

Her eyebrows arched; her lips pouted. "Well, you are not a promiser, at any rate." She went to a metal box that rested on a table. "You need more money, I suppose."

"I have to buy copper. A thousand pounds of it."

She opened the box and stood away from it. "Take what you will need."

He looked into the little chest. There were jewels and gold coins there, a small fortune but not so much as he had expected. "I will need it all—to make twenty guns."

"Then you may have it all—when you have made the twenty."

Her expression was amused and somehow wary, yet she came closer to him without looking away from him. "I will save Garnheim in any way I can, bellfounder. Whatever it costs, I will pay."

CHAPTER THREE

HE TOOK HIS DRAWINGS to Brother Michael.

The Dominican was horrified.

"These weapons are as unsanctified as any rocks in the deserts of Mahomet!" he cried. "They invite the devil, Johan—how should you trust the force of explosive powder, in which so much good may lurk, but which is so like the Devil's breath, to these unprotected surfaces?" He touched the parchment sheets where the round cross-sections of the Muhldorf cannons were drawn. "Our cannons must be marked," he said with great seriousness. "These are too smooth."

"Perhaps the devils will slip off," Johan suggested, not quite daring to make it a joke.

"An invitation to evil," the monk muttered. "An open invitation." He shook his head so quickly that the movement seemed like a shudder. "Poor Muhldorf. Leave it to me, Johan. I will write down the marks you must put on your cannons. The marks will appear in the bronze, will they not?"

"I cast so that the scratch of a fingernail will show," he said stiffly.

"Good. Come for them tomorrow."

"And the gunpowder, Michael?"

He cocked one eyebrow and held his right index finger up, like an angel in a picture pointing a moral. "Soon," he whispered happily. "Soon."

Michael's marks were intricate and covered much of what would be the barrel, from the touchhole to the muzzle—the Christian cross; a triangle to symbolize both the Holy Trinity and the union of the elements described by the holy pagan, Aristotle; quotations of scripture; and, around both muzzle and touchhole, the words "I am wholly God's."

"And the gunpowder?"

Again, Michael held up the pointing finger. "Hear what the sage Roger Bacon has written." He took a manuscript from his cupboard.

"'From the power of this salt dubbed salpetre is made so terrible a sound, that it dwarfs the thunder and is brighter than the lightning.'

"Thus the wise Roger Bacon." He rattled the parchment. "I have this from a learned man at Wittenberg, a man of great piety and knowledge in the Science." He cleared his throat. "He sends me also this, from the same Bacon:

"'Make you a powder of salpetre and of sulphur and of'—." He grinned like a child. "And of a third substance, one that I cannot, you will understand, Johan, utter?"

"Of course."

"Yes, you follow. Of salpetre and sulphur and this third substance, then, yes, make a powder, and 'the terrible flash is so horrible that if it be great enough, no human ear can stand the noise, no eye the brilliance; all must take fright and run straight away.'"

Michael studied Johan's face. Seeing more confusion than understanding there, he said patronizingly, "You do not understand yet; you can't follow this. How shall I make you understand?" Glancing around to make sure that his apprentice was not close by, he lowered his voice and leaned close to Johan, his breath sour and warm.

"The learned Bacon—he has worked all this out a century

33

and more ago, you see, but wisely, he confided his formula to a secret anagram lest the foolish and the greedy and such people as are inspired by the Devil might misuse his wisdom—the learned Bacon wrote that—even Bacon himself warns us, Johan, of those who would—let me see, I have this from another friend, it is written somewhere—aha, here, on this sheet, listen to what the learned—no, it isn't that sheet, that is a speculation upon—well, no matter. *Here* is Bacon on the sanctity of our mystery: 'It is madness to commit a secret to paper unless it be so done that the ignorant cannot read it and the wisest may decipher it with difficulty.' True. True! You don't agree?"

"Yes, yes, brother. But the gunpowder—"

"Yes, true! Now, hear what the wisdom of Bacon says on this subject of explosive powder:

"'Take salpetre, and sulphur, and *luro vopo vir utriet*, and make it thunder and lightning monumentally, and to lift great stones and dig great holes in the earth, but touch it with flame.'"

The monk looked up. He was either a little drunk or a little mad.

"He says nothing about cannons?"

"Nothing."

Johan tapped his fingertips together. He chewed on his lower lip, mouthing hairs from his beard. "Salpetre and sulphur and—"

"*Luro vopo vir utriet.*"

"A secret."

"Yes! That is Bacon's anagram to confound the ignorant and tantalize the wise. But—*I have broken it!*" His face came very close and his grip on Johan's arm was fierce. "I have broken it!"

"You're ready to make gunpowder?"

"Yes!"

"When?"

Michael glanced around again and even bent to look under a table. "On the night of the first thunderstorm, we will test it. The hideous light and thunder of my powder will be lost in the storm; thus, the ignorant will remain so. Until then—silence!"

Johan nodded dumbly.

Three nights later, he prepared to leave his house to go to the laboratory.

"Tell mistress I am going out," he said to his steward.

"Mistress is at prayers, master."

Johan nodded slowly. Pulling on a pair of gloves, he scowled at the task and pulled at the gauntlets angrily. "And my son?"

"He is at prayers, master."

He debated having the child brought to him and decided it was not worth his wife's anger. Swallowing the last of a glass of sweet wine, he threw a cloak over his shoulders and went out; when he looked back, the only lights to be seen were in his wife's rooms, where she would pray until daylight, probably, and where the boy, exhausted, would fall asleep on the stones.

Across the sky above him, the cold flare of lightning beyond the east hill glowed, boxed above his head by eaves and high gables. The wind was rising as he crossed the old chapter close and turned down along the Abbey wall; in the darkness, there was a muffled word and soft, running footsteps. Johan gripped the hilt of his knife, but hearing the footsteps recede, he knew it was only a pair of lovers or some whore and her trade.

The lightning flared far away again as he entered the tower. To him at that instant, it was like a cautionary message, a reminder of his wife's mad piety and Michael's secretive science, and, seeing it flicker through the rectangular window like dead sunlight, he was frightened—frightened for his son, left at home to endless prayer; frightened for himself. He had no right to be out, feeling his way up a dark tower stair while outside the thunder rumbled like the rising of a distant gate and the lightning spat and struck and threw messages across the sky at him.

Johan cursed when his knee struck a stone ledge; in the same breath, he begged for forgiveness—*Goddamit oh sweet Jesu forgive me*. The thunder rolled nearer and seemed to reach a crescendo over his head, and Johan crossed himself.

"Here you are!" Michael whispered from the top of the stair. A single lighted wick showed Johan his hesitant smile and the slight tremble of the lamp. Perhaps he, too, was frightened.

"Inside, quick!" *Who would follow me on such a night?* But he hurried in.

"This is a bad night for business," he whispered.

"The only time!" Michael said. His hand shook more noticeably.

"Well, get on with it, then." Johan pulled his coat close

35

around his shoulders to hide their twitching. "I'm chilled from walking," he said. "It's like February out there."

"This room is always cold," the monk said. Finding his way across the littered laboratory with the deftness of a blind man moving through a familiar room, he went to his work-table; following, Johan recoiled from each thing he touched. When the lamp was put down, he stayed near it, glad for the feeble light.

"It will come down buckets soon," he said.

"We need the rain." Michael was busy in the darkness somewhere to his right.

"I passed a couple in the Chapter Way. They'll be soaked soon."

There was no reply. He tried to picture the laboratory as he remembered it—one half-fallen wall, a jumble of broken mortar and bricks, a table with one broken leg, shelves of jars and bottles and—

"Michael? Where are you?"

There was a stir of cloth and a muffled concussion as one hard object hit another, and then a muffled word that might almost have been a curse. Seconds later, the monk stood next to him.

"I hit my head," he said blandly. "Here, take this." He held something toward Johan; thinking it was the explosive, Johan hesitated. "Take it!" Michael whispered harshly. "I have to keep it where that boy can't find it."

Johan touched a glazed earthenware jar. When he took it, he heard liquid gurgle. He felt over the thing until he found the stopper and pulled it out, and the herbal smell of the Abbey's brandy sprang up to him.

"I thought we might want it," Michael whispered. "Distillation is one of the bases of the Science."

Johan drank. Thunder rolled nearer to them, and a new flash of lightning lighted the room. He handled the clay bottle to Michael, who drank greedily.

"Now," he said. Brandy smell flowed out of his mouth, smothering his sour breath. "Now."

He lifted an iron mortar to the table and placed the oil lamp so its light shone down into it. There, like a deeper shadow inside the mortar's rim, was a fine-grained black powder. Johan sniffed. He had expected it to have an odor, but there was none.

"Is that it?"

The monk tapped the mortar. "Herein," he said hoarsely, "dwells a most potent nitro-aerial spirit."

"A spirit?"

"Aye. Or so we call it. Yes, a spirit of combustion, a spirit...I cannot explain these things to a layman. But that it is a spirit is very clear to one who understands these things." He lifted the lamp and looked down into the black dust. "This nitro-aerial spirit, I have determined, dwells within the sulphur, for it is the very principle of Combustibility. Do you understand that, Johan?"

Less frightened now than impatient, Johan said, "Yes, yes, Michael, I understand."

"Good. Now, within the salpetre dwells another spirit—a *seminal* spirit, Johan—to inspire this nitro-aerial spirit to his work, do I make myself clear? Heat and fire—a glowing coal, a red-hot iron—give life to the seminal spirit, the alkahest, we call it, after the heathen Arabs, who in turn inspires the nitro-aerial spirit, and, thus, combustion ensues— from which issues a third and most potent spirit, which is the essence of the explosion itself."

"You have already tried it, Michael?"

The monk smiled; lighted from below, his face seemed to break into a leer. "Only a grain or two. Only what I dared to test without alarming the town. But now—!" He put the lamp on the table. "Now we will test it."

He put a heavy iron dish on the table and measured a small spoonful of powder into it. "Enough, do you think? Too much?"

"How would I know?" He thought of the enormous cavity of the Black Swan, Muhldorf's great gun. "Maybe a little more would be wise."

The monk made an impatient gesture; his hand closed and chopped downward and snapped back again. "The learned Bacon says that a quantity as big as a man's thumb makes noise fiercer than the thunder." He raised the lamp and looked into the dish. "Here we have a quantity smaller than a lady's thumb, so it should be sufficient. Stand back a little, just in case."

Johan stumbled back into another table and would have gone still farther if he had not been stopped by it. Brother Michael came to stand next to him, and they stood close together, turned in toward each other with their shoulders hunched and the smoking lamp between them. "Hold the lamp steady," Brother Michael whispered. He had a long

37

splinter of pitchy wood, which he touched to the burning wick until flame sprang up along it. He let it burn for some seconds and then blew it out, and a long, orange snake of hot coal was left.

"Holy-Father-protect-and-save-me," he muttered, and he reached backward toward the iron dish with the splinter extended toward the powder. Nothing happened until he leaned still farther back, his face turned to look over his shoulder like a guilty man's, and with a yellow flash and a *whoosh!* the powder disappeared, sending a cloud of sulphurous smoke up into the room.

"Was that it?" Johan said several seconds later. He was still crouched with his back to the explosion.

"I believe it was," the monk said in a shaking voice.

Johan turned around. "It did not sound exactly like the thunder, brother."

"Well, no, it didn't," Michael said testily. "But it was a mighty light!"

"Oh, fearsome, yes. To the ceiling, I do believe. For an instant, I saw the room as clear as in sunlight, brother. Yes, a mighty light."

"And smoke."

"Yes, yes, frightful smoke. And smell, the Devil's own stink, I do believe."

"Aye." He seemed particularly pleased about the smell. "A most diabolical stink." Outside, the thunder rolled toward them. "But it did not rival that"—he pointed upward—"as to the sound, eh?"

"Not as a roar, no, brother; it was more a—well, if a huge arrow passed through the air, it might sound so. Or did it not sound like that to you?"

"Just so, yes, just so, a rushing of the air, no doubt the rapid journey of the nitro-aerial spirit." Still..." Michael tapped the table behind him. "It was not thunderish."

"No."

Michael's pent-up breath hissed out in a disappointed sigh. "Can I have interpreted the learned Bacon wrong?"

"Oh, surely not!"

"But I could have. Maybe I am one of the ignorant he meant to confound!"

"Michael, you are a student of the Science. You must be right."

Michael groaned. He produced the little brandy jug, and both drank. They went to the iron dish and looked into it;

Michael ran his finger around the bowl and showed the black soot that clung to its walls. "*Caput mortuum*," he whispered. "The dead bones of combustion."

"Aha."

Both men looked at the bones of combustion.

"Maybe—more powder?" Johan said.

Michael shrugged. "Bacon speaks of wrapping the powder in parchment. Perhaps, thus confined, thus—embraced, the spirits couple with more vigor."

Johan nodded. "Inside a cannon, I know, there is great confinement. Maybe your spirits do not love the open air. Maybe, like guilty lovers, they must couple in closed quarters." But he thought of the pair he had disturbed in the alley, and the metaphor seemed a poor one.

Michael merely grunted, wanting to hear no hypothetical concepts from a layman. He disappeared into the gloom again and came back with a small piece of heavy parchment, on whose surface could be seen fragments of musical notation; like most of Michael's sheets, it was discarded from some other function and the ink scraped off to be used again.

"There." Michael had rolled the parchment into a tube and folded one end over; he filled it with powder and twisted the open end.

"Now how will I bring heat to it?" he said.

"Well, let us pretend it is the Black Swan," Johan said. A little hesitantly, he touched the parchment, the first time he had dared to handle the black powder himself; then, having touched it and found that he was not harmed, he took out a knife and bored a small hole through. "May I?" He glanced at Michael, his knife blade suspended over the store of powder in the mortar.

"Well—ah, well, go on."

He took the black dust on the tip of his blade and placed it carefully over the hole and laid a little train of black grains along the table. Together, they backed away and Johan shielded his face with the skirt of his coat, and Michael bent forward with his splinter and touched the nearest grains.

Who-o-o-o-o-o-sh!

They had failed to rival the thunder, which seemed to be chuckling far beyond the eastern hills, but the flash had been brighter and the smoke denser, and a tail of fire had unleashed itself from the parchment tube and pointed like a terrible finger at them, while the parchment itself had sped like a frightened animal in the other direction.

"Well—" The monk's voice broke. "I've failed! That's all there is to it. I've failed!"

"Michael, we've only begun."

"No, no, this is what Bacon meant about confounding the ignorant. I have failed!"

Lightning broke and rain began to fall, first a spattering of heavy drops on the limbs outside the tower windows, then a downpour that made a constant rush of sound like the hiss of the burning powder.

"Michael, you can't know enough yet to have failed! Maybe our parchment is wrong; maybe our air is wrong, or our fire. Maybe the spirits of your elements do not like me; maybe— maybe God does not mean for us to do this." Johan crossed himself. "Maybe God does not mean for us to use guns against the Ritter."

"God does not reveal his mysteries so that they will go unused; he *means* for us to use them."

"Man knew sin only after his woman tempted him to eat of the tree of knowledge."

"Yes, yes, man ate of the tree and knew sin." The monk's voice was testy. "But he also knew other things that were *not* sin. God has put knowledge in man's way to test him, to find if he is worthy to attain the state of grace. God does not say, 'Be ignorant in My name'; He says, 'Believe in me, attain godhead through me and my saints!' He does not say, 'Be as stupid as any brute beast'! He gives us knowledge as His gift and His test; he gives us mystery, knowledge wrapped up in secrets and in signs, that we may prove ourselves worth His care!" His fingers picked at the wick of the lamp, snatching into the little flame to pull it up farther from the oil. "I'm sorry, Johan, I don't mean to scold you, but you must not let Satan tempt you into the featherbed of ignorance. We show the Fool as wearing the Devil's horns, and for good reason. No, we must persevere. I may have failed—but I have to try again."

The rain droned heavily on the trees, and the lightning, far away again, flickered like the guttering flame of the lamp. He drank more brandy, the noisy gurgle loud in the room, and, hearing the liquid in the jar and knowing it was almost empty, he handed it to Michael.

"What will we do?"

Michael drank. He lowered the bottle, raised it again to his mouth to drain the final drops.

"In the cannons," Johan said slowly, "there is a great deal

of powder, and it is held in by the metal and the ball, very tightly. What if we do the same?"

Michael lowered the bottle. Johan nodded at it and the monk stared.

"This?" he said hoarsely.

"Yes. It will shatter, but it may contain the powder enough—more than the parchment, anyway."

"No, no—I see now. Yes, but we will put the cork in, and the fearsome explosion will expel the cork like the ball!"

"The jar isn't metal; it will shatter."

"No matter if it does. How will you set the fire?"

"I will make a hole."

Johan turned the bottle upside down and began to bore a hole through the unglazed bottom. "I think it will shatter," he said.

"I think it will not." The monk's old enthusiasm had returned. "It is the powder's purpose to expel the ball; the spirits know this! The violence of combustion will expel the cork and the spirits will rush out. And what if it does break? It's an old jar."

He poured the black powder down the throat of the jar until it would hold no more, a cup of the mixture going into the little container. The wooden stopper followed, pounded in by the heel of Brother Michael's hand.

"And there we are. Very like a cannon, I think, Johan. Very like!"

He tore a small scrap of parchment and rested one end on the table and the other end on the hole that Johan had made.

"Thus," he said as he prepared another splinter of fatwood, "we will be perfectly safe, for I will stand five feet away and light the end of the parchment, which will burn to the hole, giving me time to hide. It will be quite, quite safe, Johan."

The bellfounder was careful to place himself behind a heavy table in the farthest corner of the laboratory with an oak chair pulled between him and the clay cannon. Brother Michael was humming happily to himself as he dipped the splinter in the flame. "Ready, Johan?"

"Ready, brother. In God's name, come behind this chair as soon as the parchment is lighted."

"Oh, I will, I will! Though it will be quite safe, you will see. Cover your ears, however, Johan, and I will do the same, for it is the hideous noise we have to fear and little else, for so says the learned Bacon!"

Johan had less faith in the learned Bacon than in his own

41

experience of fire and force, for he had seen thick molds explode from steam inside when the molten metal was poured, and he had the pawprint scar on his chest to remind him of his knowledge. He trusted practice, not theory, and he suspected that the learned Bacon might never have tested his anagram even so far as he and Michael had that night. He knelt behind the heavy chair like a man praying in a church, his hands clasped and his head bent, and while Michael hummed, he mumbled prayers to St. Eloi.

"Done!" he heard Michael call, and Johan could hear the quick scuttling of his race across the laboratory toward him, his haste suggesting that he, too, had qualms about mere theory. Breathless, he threw himself behind the chair and crashed into Johan, and the two knelt together, their shoulders and head pressed together by the narrowness of the chair as if they were conspirators.

Johan's face was screwed up as if he had tasted vinegar. A second passed, then two.

"The parchment has gone out," the monk whispered.

"How can you tell?"

"I don't smell it burning."

"It's a small piece; there's nothing to smell."

"I'm going to look."

"No, brother!" Johan's right hand closed over the monk's wrist. They waited, holding their breath.

"*Now* I will look."

"Maybe the parchment was damp, brother."

"It has gone out, or it burned to the jar and not had enough heat to excite the alkahest. Oh, God help me; I have failed again!"

"Brother Michael, please—"

"Let me go! I will look!"

He pulled his arm loose. Gathering his skirts in his left hand, he boosted himself upright, pushing against the chair arm with his right. Johan, still crouching, turned to look up at him.

"I think—" the monk started to say, squinting forward toward the far corner of the room.

Johan had heard great trees felled; he had heard a giant crucible break loose from its supports and boom against the earth; he had heard the noise of the storm at its peak. But he had never heard a sound like this one—a roar briefer than any thunder, louder than any falling tree, mingled in its after-echo with breaking glass and falling furniture. Johan's ears hummed as if he had stood in the bell tower when the great bell struck. He was aware of a brilliant light and then of the gagging stench of sulphur.

He looked again at Michael.

The monk was standing farther away, driven backward by wonder or fear, his happy, marveling face lit by flames from the other side of the laboratory.

"Heavenly God be praised!" he cried. "I have done it. I have done it!"

Rapt, he brushed his hand idly across his forehead to mop at the blood that poured from a long, raw wound.

CHAPTER FOUR

FROM HIS ECSTASY at the moment of the explosion, Brother Michael passed into a period of nausea and dizziness, and then into unconsciousness; roused from this, he lay groaning, with two of the Dominicans to care for him. Bled and purged, he seemed to grow no better, but begged for relief from the pain in his head. His eyes were vague, and the wide pupils wandered; even while he was coherent, his eyes wandered strangely.

"Could he die?" Johan whispered to the Abbot.

"If it is God's will."

"Reverend Father, he is the only one who knows the formula for the powder; if he dies—"

The Abbot nodded sadly. "We were novices together." His voice was profoundly weary. "Friends, as well as brothers in Christ."

"May I talk to him?"

The Abbot hesitated, then agreed. "He wanders some. He is sorely afflicted."

Michael seemed to know Johan. He looked near death—pale, unshaven, slack-skinned; the wound in his forehead was like a half-healed gash in an apple, puckered and sunken and rusty brown.

"Michael, it's Johan."

The monk grunted, his eyes still closed.

"I wanted you not to stand up, remember?" He tried to make it a joke. "Do you remember? Remember the explosion?"

Brother Michael made some sound, but it could not have been called speech.

He did not quite dare to ask the pitiful figure about the formula, and after sitting for several minutes in an increasingly embarrassing silence, he patted one of the still hands and muttered a platitude and slipped away.

"Where is his apprentice?" he asked the Abbot when they were outside.

"I haven't seen him. Bad cess, I say."

"But he may know enough to—be useful. And whatever he knows, I don't want it being drawn off by somebody else. Where might he be?"

"He was from one one of the Garnheim farms. Michael picked him out for some reason, taught him to read a little. I always thought he was good for nothing—born to hang, was what I thought. I suppose he's run off home."

Johan scowled. Concentration made him seem menacing: two thick ridges formed between his deep-set eyes, and the forehead wrinkled along the lines that were always there now, even in laughter and in sleep; when he scowled like this, he looked like an angry man about to strike out violently.

"Let me know if there's any change in Michael. I'll find the boy."

He brought in a scribe and had him write a letter to the Abbess explaining that one of the Abbey apprentices had run away and was needed for work connected "with our common interest"; would she look for him on her farms? When the scribe was done, Johan studied the letter, admiring the man's neat, clear hand. His own would have been crabbed and slow and poorly spelled; as he read, he scowled again, and the scribe, who made his living by writing letters and documents for people who could write only badly or not at all, stirred uneasily, thinking that the influential master of St. Eloi's Guild was angry with him; but Johan sealed the letter and thanked him politely and paid him well. Johan sent the letter off with a servant, and then he changed into rougher clothes and told his steward he would be in the foundry and to send his meals there for the next day.

Behind the house, between the kitchen garden and the

beginning of a leather and dyeing works, ran the little river by which the ancient swamp had been drained. It meandered in slow turnings down its flat valley and through the little city, where it picked up the freight of ten thousand humans and their enterprises and emerged through a low arch in the city wall, stained and odorous, to try to cleanse itself in the meadows below the town. Johan's property ran from Paternoster Street to the river and gave him fifty yards behind his kitchen garden, and there he had put up the sheds to store the materials of his craft, and the casting pits and the crucible and the furnaces. Inside one of the sheds was the mold for the great bell of Mouers, core and cope, preserved against that day when some unsuspected failure in the founder's art might cause it to crack or change its voice. Around it, the molds of other bells stood like silent, skirted attendants; coming to the works, Johan always made his way through the shed to stand among these ghosts of bells he had cast, to be reassured by the solidity of the huge clay molds, as if to say, *I made these; I can make anything.*

Eleven men worked under him—two journeymen, four apprentices, and five unskilled laborers, three of them indentured to him. These were *his* men, not in the way that the oath servants of the Emperor were his, nor in the way that the field serfs of the Abbey of Garnheim were the Abbey's, but his in that their very hold on a place in their world depended on his approval. His journeymen were free, but without his patronage, they would be mere wanderers; they were his lieutenants, to be consulted and listened to and only occasionally ignored or scolded. The apprentices were his special responsibility by contract, and he treated them more like bastard sons —acknowledged but not loved—and let the journeymen kick them if they were stupid. The laborers, illiterate and shiftless by his standards, were good for only the most menial and the most wearying work; they called him "master" and stood up and took their caps off when he came near them.

On both sides of his property were the houses and foundries of other metalsmiths—a goldsmith and jeweler to the east, an armorer to the west. Like him, they had journeymen and apprentices and menial workmen, and friendships and enmities existed along each level of their hierarchy, rods that bound the city together as surely as church and corporation did.

Piet, his senior journeyman, looked at the drawings he

had made and hummed to himself. Piet would one day want to borrow the money to set up for himself, and Johan would lend it to him; but Piet was cautious, and for now he would rather work for another man than for himself.

"It's a deal of metal," Piet said. It was like him to make the most obvious possible statement. He would come at the problem the gun might offer by thus circling it with platitudes, coming in slowly and at a tangent until he had the problem fast.

"Aye, half a ton," Johan said.

Piet studied the drawing some more and then said, "I never cast no gun before, Master Johan."

"No, Piet, nor have I—nor has Hans, nor anybody else in Mouers, nor anybody else for three hundred miles that I know of! Study the drawings, Piet, and tell me what you think."

Piet hummed and picked his upper front teeth with a twig. The drawings were spread out on the hard ground near the casting pit, and he circled them, humming and picking his teeth and scratching his left side lazily like a man who's just got out of bed.

"Well," he said at last, "it won't be easy."

"What would you do, Piet, try to build a furnace in the core, like with a bell, or will we heat it from underneath?"

Piet looked at the casting pit. "I'd build her of brick and heat her from underneath," he said.

"Good. I think so, too."

His other journeyman, Hans Bighead (to distinguish him from Hans Strongback, who worked in iron one street over), squatted by one of the drawings and followed the lines with his right index finger and mouthed words silently to himself. He was slower than Piet; he would probably never be a master founder, but he was reliable and steady. While Piet began to order two apprentices and the laborers about, Hans Bighead went on studying the drawings. Piet was preparing for the construction of the cannon mold under a scaffolding that would have to be altered to fit it, upon which a crucible to melt the metal would be installed. There fires would burn night and day for as long as it took the copper and the tin to melt and alloy, and then gates would be opened and the molten metal would slither down into the mold and, God willing, the cannon would be made.

While the frame was being rebuilt, Hans Bighead finished his study of the drawings and began to build the compass with which the mold would be precisely formed. Two parts were needed, one the exact size and contour of the cannon's bore, the other the size and contour of the exterior. He sawed one-inch oak to the rough shape, piecing it as neatly and carefully as a joiner might with mortise and tenon to make the full length—over seven feet—and finished each with sandstone and drawknife until the working surface was as smooth as a piece of furniture and the corner that would meet the wet clay was clean and sharp. He drilled a vertical hole through the inner edges of each piece and forged an iron rod to go through as a pivot, the whole process taking him two days; and by that time, Piet had found old timbers in the warehouse and in another, unused scaffold, and had used them to rebuild the existing one, with frames around the crucible gates and extra supports to hold the weight of the metal that would fill them; and then the workmen were set to mixing ground clay with water, three of them stirring with long paddles in a trough dug in the earth and lined with boards while the other two pounded the dry clay and fetched water and took their turns at the stirring.

For Johan, it was a time of concentration and excitement, of an intensity that only his work gave him. The making of a new bell—or, now, a new cannon—was like sex, like the birth of a child, but the moment prolonged into days, even weeks. Hours would pass without his knowing it; meals would be skipped, or gobbled when they had been long cold; outside duties would be forgotten. There was always work going on in the yard—at the moment, a string of six small bells was being cast for a chapel in the Muhldorf mother church, but that was nothing; they were cast from old molds, and one of the journeymen, even an apprentice nearing the end of his term, could see to that—but it was the new task that always gripped him and that drove him, like a lover or a zealot, to be everywhere in the yard, tense, scowling, happy.

"Master Johan, there's a fellow come."

"What fellow? Tell him I can't see him."

"He's from the Abbey, master—says Master Abbot sent him."

It was the evening of the second day. The scaffold was up, the compass finished. The laborers were grunting through a half-lewd song as they puddled the clay, their paddles slapping with the sound of a woman's hands hitting bread dough.

The boy who had come for him was frightened. "Master Abbot s-says you's to coom, master; yon brother, he's dying, thinks."

47

It took an effort to remember Brother Michael and his wound. Reluctantly, Johan looked around the busy yard and saw the work he loved.

"Tell Master Abbot I'll be there presently."

He sat with the Abbot as dusk turned into blackness and the wind hurled itself at the building as if it meant to throw it down.

"*Luro vopo vir utriet*," Michael murmured.

"What did he say?"

"Some of his alchemical secrets."

It grew dark. Johan was angry at the monk for taking him away from his work, and then, recognizing his anger, he was ashamed. Still, it seemed wasteful, this vigil over incoherence.

"*Luro vopo—Luro*...Where are the cabbages? Who took Brother Martin's cabbages?" The voice fell away; the lips moved, forming words that were not spoken. He groaned. "Surely, I have—Heavenly Father..."

He babbled. Words tumbled out, to be followed by whimpers and groans. He sighed like a man too weary to live. They put wet cloths over his hot skin and the Abbot laid another over the wound, which was oozing matter now.

"I think it is almost the end," the Abbot said. He sounded relieved and sad in the same breath.

"Of salpetre seven...seven...Sisters seven. Of days of the week, seven. Of salpetre, seven. Five and five. Of the fingers, five, so much. And seven...Papa? Papa?"

Suddenly, the ravaged face cleared and looked almost healthy again. The flesh seemed to firm, the color to brighten. Michael's eyes opened, and, seeing Johan and the Abbot, he smiled.

"Surely," he said quietly, "I have looked on the glory of God."

"Dear Michael..." The Abbot leaned over the injured man, reaching out to touch his face, but, after its moment of apparent health, it contorted and the teeth began to chatter and the lips pulled back to expose the yellow teeth. The cloth strips that had held the ravaged body down had been loosened, and now, as a new convulsion twisted the legs, Johan had to lean his weight on them to keep the monk from throwing himself out of the bed. The torso arched, strained, and collapsed; the arms fell limp; the face twisted. Only his legs continued to struggle.

48

Under his hands, Johan felt the legs go straight and stiff and quiver a little.

"It is over." The Abbot was weeping and biting his lower lip, and he looked furious.

Michael might have looked on the Glory of God, but his last expression did not show it, and with quick, angry movements, the Abbot closed the crazed eyes and molded the twisted lips into a semblance of calm.

The four last Dominicans of the Abbey of Mouers buried Brother Michael next day in the barren little cemetery behind the Abbey chapel. Johan was not there.

He slept for four hours in his own bed and was out in the yard when the workmen came an hour after daybreak to mix more clay. Work blotted out the monk's death.

The cannon mold was built over an in-ground furnace. First, a crude semblance of the cavity of the bore was built out of old pieces of brick and stones and straw, held together with the wet clay, and with a hole left in the center for the pivot rod of the compasses to turn in. Wet clay was packed around this core and smoothed until a near approximation of the bore was built up; then, with the pivot rod rotating in the hole, the inner compass was turned around the core, the clean corner that Hans Bighead had cut scraping off all excess until a perfectly symmetrical cylinder was created, its dimensions precisely those of his drawings. When Johan pronounced himself satisfied with it—when he had climbed into the pit and gone over every square inch of the shining surface himself while the compass turned and his artist's eye saw that there was no gap between clay and wood—the compass was removed and low fires were built in the pit to speed the clay's drying.

Now the dried core was greased with rendered pig's fat and a second layer of straw-reinforced clay was built up over it in the shape of the cannon itself. In bellmaking, the spreading shape of the bell made the clay settle naturally with little danger of the top's sliding off; with the cannon, however, the thicker metal at the breech end made the clay form, in its vertical position, liable to collapse as the overhang was built up. Piet cursed and shook his head the first time that the mold began to slip, and when it happened again he said, "Well, master!" in a tone that suggested that the project was impossible, but Johan drove the men to do it again. More clay was mixed, more straw brought, and the breech was built out around an armature of wood rods, and this time it held so that the damp clay, hammered in upon itself with wood mallets, became a crude double of the cannon, its surface pocked and rippled with the imprints of the workmen's tools.

"Wet it down," Johan ordered. The apprentices poured more water over the slick surface and rubbed and smoothed, and then the exterior compass was pivoted in the central hole and rotated, and the clay was scraped off and built up until the master was satisfied, and the cannon, muzzle to earth, stood in front of them for the first time.

The casting pit was surrounded with rough walls made out of lath, built on legs so they could be moved from pit to pit to protect the founder's art from any curious eyes. Johan told all his men to leave the place, journeymen and laborers alike, and when they were gone he spread out the drawing upon which Brother Michael had made the arcane marks that were to be on the finished gun. He had thought that Michael himself might make these in the clay, but that was not to be; Johan doubted that the symbols would have the same meaning if he did them—they were unsanctified, it seemed to him—but he would not bring any other monk or priest in to help him now.

He worked by torchlight in silence and secrecy. Starting at the breech, he copied the marks as Michael had made them, the triangle and the water sign, the cross and the skull, incising the symbols into the wet clay with a bone graver and wiping away each crumb of clay as it was raised. Around the touchhole, he made the concentric circles and the pentagram as Michael had drawn them, and wrote his words so that they would come up clear in the bronze. The stylus bit into the wet clay, pushing up snakes of light brown that he removed with a soft brush or blew away. Some of the marks had to be deepened or sharpened with a knife blade; some were too deep, and more clay had to be added, the compass moved again over the fault, and the cuts begun anew. He did the muzzle last, first bending to work on the expanded lip that rested tight against the top of the furnace, then lying full-length with his arms extended. For this final legend, he built up each letter as he had built up the letters around the mouth of the great bell, molding each one in beeswax and pressing it into place in the clay, then covering it with a slurry of thin clay so the finished surface would be the same as the rest of the mold. Living only in the work, he did not sense time's passage; did not acknowledge his own fatigue or the pain where his muscles had contracted too long in one position. He was astonished when he came out of the circle of lath walls at last and, stepping from the protection of the scaffold, found that it was dawn, a pink, hushed birth of day that sent a rush of pleasure through him like the warmth of wine. The first birds were beginning to call, and from over the river a rooster crowed and another answered. He smiled and rubbed his stinging eyes, and dropped to his knees to pray, clutching his hands together close under his mouth so that the odor of wet clay filled his senses again.

Wakeful as a dog when the hunters are stirring, he roused the porter and had him find what cold food was in the kitchen, splashed water on his face and hands and put on clean clothes, saddled a horse himself, and rode out of the city to the eastern hill.

Not admitting where he was going, he still knew where he would go, and he passed the hilltop without looking back and rode straight to the gate of Garnheim. He wanted a woman to talk to.

"The first cannon is molded, Lady Abbess. I will pour in six days." She looked weary and older than he remembered; she was not wearing her jewels.

"And will it shoot, bellfounder?"

"I don't know, lady. I will know when the metal cools."

"And how long to make another?"

"Three days to heat the metal if the same mold can be used; a day to pour, nine days to cool."

"Almost two weeks. At two weeks for every gun, there will not be many by Corpus Christi, I think."

She sounded bitter. She did not look at him, and he thought that her voice was the same as she might have used to disparage any tradesman. "Nobody could do it quicker, lady. If you think somebody could, you do not understand my art."

If she understood his anger, she did not acknowledge it. "How many guns will you make by Pentecost?" she said.

"Four—if the mold does not crack. Sometimes a mold will last for a dozen bells; sometimes it will crack after one. On the first one, even, though mine never do."

"It will not be enough." She moved to a window. It had come up a misty day, too warm for spring, so that vapor rose from the newly turned furrows in her fields. The reflected light was not kind to her as she stood in the window niche.

Even the wimple that bound her chin could not hide the jowl there.

"Come here, bellfounder." She had leaned her elbows on the window ledge, her chin on her clasped hands. When he stood next to her, he could smell the dried flowers that had been laid in her folded gown before she had put it on, feel even the warmth of her upper arm. Aroused, he was embarrassed, and he pressed his abdomen against the stone.

"There is the direction the Ritter will come from if he has any sense," she said. "Over the plain beyond the river. That is how an enemy will come at Garnheim. I had thought to see the slope on my side of the river covered with your great guns, bellfounder; I had thought to see them belching out smoke and fire like dragons—and now you tell me there will be only four of them." She sighed unhappily. "Perhaps I must make my own peace with the Ritter."

"You cannot!" His voice was strangled. "Your pardon, lady; but if you make a peace with the Ritter, Mouers will be cut off on three sides."

"Then I must have more than four guns."

"I am doing what I can."

"There must be twenty guns! I will put three hundred serfs on that hill, bellfounder; the Ritter will cut through them like a turtle through a flock of ducklings unless we have guns. Make me more guns!"

"Bronze is a slow metal, lady."

"Then make them of iron! Make them of wood! Make them of what you will, but make them!"

He laughed at her. His tension vanished. Perhaps because she reminded him of his wife and his daughter, or perhaps because his house was full of women and he was accustomed to touching them and giving them what little comfort he had, he patted her shoulder and said, "Well, well, I will do something," and let his hand rest on her back, and then withdrew it too quickly when he realized what he had done.

Surprisingly, she laughed, perhaps as much at herself as at him. "It is very tempting to be petted, for a change," she said. Her mouth formed into the sucking, kissing shape he remembered. "But not quite tempting enough." Her eyes came up to meet his, then swung away, a parody of girlishness. Now she was laughing at him alone.

"Did you think I meant something by touching you?" he said.

Her face stiffened. He knew the look—the amused aristocrat. She would say something insulting now; her mouth was already forming its fishlike pout to be witty.

"I touched you as I would touch any woman in my house when she is troubled," he said. Her reply, whatever it would have been, was stilled; her indrawn cheeks, her look of skepticism, relaxed. "I cannot help it if I think of you as a woman, Lady Abbess."

The Abbess of Garnheim crossed the room and stood by the heavy table that served her as a writing desk. She remained with her back to him thus and her face in partial profile; the fingers of her left hand touched the table.

"I go hunting on Wednesday week," she said languidly, "in the woods beyond the river. I will sleep in the Abbey farmhouse called Gray Stones." She looked down at her fingers. "My attendants will retire early."

In the silence, the moment stretched, tightened like a bowstring; if he blinked, if he breathed, disaster would come. He felt as if he were made of brittle glass; if he were touched, he would crack. He heard a sheep bleating, a human voice calling; he saw the Abbess, her head still bent over her shoulder. It was like an instant of his youth recalled—the exhilaration of something like love, the dizzying sense of danger, rare and delicious; yet, middle-aged, he knew that this was the best of the moments that would come. He tried to make it last by staying utterly still, and then she moved and the moment was shattered.

What he really wanted was the bittersweet pleasure of refusing her. Yet he would not. Such a thing could not be refused, although it threatened annihilation. He breathed.

The Abbess was speaking. She was asking him about gunpowder.

"I know the principle, lady." He had to control the tremor in his voice. His knees and his shoulders were weak, watery; he felt like a boy. "It's a problem of proportion and the right materials. I wrote to you about the missing apprentice. I need him, now that Brother Michael's gone."

"Can the boy help you?"

He nodded, not trusting his voice.

"Well, I will find him." Still she would not look at him. "I count on you, bellfounder. God has made you my destiny, I fear."

It was only when he was riding away from Garnheim that he realized how utterly weary he was. Peasants were on the road, taking scruffy winter goods to Mouers market day. He

53

rode slowly through them, his thoughts already leaping
ahead to the day when she would go hunting.

CHAPTER FIVE

WHEN THE CLAY FORM was dry they began to build the
cope. With the form covered with grease, new clay was laid
over it and around it, reinforced with straw, and three iron
sheets cut and hammered to shape by Hans Bighead were
forced through the wet clay until they came to rest against
the form. These would divide the cope into three sections so
that it could be lifted clear of the finished cannon, whose
bulbous shape—thicker at one end than at the other—made
it impossible simply to lift the cope away, like the mantle of
a bell. Bricks were packed around each section and interlaced
with more clay and straw until three masses were built up,
with reeds pushed in at certain points for air vents and iron
rods set in vertically to reinforce each section. Finished, the
cope stood nine feet tall, a stout brick-and-clay pillar that
looked like a blunt chimney rising from the casting pit. Then
Piet and an apprentice took four iron hoops that had been
shrunk to size and hammered them down over the clay shape
so they held the sections tight together, and fires were lighted
in the pit to dry the ponderous mass.

It took forty hours to fire the cope so that it was as hard
as a jar and rang under a hammer, and when Piet and Hans
Bighead told him it was ready he jumped down into the pit,
the ashes of the fire hot against his shoe soles, the clay me-
tallic and hot in his nostrils; and when he was content with
it and knew the clay was hard, he gave the signal for the
iron hoops to be pulled off.

Long spruce poles were fitted into recesses near the top
of each section and then the hoops were hammered up from
below, and when the laborers had sweated and hammered
and burned themselves on the hot metal and the hoops were
free, it was time to lift the cope away.

"Pull away!" Hans Bighead shouted. Chains ran through

a sheave to a yoke of oxen from a rod in each third of the cope. The oxen moved, their hooves striking up dirt from the yard floor, and then they strained forward and the chains began to run, and slowly, slowly, with the journeymen and apprentices and laborers and even Johan straining at a rope, the three sections were pulled out and lifted, held together at the top by the spruce poles in the hands of the seasoned apprentices, lifted free at the bottom by ropes in the hands of all the others. It went up until the cannon mold stood stark and clear, and then the three sections were hung on the chains, and their bottoms were pulled wide apart by the ropes and tied off, and Johan could climb a ladder and examine the inside of each with a torch and know that every mark that had been incised on the mold had been cast in reverse, exact and true, in the cope. Satisfied then that there were no flaws, no cracks or bubbles, he ordered the mold—the clay replica of the cannon—lifted off the core and destroyed; and when the three-sectioned cope was again lowered into the pit, centered precisely over the clay-and-brick core, and the hoops hammered down to join them into one mass, the empty space between core and cope was precisely that of the cannon that was about to be cast in bronze.

It took three more days to melt the metal in the crucible over the casting pit—eight hundred pounds of copper from Rammelsberg, a hundred and twelve pounds of tin from the mines of England, imported through Bruges and Cologne with a doubling of price at each change of hands, plus twenty-eight pounds of zinc from the Low Countries. The metal started its melting slowly, the copper ingots toppling suddenly into a liquid red pool, chunks of tin joining them in silvery curves that lay on the glistening rust-gold like sunlit reflections, until they were puddled by the laborers' long rods into a constant alloy of dull yellow. Because the metal had to be tended day and night, the members of St. Eloi's Guild and their apprentices were excepted from the city proscription against work after sundown, and so there were always three men on the scaffold, their bodies in the dark night lighted from below by a golden glow, their torsos bare despite the chill night temperatures.

At the end of the third day, he knew the metal was alloyed and he ordered the gates opened, and the liquid bronze began to run down into the mold with a sound like a giant swallowing. Gas rushed out of the vents and burned blue in the dark. The stink of hot clay and burning grease filled the yard.

With relief, he saw that the cope had not cracked and no metal had seeped between its sections. Steam came from the vents now; the last moisture in the clay would be vaporizing, the clay drying to a dangerous brittleness; the last beeswax of the letters he had put on the cannon mouth would be burning away, and the last vestiges of the grease that separated core and mold and cope would be bubbling from the vents. A cloud of smoke and steam surrounded the casting pit, over whose top the journeymen paced nervously on the scaffold, while the laborers, bare to the waist, waited with their gloved hands on the rods of the pouring gates. The last of the gas burned blue; the metal gurgled once and was still, and Piet turned to look into the crucible and then clutched the railing of the scaffold and looked down at Johan.

"Done, master! She's full!"

He circled the casting pit with one of the apprentices, who held a torch for him. The clay cope glowed, hot enough to burn through any flesh that touched it. He looked for a tell-tale globe of metal that would show where a crack had started, for a sliver of bronze between the hooped sections. He prowled, bent, searching, intent.

"Done, in God's name!"

A cheer went up from them all, and the laborers and the apprentices were slapping each other's backs and laughing while Piet and Hans Bighead shook hands on the scaffold; Johan's daughter and his servants brought out food, meat and beer and fresh bread and smoked carp from the river, and they all ate and laughed and talked over and over about the pouring and the making of the novel three-part cope, the weight of the metal, like men who had been through a battle together. His son had been brought out to see the pouring, and now he let the boy stay up and eat with them, his face flushed and happy as he talked about the flames he had seen shoot from the vents when the metal had rushed down the throat of the mold.

"It was all black and red," he said, hushed as if he were telling a ghost story. "Everything black, and the red where the flame jumped out!"

"Aye, boy," his father whispered, hugging him, "black and red, that's the founder's world." Johan was a little drunk, and he pulled the boy to him fiercely. "You don't know the art until you've stood all night, waiting, and then seen the fire against the dark!"

He wanted a woman. When the food was cleared and the

boy had been taken away, he went to his wife's rooms, but her sleepy women told him she had prayed and was asleep, and he turned back to the yard, thinking to find one of the other women there, but the place was empty and cold. Suddenly depressed, he took blankets from the stable and lay down on a pile of straw among the old bell molds, nursing his sense of rejection like a prize, and fell asleep thinking of the Abbess. Like an animal, he slept for eighteen hours, and when he woke it was night again and he went off and found a whore in Old Town and left her as soon as he had finished.

Waiting for the metal of any casting to cool made them all jumpy. The cannon would take nine days. Piet was dull-witted and too quiet; Hans Bighead knocked one of the laborers against a wall for some stupid mistake. Johan walked among them and found himself criticizing faults that did not exist, and he shut himself up in the house and tried to keep his own bad humor away from them.

Two days after the cannon was poured, Brother Michael's apprentice was brought in to Mouers. Two of the Garnheim peasants brought him with a rope around his neck like a cow being walked to market, and they made a game of slapping him with the loose end of rope and shouting, "Hoo, bossie," and jerking him away from the roadside as if he might stop to browse. One of the louts had a letter from the Abbess, a curt, beautifully printed message thanking the bellfounder for his aid and committing "one Cob, a slave's son," to his use; there was no mention of any intimacy. Johan folded the letter and put it in his purse and scowled at the boy, who was trying to keep up his cheeky air despite his fear of the scowling bellfounder.

Johan gave each of the peasants a penny and took the rope with which the apprentice was tied.

"Mark he don't gore thee with 'ees 'orns, maister," one said.

"Aye, 'e ain't 'orned, that one." The two men laughed, their red faces split with cruel, happy grins.

"Maybe ought to be gelded, that one," said the first, and the two men punched each other and roared until they saw that Johan was not laughing with them. Sobering instantly, they bobbed their heads at him and backed away, mumbling their subservience.

"Tell Lady Abbess that Johan of Mouers says you did well."

"Ah, thank thee, maister!"

He saw them leave, and then sat quietly in a backless armchair in the middle of his sitting room, the boy's rope in his big hand.

"What's your name?"

"Cob, maister. Son of Mak of the Apple Farm."

"Do you know that your master is dead?"

"Aye, I do that."

"Do you know you can be branded for running away?"

"Nay, maister, di'n't run off, see—was sent; my maister, yon monk, he sent me off. I di'n't run, no."

"What did he send you off for?"

"Why, for them charcoal fellows, to see would they burn willow charcoals for him."

Johan had no doubt that the boy was a practiced liar, like all his class, as shifty in his thoughts as an animal covering a track. He could return Johan's stare with a perfect counterfeit of honesty.

"If you lie to me, I'll have you whipped."

"Nay, maister—"

Johan swung the rope and struck him lightly across the face. "I won't be lied to, Cob! Now, you know what happens to runaway apprentices, do you?"

"Aye, maister." His head was low. "But I wa'n't proper apprentice to yon dead monk, no."

The rope swung slowly from Johan's fingers. "No?"

"Was never no papers, mark you, never no writing. Only him and my da nattered and they told me, 'Go to yon city, do what yon monkish fellow tells thee.' So I come and I done good for him. Daft business."

"What?"

"Why, yon devilish marks and stinkings and all, maister—a daft business, I say."

"A runaway apprentice with a runaway tongue is sure to hang. Don't they teach you respect on the Garnheim farms?"

The boy grinned. "Aye, yon Lady Abbess'd teach respect to the Devil—got a stocks and a whipping tree and uses them regular. She's a wonder for respect, maister!"

"Why did you run away, Cob?"

"*Di'n't* run away, maister!" He flinched as the rope swung toward him. "Told truth about the charcoal! But—I did stay away some, truth; I stayed off to home and thereabouts. I feared that business yon dead monk was up to, maister."

"What business was that?"

"Why . . ." The boy swallowed noisily. He shifted his weight

58

and wiped his sleeve across his forehead. He smelled like unwashed clothes that have lain a long time, damp and sour. "Why, I guess it was conjuring, maister."

Johan struck him again, surprised at his own anger and then aware that the boy's credulity had touched some secret fear of his own. "He wasn't conjuring, you ox! He was a brother of the Church!" He whipped the rope across the thin shoulders. "Why would a monk conjure?"

"Don't know, don't know, maister! But he was always burning of things and making stinks and smokes. Sulphur, he burned sulphur near every night! It was terrible, maister—his secret books and all! Was frightened terrible, Maister Johan."

Johan sat down and let the rope trail on the floor. "Can you read, Cob?"

"Not read proper, not what *you'd* call reading. Can puzzle out yon monkish secret marks."

"Brother Michael's marks?"

"Aye, them little pictures what he drew. The Virgin and the river and all."

"Did Brother Michael teach you how to do things in the laboratory?"

"Oh, aye, maister! Learned to lixiviate and precipitate and boil off vapors, and all them. Learned to read the signs, the change of colors. Learned to make salpetre from rime and all."

"Did you ever see Brother Michael make anything with salpetre in it?"

The boy hesitated. "Nay. But I know he did it."

"What did he mix?"

"Don't know. Would never let me watch, that fellow."

He looked at Johan with his honest eyes, and Johan distrusted him. "But you do know what he mixed, don't you?"

"Nay, how would I know? Not me."

Johan picked up the rope again. "Cob, if you lie to—"

"Nay, maister—"

Johan struck once, twice, across the face and neck, and when the boy hid his head in his arms, he began to beat him over the ribs.

"Tell me the truth!"

Johan pushed him against the wall, lifted him off his feet and slammed him into a beam. "Tell me!"

Blood was running from Cob's mouth and one eye was closed where the end of rope had slapped across it. He lay passively in Johan's grip, cowering like a hound that is regularly whipped.

"Tell me, you peasant ox!"

"I daren't, maister! They'll come for me!"

"Who'll come for you?"

"Them demons. They come for yon monk, they did—come and took him in the night! Took him body and soul down to Hell, so folk say; was no body to bury, they say—the monks, they made sham of burying, but he was gone straight to Hell for conjuring up demons!"

"What do you know, that they'd come for you?"

Cob's voice turned flat and hopeless. "I snuck up to watch him one night. I seen him. Mumbling to hisself, 'Seven and five and five,' like that. And he mixed salpetre and sulphur and charcoal and made a great fire and stink, and I think a demon come in that fire, because I was near blinded, and I took fear and run off then."

Johan let the boy go.

"Can you make salpetre? Make it properly, I mean?"

"Aye, maister—done so for yon dead monk."

"If you lie to me, I will give you to my apprentices, and they will strip you and beat you with hot iron rods, do you understand that?"

"Aye, maister."

"Very well." He went to the door and shouted down the stairs for a servant and went back to his chair. When a woman servant appeared at the door, he stopped her with a lifted finger and she waited placidly. "Cob," he said quietly, "I have it in my mind to make you my servant. I'll make it right with your father and with the Lady Abbess. You will live in one of my barns and make salpetre for me; if you are a good boy and do it well, I will give you a new set of clothes and see to it that you eat beef once a week. Would you like that?"

"Oh, yes, maister!"

"And if you do your work very well, I will get another boy—maybe two—to work under you, and you can whip them when they are bad. Would you like that?"

"Oh, yes, maister!"

"Very well." He beckoned the servant. "Go with this woman and do as she says." To the servant, he murmured, "Wash him and put him in the stable until I find another place. Mind he doesn't run off."

She curtsied and went out, cuffing the boy because he would not step aside for her to go down the stairs. Johan crossed the house and started down another flight of stairs to the street. Halfway down there was a landing; a door opened there and his wife stood staring up at him.

"Well? I'm just going out, Katrin."

"I heard you talking about demons." She spoke softly, but the words were an accusation.

"I was talking to a stupid peasant."

She stared at her hands. "I was sleeping. St. Francis came to me. He showed me his wounds. I woke up and I heard you talking about demons." She looked up at him. "You are bringing the odor of the Antichrist into my house!"

"Now, Katrin—"

"St. Francis has given me a warning." She shook her head and muttered something to herself. "You'll see."

"Not now, Katrin."

"Not now! *Not now?*" She swayed and clutched the doorpost. "I gave you the warning that St. Francis has shown to me, and you tell me *not now!*"

He pushed past her. "I have business in the city."

"God has business for you in this house!"

He went on down the stairs. Wanting to say something to her to close the gulf between them, he turned and looked up. She was gone.

He went to the Rivergate and strode along it to the lawyer's house, a three-story timbered building that rose straight from the edge of the little canal that ran down to the river.

"I want an indenture. One of the Garnheim serfs. The Abbess won't make any trouble."

"Male or female?" the lawyer said blandly.

"A boy. His name is Cob. I want him bound fast, do you follow? *Fast.*"

CHAPTER SIX

THE ABBESS OF GARNHEIM had a hard, lithe body that was kept lean by riding and hunting—not at all the sort of plump, comfortable body that Johan usually admired. There had been an intensity to her lovemaking that was almost hysterical, as if she had feared missing her pleasure by being too slow or too lazy; in her climax, she had cried out almost angrily, the way one might cry out if things had turned out as badly as one feared. Yet afterward she was quiet, as if with satisfaction. Eyes closed, head turned away, she seemed, like him, to be savoring that weakness.

He swayed his torso back to look down at her. Wanting to reach her, wanting intimacy, warmth, he supported himself on his hands and looked down at her, a smile crinkling the corners of his eyes, but she did not look up. His wife—in the old days, in the old days—would have turned and smiled, would have made some smooth-worn joke. He rolled away and lay on his back, and almost instantly she lifted her legs and flipped herself forward off the bed like a tumbler at a fair, her buttocks hitting the coarse mattress with a bounce that propelled her upright. She walked behind a screen, her naked back straight, her toes pointed as if she were walking a straight and narrow line. He heard her urine splash in the metal pot her nuns had put there, and seconds later she reappeared with a wool gown over her shoulders, her left arm still struggling to enter the sleeve. She poured wine for herself and cut a slice of cheese but did not eat it.

"What am I to call you now?" he said. He meant it as a joke. "Still my Lady Abbess?"

She ate the cheese, sipped the wine. Her mouth formed the kissing shape. "I am still the Abbess of Garnheim," she said coldly. "I do not expect my horse to call me Sweet just because I have ridden him."

He sat up. His lower jaw was tight with anger. "I will not call you 'my lady.' Do you understand?"

She turned slowly. "I can have you whipped," she murmured.

"I am not one of your peasants."

"You are a perfect peasant. You fuck like a peasant."

Shocked by the word, he muttered, "I am not a peasant."

"In fact, you fuck like a dog. Jump on, rut, finish."

"I am not a peasant!"

"It is uncouth to raise your voice. My ladies will hear you and will be distressed; they know you are here, but they do not want to be reminded of you." She poured herself more wine and looked him up and down as if she were appraising his body with some thought of buying it. "Who *are* you, after all?" she said.

"I am myself."

"But where do you come from? Had you parents?"

"I was a foundling."

"Dear Mother of Christ, I have allied myself with nobody!"

"I am somebody! *I am me!*" He sat up angrily. "I am what I have made myself, not what my parentage has given me!"

She sipped, chewed, nodded. "As I said, you are a peasant."

He swung his legs over the bed and stood up. "I shouldn't have come here." His shirt was on the floor, and he bent to pick it up. "You're the one who talks like a peasant, not me." Struggling into the shirt, he ripped the shoulder seam, and he lunged harder, hearing it tear with perverse satisfaction.

"Surely you're not leaving, bellfounder."

"I should never have come here." The hem of the shirt fell to his knees. He looked around for his hose, and, finding them, looked up at her. "I don't *fuck* well when I'm angry."

She shook herself out of the gown and walked naked to his side of the bed and put her wineglass down there. "Come," she said, "I'll put the lamp out and you can pretend I'm someone else you're not angry with."

"I do not need to pretend."

She shrugged. "Then I will pretend *you* are somebody else, like last time."

He struck her across the left side of the face with his right hand, pleased to see that the blow frightened her. He began to pull up his hose without looking at her again; the thin wool clung to his big thighs. He gave it a last yank and pulled up the flap that covered his groin and began to lace it to the hose. When he was done and the shirt had been tucked in so that it bulged over the top of the hose, he glanced at her. The moment their eyes met, she said, "I can have you killed."

"Well, lady," he said, falling into the old term unthinkingly, "you can have me killed and you can appeal to church court and be pardoned; yes, you can have me beaten and killed. But you cannot have anybody else make your cannons for you." His eyes flicked over hers, then went down, past the small breasts to the lean stomach and hips. To his surprise, he was instantly aroused.

She laughed. The ironic pout returned. "Well," she said. She shrugged and began to shiver, and she hugged herself, pushing her breasts together so that a long, sharp shadow folded between them. "Well, you have struck me. Well, it is not Doomsday, I suppose. I will strike you one day, and that will not mean much, either." She became grim. "But I will not be treated like your woman!"

"Woman was made from man's rib; woman is man's—"

"I was not made from your rib! I will not be ruled—nor struck, either, except by way of play—nor cuddled nor chucked under the chin nor cooed at like some dolly!" She snorted. "Woman is made to serve, aye, so we are taught. Well, I will not serve you. I will serve myself; I am your better in everything, by right of birth, by my intelligence, by my—" She clutched her hands tight, the arms crossed over her breasts. "Oh, God! if you make me weep, I *will* have you killed!"

"It is yourself will make you weep, lady."

She wiped her eyes by pressing the fingers of each hand into them as if she were hiding her eyes to play a game, and then, wiping them to the sides, she looked at him, glanced down, began to laugh when she saw his codpiece. "You lied, bellfounder," she said. "You can make love when you are angry."

He hesitated, then began to laugh with her. "Come to bed," he said, pulling off his shirt.

When they lay together, content for a while, she sprawled across him. They were quiet, and then she said, "What is your woman like?"

"My wife?"

"Aye."

He was quiet. "She had a vision," he said after some seconds.

"Do you tup her still?"

"No." He rolled his head to the side and looked into the shadows. "She dreams of St. Francis and his wounds."

"Yes." She sounded contemptuous, but behind the contempt was sadness and despair. "I have a nun who dreams of the end of the world. The seals will all be broken; the great beast will appear; there will be a sound as the world is rent asunder. The Abbess will lie down with the bellfounder."

He touched her head, but she shook his hand off impatiently.

Toward morning, her mood was different. The first birds were beginning to call, low and drowsy; at a distance, a lark sang. Coming to him from the window, she moved her mouth along his chest and down to his navel; her hand touched his testicles, his penis. She began to chuckle.

"Tell me about your great gun."

"It has not been taken from the—stop that!"

"Nay, I shall but make it salute me." She leaned back and looked at his erection, over which her hand moved slowly. "And I had one of these, I'd tup the world," she murmured.

He caught her wrist. "And you had one of those, we'd not have had such a pleasant night."

He felt her shrug. "There are more roads to pleasure than you've ridden, bellfounder. When will you shoot the cannon?"

"When it is cooled. Perhaps next week, but I have to find a private place."

"Bring it to Garnheim. The woods by the fishweir are empty. There is a little keeper's cottage there; I will meet you." Her lips brushed his; her tongue came out. With her hand still in his groin, she swung her right leg over and straddled him. Her breasts touched his chest; for two long seconds, their eyes were close and staring into each other; then hers closed and her head dropped to his shoulder and she was alone and lost to him.

He left very early to save her attendants the embarrassment of seeing him. The elaborate stratagems of her world depressed him. Riding homeward, he thought of the implications of the affair with her—how he would confess it and to whom, how he would hide it from his guild-fellows and the city. He decided that he would confess to the Bishop. "I have committed adultery....I have caused a nun to break her vow...." The fault was not solely his, however.

He thought of the sin of lust. He thought of it as it would be costumed for a pageant or a play, perhaps for some allegory that Brother Michael might have written: Lust carried in a hammock or a bed, her dress (for Lust was always a woman) voluptuous and shocking, bare arms and thighs showing, Lust with a cooing voice like the cheap whores who call from the upper windows in Old Town.

I have committed the sin of lust. I have also committed the sin of pride, for all sin is pride, pride in defiance of God.... Pride was dressed in peacock's feathers, all eyes and show, boasting.

I have not given in to envy; I envy no man. Nor to anger, though I slapped the Abbess. Was that anger?

He saw the scene as if it were an allegory incised upon the blue-green surface of an old bell—the two nude figures, the man striking the woman while Lust and Anger looked on, smiling....

I have not been seduced by greed; I am not overambitious.

I am not a miser. The Franciscans say all pursuit of money is greed, the love of the city of man instead of the city of God. Still, I do not think I am guilty of the sin of greed.

Sloth is a stranger to me; if anything, I work too much.

Gluttony? Nay, I like meat, but I am no glutton; the Bishop is more the trencherman than I.

The thought brought another picture, a banquet of the Seven Deadly Sins—the Bishop as Gluttony, food piled around his overstuffed body, his fingers greasy, his hair stiff with congealed food that had been rubbed there, his clothes a putrid mass of spills and droppings; the Abbess as Lust; the Franciscan monk, surprisingly, as Envy, not at all the way he had ever seen the man, but there he was, his face peering like a ferret's from the head of Envy; one of his apprentices as Sloth; a goldsmith in the next street as Greed; his wife— *why she?—*as Anger—*Anger? but Anger is a man; she has no sins; but maybe her piety makes her angry with men, poor woman.*

Pride dominated the picture—Pride the paradox, for Pride, though a servant, was the only one standing. It was Pride who served the banquet of sin, yet it was Pride who was host, as well; it was Pride who sneered at Gluttony and leered at Lust, who offered spiced foods and wine to heat the blood of Anger, Pride who let Gluttony gorge and Sloth snore, and Pride who whispered lies and gossip to Envy.

His own was the face of Pride.

He reined the horse. He had topped the hill above the city, and now he could look down on it. A thin mist was rising from the river, like steam from a pudding; early sunlight cast long shadows from behind him, turning the church tower into a long finger that pointed up the hill across the valley.

Mouers stood within its walls like a picture of a city, self-reliant and distinct. It caused him to smile, to stand in the stirrups and look proudly over the city that he loved, blotting the Banquet of Sin from his mind. And then, sitting in the saddle again, he remembered and recognized in the swelling of his heart that pride in the city of man that was the root, the preachers said, of all sinfulness. He tethered the horse to a stunted tree and knelt in the dew-wet weeds by the roadside and prayed. *Forgive me, God forgive me, I have sinned most terribly....* When he was done, he knelt for some seconds, his face turned up. His prayers were leaden. He was mired in pride. When he looked again at the city, he was glad.

Johan of Mouers rode home. Twenty yards from the East Gate, the muffled thud of his horse's hooves changed to the crisp clang of iron shoes on cobbles; when he passed under the gate and into the vaulting of the city wall, the hooves echoed and even the sound seemed proud to him, the sound of a conqueror.

He rode through his back gate and into the yard and walked at once to the foundry, where the cannon mold stood, ready to be opened. He thought of the core, filling the cannon barrel; it was impossible not to be reminded of intercourse. He grimaced. The Abbess disgusted him at that moment. Still, he would meet her again at the keeper's cottage.

Pride would go on serving Lust.

He touched the mold. The clay was hot.

A sound from his house turned him around. The sound came again, and he recognized a woman's voice, the tone urgent and probably frightened. It might be one of the maids screaming at another; it might be his daughter, a harridan when she was waked. Still, he hurried from the casting pit toward the door.

"Master!" His wife's maid was at a second-story window. She still wore a sleeping cap and smock; the swell of her breasts under the gathered bodice drew him. *Lust.*

"What is it?" Fatigue made him short-tempered. "What is it, you silly bitch?" *Anger.*

"It's the mistress, sir! She's hurt!"

He ran through the kitchen and up the narrow stairs. The maid was waiting for him by his wife's door; her right forearm was drawn across her breasts as if she feared he might strike her. Her eyes were swollen with sleep.

"What's happened?"

The girl swallowed. She was a broad-faced, shrewish piece who was usually to be heard lording it over the other maids, but now she was as meek as the cat.

"Mistress's hurt herself." She looked at the closed door. He pushed past her, smelling her warm, sleepy body, a smell like a child's, and tried the door, expecting it to be locked. It opened at his touch.

His wife was lying across the bed on her back. Her breathing was extraordinary, labored and tedious. Her arms were spread and the hands lay palms up, and from their centers welled dark blood. There were blood spots across the tiled floor, streaked in several places by footprints, but not so badly that the trail of blood could not be followed back to a small

67

table on the far side of the room where she sat sometimes to read *The Life of Our Lady* or to write pious prayers to send to other pious women. The inkstand on the table was one he had commissioned to be made for her; it stood a foot high, made of lead with brass inlays, its top a crowned brass spike three inches long. The spike was smeared red now, and he grimaced as he understood how she had smashed her hands down over that upturned point.

"Get the doctor," he said to the girl. "Move, you goose. Or send the stableboy; he'll be faster."

He bent over his wife. Sweat glossed her face; under half-opened lids, her eyes rolled upward.

He tore a strip from the bedsheet and began to bandage her right hand; when he lifted it, he found that there was a wound on the back of the hand, too, where the point had gone through. Blood soaked through the bandage, but he went on winding as if to hide it.

"The boy's gone for Doctor, master."

"Good." He tore off another strip. "Fetch wine for her." He began to bandage the other hand. "Katrin," he said softly. "Katrin, it's Johan. You'll be all right, hear? I've sent for the doctor."

Her tormented breathing did not ease. She did not look at him. She slowly raised her bandaged right hand and looked at it, instead; from below the strips of cloth, a rivulet of dark blood started down her arm, twisting like an animal doubling on its track.

"It will be all right, Katrin. You had one of your dreams. You fell on something."

He tucked the cloth strip under itself and tied a loose knot and put the hand back on the stained bedclothes, and when he looked at her face again, the eyes were closed and the mouth was open and smiling slightly, and her breath came through it hoarsely. She was sleeping like a drunk.

He had food served to him in a room at the back of the office, whose window looked out over the foundry and the casting pit where the cannon stood stolidly. A maid scuttled in and put food down near him and disappeared; from the rest of the house he could hear quick, muffled footsteps and the unintelligible rumble of voices. When his daughter came into the room he had still not eaten, but sat in an armchair by the window, looking out at the cannon.

"Where were you all night?" she said without prelude.

"I am weary," he said.

"Where *were* you? She was frantic. And now this!"

"I told her I would be gone all night."

"Where? Where were you?"

"Let me be, Margit; I'm weary."

"She had the Franciscan brought to her. I could hear them in her room, praying, preaching at each other until I thought I'd scream! I couldn't sleep. How could I sleep, with my father out God knows where all night and my mother closeted with that half-crazy friar? But who cared about me? Who cares if—"

"Shut up, Margit."

"I won't! I'm engaged to be married. What if folk hear my mother has gone crazy, my father is out whoremongering all night long? I try to be respectable, but what if—"

He swung his left hand, rising from the chair as he swung, and hit her under the right side of the jaw with the open palm, the movement bringing him up so that he was crouched, bearlike, his coat hanging open with its fur collar ruffed above his thick neck. "Get out," he said almost kindly. She started to weep and ran out.

Minutes later, the doctor came and told him that his wife would need care. He had prescribed poultices; her women knew what to do. He would be back in the evening, perhaps a little late because an engagement might keep him. When he went, Johan remembered that the doctor was a bachelor, and he felt a pang of yearning for the irresponsible life the man must lead.

Envy.

CHAPTER SEVEN

SHE WAS NEVER LIKE other women after that. The wounds would heal, but they would leave lumps of scar in her palms, perfect circles like targets. The scars would itch; in bad weather, they might give her pain.

She stayed in bed for three days with her women around her, visited by the doctor and the Franciscan and certain pious women. When, on the fourth day, she appeared in the house again, she was pale and she looked like a woman who had just given birth, haggard and swollen-faced.

She took vows of poverty and humility, and her part of the house suddenly became a convent of sorts. There were always women he didn't know there, often the poorest and meanest of the city, dregs he would have preferred to have out of his sight. Yet he said nothing. He earned himself some sympathy from his guild-fellows, and if it angered him at first that it was his money that made it possible for her to turn his house into a hospice, he quickly conquered himself. Some of the credit in Heaven might be his.

He confessed his sins to the Bishop. The Bishop was furious with him and with the Abbess, but he did not refuse to give the penance with which Johan would cleanse himself. His rage was evident in his voice, but he did not refuse relief.

"This is a grave sin," he muttered. Johan could tell that his jaws were tight with anger. "You have put yourself and her in peril." He seemed to wait for some response; then he barked, "Well?"

"I am heartily sorry, my lord."

"Is it love, is that it? Do you love her?"

"No, my lord."

"Well, what, then? Do you rut like an animal, is it merely lust? Well?"

"I—I don't know, my lord."

"You must never do it again. Well? Do it again and you are damned eternally, do you understand? Well?"

"Yes, my lord."

But when he dined with the Bishop that evening, the cleric's mood had changed, as if he had put off his rage with his robes. He seemed amused.

"Is the Abbess satisfied with your work, bellfounder? Do you think she is happy with the way you wield your tool?"

Johan picked at a chicken he was pulling apart. "I don't think I want to talk about it outside the confessional, my lord."

"Come, come, don't get grand with me; I am asking you, does the lady like your swinking?" They exchanged a long look, and the Bishop, finding Johan unmovable, shrugged and looked away. "I meant only that we might unlock her treasury more easily if she was happy with you. If your key fits her lock, I mean."

Johan said nothing. He poured himself wine.

"Has your wife any suspicion?"

"I think not."

"They tell me she has had a vision. In Muhldorf, they say she was miraculously gifted with Our Lord's wounds."

"She mutilated herself on an inkstand."

The Bishop widened his eyes in mock astonishment. "Skepticism, bellfounder! Tut, tut! This is what comes from associating too intimately with the nobility."

"I do not doubt that my wife has been touched by the Holy Spirit. She's a good woman. She gives her life to God. But that she mutilated herself on the inkstand, I do not doubt that, either."

"They say she touches for the cure of disease. Is it true?"

"There is always a crowd in my house. Maybe she touches. I have not seen it."

The Bishop made a noise with the tip of his tongue and his teeth; he sounded like a squirrel. He looked down his nose at his knife blade, twisting it so that it would catch the candlelight. "I do not want you to abandon your wife, Johan."

"I have no thought of it."

"Whatever she does, whatever all this means, you must be man and wife—in appearance, anyway. I don't want you to be a bad example."

"I think I know my own responsibility."

The Bishop nodded. He stood up, patted his belly, stretched. "What of the cannon?"

"We pulled it from the mold today. It's perfect."

"When do you shoot it?"

"Next week." He glanced up defiantly. "Beyond the fishweir woods of Garnheim."

The Bishop sat down, sank back in the chair. His mouth was pursed up, and for a moment he was fleetingly reminiscent of the Abbess in the expression; then the resemblance vanished and his mouth, set in its wiry tangle of beard hairs, looked to Johan like an animal anus. The Bishop stroked his mustache. "I can shrive you, bellfounder; I can warn you of peril to your soul. But I can't help your earthly life." He reached for the wine. "The Abbess can never be a happy woman; she can never make you happy. She hates the world, and yet she's entirely of it; she shouldn't be an abbess, not even a nun. If it weren't for the Ritter and his menace, I'd demand that she renounce—." He looked into the wineglass and sighed bitterly. "I need her worldliness just now. Her money."

"The times are bad."

The Bishop turned the cup. The lights, reflected in the curved metal, winked on the walls. "There was a baby born at Muhldorf last week with teeth like a cat's. I saw it. Yes, the times are bad."

"Maybe my wife is the best of us. The holiest."

The Bishop's laugh barked. "What a creature you are, Johan! Your wife becomes a nun; a nun becomes your whore!" He laughed on, the sound wild and loud in the small room. His frank stare seemed to dare Johan's anger. When the laughter had run out like the last of the liquid poured from a pitcher, he reached again for the wine. "Are you afraid, Johan?"

"Yes."

"So am I. God means for us to be afraid, that's why he sends these signs. He doesn't mean for us to be happy."

"I am not happy."

"No, nor am I. Nor is the Abbess. We are three good, miserable sinners. Our sins make us unhappy, and that's the way God wants it. Would you have it other than the way He wants?"

Johan refused the wine with a shake of his head. "I saw my wife yesterday with some of her women. Her hands were all bandaged; she looks sick. But she was happy."

"Your wife is not a sinner. Nor is she the one who is going to save Mouers from the Ritter."

"Then maybe God means for Mouers to be taken by the Ritter. She seemed so—at peace. Peaceful."

They were both silent. The candles guttered as if a gust of wind had blown through the room; far away outdoors, a shutter banged. Johan touched his forehead and then looked at his fingers as if he expected to find blood or paint or dirt there. "I'm burning up," he said.

"Too much wine."

"I must go home."

He stood up. He swayed and supported himself on the table, suddenly dizzy. "Are you coming to see the cannon tried?"

"For as long as I can spare. I won't stay the night." The Bishop's voice was dry.

In the morning, Johan was feverish and short-tempered and his head ached as if he had drunk too much, but there was burning at the back of his throat and his nose that told him he was sick. He went out nonetheless and told Piet to prepare the mold to cast a second cannon. Ingots of copper had already been piled in the crucible, waiting for the fire.

There was a knot of people at his front door, one of them a man whose face was covered with boils, another with an ulcerated arm that was oozing matter. Across the street, the wife of the whitesmith was looking down from her balcony with disgust, and, seeing him, she made a face and turned away.

"Have these people put inside," he told the steward. "The neighbors shouldn't have to look at them."

"What will we tell people that come to see you, master?"

"Send them around to the works. Move my office out there."

He left instructions that a narrow bed and his worktable and his clothes were to be moved to a small room over the storage shed, and then he went up to his wife's side of the house to tell her that he was leaving overnight. She hardly noticed him. He kissed her cheek; she smiled. Going out, he met his son and embraced him, wanting for a moment to take the boy with him and then thinking of the Abbess; he let the boy go and watched him move into his mother's room for prayers, and then he went downstairs and out to the yard and got on the horse a servant was holding for him, and, with a boy following on a mule with his clothes, he rode out of the city.

The cannon had gone on before him a day earlier, hidden in a cartload of scrap metal so that there would be no questions; Hans Bighead and an apprentice had gone with it. Components to make up gunpowder had been sent still earlier, the now self-important Cob personally carrying the six pounds of salpetre he had made in the remains of Michael's laboratory.

Johan rode hunched over like the sick man he was, passing the spot where he had knelt to pray without a glance, seeing only the horse's mane and the road slipping by beyond it. A painful cough came up from his lungs, and his shoulders ached fiercely; when he touched his forehead, there was sweat there.

At Garnheim, Cob had collected a keg of sulphur and four bags of charcoal and was ready to set out again. Led by one of the nuns, they rode in silence, the nun disapproving and hard-faced, Johan sick, Cob too full of himself to speak to the boy who brought up the rear on the mule.

"So, you really are sick, bellfounder," the Bishop said

73

when they had crossed the river and ridden down to the meadow by the weir.

"I feel like death."

"You look it, too. Want to postpone the test?"

"No. I'm not that sick."

Cob was mixing the gunpowder behind a screen of small trees; only Johan and Hans Bighead were allowed to watch him as he dipped the elements out of their containers and mingled them in a tub, reaching in sometimes up to the elbows with his bare arms; when he lifted his hands out, they were black. At Johan's command, he expertly rolled a cylinder of bark and plugged it and filled it with gunpowder, and then self-consciously put it on a stump and touched it off. The explosion and the rolling smoke delighted the Bishop, who was standing twenty feet away, and the Abbess, who, sitting under a canvas pavilion like a lady at a play, applauded.

The cannon had been lashed with heavy rope to a double plank half again as long as the gun; the plank was pinned to two oak beams, on which the apprentice and Hans Bighead were piling large stones.

A pound of powder was put in the cannon's mouth and pushed down with a tool that Hans Bighead had made; Cob sprinkled powder in the touchhole and then dropped a coal on it with a pair of tongs, and the cannon spat and hissed and a vast amount of white smoke and sulphurous stench rolled out. Johan coughed and feared he would strangle.

"You should be seen to," The Bishop said. "Put off the test."

"I will be fine."

Late in the afternoon, when they had tried two larger charges of powder but no ball, the last with a wad of dried moss that had contained the explosion sufficiently to make the gun roar instead of hiss, Johan ordered the cart in which the cannon had been carried to be pulled up opposite the cannon's mouth, some hundred feet away. The gun was loaded with three pounds of powder and two double handfuls of round pebbles that Hans Bighead had picked up along the riverbank. There was some discussion of what the cannon should shoot—arrows, the Abbess said; the Bishop held out for boulders—but Johan decided on the stones, because he wanted to know if a rain of small projectiles would be useful against a mass of men rather than a single crushing shot. A ball of moss was pounded in on top of the pebbles, and Cob pronounced himself ready. He sprinkled more powder into the touchhole, his hands shaking and his face white.

Hans Bighead and Johan looked down the barrel from the breech. The gun had no sights—none of them had thought of sights—so that only the general direction of the bore was discoverable.

"Shall I have the horse unhitched from the cart, master?"

Johan tried to clear his throat. Unable to speak, he waved his hand and shook his head. *Get on with it*. The journeyman bent over the cannon again.

"The horse has moved the cart now, master."

The Bishop tittered. Johan waved impatiently and the apprentice ran forward and forced the horse to back the cart into the cannon's path. All the time that he was out beyond the muzzle, the young man kept his frightened eyes on it, and he had to be shouted at to keep from backing the horse too far. When he ran back, the tired old nag followed his retreat with its eyes, head lowered, great belly drooped almost to the ground under its wretchedly curved spine. It was a worthless horse.

When the cannon went off, there was no simple hiss, no muffled bang. With Hans Bighead's arm extended fully, the five-foot-long rod he had fashioned to hold a coal had hardly hovered over the touchhole when the gun fired and the entire carriage shook and some of the rocks rolled off the oak beams; the gun itself could be seen to rise from the planking against the restraint of the heavy ropes, as if it meant to fly away. A concussive roar, painful and loud, came from it; too late, the Abbess covered her ears. The gun fired and then it was over, so quickly that they were not prepared, and in the same instant they heard the rattle of the stone shot against the cart.

The smoke wisped and twisted and slowly retreated from the line of fire. When they could see it, they found that most of the canvas top had been ripped away from the cart. The near wheel, which had been made of overlapped pieces of oak, was split in half and the cart had sunk to the side on it; as they watched, it slewed forward as the horse, his near back leg buckled, began to sink, blood running from three holes in his drooping belly; then, with a maddened whinny, he tried to rise and run, but the leg buckled again and he crashed to the ground, to thrash and buck and beg for release from the agony they had caused him.

The Bishop, seeing the damage, crossed himself.

The Abbess turned angrily to the men around the gun. "See to the beast; are you blind?" she shouted, and the apprentice ran toward it, pulling a heavy iron maul with which he tried to kill the frantic animal, his first swing partly missing and breaking its jaw, the second missing entirely. Hans Bighead came up and took the sledge away and with a single clean blow dispatched it.

They walked toward the cart like communicants in a procession, the Bishop first, all kept by an unspoken fear from walking directly in front of the gun. They processed around the horse and around the cart.

"This is a fearful thing," the Bishop said hoarsely.

Johan walked back to the gun, then up to the cart again, trying to see if any shot had fallen short. "Tomorrow," he said in a hoarse caw to Hans Bighead, "we see how far the stones spread. We'll set up boards"—he pointed beyond the dead horse—"until we find how wide it shoots." He tried to clear his throat. "We'll have to try a heavier charge. And more shot. Until we know—" He blinked. Sweat was trickling down his left temple. "Until we know how far, how much—how well she'll shoot."

"Awesome," the Bishop murmured.

"It will be awesome," the Abbess said, "when there are twenty more like it." She looked down with distaste at the dead animal. "Though I am somewhat impressed with the effect, I confess."

That night, Johan lay in the farmhouse by the fishweir wood, half-delirious for part of the night, convinced that piles of metal were growing on the foot of his bed. The coverlet seemed to thicken between his fingers, to grow huge, big enough to crush him; then it would recede, leaving piles of scrap behind it to weigh down his legs so that he moved them with difficulty to cooler spots between the sheets. The Abbess hovered near him; she mopped his chest with a wet cloth, then his legs and feet.

"Make them stop," he whined. He sounded like an old man.

"Stop what?"

"Make them stop. All that metal. Make them stop."

"It will go away. Sleep. Go to sleep."

"Make them go away."

In the low hours of the morning the dream changed; he had an erection: she mounted him, torso rigid, kneeling, upright, head thrown back. He saw her as at a distance. If he

76

had tried to reach out, he thought he would not reach her; she would have been too far away. It was the same as with the coverlet, but now it was distance that was expanding. Still he saw her with his fever's clarity, watched her and understood what her solitary writhing meant. It mattered not at all that he was sick, bad-smelling, incoherent. He served the purpose: she was damning herself.

"Go away," he whispered, but she didn't go until she was done.

When he woke it was just daylight. The room was cold; he was uncovered and naked and chilled. He rolled over on his belly and pushed himself up and put a leg over the bed so that he could slowly get to his feet. He thought it might be evening, not morning, but when he got to the window he saw the gray dust of frost over the grass and knew it was morning. He went back to bed, to huddle under his cloak until his servant brought wine and a hot cloth to wipe his teeth with.

"Will I send for doctor, master?"

"Nay, nay, I am better."

"Some told me I wa'n't to sleep in the room, maister." The boy was frightened. "I'da been here to tend to you, but sister there, she tole me not to tend you."

"One of the nuns took care of me."

"Glad of that, maister. Thought I done wrong."

"Nay, you didn't do wrong. Hand me the wine." He leaned his bare shoulders against the cold, whitewashed wall, because there was no headboard to the bed. His breathing was a harsh rasp. "Tell Hans Bighead I'll see him in the field when he's eaten. And tell Cob I want sulphur to breathe!"

He fired the gun three times that day—as often as they had gunpowder for. On the last shot, the cannon broke its ropes and bucked like an angry horse. It was slow to load and impossible to aim, but he had proved that it could be shot and that it would kill. He had another cart brought and the cannon loaded into it, and he saw it started back on its journey to Mouers with a guard of two of the Bishop's men riding behind it.

"I want more gunpowder," he told Cob. "Much more gunpowder. Tell Hans Bighead what you'll need; we'll buy it."

A servant told him that the Abbess of Garnheim had ridden back to her abbey, and he lay alone that night with the servant outside his door, and in the morning he rode back to Mouers with a cough and a bad throat, spitting foul-tasting

77

matter on the ground as he rode. He went straight to the room above the storage shed and went to bed, telling the boy to bring him more comforters and wine and hot broth, and he slept most of the night and much of the next day, waking twice to kick the boy and tell him to fetch more broth, and that evening he felt well enough to dress and go out.

He went through a side gate of his garden and stood in the gloom under two apple trees that were just coming into blossom. Three women were moving slowly down the garden toward him. They seemed to have no means of propulsion, but to be moved invisibly, magically, over the walk between the beds of dead herbs and bare, wet earth. A murmur rose from one of them—prayer or recitation, he could not tell.

One of them was his wife. As she came closer, he bent his head.

"Bless you," she said. It did not seem like her voice. Looking up with his head lowered, he saw that she was smiling faintly; their glances met, and her smile grew to one of happy recognition. She slowly bobbed her head to him—a parody of his own bow, perhaps? Or was it a more thoughtful and benign gesture—forgiveness? Acceptance?

"Good evening, Katrin," he murmured.

She put a finger to her lips and smiled again. One of the women was reading. He took a short step backward so that his heel sank in the soft earth and the apple buds framed his face, and the three women moved on and were lost in the twilight, the murmur of the voice like a cooing bird for some time after they had turned a corner and passed from his sight.

He ate alone in a room at the back of the house. Creakings and muffled voices seemed to come from all around him, and he realized that the house was full of people.

"Send my meals out to the works after this," he said to the steward. "The room where my things are."

The man bowed. He was sixty, indifferent. He had given up on Johan the Bellfounder.

"Send out wine and broth at midnight."

Curiosity took him through some of the downstairs rooms; people he did not know looked up guiltily or angrily and then looked away. Passing along a corridor, he heard the sudden, sharp noise of two voices striking against each other in argument. He located them down another corridor that led to the servants' rooms, and he took two quiet steps along it. One of the voices belonged to his wife's maidservant, the wide-faced girl who had called him when she had mutilated her hands; the other belonged to one of the common maids. Their wrangle was an old one—duties, rank, their places in the order of the household.

"Do you both want to be whipped?" he said sharply. The wide-faced girl was weeping; surprised, guilty, she stopped. The other one froze with a triumphant smile fading from her face; her breathing came and went loudly.

"How dare you make noise in my house! Well?"

They stammered and babbled but no sense came out. There was no sense to be made of it; they were simply clawing at each other.

"Go!" he said to the housemaid. "Leave me. If you ever do this again, you'll be whipped and put out of the house."

The wide-faced girl had stopped crying, and now she looked frightened and angry, but she was calm. "My mistress has no need of me any more," she whimpered. "She has those women to tend to her now. I have no place."

"I will send you home."

"I want my place here. Please!" She had a very broad forehead and a pointed chin, and the top half of her head looked too large for the rest. She was almost a monster, and yet she was curiously pretty.

"Has my wife sent you away?"

"No! But when I go to her, there are always the other women. There's no place for me. She doesn't care about her hair or her dresses now. She makes me pray or help her with the sick ones. Some of them are disgusting!" She wept again. She dropped to her knees and bent far forward to rest her head on his foot; her hands clutched at his ankles like briars.

"My daughter has her own maid. You'll be better off at home."

"No!" She twisted her head to look up at him. "Please don't send me back to that!"

He pulled away. "Continue on as my wife's maid, then, until she sends you away herself. If there's nothing for you to do—then do nothing. But don't wrangle in my house. I'll tell the steward not to give you duties with the common maids."

He hesitated. He felt weary and weak from his sickness, light-headed with illness and fatigue, yet his heart was pounding and he knew that he was enjoying the familiar thrill of temptation. "Bring me sweet wine after vespers. I will be in the room above the shed." He looked down at her. "What is your name?"

"Greta." She lay on the floor as if she might go to sleep there forever; when he looked back from the end of the corridor, she was still lying there, watching him.

The journeyman Piet came to him just at dark. "I'll be ready to pour metal sometime in the morning, master."

"So soon?"

"We're almost melted."

"It seems too soon. The mold could be cool yet."

"It's hot. I've had the fires very high; I knew you was in a hurry."

"Very well, call me when you're ready. Mind you knock first."

As Piet was going out the low door, Johan said, "And Piet?"

"Yes, master."

"See my son is there to watch the pouring. Tell the steward he is to be there."

CHAPTER EIGHT

WHEN THE KNOCK CAME, he was awake. He signaled the girl to silence and called out, and Piet's voice, muffled by the heavy door, said that he was ready to pour metal.

"Has my son been called?"

"I'm just going now, master."

"Then go."

He dressed by the light of a single lamp. The girl's wide, feral face was always turned toward him as he moved around the room. "Why do you look at me?" he said.

"I don't know."

"Then don't do it." He tied the strings at his throat and reached for his heavy coat. "Do you want to come back here?"

"Yes. Tomorrow?"

"No. The night after. Go back to your room now."

"I'll wake the others. They'll ask where I've been."

"Tell them you've been with my wife. Tell them you've been praying for their souls."

The air was cold enough for frost. He worried about the apple blossoms, then thought about the women as they had glided through the garden toward him. There was no moonlight and he could not see even the silhouettes of the trees above the wall, but he could smell the damp earth that had been turned over.

He went down along the building and walked to the casting pit. Above the cannon mold, the furnace turned the misty air a coppery red, while in the furnaces fire glowed hot orange against the deeper blackness.

His son was led out by Piet, still in his nightclothes and with a fur wrapped around him, from which his head emerged like a wobbly doll's. He stumbled. Johan went to him and hugged him, fur robe and all, and the boy stirred and tried to pretend he was awake.

"Wine," Johan said. An apprentice ran toward the house.

Johan sipped wine and gave the boy some to warm him. The laborers were moving around the pit, checking the shoring and the brickwork at the base; above on the scaffold, Piet called down orders to them and shouted at the apprentices. Satisfied at last, Piet leaned over the railing and called, "Ready, Master Johan!"

Johan drank, swallowed.

"Pour!" he bellowed.

Piet waved and shouted an order at Hans Bighead. Three of the laborers were already at the long rods that would open the gates. They reached up to grasp the oak handles and then, on Hans's command, they wrestled the long rods back, and inside the casing above the mold the gates opened and the molten bronze began to flow.

Tired, sleepy, still sick, he was nonetheless the most sensitive to any trouble and the most worried. He knew at once the look, the sound, even the smell that the cracking mold made—first, an indefinable change in the surface of the cope, caused perhaps by the first steam through a pinhole there and bits of clay and a wisp of smoke, a mere obscuring of the exterior; then, sometimes, an actual coloring of the clay with heat; or, if the metal had come up that high inside the mold, a glimpse of the liquid metal through the hairline crack. This time, the sequence was very fast: he had hardly dared to recognize the first wisp of steam when the entire rent, a jagged line eighteen inches long, turned bright red like a stroke of lightning down the mantle as the metal filled it, and, held for an instant by its own surface tension, seemed

81

to check; then metal began to trickle, then to gush over the outside of the mold and harden, to be buried under more molten bronze as the fiery liquid, meeting the night air, popped and bubbled and exploded.

"Close the gates!" he screamed. The effort made his ears hurt. He threw the wine cup from him as the metal began to shoot from the crack. "A crack! Piet, close the gate!"

The laborers still held the gate rods, and now one of them, an experienced man, began to shove his rod back in, but the other two stared stupidly, one of them even leaning on the gate handle like a side of meat hanging from a hook.

"Close the damned gates!"

On the platform, Piet was cursing. Johan ran toward the nearest gate rod. The metal spat and hissed; the crack lengthened and clots of metal shot twenty feet through the black air like falling stars; one landed on his cloak and began to smolder. He pushed one of the laborers away, smashing the man into the brick buttress of the pit, and grabbed the rod with his bare hands and began to twist it home. He felt the grating resistance of metal on metal, pulled it out and thrust it back again, twisting and vibrating it to move the gate in its slot.

"Get the boy out!" he bellowed. His son was still standing there, hypnotized by the hot sparks that were landing at his feet. "Get him out!"

He leaned on the rod with all his strength and it ground into its tracks and the gate closed. Johan let go, staggered past the next gate, where Hans was slamming it closed, and went around the pit to look at the mold. The crack had widened to a full inch, and a foot down it a whole chunk had come away and metal was sliding out like a red tongue, an obscene, fiery slither that oozed over the ground and at last congealed in a great, formless mass around the floor of the pit. One wood support had caught fire and was being doused with water.

Somebody was screaming, the sound trickling off and then surging into a scream again. Johan spun about and saw one of the apprentices on the ground, Piet and a laborer bent over, trying to keep him from clawing at his face. They held his hands and wrestled with him while he tried to pluck the fading red bronze from his face.

It was the apprentice he had cast as Sloth. He was all activity now—throat screaming, arms thrashing in their grip, back arched in agony. A bursting bubble had splattered on his face and neck, setting his shirt on fire and taking off his skin. Johan touched the old scar on his chest and felt sick.

"Put out the furnaces." Johan sagged against a buttress. "Put out all the fires, in the name of God." He stopped one of the laborers, surprised that his hand hurt when he touched the man's bare arm. "Go for the doctor."

His son was standing in the shelter of the storage shed, his fur cloak pulled tight around him, the cloak encircled by a pair of bare arms. It was Greta, whose feral face looked over the boy's shoulder. He clung to her, his face buried in her shoulder.

"He's fine, he's only frightened," she said. "He's fine."

"Let me see." The boy turned. Johan saw nothing, then found the tiny mark just above his right eye, hardly larger than a pinprick, where a bit of metal had struck him.

"Does it hurt?"

"What? I didn't feel anything."

Johan grasped his face in one big hand and turned the head, screwing the boy's face up in pain. There were no more marks, only the single, tiny scar he would always carry.

"Put him to bed."

She studied him, knowing that he was angry with her. "I heard the shouting; I had to cross the yard," she said.

"Tell them you were the first to wake up, that's why you weren't in your bed." His anger faded; he put his fingers in the boy's hair and pulled his head to him. "Go to bed," he said softly.

The doctor came and tried to apply a soothing grease to the apprentice's face, but the skin came off like the skin of a spitted chicken, crisp and blackened, and the boy, slothful no more, screamed and thrashed, and Johan had him carried into the cellar and sent a message to his wife, asking that she go down to him. Perhaps her touch, which the sick came for, would soothe the wretch.

The furnace fires were dying. The metal, solidified but still hot enough to cook flesh, steamed when some of the water dripped on it, and he had a railing thrown up around the pit until the metal would be cool. The workmen kept away from him, working quickly and without noise.

"Shall we lift it out of the pit, Master Johan?" Hans Big-head stood a body's length away from him, while Piet was not to be seen.

"Where is Piet?"

Hans shrugged. There were smudges on his face, and the

front of his leather jerkin had stiffened with the heat, and
its edges were curled like the scallops around a piecrust.

"I want Piet."

"It ain't his fault, master; the signs was all correct, metal
looked ready for casting, mold, she was hot—"

"Send him to me."

Hans hung his head. Again he muttered. "Shall we lift
her out of pit, Master Johan?"

Johan looked at the obscene mass around the mold. "No.
Leave it."

"Can lift it with yon chains, Master Johan. Can get her
out of there and start a new mold."

Johan shook his head. "Tell everybody to get some sleep."
He looked at the pit. "It's God's will that we not make it."

There was an oak tun at the corner of the shed, half full
now of rainwater from the eave, and he leaned his groin
against its lip and bent forward to push his hands deep under
the water. His palms stung fiercely, even in the cool water;
when he raised his arms they began to hurt still more and
he thrust them under again, his forehead pressed against the
side of the building, and in that position the doctor found
him.

"The boy can't live, I'm afraid," he said, hardly looking at
Johan. "Your wife is with him. She called the friar."

"How long?"

"The burns are very deep." The doctor cleared his throat.
"He has started to bleed."

"Well. I'll make it right with his parents. Somehow."

He let the doctor apply salve to his blistered palms and
then he fell into his bed and slept, drugged with fatigue and
failure.

"It is impossible!" the Bishop shouted. "Impossible! I don't
believe it—a month at the most until the Ritter takes the
field, and you say you will make no more cannons!"

Johan of Mouers sat stolidly, his bandaged hands on the
table in front of him, their white thickness faintly ludicrous,
like the oversized paws of some animal. "I did not say I will
not, my lord; I said I could not."

The Bishop wiped his hands down his face, forehead to
chin, letting the fingers pull the lower lids down horribly; he
groaned with exasperation. "You astound me! You, of all
people!" He pointed a shaking finger at Johan. "You told me
three months ago you would do anything to save your city!"

"And so I would."

"But you will not risk your reputation," the Abbess of Garnheim murmured. She was at her haughtiest, her chin tilted, her jaw tight so that the words seemed to struggle from her teeth sideways. "One failure, and you cringe. Is it the opinion of the city that you fear, bellfounder? Or are you simply timid?"

The Bishop glanced at the ceiling and tapped his fingers on his belly as they glared at each other; the Abbess's face was aloof, but she was flushed.

"I do not expect either of you to understand the meaning of what happened in my foundry," Johan said quietly. "Only another founder could understand. But I lost an apprentice; the boy died this morning. I lost a journeyman, who was responsible and who has run away." He glanced down. "I have lost my hands—for a month, the doctor says; but I think less. I heal fast." He looked at her. "I lost the mold for the great gun. Now, I would have to begin again, all of it over again—making the mold, drying it, praying that it will not crack—by the time I was done, as my lord has said, the Ritter would be in the field." His eyes met hers; he looked away. "I am not timid, lady; I am practical. Maybe you don't understand the difference. But without a miracle, I would make no more than two great guns before Corpus Christi. And miracles do not seem to be working for me."

The Abbess's head jerked like that of a nervy horse. "We will need twenty great guns, at least!"

She began to chatter about oaths and honor. She would work herself up, he supposed, into a rage. He did not listen.

The Bishop growled in counterpoint. He agreed with her and added his own outrage, the two of them egging each other on in mounting fury like two cats mating in an alley. They sputtered and fumed. They looked for other solutions—an ally of the Emperor's would come to their aid; her relatives would be persuaded to send troops from the north; the anti-Pope would preach a crusade against the Ritter; the...

When he thought they had gone on long enough, he leaned a little forward along the table and pulled the wine pitcher toward him. It was a very fine one that held about two quarts, made of glass with a metal foot and a metal cover and handle. Picking this up by the foot, he swung it back and down so that it exploded on the table and wine and shards of glass splattered over the Bishop and the Abbess and Johan himself. The Abbess screamed and raised her hands, the corners of

85

her mouth pulled down in fear; the Bishop reared back and all but tipped over his chair, and when he recovered he was half out of it with one hand on the table and one leg stuck out as if to flee.

"My Lord Bishop," Johan said slowly. "My Lady Abbess." He looked from one to the other of them. "The time for nattering is over. Sit down, my lord. My lady, you will be none the worse for taking your hands away from your face; the damage is done."

If she had once had the face of Lust, it had metamorphosed into Anger. He hardly looked at her.

The door opened cautiously and one of the Bishop's servants looked in. "Leave us," Johan said. "I spilled some wine."

The man vanished. Behind the Bishop, the sun turned the panes of glass that looked out on the square bright pink, and the light, falling through them, fell at an angle across both Bishop and Abbess and turned them ruddy-colored.

"The time has come to change." The Abbess would not look at him; the Bishop would, and was offended. "My lord, I want to hear no more from you about great guns; it is too late, and I know more than you do of such things now. You are my authority and my guide in matters spiritual—but you are not a cannon-maker.

"My lady, talk to us no more about how many guns we *must* have. So long as you pay, you may expect our help; but pray command no more.

"My Lord Bishop—my Lady Abbess—henceforth my foundry will make only small bronze guns, not great guns, not cannons to knock down the walls of Jerusalem with, but small guns such as three men may fire and two men may move from place to place. I will make two molds, and in a month I will make a dozen of such little cannons; six of them will go on the city walls with the great gun already made."

Her eyes widened; her right hand tightened into a fist and she opened her mouth to object.

"You will be repaid, lady, from the corporation and the guilds. The matter is closed.

"One of my journeymen with three apprentices can make these little cannons. They will serve well enough."

"But this is—" the Bishop began.

"If you please, my lord, I had not finished." Johan looked at his bandaged right hand, on whose palm a winestain lay like blood. Near its center there was a sliver of glass, which he worked out of the fabric as he talked. "It is God's will that

I not make great guns. It is God's will, perhaps, that I find some other way.

"Do not interrupt me, please, my lord.

"Instead of great guns, I will make the dozen small ones—swallows, if they are compared to the great hawk I cast first. And I will also make fifty little guns so small that I have no name for them, but if the small cannons are swallows, they will be as wasps. Indeed, I will make them so small that one man will hold and fire them."

The Bishop's mouth was open. A sound like a low dog's growl came from it and formed into speech. "I think you're mad." He giggled and looked at the Abbess. "I think he's gone mad."

"No, my lord, I am very sane. I am not bemused, like you two, with romances and histories and tales of great battles. I simply want to knock down some men-at-arms and some horsemen, not to capture Mahomet's capital."

"Who will shoot these little guns of yours?"

"I will train them, my lord. Craftsmen, guild-fellows—I'll find them."

When she could speak, her voice was horrified. "You mean to give these pipsqueak guns to *common people?*"

"Aye, lady, for they will be very common little guns."

"To shoot at horsemen? *Knights?*"

"Aye. And their horses."

She laughed; she seemed relieved. "Their armor will repel your little pebbles."

"I think not."

"Of course it will!"

"If it will, then you will lose Garnheim."

"Better to lose it than to see p-p-*peasants* shooting down noble horsemen! It is b-b-blasphemy!"

"Nay, lady, I think it is God's will. Why else would he have cracked my mold?"

"Oh, it is impossible!" she wailed.

"Johan," the Bishop pleaded, "my son—"

"My mind is made up, my lord."

"But you're giving us insanity! What are you thinking of?"

Johan smiled sadly. "I am thinking of what can be done in four weeks. I am thinking that casting big guns in bronze is too slow, so I will cast a few little ones; but welding these very little ones, these wasps, in iron is fast and cheap, and there are ten smiths in Mouers who can make them under my direction. I am thinking that it takes a month to train the wretchedest gun crew in Christendom, but I can teach a man to shoot one of my handguns in a third of that time. I am thinking that a great gun takes as much gunpowder in one shot as my powdermaker can make in two days, but these handguns will shoot twenty times for the same amount. I am thinking that you two believe in grand gestures and beautiful ceremonies, but I do not—and death does not, and battle does not! The Ritter will come with his army, and he and his half-dozen knights will ride their horses and be noble and very proper and very deadly, and his men-at-arms and his peasants will fight like animals and hack us all to pieces like any heathen from beyond Jerusalem! We have no knights to fight with his knights; we have few enough crossbowmen, fewer still of longbows. Well, we will have men armed with a weapon that Josef Redhand, nor any other Ritter, either, has ever seen—not one big cannon that will make great fire and smoke and send some boulder three hundred yards, but fifty little guns that will, I tell you, kill a horse or a peasant or a man as well as any clothyard bolt that was ever shot from a bow!"

The Abbess's nostrils were flared with anger, but there was something almost of pity in her face, too. "Johan—" she began, her voice pleading.

"It is too late!" His bellow filled the room and made it echo and resound. "Take it or leave it!"

They began to speak at the same time, the two of them. He let them talk. An hour later, they were still trying to deny the coldness of the facts he had given them. The servant brought in fruit and cold meat and bread, and when it was eaten and the table was littered with crumbs and the Bishop looked dizzy with fatigue and wine, they had succumbed to the inevitable. Not to the wisdom of his argument, not to the practicality of his idea nor the power of the city and the guilds behind him, but to the inevitable failure of other alternatives. The Bishop was praying. The Abbess wept.

"Amen," Johan murmured when the Bishop had finished. He let a moment of silence pass to make a bridge between piety and practicality, and then he swung to the Abbess and said, ignoring her tears, "The hand-cannons will cost seven kosters each."

"Do you dare," she said slowly, "to beg me for money for a folly that I loathe?"

He nodded. "I do. I must. I will do the work for free, my

lady, but my fellow craftsmen cannot. I must have three hundred and fifty kosters for the hand-cannons and another hundred for salpetre and sulphur; and as the gunners will be freemen of the city, they will have one koster each for each week of training and another for each week they are under arms, and some small bonus for any fighting that they do."

"I will not give a penny. Let your *free* men fight for free!"

"You must. If you do not, there will be no Garnheim and no Mouers, and your own freedom will be only a memory. My Lady Abbess—*please.*"

The Bishop was gnawing on the knuckles of his right hand as if the fist were an uncouth piece of meat he had been served, as if he were Gluttony in truth, so reduced that he gnawed himself. "Oh, give him what he wants. He's our only hope, God help us."

The Abbess, like a cat stretching, straightened and lengthened her spine and sat rigid with her hands pressed against the chairseat on each side of her hips. "Very well. I will pay for these guns and the sulphur and the powder—but not one groat for free men to man them! My Lord Bishop and I will find young gentlemen to fire them."

Johan looked at the Bishop. The cleric was nibbling his knuckles again and looking worried. "Well, my lord?"

The Bishop muttered something about time and the lack of sympathy among the local nobility. He would not meet the Abbess's eye.

"Then I will find them," she said.

Johan bowed his head gravely. "So be it." He tried to smile at her. "But the Lady Abbess will provide the four hundred and fifty for the guns and the powder. And, as time is essential and craftsmen do not work for nothing, the sooner—"

"Yes, yes, the sooner the better! You will have your wretched money, you and your fellow tradesmen! You may send a man for it tomorrow to Garnheim—*your representative* will be most welcome there." They looked at each other. She would not be stared down; indeed, she straightened even more as she stared at him with hostile eyes. It was he who broke it off, with the slightest of shrugs and an impatient sigh.

"Thank you both," he murmured, and stood up to signal that their meeting was over, although they were gathered in the Bishop's house and had eaten the Bishop's food.

In the courtyard, she was stepping up on the mounting block when he went out, her horse waiting quietly with his head held by one of her farmers. She mounted and said something to the man and he started to lead the animal off, but Johan, stepping into his path, stopped him with a touch and stood close by her knees to look up at her, acutely aware of her body under the folds of her gray gown.

"I may not see the Lady Abbess again," he said, "and I wanted to say that I hope we won't part as enemies."

"If we do not meet again," she said, "I will not quite weep."

"Then say we do not part enemies."

"I cannot tell the sun to stand still and I cannot say that black is white; why should I say we are not enemies? We are as thorough enemies as any two creatures on this sad earth, I think."

The horse shied and the farmer spoke soothingly to it; Johan never took his eyes from hers. "Well, then—say at least that you forgive me, as I forgive you."

"I do not want your forgiveness! It is not your *place* to forgive me!"

He stood with his left hand on the saddle only an inch from her dress; he saw her breasts rise with a breath and he was aware of the still world around them—a hawk wheeling overhead, a bee buzzing somewhere behind him in a flowering shrub, the courtyard fowl pecking in the straw and dirt beyond the horse—and then the air vibrated with the first stroke of the great bell of Mouers, and the moment broke.

"Vespers," she said. "You detain me."

He stepped back. He remembered afterward having given some signal to the farmer, and the horse moved away with the Abbess swaying gracefully in the sidesaddle, one hand on the dappled flank behind her. She never looked back at him.

CHAPTER NINE

HE BEGAN NEXT DAY to oversee the construction of two molds to cast the small bronze cannons, and in the morning he sent Hans Bighead out to Garnheim to collect the money from the Abbess. Hans was a strange choice, but the only man he had; Piet was gone nobody knew where, terrified that his master would punish him for his misjudgment with the second gun.

Within three days, Johan had paid advances to five blacksmiths to begin the welding of the little iron hand-cannons. Gathering the five and their journeymen around a forge, he instructed them, patient step by step, in the way that they were to make the reinforced tubes from bars of raw iron. Heated and hammered flat, these bars were turned into strips thirty inches long and an inch wide, with slightly beveled edges so that they were trapezoidal in cross section and three-eighths of an inch thick. Ten such strips would make one gun by welding them, bevel to bevel, as the staves of a keg are laid together to make a circle, the ten held temporarily with wire hoops. Heated to near-white weld heat, they were hammered to an iron plug that filled one end and extended six inches below it, and then the welded barrel was put aside to cool.

Other iron bars were flattened and hammered into circles and welded tight like the iron rims of wagon wheels; then, heated again to less than weld heat, they were hammered down over the stavelike iron bars and the plug until a solid second tube was built up around the first, one made of hoops and the other of longitudinal strips. Shrinking as they cooled, the hoops compressed the strips and formed a gun barrel of great strength.

The projecting end of the plug was then hammered and shaped to form a collar, into which a twelve-foot ash staff like the handle of a pike was fitted; and, with nothing more to be done but the drilling of the touchhole, the "hand-cannon" was complete. Even with the many stops for questions and explanations and discussions, even with the cajoling and pleading and soothing that had to be done to cope with the fears of the smiths, who had never worked on such devil's instruments before, it took one master and two helpers less than a day to make a gun.

"The next will take you half a day; after that, they will come quicker and the work will be better." He let his eyes roam over the smiths in the forging shed. "All of you together will make fifty of these little cannons in two weeks."

"And you'll shoot fire from these?" one said suspiciously.

"Aye, and ball."

"I'd as lief use it to club some fellow on the pate," the

smith said, and they laughed; yet, from the remark came the idea of fixing a spike on the opposite end of the shaft so that the gunner, when his shot was fired, could reverse the shaft and brace the cannon barrel on the ground to fend off attacks.

"Seems daftish to me, Master Johan," said one of the smiths, "but you got a head to your shoulders, I know that; and you're paying good money, so I'm with you."

A week later, they were making two handguns a day each, some of them three; some had tried to improve his design by pouring molten lead or brass into the gaps between the iron staves; still another, who had seen the one great gun—now named the Goshawk—fired from the city wall and had at once grasped the need for strength at the breech, had begun to taper his strips and hoops so that the gun was lighter without sacrificing breech strength, and thus easier for the gunner to carry. A last improvement came after they began to shoot the guns, when one journeyman, inadvertently putting two loads down his barrel out of nervousness, had his gun shoot twice, the shots half a second apart, and his master lashed the gun to a cart and loaded six charges and shot down it with a bit of tow running between shots and a second touchhole drilled where the top charge was, and the gun bucked and kicked and fired out six shots like a roman candle, the projectiles spreading erratically over the section of wall they had chosen for a target so that it was pocked like a cliff where mud swallows build.

Thus, there were differences among the guns, and anyone who watched the whole process as Johan did knew which guns had been made early and which late, and even which smith had made which guns. When they were all finished, they were taken out to the fields beyond the wall and fired with double loads. Four of them blew up, their hoops bursting and the iron staves swelling and peeling back like flower petals; five others cracked, and three had swollen spots in the barrels because the balls had not been hammered down properly on the charges. But these were all replaced, and only two men were injured by the accidents.

Two weeks before Corpus Christi Day, the smiths and founders of Mouers appealed to the city corporation for a charter for a new guild, to be known as the Holy Brotherhood of St. Barbara, and Johan unfurled a flag that the broad-faced girl and two other maids had been working on, whose device was an angel with a flaming sword and a man with a hand-cannon and the motto "With God's help, Man's fire."

Frightened by the news that the Ritter was actually preparing to march on the city, the corporation quickly chartered them, their willingness enhanced by the gift of the great Goshawk and six small Sparrow guns by Johan the Bellfounder; and on the Thursday, the Brotherhood of St. Barbara set up temporary quarters in Johan's shed, with him as Guildmaster and Hans Bighead and two smiths as his First Men.

The Brotherhood of the Gunmakers and Cannoneers of St. Barbara processed to the mother church of Our Lady of Mouers on Corpus Christi Day behind its Guildmaster, with its banner carried ahead. Forty-one of the guild-fellows carried hand-cannons over their shoulders. At first nervously amused, then awed, their townsmen looked on in silence as they marched up the hill to the church and stacked their weapons against the side of the Dean of Chapter's House in the old Close. If anyone thought them odd-looking or crazy, he said nothing; every smith of importance, as well as forty of the healthy journeymen and apprentices of the town, had marched.

Afterward, Hans Bighead and three others gave an exhibition of shooting in Old Moat along the city wall. With a target set up thirty yards away, they fired the awesome new weapons before people who had never seen a gun or gunpowder. The gunners kept a wire glowing in an iron brazier full of burning coals, and, holding his weapon by the ash shaft, one gunner lowered the muzzle until a second gunner could pour down powder and follow it with an iron ball almost the size of the bore and six small balls, or pebbles, or pieces of old horseshoe nails, and then a wad of moss that was tamped down with a wood rammer. The second gunner then retired behind the master gunner, who took up his glowing wire and advanced toward the target, the muzzle elevated and the iron point dragging in the dirt behind him. On command, the gunner knelt, leaning back to force the point into the dirt, and held the shaft under his left arm. With his head tilted so that his left eye could sight along the barrel, he raised his right hand with the hot wire and then plunged the wire into the touchhole.

Two shots out of three, the guns fired.

The crowd along the wall and sitting on the grassy margins of the dry moat applauded every shot, groaned over every misfire. When the horse-shaped target was struck, they cheered and whistled and nodded happily. Smoke rolled along the dry moat in choking billows, obscuring the target to add to the drama of the shot and causing shrieks and coughs and cries. In all, the marksmanship that the Brothers of St. Barbara showed that day was remarkable, and only the most uncharitable of enemies would have suggested that Johan the Bellfounder, who was marking the hits, found more holes than there were balls to fire.

The instant popularity of the showy weapons and of the men who fired them pleased the city corporation, and they called an extraordinary meeting to pass three ordinances that were proposed by the Mayor after an unpublicized meeting with Johan:

First, that no man, be he master smith, journeyman, apprentice or stranger, shall attempt the making of any weapon called a gun, neither great guns nor small, nor ribaldekin nor cannon nor bombard nor firepot, unless he be duly taken into the Brotherhood of St. Barbara, according to their lights.

Second, that no man, neither in his own house nor in this city nor in the boundaries of the city's farms, shall own or have or carry or use any gun or cannon of any sort, unless he is a member of the Brotherhood of St. Barbara, according to their lights.

And third, that for the defense of this city, the corporation may demand of the Brotherhood of St. Barbara no fewer than ten little gunmen and eight great gunners, with their pieces and powder and appurtenances, which men shall have the same privileges identical to our waits and longbowmen and city watch; to whose support the corporation will pay to said Brotherhood yearly the sum of thirty kosters, and one koster per day per man when he is under arms, and one koster per day per gun, when they are called to its defense.

When, then, a trickle of gentlemen and small nobility appeared in Mouers to claim that they had been requested by the Abbess of Garnheim to come there to man certain cannons and guns that were being made for her by artisans of the city, the gentlemen and small nobles were told politely that they would be breaking two of the city's laws if they so much as touched any weapons. The gentlemen and the small nobles left, and when an angry letter came from the Abbess of Garnheim, it was referred to the Guildmaster of the Brotherhood of St. Barbara, who must have explained matters to her, for she did not write again.

CHAPTER TEN

HE WOKE DRY-MOUTHED and frightened. His heartbeat was rapid from fear of the dream, and he heard himself groan aloud. His right hand groped over the bed, found the warm solidity of flesh, withdrew. "Are you awake?" he said very low.

"Yes."

"I fell asleep."

"I know."

He sat up in the darkness, put his head in his hands. "I had a dream."

"I heard you making sounds."

"Did I talk?"

"No, only sounds. You whimpered."

"Like a peasant, you mean?" he said bitterly.

The linen of the bedclothes whispered as she sat up to embrace him from the back. "Don't," she whispered. "Not that. I am so weary of all that just now."

"But tomorrow, I will be a peasant again, eh?"

She said nothing. He felt her kiss the back of his neck, then turn her head so that the other cheek was on his shoulderblade. "Tell me your dream," she said.

"I saw a beast. I thought it meant to kill me."

"What sort of beast?"

"A—like a horse. With eyes of fire. But all white, white all over. I had aimed my hand-cannon down the hill at a horseman riding up at me—I knew he meant to kill me, and I fired. He fell. And there was the white beast, eyes like coals—"

"Was it the rider's horse?"

"No. I think not. It was—it was Death's beast, I think."

"Your death?"

He shivered. He tried to remember the dream completely. "No. All death."

She clutched him tighter, as if she understood his fear. "What did it do?"

"It saw me and turned away." He sighed deeply and clasped her hands where they rested on his shoulders. "I thought I was the only man left alive in the world!"

"Was I in your dream?"

"No." He was able to smile a little at that. "I have different dreams about you—my lady."

"No more of that—no more!"

He had come to her after midnight, forcing his way into the Abbey and along the silent corridors to her apartments. He had to see her, that was all he knew. And she, facing him, put her anger aside and kissed him, and they were both as gentle with each other as two children.

"A strange night," he murmured.

"It is almost dawn."

"I must go."

He dressed slowly. Behind him, she moved quietly about the room; when he went to her, she was clothed. "I meant to hate you," she said. "And I will still, I think."

"In the light of day."

"Well..." He held her shoulders. "I had to come. I thought you might hate me for that. But I had to come."

He felt her nod. She rested her forehead against his face. "I'm happy that you did. If you hadn't—I would have come to find you." She kissed his cheek. "Goodbye, bellfounder."

He went out and down the spiral of stone stairs, and as he passed the arrow slits, he saw the first light of dawn over the Abbey farms.

The sun rose like a heated coin from the downs that stretched away to the east from the Abbey. The Ritter Josef Redhand, having moved out of his own lands ten days before, had come by easy marches to a strong position on a hilltop facing Garnheim. During the night, he had fortified the hill with shallow earthworks and gabions and had thrown an abatis of felled hawthorn trees around his western flank. With this as a fallback stronghold, he moved out at dawn, down into the valley between his hill and the Abbey's, and by the time of the matins tolling of the great Mouers bell, which was clear even at that distance through the summer air, his force was in battle order on the east side of the shallow

96

river—eighty men-at-arms on his left and a hundred more on the right, with twenty mounted men in armor at the center. Defensive pikemen curved behind the center to each of the flanking units, while between the pikemen and the horsemen were fifty longbowmen, and at the river's edge was an uneven gathering of two hundred of the Ritter's serfs, armed with brush hooks and boar spears and agricultural tools, a mere mob to be thrown as a first wave at the defenders. Prevented from running by the horsemen, the serfs would be nudged forward—whipped when they had to be—like a moving hedge to entangle the enemy's first line.

From the window of the Abbey, the Abbess watched the Ritter's lines form. The Abbey buildings had no outer perimeter of moat and wall, but the walls of the buildings themselves were joined and were without windows for two stories, except for arrow slits and a bastion at each corner. Twenty mercenary crossbowmen occupied these positions, supported by thirty more foot soldiers hired by the Abbess and commanded by two of her cousins. She had the most obvious contempt for her relatives, and in a direct attack she would command the mercenaries herself, but it seemed important for the sake of form to have her cousins as the nominal captains of her garrison.

Looking down over that slope, the same one that she had studied with Johan seven weeks before, she saw the Ritter's army as a prickly jumble of toy figures, so distant that their movements were lost and they seemed frozen in the attitudes of a naive child's idea of war. The morning was bright and the day promised to be hot; neither mist nor distance blurred their clarity of outline, and even the far horizon where the downs rolled lazily against the sky was hard-edged. The river crackled with light in front of the Ritter's troops, brilliant as her lost jewels where the water rippled over the rocks where her trout lurked. Closer, the gaps in the hedgerow where she sent her hawks after doves had been filled with felled trees to break the movement of the oncoming enemy, and at the nearer edge of a field bounded by the hedgerow, the Garnheim serfs and freehold farmers waited, armed like their counterparts across the river with the sharp tools of their labor. Other mercenaries and another petty gentleman waited behind them. They would take the first shock, unless they ran.

Behind them, the close-cropped meadowlands rose to the Abbey gate. Dotted normally with sheep and cattle, the slope was dappled now with the rapidly shifting colors of three hundred men: to the north, the city longbowmen were just moving into a position from which they could retreat toward Mouers, their blue-and-yellow livery brilliant against the green grass; to the south, a hundred volunteers from Mouers and its freehold farms stood or prayed or paced, none of them mounted but all of them armed with some sort of spear and a cutting edge; in the center, the six little Sparrow guns were lined along the slope like parodies of the armament she had thought to see there. Each gun had its little crew, mixing powder, laying out rams and ball and swab, checking and rechecking the braziers in which the cannon lighters were kept hot.

Behind the cannons were the Brotherhood of St. Barbara. Their standard filled gently with a breeze and rippled slowly over their heads. The hand-cannons were invisible in the grass at their feet; the second gunners nursed their own fires—many of them simply footwarmers that the Mouers women used in winter when they went visiting—while the gunners paced and some sprawled in the thick grass, as seemingly lazy as if they were picnicking in a meadow.

Behind the hand-cannoneers, the Bishop and three other men waited. In full chain armor, they had not yet put on their steel casques or mounted the horses that were being held by grooms. They were talking among themselves, four horsemen to face twenty; the Bishop was pointing down at the Sparrows, and then Johan detached himself from a gun crew there and made his way slowly up among the Brotherhood, speaking to this one and that, squatting to look at a handgun and to make some remark to the man who would use it.

Passing under the standard, he looked up and crossed himself and then he turned up the hill toward the Bishop. He knew which window was the Abbess's, but he could not see her in the shadow; still, his neck turned red and he felt his face grow hot as he moved, alone and very visible, across the open space between the standard and the little group of dismounted horsemen.

Johan, like all of the Brotherhood, wore a simple tabard of black and red—such livery as a wife or a daughter could sew in a day, red above and black below, divided on the diagonal from the left shoulder to the right hip.

Johan bowed his head. "My Lord Bishop."

The Bishop acknowledged him with a nod. Johan knelt

and asked for his blessing, and the Bishop prayed and Johan stood up.

"Shall we stop them, do you think, Johan?"

"If God will it, My Lord."

The Bishop grunted. "If the Pope at Avignon is God's deputy, as he claims, then we're all done for."

There was movement along the front of the Ritter's line, a billowing of the mass of men toward the water.

Johan watched them, arms folded. "There were two hundred people at my house when I left it last night. Praying, fasting. Armed men. They say they'll defend my wife as long as they can lift their arms. They say she is a saint." His head came up as he watched the Ritter's right flank begin to flow toward the river's edge. "They say that they will be forgiven their sins if they die for her."

The Bishop shifted the casque in the crook of his left arm as he, too, watched the Ritter's little army advance. "Their piety is admirable. Their theology is a little weak." He turned to the three men in armor behind him. "Mount up!"

The Ritter's knights came in a line down to the water's edge and splashed into the river, their horses' prancing feet sending up cocks'-crests of spray around them. Easily identifiable by his big silver-gray horse and his crusader's cross, the Ritter rode at their center, a squire with a white pennon on his right. He carried his lance at forty-five degrees, an implied threat to the serfs who were wading across ahead of him; behind him, the pikemen came more slowly and formed a defensive crescent on the Abbey's side of the river, ready to defend the crossing against counterattack.

Johan moved ten yards down the slope, taking a position alone between the mounted men and the standard. At his signal, the master gunner of the Sparrows bent over one of the guns and touched a smoldering wick to the hole, and the little gun, aimed and reaimed during the quiet morning, threw a two-inch ball at the advancing serfs. The master gunner moved to the next gun, sighted and fired, then went along the line; the first shot was high and splashed in the river behind the pikemen, and the cheers of the Ritter's footmen came back like a derisive challenge. The serfs and men-at-arms, reaching the first hedgerow, began to tear down the bulwarks that had been thrown up there, making gaps so the horsemen could pass through.

The Sparrows banged. The first man fell to one of Johan's cannon, an unmourned, unassuming serf who was wearing

99

nothing but a smock and a pair of soft shoes and who died in the instant that he felt the ball strike his collarbone. The Ritter's peasants were terrified of the cannons' noise, but they were terrified, too, of the Ritter and of his retributions on their families if they ran, and most of them went forward even after the first man was hit, only a dozen of them who were close by taking flight because of what they had seen. The others ran across a seeded field toward the Garnheim farmers, shouting to urge each other on.

Grass and mud splattered from a Sparrow shot twenty yards behind the Ritter, and when bits of earth rained down on his armor with a sound like hailstones, the Ritter turned angrily in the saddle and looked back where the shot had landed, then lowered his lance and cantered forward as if to challenge the force that dared to reach out so far for him.

One of the Sparrows on the south end of the line would not fire, and its crew was trying to pry the ball out to get at the powder and reload; the others, overheating, had to be cooled with water, swabbed out and let stand unused until they were fit to shoot again. Johan ordered the crews to ready small shot for them instead of ball. He had lost his hat somehow and his gray hair was tangled by the wind, but he was oblivious; scanning the oncoming force, he was as totally engaged as if he were casting a new bell.

The wave of peasants flowed toward the Garnheim serfs, and their line bulged out to meet it. Light flashed from scythes and brush hooks, and the shouts of frightened men came clearly to the Abbey windows. Untrained, desperate, the serfs on both sides fought with a brutality born of terror. Both groups would have disengaged, but to turn and try to run was an invitation to be cut down; it was safer to fight through the opposing line and huddle behind it, and in minutes, a third of the Ritter's peasants had cut through the Garnheim line and stood panting at the foot of the Abbey hill, while almost an equal number of the Garnheim farmers found themselves isolated between the Ritter's line and the distant pikemen. Wisely, they straggled toward the southern edge of the field, where a grove of trees offered some protection from the men-at-arms on the Ritter's flank.

The mounted knights swung to their right and passed behind the men-at-arms and the peasant stragglers, while the Ritter's longbowmen began to drop arrows close to the cannons. A flight of arrows was returned instantly from the city bowmen, and within seconds the two groups of archers were firing at each other, while arrows continued to buzz down among the cannons and Johan saw three men fall within seconds of each other, victims of two or three bowmen shooting together.

The Ritter's foot soldiers broke into an easy run, urging the serfs on, driving them with the flats of their swords when they could.

Two of the Sparrows roared, too soon. Johan groaned, knowing that the metal scrap and pebbles would fall short, too scattered to be effective. Another fired, and then another, and five of the attackers stumbled and fell and men around them wavered, but then came on more strongly up the north slope, leaving the hill in front of the guns open except for a few bewildered peasants who turned and spun in front of them like dancers.

"Hold fire!" Johan bellowed. "Hold fire, you fools!"

One of the gunners looked at him, his face glazed. A man in the St. Barbara's colors lay in the grass next to him, an arrow through his cheek and jaw. "Hold fire!" Already hot, the guns would be inoperable within minutes; two were out now, one with its crew dead. At the north end, a gunner tried to ram powder down the hot tube, and the powder caught and burst out the hideous flame that Johan remembered from the laboratory with Brother Michael; holding his blackened face over his hands, the man screamed and started to run along the line of guns.

One Sparrow roared and men went down in the Ritter's line, and then the soldiers closed with the Mouers volunteers and then with the gun crews themselves, and the cannons were useless.

The Ritter's knights wheeled to their left and started at a canter for the gate of Garnheim, angling across a corner of the melee so that they would cut behind the Sparrows. Coming on, they spread into a fifty-yard curve, a crescent whose points turned back toward the river. The futile gun crews on the far end away from them, not under attack as yet, were trying to bring their cannons to bear on the horsemen, but there would be no time. Behind him, Johan heard the Bishop give an order to the mounted men with him.

"Brothers of St. Barbara!"

His voice rang above the shouts and screams.

"Handgunners, form up!"

The crouching men lifted the weapons from the grass and trotted in a sinuous line at an angle to the hill, bringing the

101

farthest man almost to the Abbey wall while eleven gunners on the other end moved behind the first line and crouched directly between Johan and the banner. The second gunners crouched, their second loads ready on the ground in front of them; and Johan, watching the oncoming horsemen, knew that the second shots would never be fired.

The horsemen reached full gallop; the distance to the first guns closed to sixty yards.

"Gunners, ready!"

Forty yards. The curious weapons came up at an angle, their long points thrust behind in the ground. To the Ritter and his knights, they must have looked like pikes or some curious obstacle to the horses.

"Fire!"

They fired along a line two hundred feet long, with nine gaps where the weapons misfired. Behind them, moments later, the second line shot. Six of the superimposed-load guns shot, their rapid sequences popping after the other guns had finished, their gunners holding the bucking staves and spraying shot toward the dust cloud of the horsemen. One gun split, despite the earlier testing; one snapped its staff because the frightened gunner leaned on it when the charge went off. Yet, thirty-eight of the little Wasps buzzed, and the white smoke sprang into the gap between the guns and the horsemen and for two full seconds gunners and horses and mounted men were hidden, and then the smoke began to move away in a long coil, a caterpillar crawling slowly southwest along the hill.

Johan was dimly aware that there was no center any more to the Ritter's line of knights. Five horses, four of them with riders, charged out of the end nearest the Abbey wall; a larger number came out of the smoke down the hill, but they veered away as soon as they were clear, and, after a faint-hearted pass toward the Mouers archers, turned and swung west and downslope, cutting into the Mouers volunteers spitefully as they retreated toward the river.

"In His name!" the Bishop bellowed. Horses thundered by on both sides of Johan as the Bishop, casqued now, lance at side, clattered out, and in the angle of the Abbey walls the four knights met the Bishop and his allies, and three men of each side passed through and wheeled, returning with mace or sword to close in a dusty tangle.

Johan staggered down to the standard. Five of his gunners were sprawled around it, two of them dead of arrow wounds,

102

the other three smashed by the other horsemen who had ridden out of the smoke and fled, slashing at anyone on the ground as they went.

But the center of the Ritter's mounted attack had broken. Panicked horses balked and circled, while one man was still trying to remount despite his armor, despite longbow shafts that buzzed around him. Three knights were still in the field, trying to quiet their mounts enough to ride away, while two others cantered along the hill at right angles to the line of attack.

In the very middle of the line, two horses and their riders were down and utterly still. One was the Ritter's squire, his pennon trampled in the dirt twenty feet away. The other was the Ritter. Three shots had struck his chest, one his casque, and four others his shield; three had hit his horse in the body and one had broken the right rear leg.

"Dear God!" The Bishop had ridden up next to him and dismounted, his face red and sweaty from the casque.

Out of the disorder beyond the ruin of the mounted charge, the remaining horsemen were organizing a withdrawal. They could have formed again and come up the hill, perhaps, but their ignorance of the little weapons and their astonishment deadened their brains, and they had no way of knowing how many of the little cannons remained to be fired. The Bishop mounted and spurred his big horse downslope, followed by two of the three men who had ridden with him, and they routed three enemy horsemen without ever coming close enough to fight. Coursing then along the hill, the Bishop sealed off any further attack on the north slope and came up behind the Ritter's men-at-arms, driving them away from the Sparrows and the gun crews.

The Ritter's peasants fled; his knights, too shattered now to try to rally them, fled with them toward the river, and, seconds later, the right flank of foot soldiers began to back down the hill. The Mouers volunteers charged at their right and pinned them against the Garnheim farmers, who hacked at their rear and grew more brutal and bloody as the enemy weakened. A minute, two minutes of carnage, and the men-at-arms surrendered; three of the Sparrows fired, and the withdrawal became a rout that fled pell-mell across the river toward the dead Ritter's fortified hill.

Johan of Mouers walked down the slope to the Ritter's body. Unthinking, he carried the St. Barbara's banner and planted it beside the mass of the dead horse, under which the

Ritter's body was crushed and twisted so that his torso, with its crusader's cross bullet-pocked and stained, was torn and wrinkled. One of the handgunners ran up and grabbed the fallen pennon, and, carried on the back of another man, he tied it to the staff of the banner just below the guild standard. Around it, the gunners leaned on their curious weapons and gazed at this wonderful ruin they had accomplished; and they knelt and waited for the Bishop's blessing.

He rode up and reined in. He handed his casque to Hans Bighead and wiped his streaming face, looking off beyond the river, where the last remnants of pikemen were wading across and straggling up the hill.

"This afternoon," he said triumphantly," we will take the Hawk from Mouers wall and plant her across the river and see what she will do to fortifications!" He stood in his stirrups and looked around him, where the cannon crews and the Mouers volunteers and even the Abbess's mercenaries were kneeling.

"Now have you my blessing indeed!" he shouted. His face was bright with a fierce, boyish grin. "May the blessings of God and of his only son Jesus and of the Holy Spirit be on you all this day, for He is with us!"

They crossed themselves and stood up. Some cheered.

"Johan." The Bishop settled himself in the saddle and smiled down at the bellfounder. "You were right. I admit it. I will tell all the world about it. Johan, you are going to be a very famous and a very rich man!"

And Johan of Mouers, who had come down the hill to savor his triumph, knelt by the dead Ritter's side and studied the cause of his wealth and greatness. One horse leg, like a log, lay under the knight's left side and rolled him partway over; his right arm, as if flung up, curled above his head. His casque had fallen or been taken off, and the face there was not the face of evil incarnate that Johan had hoped for, but the face of a dead old man, thin and lined and somehow innocent. Johan's triumph fled, and he knelt by the head of the great man he had destroyed, and wept.

"God forgive me."

Tears on his cheeks, he stared at the bloody wounds in the crusader's tunic.

"What have I done? What have I done?"

104

CHAPTER ELEVEN

THE RISING SUN STRUCK through his wonderful colored window like a shout, like God's affirmation that his way was right, and the spill of color across the tiled floor was like a carpet that had been unrolled there by the morning. At fifty-two, he could not see it so well as some, but it was still a delight to him. He was old, he told himself; fifty-two was old. The crash of cannon had blurred sounds for him, too; sometimes he had to ask people to repeat what they said. *But life was good!* Wealthy beyond the dream of any other man in Mouers, the equal of any noble in the Empire in the respect he was given: he had what he wanted. Or most of what he wanted.

His new house was a palace. Even his old friend the Bishop of Muhldorf and Mouers envied it; now, when he came to Mouers, he stayed at the *Niugewehrhus* of his good friend Johan Bellfounder, and left the crumbling Dean of Chapter's ruin to his secretary. Johan's foundry and his try-fields stretched a quarter of a mile down to the river now, and he owned a proving ground for cannons beyond the city, and, a mile downstream, a gunpowder works that sold its product all over Europe.

In eleven years, death and war had made him rich, and they had made him famous. Johan de Mouers was a name that every cannoneer in Europe knew. Attached to no prince, he sold where the money was best; he sent out his own ambassadors and went about himself like a nobleman. He had sold great guns to England, ribaldekins to Valois, gunpowder to Bohemia, hand-cannon and small *ingenia* to van Arte-velde's rebels before the battle of Roosebeke. With a dozen other gunmakers, he dominated his craft. They were too few to satisfy all buyers along nice political or ideological lines, and so they crossed them at will and even sold, sometimes, to both sides in a conflict. Like bankers, they were true internationalists. ("And like churchmen," the Bishop had said with satisfaction. "Money, God and guns—yes, those are things that cross all borders.") And their customers expected them to disdain small loyalties. Only the most narrow-minded zealot would expect a gunmaker to take sides any more than one of his guns did.

The colored glass of the window changed subtly as the sun rose. He had commissioned it in Paris as a monument to Katrin, his first wife, the saint who had died six years before. His second wife had approved it, for such a magnificence was a proper display of her husband's wealth. Matilda, second wife of Johan de Mouers, was the older daughter of a minor noble who had decided she would never marry and who had been delighted when Johan had found her through a middleman. It had been a good match—a perfect match, many said. He had money, and she had a coat of arms.

"Well?"

He responded gruffly now to a knock. The gruffness came because he knew it would be his son, Rolf, with the day's correspondence.

"Good morning, Father."

Johan grunted. His bitterness toward the young man was almost palpable. Like a bad taste, it came up in him whenever they were together. Johan missed sorely that little boy who had huddled in his arms and who had ridden on the saddle in front of him. He wondered now where that boy had gone, and how this cool young stranger had been put in his place.

"Letters, Father. From Hamburg, Köln, Muhldorf—"

"The Bishop?"

"It has his seal."

"Give it here."

"Also one from Bergen—"

"Yah, what do *they* want?" He made it sound as if Bergen were his enemy and possession of the letter were somehow Rolf's fault. The Hanse towns were actually his best contacts, not only because they bought bells and cannons, but also because they could supply enormous reserves of credit.

"I haven't read it. Naturally."

Johan grunted again. He had forbidden Rolf to break any seal. Nonetheless, he suspected that the young man lifted the seals and put them down again with a hot knife. At least, Rolf seemed to know far too much of Johan's business.

"What else?"

"The usual—guildhall seal on this one—then something

106

from Garnheim Manor Farm, that means that peasant Dik, stirring up the other peasants again—"

"If he's writing me a letter, he's not stirring things up, you fool!"

"It looks bad, getting a letter from a peasant."

"Not half as bad as some of the things you do."

"I don't see that attacking me, Father, is germane to—"

"Who gives a shit whether I get letters from a peasant when I've got a son who's famous far and wide for fucking everything that moves?"

Rolf never blinked. The novelty of being shouted at had worn off. He even smiled a little, maddening his father even more.

"Get out!" Johan bellowed.

Rolf arched his eyebrows in a way that his father hated and left the room. He trailed a whiff of a musky scent he had brought back from Brugge the summer before. A luxurious dresser, he wore sleeves of a fullness at the elbow that was almost scandalous in conservative Mouers, and the linings of fur and silk made older merchants whisper. Johan despised the foppery and could not understand why women seemed to find it so irresistible. Women fell on their backs when Rolf so much as approached them, it seemed, like so many cats wanting their bellies tickled. Already he was rumored to be father of more children than Johan was; most galling of all— it was worse than galling; it was a burr worn right against the skin, like a penance—three of Rolf's bastards were boys. Johan had made only one boy. An astrologer in Bremen had told him that it was in his stars that he would cause the death of many men, the life of only two; with Matilda, he waited eagerly for that second son to appear. Meanwhile, his son Rolf engendered boys with ease; he had only to exhale, it seemed, and pregnancies began.

Johan held the pieces of correspondence close to his eyes. No one else was there; there was no need to pretend.

Hamburg and Köln were accepting bids on so-called "monster guns." They were the fashion now, every city wanting a bigger gun than its neighbors. *Not that they're worth a damn in war,* Johan thought grumpily. He had proved at Garnheim what small cannons and handguns could do. Still, if cities wanted to spend their revenues on huge cannons, he would be the gainer.

Should he bid on a gun of at least seventeen hundred pounds for Hamburg? Maximum cost would be one penny *tournois* per pound in *"cuprim* or its family of metals," a vagueness that made him wrinkle his nose in distaste. He would have to consult with his yardmaster. For himself, he was bored with big cannons. He would rather make one more wonderful bell. Or fight one more Garnheim.

Köln wanted a gun "at least as big as that called Groz Grete in the town named Frankfurt," but their budget was miserly and he threw the document down in disgust. The letter from Bergen was in code; he would have a clerk decipher it. All about metal prices and the effects of Richard the Second's reign on English tin.

He passed over the other correspondence and came to a small letter with an unfamiliar seal. It had traveled in a beautiful little case of tooled and stained leather. He brought the seal close to his eyes; it was familiar, after all. He frowned. *A swan, a cross, and a star. Where have I seen it?*

Holy Jesu, the Abbess of Garnheim!

Understanding brought it all back to him with a flood of pain, like the opening of an old boil. Her lithe body, her cruel wit, her contempt. The battle.

Sweet Jesu, forgive me for still lusting.

She had left the Abbey forever as soon as the battle had been won. The Bishop told him later that she had petitioned her order to be relieved as Abbess; later still, he had heard that she had undertaken a pilgrimage of great piety and expense to shrines in Bohemia and Italy.

He had never got over her. Even with another woman in his bed, he sometimes thought of her.

He looked in the leather pouch for the record of the letter's travels. It had been on the way for seven weeks: two merchants had brought it to Mouers from Mecklinbirk; a minor noble had had it from Prague to Mecklinbirk in his baggage; it had reached Prague by way of Lienz and Salzburg, up through the March of Treviso from Ravenna.

So, she was in Italy.

He broke the seal and unfolded the stiff, thin sheet of scraped hide.

From the Mother Governor of the Convent of the Holy Sepulcher of Vis'Adriatico, near Ravenna; to Johan Bellfounder of Mouers in the lands of the Empire of Holy Rome. The fourth day of April in the fifth year of the reign of His Holiness Clement Seventh, and of Wenceslas, King of the Germans, also the fifth:

I commend to your care and conscience the training for five years of a boy, namely one Cosimo, called Tedesco. I require that you will feed, clothe and educate him in your craft as is proper to one of his station, which is to say the son of good house; to which end I will send three crowns Florentine *per annum*. At the end of which period, knowledge of cannons and sieges and all such being his, he will be returned to me. I require that he be raised in piety, being intended for orders. If any of this please you not, provide for him as for the child of a revered colleague, and send him to me again at this place and you will hear no more of it.

Sent this day and dictated by
Alys de Monckton, Lady Mother
and Governor

Johan sucked air between his upper front teeth. His heart was beating as it had when he was first about to meet her alone—as if he were again on the way to the hunting lodge. *Dear God!* She was very deep in his skin, not a burr but a blade. Peasant bastard, she had called him, and he thought he had hated her for it. Now this—and a heartbeat as if he had run a footrace.

He piled the letters neatly according to their subjects, picked up the two from Köln and Hamburg and left the room. He hid her letter in a secret recess.

From his room, a private door led directly to a second-story bridge over the alley separating his house from his outbuildings; an enclosed corridor led from the bridge to a corridor above his stables, over the brewhouse and the springhouse and two of his barns, to the upper story of the bellshed, on whose vast first floor the copes of the mighty bells still waited. They waited long years between uses, now, for there was more money for guns than for bells, yet he could never walk above them without thinking of them, of their shapes like widespread skirts, like hips with cloth falling from them—the lovely, pregnant shapes of his bells, waiting to give birth to music.

He entered the enormous room that took up the entire loft of the copehouse. It was lighted with windows along both long sides; at one end, two journeymen worked at a long table, plotting drawings of guns and carriages that would then be laid out on the floor. At a small table at the side, the yardmaster sat with his back to Johan's private entrance; when spoken to, he jumped.

"Didn't hear you! Gave me a start, master!"

"Look these over." Johan ignored the man's embarrassment. "I want your thoughts by tomorrow." He threw down the letters.

"Something you think well of, master?"

"If I already knew what I thought of it, I wouldn't ask your opinion." Josef, the yardmaster, was too cautious and too servile to please Johan. He would have preferred Piet, but Piet was dead, or so he had heard—killed at Gevaudun with the free company he had served as gunner.

"I'm bringing a new boy into my house," he said to Josef. He was trying the idea out to see how it would sound.

"New apprentice, master?"

Johan hesitated. "No, not exactly." Josef needed definition. Josef disliked ambiguity. "My cousin's boy," Johan lied. "Wants him to learn the business."

"Ah!" Josef was satisfied. He understood cousins and sons and such things.

But Johan was not satisfied with the lie he had told. The Abbess's letter had disturbed him profoundly, confused him. He tried to lose himself in routine, and he went about his regular inspection of the works—looking over the journeymen's shoulders as they made their drawings, staring down into the pit of a new casting with Hans Bighead, examining a small house-bell cast by one of his apprentices as a test of his progress. The apprentice trembled as Johan touched the inner surface of the bell with big, rough fingers that could find a flaw as small as a hair.

"Feel that," he said to the boy. He put one of the trembling fingers on a roughness where the core was not perfectly smooth. Johan patted the boy's shoulder. "Melt it down and start over." The boy burst into tears.

At his wharf on the river, two blunt-ended little ships were tied up to unload cargo. They were equipped with a single mast and oars, and they could navigate the shallow stream both against the current and with it, right down to the Eger and into the Elbe. They were offloading copper in

110

small ingots, Sicilian sulphur in wood casks, two blocks of English tin. The sulphur would be loaded into his own barge to make the trip down to the gunpowder mill; the rest would be used at the works.

Today, he skipped the carpentry shed and cut across to the smithy where a wrought-iron wall gun was being made. Some of the members of the smiths' guild had objected to his bringing ironworkers into his yard with their forge; it was a change from tradition and a threat to the order of things. But he had made a payment to the guild and now had his own forge; he had even brought in an armorer last year. Now he watched the forging of the wall hook that would control the little gun's recoil and then went on—along the rear of a storage shed, around the duck pond, behind the stableyard and out to the street, passing under the same bridge by which, two hours before, he had gone from his room to the works. The problem he had carried with him then was no more solved than it had been.

To his right, sixty yards away, was the Mouerswand, the old city wall; to his left an equal distance was the Niu-Mouerswand. He could brag that Mouers had grown while other cities were stagnating, and it was his gunmaking, and the other crafts affected by it, that had brought the city such prosperity. "Proud as a Mouersman," they said in other places; they even said it to his face. *Pride, always my abiding sin.* Well, let them mock; there was not another city within the Bishop's see that had pushed out its walls in that century. His fellows, as if to acknowledge his responsibility for their sin of pride, called the new street after him: Johanstraza.

Four timbered stories high, his house rose above the new part of the city like an arrogant face. Its many windows were a mockery of the window tax. Everyone, even strangers from a strange culture, would know that it was the house of a great man.

Three stone steps up from the street, a massive doorway enclosed an entrance like a tunnel. The symbols of his life were carved in intricate patterns around that doorway: bells and cannons mingled on the portal, and around them were twined ropes and flowering vines, and, along the vines, as if they were pathways, walked and ran and danced the people of his time—lovers and soldiers, acrobats and priests, a nun and a cannon-founder. He had made the drawings for many of those carvings himself, laid them out as he would have laid out the decorations for a bell, and he knew better than

111

anyone the intricacy of their symbolism and the looming importance of the figure that loomed, larger than any, above the keystone—Death. Death held his hook like a banner. At his feet, open coffins waited; behind him, a strange white animal reared. Was it Death's mount, this horselike creature with horns like a deer? Or was it something like the unicorn, unreachable and magic? The vines twisted toward it and the figures walked and ran and danced, his whole little world moving toward Death and the white beast through his bells and his cannons.

It was his secret, but he knew which figure was himself there, and which his saintly first wife, who wore a secret smile and preceded him toward Death; he knew which was his second wife, leaning over a vine as if it were a garden gate and beaming at the world; he knew which was Rolf, who was eyeing one maiden's broad behind while he stroked the breast of another; and the Lord Bishop, in full armor under Christ's banner; and the Emperor and both the Popes and the brothers of St. Barbara and all the others who were marching with him toward the end of the world.

And the Abbess of Garnheim was there, too, looking down at him as he passed as if from a wayside shrine.

Had he, he wondered, unwittingly put this boy she was sending to him among the vines and the cannons? There were some impish faces there, peeping out among the leaves—one in particular that attracted him now, just behind the Abbess's left shoulder. Was that the boy she called Cosimo? And was there, then, a secret within the secrets of his doorway, a joke about the bellfounder himself, who half knew, half feared this boy from nowhere?

People were coming and going along the corridor that led back from the great doorway—apprentices with messages, servants, small merchants seeking contracts, two priests. He knew them all, nodded to them all, kept himself apart from them all. The corridor was like the carving outside, all microcosm and allegory. Up the broad wood staircase he went, through a plain arch, and into the rooms where his wife spent much of her days. The problem of the boy was still with him, but he tried to wipe away his frown as he came to her. In truth, his second wife was dear to him as Katrin had never been. She touched him. She had touched him on the day of her wedding, when, a thirty-year-old virgin, she had first lifted her veil for him to see her plain, hopeful face. Her broad hips and her tiny breasts stirred him almost to the kind of

112

love one feels for a child who has been hurt; in bed at night, lifting her gown and sliding his hand between her legs and hearing her pleased sigh, he was touched to think of her astonishment and her fear the first time.

She had had two babies in four years, both stillborn. Those deaths were bitterness to him, and yet he felt it as deeply for her.

He wanted another son—one legitimized by her father's title. She wanted it, too, she said, and took it as her failure when she did not conceive again.

When he came upon her suddenly now, she blushed. She made him feel guilty. He had been thinking of the Abbess.

"Shall my women leave?"

"No, no. Let's talk a little apart." He drew her to a window at the end of the long room; at the other, the women went on sewing and whispering together. *What do I mean to say?* he wondered. He came to her often like this, to talk and to find in the talking what nagged at his consciousness.

"Is it Rolf, Johan?"

"Oh, Rolf!" It always could be Rolf; half the town talked of Rolf, he knew. Rolf the bastard-maker. There was a dirty little song about it.

"He needs a wife," Matilda said firmly. Oddly, she had no fear of Johan, for all his greater age and his wealth and his gruffness, and no disdain for his common blood, either. "If he married, he'd settle down."

"Or compound his sins."

"Most men are satisfied with what they have at home." She blushed again. "He is not a bad young man," she said quickly.

"Bad enough. But I agree, he ought to marry. It can't hurt him. And it might do him good. Good for the foundry, if I could make the right connection with a marriage."

She was timid now. She had an idea, he could tell. "I may have a suggestion."

"Aha."

"The cannon-maker in Mons. He has a daughter."

"*What?* Den Hoeck? He's my worst competitor—and a great thief, to boot!"

"Hush!" She looked down the room at her women. "He isn't a thief. He beat you out of two contracts last year, is all. And if he's a competitor, what better reason to marry his daughter?"

"He's as common as dirt," Johan said judiciously. "Now,

113

I'm common, but I know what manners are, eh? They say den Hoeck is a pig—no more polish than Hans Bighead."

"The daughter of a very common *rich* man might be a very great lady. How can you tell?"

"Rolf would hate her if she weren't a tasty piece, you know that. He has an eye. Damn him."

She joined her hands in front of her so that they seemed to protect her groin, and, swaying a little back from him so that her wimpled face was made fuller and younger, she said gently, "It would cost very little to send a man for her picture, husband."

Was it the posture? The almost nubile coyness? For whatever reason, he wanted her, and, never a man to temporize, he said, "Go to the bedroom."

"Husband, why? What did I say?" And then she understood him, and she was shocked. "I can't!" In almost four years, they had never made love in the daylight, and she had never let him see her naked. "It's not decent."

"Decency is inside the head. Go to the bed. I'll be there immediately." He grinned. "Matilda, as your husband, I order you!"

"But—what about Rolf and the den Hoeck girl?"

"We'll talk some more. Afterward."

When he entered the bedroom, she was hiding under the covers, and she demanded that he lock the door in case a servant came in. He stripped, revealing an enormous tumescence. She tried not to look at it. Unmoved by her pleas for decency, he whipped back the bedcovers and looked at her, pink and plump, womanly as Venus from the navel down and tapering to an almost childlike narrowness of shoulder, with breasts that were hardly more than engorged nipples. "We've been married for years," he said righteously, and knelt on the bed and kissed her thighs. Then he behaved as he might have in the old days to a woman he had pursued for a long time, one whose pleasure had to be catered to so that she would know that her surrender was worth it. Pleased, astonished, perhaps a little frightened, Matilda passed from confusion to pleasure to an enjoyment so gusty and improper that he had to laugh. When he entered, she groaned; she gripped him, and left four long scratches down his back.

"I didn't do that!" she cried when they had uncoupled, many pleased minutes later.

"Of course you did. Is the skin broken?"

114

"I couldn't do that. I couldn't have!"

"It wasn't the cat, my sweet." He rolled on his back and stroked one of her nipples, which hardened at once. No longer caring so much for propriety, she watched his fingers, then pressed them to her lips.

"I'm a wanton," she whispered. "Not really, I know. I'm making fun of myself. But God must love such pleasure in a marriage, don't you think?"

"It's one of His blessings, yes."

She kissed his fingers again. "Now talk to me." It was as if she knew exactly when the knot in his mind would loosen.

"There's a boy being sent to me. I'm trying to think what to do with him."

"Who is he?"

"I think he's my son."

Not by so much as the slightest contraction of a finger did she betray any jealousy. "Don't you know?"

"No, nor ever will, I think. I'll have a better idea when I see him—his age, all that. And it's the sort of thing she'd do, send him back to me without telling." He squeezed her fingers. "Do you want me to tell you who she was?"

"When you're ready. I don't dare ask."

He looked away out the open window and exhaled slowly. "Maybe, after I've seen the boy. I don't want to hurt you, Matilda. What do you think I should do with him?"

"Why, do as you're asked. If it's an honorable request."

"Yes, of course. If it's an honorable request."

"Should it not be? Wasn't she an honorable woman?"

He watched a cloud sail into the window's picture, forming, re-forming, making indecipherable allegories in the sky. "I was never sure." He gripped her hand and said with sudden fierceness, "You're worth ten of her!"

CHAPTER TWELVE

THE BOY HATED Johan the Bellfounder. His hatred made him anxious to meet the man. He rode north, driven by a strange mixture of a child's fascination and an old man's suspicion to meet and to know this monster whom he had been raised to hate.

His tutor rode beside him, a young Dominican of very noble blood from Naples. The two chatted in Italian and Latin, their talk that of two ascetics contemplating the Devil's work in an imperfect world.

The boy hated five things: impiety; the false Pope at Avignon; peasants and so-called "free men"; intellectual stupidity; and opposition of any kind. These five hatreds made him, at ten years and four months of age, the enemy of France, Scotland, Spain and the Kingdom of Naples; of Wykliff and all who followed his ideas: of the lower two-thirds of the population of all Europe; of ninety percent of the remaining upper part of the population, who were not intelligent enough to carry on a conversation with him; and of all adults except his tutor, who never opposed him for fear he would lose his post, and the Lady Mother Governor of the convent in Ravenna where he had grown up, for she never opposed him but always led him. Such enmity might seem a large burden for a child of ten, but he carried it almost blithely. He did not seem much like a child in many things. After all, he had debated the ideas of Wykliff with two doctors of the University of Padua and had been applauded; what need had he of childish things?

The boy hated Johan the Bellfounder because he had been taught to hate him, and he had been taught to hate him because Johan the Bellfounder epitomized the evils of the world. There was no doubt of this; beyond question and beyond debate, this was so ingrained that it was almost—*almost*—unshakable.

He had no idea that Johan was his father.

Before the sun was even a finger's breadth above the horizon, the birds began their morning music—God's harmony to the pious, God's renewal of drudgery to the oppressed. The birds cared for neither piety nor drudgery, but sang in a merry cacophony—whistles of blackbirds, trills of larks and thrushes, croaks of herons, the first restless groans of baby crows in the nest. The merlin went hunting with a shrill scream; the songbird answered with its song—and died.

To Rolf of Mouers, son of Johan the Bellfounder, the birdsong was a signal to live again. He liked to wake. Sleep was welcome when it came at night, but it was a garment to be thrown aside at first light; after sleep, a world of good things waited—food, motion, sex. He stood at the open window of the timbered house, naked, and scratched a shoulder as the morning air bathed his face. A flea had nipped him there. In the bed behind him, Gilda still slept. She was his mistress, or so she called herself; she was also the owner of the flea. Rolf and Gilda had made love four times since sundown; now he moved to the bed and carefully slid the cover down her body to look at her big breasts and her vagina, presented as if for his study between widespread legs. Without warning, he leaned over her and entered her, and she woke, not with pleasure, but with surprise.

"You're a bull," she complained when he was done. "Other men don't do that, I'm sure they don't." She had been a virgin when he had first found her, fifteen and not unwilling. She had had no prospects but marriage to another peasant. She could still marry a peasant.

"I love to do it."

"Other men aren't like that."

"How would you know?"

"I asked! I asked my mother. I asked my girlfriend; she's married. The first year, they did it a couple of times a night, she says; now, they do it every few nights. Not like you."

He wiped his groin with a piece of linen, realized too late that it was one of her underskirts. "Buy yourself a new one." He tossed it aside.

"Will you be back tonight?"

"No."

"Why not?"

He paused, his shirt held over his arms, ready to pull it on. She should know that look—steady, cold, the nostrils flared. "Don't whine at me, I've told you!"

117

"I'm sorry. I thought you were coming back."

"My father wants me to go to Prague. A deal we thought was settled, now they want..." He let it trail away; he never told her about business. "I'll be getting ready to go away."

"Prague! You never told me. How long?"

"Maybe a month." He kissed her off-handedly. "Have your mother come to stay, if you want—but remember, I don't want her getting any ideas about making it permanent. When I come back, out she goes."

"I know."

"No parties, no men. Have a girlfriend for a few days if you want. Or go into Mouers."

She was kneeling on the bed with her long, handsome legs tucked up under her, her short-cropped hair fantastically at odds with that lush body, for it looked almost boyish. She had had it cut short so she could wear a lady's headdress. People said she gave herself airs. "Did you love me so much last night because you're going away?"

"I always do it that much."

"Not with me."

He combed his shoulder-length hair, checked his purse. "I didn't say it was with you."

Over a stone bridge and under the walls of Garnheim Abbey and down a dirt lane along the river he rode, his horse's hooves making soft kissing sounds, hunched in thought and oblivious to the glory around him. Perhaps because he had been born to luxury, he lacked his father's acute pleasure in country things; yet he truly loved his life. But there was no stopping for him at the hilltop shrine to pray in gratitude—nor was there any tortured conscience yet, either. Women, food, business—was that the order of his pleasures? Ruthless in the pursuit of all three, he loved the chase and the victory, but he had no pleasure in recollection, and so he always began the pursuit again. Prague lured him now with the promise of new business. And new women. And new food.

His route crossed the river again at a ford and led along the edge of the narrow fields that were separated by hedgerows where birds nested and rabbits cowered. These were the fields of Garnheim Manor Farm. He looked them over for new women. What a wonder it was to him—*little girls grew into women!* That baby there, sucking at its mother's breast, or that three-year-old in the mended smock, or that pinch-faced ten-year-old could grow up to be the most delicious

118

thing under God's blue dome! And he had twenty years of them left to him, at least—twenty years of women who were now little girls, or even unborn.

Three fields without hedgerows showed a common tenancy, and at their corner was the rich peasant who owned them—a man wealthy enough to increase his lands, to possess a plow and an ox and a village house. This was Dik of the Manor Farm Village—Dik the troublemaker. He had sent a letter to Johan, something written for him, Rolf was sure, by a scruffy Franciscan or some other friar traveling out of Bohemia to preach the latest crazed mysticism. All of it was nonsense, and all of it was really aimed at stirring up the peasants against their betters.

"Master Rolf," the man said by way of greeting. He made no pretense of touching his forehead as the other peasants had.

Rolf rode past him, then changed his mind and backed his horse crabwise toward the peasant. "You wrote to my father, I believe."

"I sent a letter, yus."

Rolf had read the letter. Not because Johan had wanted him to, but because he read all of his father's letters—in secret, of course.

"It's a crazy idea, Dik, to want to train the Manor Farm peasants to arms. We'll have no part of that."

"Men want to protect their homes. And their women."

It was an impudent thing to say to the district's leading womanizer, but Dik's face was bland.

"The peasants are protected by their masters, just as it's always been."

"Times are changing."

"Not enough that St. Barbara's Guild would train peasants to arms."

"That what your father says?"

"That's what *I* say! Send us no more letters, man!"

He jerked the horse's head to the left and jabbed its sides with his heels, leaving the peasant in a little shower of dirt. When he looked back from a bend in the road, Dik was still there, leaning on his rake. *Like Death with his brush hook,* he thought idly. Reminded of his father's carved doorway, he thought of the picture of Death there. *Death is a peasant, for he always carries a tool.*

"Damn Dik, anyway!" he muttered. *Damned troublemaker. Where was the Inquisition now?* Last year it had come

119

to Merndl, piddling away its attentions on fidelity to some damned papal bull that didn't matter a damn, when half the countryside was full of friars preaching heresy and pilgrims running to see fake miracles and peasants wanting to be trained in arms. *Well, Dik was right about that. Times are changing!*

He rode on to the gunpowder mill, where Black Cob was bellowing at three workmen who seemed unable to crush charcoal the way he wanted it. Under his brutal tongue, they slouched like bodies hung from a gibbet. *Spineless,* Rolf thought.

"I want to talk to you, Cob."

"Aye, sir. Sorry you came to hear all that shouting, Master Rolf."

Behind them, the huge waterwheel groaned and creaked like a dozen men on the rack.

Black Cob had been a serf named Cob once. Rolf had heard the story so often he was thoroughly bored with it.

"I'm going off on business for the house, Cob. There'll be a question of providing powder for a set of guns—say for three years, that's what I'll try to contract for—give me a figure I can bargain with, will you? Give me a low and a high on our cheapest grade, enough for a great gun and three crows."

"Active fighting, Master Rolf?"

"No, decoration, mostly. Civic thing."

"But some saluting and practicing and all, yah?"

"The usual."

"Price of sulphur is up, Master Rolf. That last lot come in at—"

"I leave that to you, Cob."

Johan had seen something in the serf that Rolf would have missed. When the frightened boy had been pacified, a strong mind had shown itself. Johan had seen that he learned the rudiments of writing, and now his crabbed messages, mixed in with all the strange gibberish of alchemical symbols, were strewn over his office at the works. It was said that he corresponded with alchemists in other parts of the empire, but Rolf could not believe it.

"That's about right, then, Master Rolf." Cob handed him a folded scrap. "Got a moment more, have you?"

"What for?"

"Been looking to improve the powder—keep it from going all to Hell in storage, and all, you know. Got a minute?"

"I'm no good at any of that. Better tell my father about it."

"I thought you might take him the message."

"I'm not a messenger."

"Very sorry, I'm sure, Master Rolf."

"Quite all right. I just don't want to go into all that."

'"Right you are. My apologies for my mistake, sir."

Black Cob's voice was bland, and when Rolf rode away, the powdermaker was haranguing his workmen again as if the matter he had raised was quite forgotten. For Rolf, it was; he meant to tell his father of it that night, but he would forget. Black Cob would not.

Rolf could not understand that a man as uncouth as that could be sought after by other gunmakers; to him, Black Cob was simply another laborer in a world of laborers. Rolf disliked the dirty, manufacturing side of the business, anyway: for him, work was work, men were men, one gun was much like another. The thrill of business was in making and closing contracts, in beating out competition. Rolf had his own dreams for the House of Johan, but they were not dreams of better gunpowder or stronger guns, they were dreams of a vastly expanded network of agents and suppliers, through whom money flowed without middlemen.

Halfway to Mouers, he saw a girl by the roadside. She was new to him; perhaps she had just matured into that coltish body. He smiled at her. She was sixteen. She had never talked to a gentleman before.

A week before the boy Cosimo and his tutor deigned to tell Johan that they were nearing Moeurs, Johan knew precisely where they were. The agents who were paid to keep him aware of shifts in politics and shifts in prices would provide trivial information, as well, for another fee. They could find people, predict their routes, bribe others to direct them this way or that, even find the right sort of men to kill them, if such a thing was wanted. Thus when the boy and his tutor attached themselves to a gentleman retainer who was heading toward his lord's hold in Brunswick, Johan knew of it within four days, and the gentleman retainer was shortly thereafter given a purse and a pretty little dagger and persuaded to alter his route so as to pass closer to Mouers. The tutor and the boy congratulated each other on finding this rare person who was going so near their destination, although they found the gentleman himself coarse and unlettered. Jo-

121

han, meanwhile, studied them by proxy and watched their approach in his agents' letters as a magician might have watched them in a magic pool.

"Tutor is powerful in his influence, talks to boy in Latin or Italian and always apart. Boy sealed off from other folk. Tutor sends reports by letter to Mother Governor at Ravenna."

More money was spent; in a few days, the tutor's letters were being intercepted and copied for Johan's scrutiny. They were the usual tedious stuff—sights, thoughts on God's mercy, God's intentions for the world, God's hand as manifest in all things, reports on the boy's health, his wittier statements, his learning.

The agents' reports were more interesting:

"Boy is of a dark nature. Speaks mannishly and of elevated things. Disputes theology. A child in stature only....

"Likes roast fowl, apples and cider; refused fish and beets. Struck a servant who spilled his food....

"Being the Sabbath, they did not travel. In prayer all day. Boy chided his tutor for Sabbath napping....

"Boy said, 'These folk need whipping....'

"Boy said, 'There is no holiness here....'

"Boy said, 'Children are devils, and women are devils' dams....'

"Boy said....Boy did....Boy went..."

Forewarned by his agents, Johan arranged to be away from home on the day that the boy and his tutor arrived in Mouers. He found himself so anxious to see the boy that he distrusted himself. He went out to the gunpowder mill and spent half the day with Black Cob, and when he learned that Rolf had been there and had not told him of Cob's new project, he was cold with anger.

"I'd have come the day I learned of it, if I'd known, Cob."

"No matter, Master Johan. He had much on his mind."

"Aye—oh, aye!" Johan examined the coarse grains that Cob held in his palm, so unlike the black dust of conventional gunpowder.

"Will it burn?"

"Oh, indeed! Better than the other."

"Why?"

"I don't know. Maybe in each grain the three spirits are bound up more closely together; or maybe there is a spirit in each grain."

It was like roughly ground wheat or coarse meal. "How did you make the grains?"

"Added water to make a slurry of the old powder, dried it with stirring—how the men blathered at that!—but I can put a paddle to the waterwheel and do it that way, if we come to making it. It comes out of the bottom of the pan, a stuff like black leather. Then we crush it into grains like this."

"Expensive, two more steps in the making. And then what have we got?"

"If it blows, master, we got a gunpowder you can store forever without she separates out. And she fights off the damp better."

"If it blows."

"It'll blow, master. Better than the old."

"Well—we'll prove it, then. Send two barrels out to the try-field next week. I'll haul a crow down there."

"She'll prove, master. She's the best gunpowder in Germany!"

What had been the "secret" of gunpowder was a secret no longer, and every gunner worth his pay had his own formula for mixing the explosive. The results all suffered from the same dire weaknesses, however: they were vitally vulnerable to damp, and in transit they settled out into their components. A barrel of gunpowder that left Mouers as a good explosive might arrive a hundred miles away after a jolting wagon trip as a barrel of three distinct layers, with the top almost pure charcoal. Gunners put all sorts of stuff into their mixtures now—flour, charcoal of all sorts of wood, even ashes and lye—but the problems remained unsolved.

"There's a good bonus if it works, Cob. If it truly works—if it's that different, I mean—you'll get a farthing on every barrel that I sell."

"You're a good master. I was going to ask for half that. A good master."

Johan rode out toward Garnheim Manor Farm and then over the river toward the Abbey. Wryly, he reflected that Cob was a really very dangerous man—a peasant with knowledge. Scientific knowledge should be the province of the Church, he knew. *Well, I'll tell the Bishop about it.* He grinned. The Bishop could justify anything. If Cob's gunpowder worked, the Bishop would think up a reason why it was all right for a common workman to meddle in the Science that was supposed to belong to the Church.

He thought about the boy again. He was killing time now,

123

running out the day. He rode up to the Abbey and looked over the old battlefield, and then went on for several miles to the house where he knew Rolf kept a woman. There was a tall, handsome girl at the window now; she looked out boldly at him. *Dressed too fine for this place. Sweet Jesu, she's a piece! Dear Lord forgive me using Your name like that.*

He rode back along the edges of the fields of the Manor Farm, looking for Dik, but he was away at another field that day. At least he would know that Johan had looked for him. *Undo some of the damage my damned son did.* Not that Johan approved of Dik; the man was a troublemaker, and he would end up on a gallows one day. But it was better to know what such a man was thinking.

He rode back along the river, past the gunpowder mill again and up over the hill where the river made a great loop before reaching the city. The last workmen and travelers were hurrying into the Westentor already, and in the city's meager suburb, shutters were going up against the terrors of the night. There was little ease in the world, ever, and even in their own houses, men were not at peace.

Vespers bells rang. He could hear them and recognize four that he had made. The bell sound was taken up by smaller churches in a dozen towers, spreading, gaining variety, like the birdsong of first light, when the sun is a sliver on the horizon.

The horse went eagerly toward the city now. Johan shivered as he passed into the damp shadow of the Westentor, and then, shivering again with pride, he turned the animal into Johanstraza.

The day was over.

Johan resisted sending for the boy that evening; instead, he went straight to his business room and sent a servant from there to Matilda. She came to him at once, and, without asking him, ordered his supper to be sent to him.

"What about you?"

"Later. You'll eat again, anyway."

He smiled at her, sighed wearily. "Have you seen the boy?"

"Yes."

"Well?"

She studied her hands. "He'll be difficult."

"All children are difficult." He thought of Rolf. "Does he look like me?"

124

"No. Only the eyes. That look of not fearing anything in Heaven or earth."

"Matilda, if it will trouble you, having him here..."

"No. I've thought about it. If he is your son—well, the astrologer said you would have only two, and he would be the second. So I—would not bear you a son."

"That's just trickery." But he believed it—portents, omens, predictions. He knew that they came true. "I can send him away."

"No, what would it change? It is all in God's hand."

"You're smiling! What are you smiling about? Come, tell me."

She held her plump hands over her tiny breasts. "I missed my flux this time. I think I'm pregnant again. It would be that time that you—that we—during the day, remember, you—"

"I remember." He kissed her and let out a rumble of laughter like the sound of a great gun's carriage going over a bridge. "I remember!"

He summoned the tutor and the boy to him early the next morning, when the sun was casting the many colors of his window over his floor, like a carpet of his pride spread for them. A servant flattened himself against the wall to let them in, the tutor first, a pop-eyed, sallow, humorless Neapolitan whom Johan merely glanced at.

The boy was sturdy, and he would be broad-shouldered. His long hair was very dark, like the Abbess's. Johan's lengthy scrutiny was returned with a gravity and a directness that would have been insolent in a man; in the boy, it had an almost comical effect, for it mixed solemnity with childishness in the way that has to cause laughter. Johan grinned; the grin was not returned.

A wide forehead, from which the nose dropped almost straight, without an indentation at the bridge; very wide-set eyes with prominent circles under them; a mouth with thick lips and small, even teeth. The face was intelligent, but above all, it was stubborn.

Johan looked at the eyes to see what Matilda had seen there. *Pride. Of course.*

He is mine!

CHAPTER THIRTEEN

THE WEDDING of Rolf de Mouers and Elsbet den Hoeck consumed the energy of the city for a week. Guests and their retainers took over every vacant room within the walls, and some stayed as far away as Garnheim; even the churches were full because of it, not only on the Sunday before the ceremony, but for the special processions of St. Eloi's Guild, when the smiths and metalworkers from as far away as Riga marched under their banners to mass, and of St. Barbara's Brotherhood, with its guns and its fellows from other places and a new statue of gilded wood that the bride's father had sent, to the new church of St. Barbara's Outside the Walls. Ovens were filled with breads and cakes and meat pies and pasties; butchers massacred cattle in the shambles; the public spits in Grozplaatz and Meatman's Street kept turning all night long; hawkers and actors and tricksters and roisterers roamed, drawn by the crowds, and they drew bigger crowds.

The gifts filled two rooms of the great house in Johan-straza—gifts from the guilds, from the guilds of Prague and Mannheim and Mecklinbirk; gifts from gunmakers in Mons and Brugge and Antwerp and Leiden, even from London in faraway England, all sent because of their contacts with the bride's coarse father; gifts like the chalice that the Bishop of Muhldorf and Mouers had brought for use in private mass; gifts from even the peasants in the farms beyond the walls, who had given a half-penny each to buy a trestle table for the wedding of the son of the man who seemed to treat them like human beings.

Mouers had never seen such a gathering of nations: Russians who had traded with Rolf and Johan at Prague or Riga or Konigsbirk; Estonians; Norwegians and Swedes from the Hanse; Englishmen; an Italian, thought by the ignorant to be representing His Holiness but actually a representative of a Venetian bank, a far more meaningful mission; Germans from every province and duchy in the empire; and even several Frenchmen whose tastes in gunmaking had leaped over the barriers of politics and papal schisms. The city swelled inside the Mouerswand, spilled out over it into tents and shacks and rough-board booths, and throbbed like a full heart.

The wedding had been postponed twice—once, so that Matilda could give birth. Despite the astrologer's prediction, she had prayed for a son and had sent a gift to a shrine in Bohemia; she had carried herself like an egg and was almost an invalid for the final two months. She had produced a girl of apparent health and vigor. Matilda herself hemorrhaged and was supposed to die, but rallied. When it was clear that both she and the baby would live, Johan proclaimed a holiday at the works, and he went up to the mother church and prayed in the chapel he had founded in the memory of his first wife, Helic Katrin as they called her now—St. Katrin, some of the peasants said.

It was some months after the wedding that Matilda began to suspect that her vigorous daughter, whom she had called Friede, was not a normal baby; and it was a year after that before she knew that the infant was deaf and dumb. The discovery made her quiet, pensive—and, finally, wise. Johan, deep within his consciousness, knew that she was a holier woman then than Helic Katrin had been, for Matilda's acceptance was of a world that made her suffer.

The other postponement of the wedding had come because of the bride's father's insistence that every term and nuance of the marriage contract be written out, with each detail written as much as possible to his own advantage. Johan cried despairingly that the lawyers had worn a track between Mouers and Mons with their travels; the boy from Italy, Cosimo, observed wryly in his slightly accented German that the College of Cardinals could pick a new Pope more quickly than Rolf could arrange for a wife. And then he added that the cardinals had only one anti-Pope to deal with, but Rolf had God knew how many anti-wives. As always at such remarks, his tutor had made a face, and any expression on his froglike features made them even uglier than usual. The tutor disapproved of any remark that suggested contact on a human level.

Johan, however, welcomed the boy's jokes. He repeated them to his colleagues (even the one about the anti-wives) in the guilds and the corporation, and Matilda, recuperating now from the birth in a big bed set up in a downstairs room, had the boy brought to her every day, and they would sit and chatter and laugh like two old gossips in a sunny doorway.

"You don't have to humor him," Johan said, but he was pleased.

"He's the only son I'm going to have," Matilda said. "I believe your astrologer."

"Yah, but it was *me* he was predicting about."

"Well, it's you will engender only two, and me who bears your children; I swear I'll never have another man about me!"

When Johan was alone with the boy, he said, "Do you like to be with my wife?" He had taken the boy up on his saddle to ride out to the gunpowder mill.

"Yes. She is a lady. Her father is a knight!"

"Well, she is my wife, too."

"Yes, but she is a lady because of her father, not because of you."

"But I am as rich as a noble. I am like a noble in Mouers."

"But only *like* one. Words either mean a thing or they don't. That is what you learn when you are a foreigner."

Johan frowned down at the dark hair that curled against his beard. The child always seemed so innocent, but it was certain that he was not. "Well, my wife, who is noble because of her father's little title, then. Do you like to be with her?"

"Yes. I like to make her laugh. She says I am practicing my wit for all the girls I will meet."

"But you don't plan to meet many girls, do you?"

"I will never marry."

The boy was prudish. Johan already knew this side of him from other walks and rides. Cosimo had an aversion to most women, showed no signs of that pre-adolescent flirting that had been the first indication of Rolf's coming rage for women. Cosimo had been told so often that he was to be a churchman that he no longer questioned the idea.

"So, you like to talk to my wife because she makes you feel witty. That isn't so much liking to talk to her as it is liking to listen to yourself, is it?"

Cosimo turned to look at him. He was pressed so close on the saddle bow that they might have kissed. After studying Johan's face, he said, looking ahead again, "Sometimes you say things I don't expect." The boy had a streak of perverse honesty that made him say things that were not necessarily to his own advantage. "That isn't the sort of thing I want you to say to me."

"Maybe you should write out my words, then, and I can memorize them, like I do for the Corpus Christi play."

"I'd like that! Then you would always say splendid things about me!" Cosimo laughed. "What do you play at Corpus Christi?"

"I used to be Abraham, when Rolf was a little boy, and he was Isaac. Then he got too old. Would you like to be Isaac?"

"Oh—if you want me to. It's only pretend, isn't it?"

"Yes."

"I like *real* things. I will be a great man *really*, not just in a play." And then he tipped his head back so the curls brushed Johan's beard again, and he said, "But you know, I have conversations inside my head a lot. Just like a play. And that's pretend, isn't it? But that way, I know exactly what you will say."

"Ah, you have conversations inside your head with me?"

"Yes, you more than anybody."

Johan laughed, delighted that the boy thought of him so much. "Which do you like better, the me inside your head or the real me?"

The reply was coldly casual. "Oh, liking you is not the point."

It was such remarks that jolted Johan back into the deep suspicion with which he had first greeted Cosimo. He found himself liking the boy, and then he would be startled by his brilliance of mind, startled by his intellectual cruelty. Johan knew lords and princes, and knew them well enough to believe that they were not like common people because they did not think like common people. Cosimo thought like a prince.

"Do you have the whole world inside your head?"

"No! Only the ones who matter."

"How do they matter?"

"They're the ones who can help me. Or hurt me."

Spoken like a prince.

At the gunpowder mill, Cosimo studied Black Cob's diagrams and listened to the man until he seemed to understand what was being done, and then he grew bored; minutes later, Johan saw him outside the window, engrossed in a bird's egg. Yet, he believed, the boy would remember what he had heard that day about trying to make grained gunpowder; perhaps, ten or twenty years hence, he would take that knowledge out of the attic of his mind, blow the dust off it and use it.

Johan's negotiations with den Hoeck had dragged through

the summer and into the autumn. To Matilda's dismay, they were still being haggled over when she was well enough to leave the downstairs room where she chatted with Cosimo. On they dragged through the first snow, past Christmas and the New Year and into bitter February.

"We will make a whole generation of lawyers rich!" she groaned. "What have I got you into, husband?"

"A good marriage contract takes time. My lawyers told me that."

"How is poor Rolf bearing up?"

"He's surviving," Johan said with some bitterness. "Putting his usual poultice on the wound." Rolf had glanced at the bride's picture and said nothing. He had visited her and her family at Mons, and had come back without comment. He clearly felt that this wife would do as well as any other.

"Rolf *is* better these days," Matilda said hopefully.

"Let us hope his confessor thinks so."

"He seems to be at home more."

"I'll see to the maids."

"You're so cynical about him, husband."

"About Rolf, yes, I am."

Indeed, he had become cynical about many things. It seemed to be the times; everybody was suspicious, everybody was cynical. It seemed to be an age of skeptics—or, rather, an age of faith that had become so divided and redivided and subdivided that to believe in any one splinter of faith was to show a profound and cynical disbelief in all the others. Trust seemed impossible; men did not even trust themselves. Husbands did not trust wives, nor fathers, sons; contracts were drawn up to define even these family connections that were supposed to be defined by blood and love; they were the delight of lawyers—all good cynics themselves—and the despair of everyman. As in the last days of Rome, lawsuits abounded, and no one went into a new relationship without his written contract.

At last, when the end of winter brought the completion of the haggling over the marriage, the contract was as thick as a book of hours and as loaded with dangling ribbons and seals as a treaty of peace. In essence, it gave the bride's dowry to Rolf and Johan, but it provided a sizable penalty if Rolf could not sire children; as well, old den Hoeck had insisted on a clause that specified reversion of the dowry to Elsbet if Rolf died before his eldest child reached twenty-five. There were other clauses that Johan did not like, for they brought

130

Rolf's children by this marriage under the influence of their mother too much, and so of the den Hoecks; Johan doubted that the pinched-faced little girl in the painted miniature would be anything but a proxy for her father and her brothers if Rolf died. Yet, in the end, it was a good marriage—on paper. He could pray for its happy conclusion.

Johan and Rolf got somewhat drunk together after the contract was signed. Those seals and signatures seemed to free Rolf of his father's domination; or perhaps he had decided that his father could be more easily dealt with as an equal than as a father.

"What did you think of old den Hoeck?" Johan asked hoarsely.

"I wanted to reach for a boar spear."

Father and son laughed raucously together. The servants thought they were fighting, as usual.

The bride came up to Mouers by river, like a shipment of goods. With her were two widowed aunts and five servants, an older brother and a hard-faced Flemish priest. She was fourteen years old. A tiny figure in an enormous sable cloak, she stepped to the quai, where half of St. Eloi's Guild were waiting with Johan and Matilda and their servants, and when she came down off the stone curbing to their level she seemed to sink so far into the furs that it looked as if she had fallen to her knees.

"Dear Mother of God," a voice murmured in accented German, "they've sent the runt of the litter!"

Some of the servants gasped. Matilda looked shocked. The remark was too close to home, for not only was Elsbet den Hoeck tiny, she was also remarkably feral of face; in its wreath of dark fur, the little pale mask looked like that of a newborn fox.

Johan's face closed up when he heard the boy's words. It was not the remark itself, but the malice in it. It was malice aimed at Rolf, whom Cosimo despised; now that malice was to include his wife. Johan turned his head slowly toward the boy, and his expression said it all: *I will deal with you shortly.*

The widowed aunts and the priest justified the expense of sending them when, on the wedding night, they witnessed the consummation of the marriage. It was all written out in the contract, and had not even been one of the contested clauses. The groom had to demonstrate, in the presence of these witnesses, his potency; the physical consummation must be witnessed so that no claim for annulment on the grounds of nonconsummation could threaten the financial arrangements. The two women stood on each side of the bed, the priest at the foot; in the bed itself, the foxcub lay like a trapped wild thing, her shaven head very still on the big pillow and her eyes, enormous, flicking from aunt to aunt as if she expected them to save her. Small fingers showed at the top of the comforter that she had pulled over her nakedness, but not even that would do; at a signal from the dour priest, the women straightened the tense fingers and pulled the cover away.

Rolf had given up other women for an entire week. It had been the Bishop's idea, a nod in the direction of chastity. Now, when he took off his shirt, there could be no doubt of his potency; it was said afterward that one of the aunts gasped and the priest looked faint, but all that may merely have been part of the legend of Rolf's sensuality.

The bride did nothing, said nothing. Her aunts arranged her body and Rolf went to work—quick work, for abstinence had made him ready. The ejaculation was duly noted, the bride's blood, the penetration. A document was signed and wine was served. The priest blessed the pair and he and the aunts went away.

Rolf sat on the edge of the high bed. The foxcub was hiding under the comforter again.

"I didn't want to hurt you."

"I'm fine." Her voice was a little fuzzy. She had had two glasses of the wine before coming into the bedroom.

"It will be easier." He had decided to be straightforward; there came a time for that in all deals. These were the first words he had ever spoken to her alone. "The sooner there's a baby, the better."

"I know. I'm ready."

"I want lots of sons. I have plans."

"All right."

He was not at all sure that she understood him, for her language was heavily tinged with Flemish, and she had been studying German only since negotiations had reached the serious stage.

"You understand what I'm saying? Babies, yes? Babies? Lots of boy babies. Girl babies no good. *Boys.* Got to have one right away." He finished his wine at a gulp. There was a heavily worked pitcher of Venetian glass and gold on the table, and he took it up, thumbed open the lid and poured himself another glass of wine, then set the pitcher on the floor next to him. He was naked. "What I'm saying is private, understand? Private? *Privé?* You're my wife now and you'll do as I tell you. You swore it in the church, you swore it in the chapel of my sainted mother. Helic Katrin, she was my mother."

He was a little drunk himself, or he would not have said that about his mother, who was a dim figure whom he remembered with more resentment than awe. She had been a dreadful mother, or so was the conclusion he had reached at her funeral; anyone who thought her a saint was a fool, for how could somebody be a holy saint and a bad mother?

"God will punish you if you do not obey me, Elsbet. You understand me? *Le bon Dieu vous punir, comprenois?*" His French was not good, but it was better than his Flemish.

Wide-eyed, she nodded. Her face *was* like a fox's, he realized, triangular, very broad at the forehead. *Elsbet the Fox.*

She understood him well enough. Everybody had been telling her that God would punish her. It was all that she had heard since the contract had been signed. It would have been easy for her to conclude that the principal end of marriage—for a woman—was divine punishment.

"I want a son. To fix my father, you see? I can't trust him. He may get an idea in his thick head. He's funny. About that boy, for instance—that snot-faced Italian. *That* boy. My father's got something going on in his head about him. I can tell. Well, that won't fit in with my plans for our sons. Get it? Never mind. You don't have to understand. Just start having the babies. No babies—back you go!"

He was quite drunk. He knew it, dimly, but he did not see how it was his fault or why he should do anything about it. He heard himself repeat the same things for the third and then the fourth time. The wine pitcher was lying on its side by his chair and a ribbon of shiny liquid led from its neck down the slope of the room to the corner. He was drunk and there was nobody to tell him so *because he was married and when a man was married he was a master at last!* He looked at his new wife and was astonished to find that she was asleep. Like a child, she had simply faded away, perhaps exhausted by the week of ceremony. It was in his mind to get up at that point and dress and ride off to spend the rest of the night with his mistress, but when he tried to stand he lurched to one side and fell heavily against the bed. Catching himself on the furred comforter that she still held tight at the top with her small hands, he pulled himself up straight

133

and found that he was bending over her. She slept on, indifferent to him—her mouth was a little open, and from it came a shallow breath, warm and sweet-smelling and faintly vinous, the breath of a child who has been told a story and given a glass of wine as a treat and been put to bed.

"Little fox," he muttered. Real tears formed in his eyes and ran down each side of his nose; he wiped them away with a knuckle and touched her triangular face, the tears leaving a shiny mark on the high cheekbone. Like many otherwise callous and narrow-minded men, he was a sentimentalist in his drunkenness. Companions would say that he had a good heart, and people who wanted to think well of him would say that his real tenderness came through only when he had drunk enough to let his armor fall. They would be wrong, of course: drunken sentimentality is no more real than drunken courage.

"Called you the runt of the litter. Little bastard!"

The thought of the Italian made him furious. He wanted more wine, too. Out of the bedroom he went, still naked, down the dark corridor and through the passages of his father's proud house, looking for the Italian so that he could kill him. He was too drunk, however, and he got lost, and then found his way again to the kitchen, where two cooks were working to prepare the early meal for eighty guests. They wrapped him in a cook's gown and fed him beef and bread, and he made them bring him more wine, and when he looked up next his stepmother was standing near him. She had a proper gentleman's robe over her arm.

"Poor boy," she said. He rather liked his stepmother, just at the moment. She was mostly cheerful, and she was *there*, not at all like the emotionally absent nonentity who had been his mother. "Finding it difficult to be a groom, are you?"

"Havin' a lid-liddle—a little meal. Have some?"

She settled herself next to him like an old crony and picked at the meat with her fingers and drank some of his wine.

"You're a good woman," he said.

"You told me that."

"Wha'?"

"Twice. You're repeating yourself. You're very drunk."

It seemed to him very important to tell her that he liked her and that she was much dearer to him than Helic Katrin had ever been. In fact, he wanted to tell her that he hated his mother. She might be offended, however, and he did not want to offend her.

134

"Where's my father?" He must have been asleep; he found that he had to force his eyes open to see her.

"In bed."

"Your bed?"

"Don't be a bad boy."

"Wants a son—I know! Still at it, isn't he? Old goat. Foxcub and a goat. Little bastard called my wife runt o' the litter. Because she's—young and because—very *small. Very* small. Virgin, too. Whoo!" He was able to see her if he held one eye closed and the other open. "Now, you and I could make sons. Not m'father. Too old. I'm *full* of sons! We could. I like you, see?"

"You're raving."

He was aware of being carried along a dark corridor where the candlelight played on the walls like waving flowers; then he was on a bed and the room was quiet.

"Go to sleep now. You're a bad boy."

He reached for her and caught a handful of cloth. "You and me," he muttered. She had very plump thighs, wiry pubic hair. She kept saying, "Don't—don't—you fool, don't—" very softly and calmly; when he thought she was next to him and he could roll over and be on her, she was gone. "Matilda?" he said. The room was silent and black, and he fell back on the bed and slept. He woke to feel for the body that should have been sleeping next to him—any body—but he was alone and again he sank into oblivion.

CHAPTER FOURTEEN

ALYS DE MONCKTON, Mother Superior General of the Cistercian cloister of Vis'Adriatico, smiled with relief and turned from the window to pour herself wine. Below her, the train of the Bishop of Ravenna wound away down the hillside like a painting of a procession. Miniature horses and mules carried miniature riders, far away but perfectly clear as if in one of the new paintings from Florence, down into the valley where the diminishing road's clean and almost geometrically perfect curve bent out of sight. Beyond the hundred acres of timber there, the road went up the far hill again like a curved knife edge pointed toward the distant towers of Ravenna.

An episcopal visitation was always a strain. Even for a strong woman, the days of questions and audits were a strain. The departure was always a relief; when it was coupled, as it was now, with a letter of high praise, the relief became a sober joy. She was a good manager, and the Bishop knew her value. As for the petty complaints of a few of her nuns—that she was too strict with them and too lenient with herself; that she put their dowries to her own use, or at least bent the concept of what good conventual use should be; that she had favorites—the Bishop and his aides heard such whining at every convent in the diocese. Let them complain; it was a proper venting of the frustrations of the cloister.

"Sister Anna!"

"Yes, Reverend Mother."

"No more business today. Sister Blessed Trinity is to take my place at dinner and do the reading; I will be served in my own quarters. No visitors, unless Father Tadeo chooses to ride over, in which case he is to be brought up by the private stair. You may announce that the Bishop has granted us two days of holiday in the coming year; I will choose them when I am satisfied that the sisters are content with each other. All sisters not assigned tasks this evening are to go to their cells at once after dinner and pray in gratitude for the Bishop's keen appreciation of the Mother Superior's stewardship. You may go."

"Yes, Reverend Mother."

The breeze from the window had been perfumed by some blooming tree. She shivered with the pleasure of it. Passing from the window to her high reading desk, she saw the rippling reflection of her dress in a pane of glass; unthinkingly, she stroked the lines on each side of her nose and mouth. *I am growing old.* The idea was almost amusing. She did not like her aristocratic face any more. It was still a good face—intelligent, intense—but it was no longer young enough.

She stood to read. There was the monthly letter from Cosimo's tutor, and, with it, a note dictated by Johan to a scribe.

She knew what the tutor would say without having to cut the seal, knew the faintly sour tone, the hint of personal grievance left to the end ("These folk do not like me much,

I fear"), knew the hope that he would be brought back to Italy.

Alys de Monckton knew that the tutor's letters were opened and copied for Johan. It amused her that Johan could read the man's dislike of him; such insults served her purpose.

But what is my purpose? Once she thought she had known. Hating Johan for his love, she had fled the Abbey when she had seen him destroy the Ritter that day at Garnheim. It had appalled her to see mounted knights brought down by a commoner; it was too like the emotional fall that she had suffered. To be sure, peasants in battle now and again unhorsed a nobleman with their pruning hooks, but that was a matter of numbers and was clearly an act of God, Fortune's wheel turning for men to see and learn from; this shooting down a mounted knight with a handgun was a blasphemy. She had fled from it as she might have fled a plague and had gone to a shrine to pray. A little recovered, she had realized that her menstrual period was late—or missed; she had started south to seek the help of two wealthy cousins, and by the time she had got to Milan, she had known she was pregnant.

She lifted the seal on Johan's letter. "...know your ladyship will be pleased to learn of the boy's most gratifying progress in understanding my mystery...."

To have a child by a common artisan! She had shut herself up in a half-ruined family estate. *To have a child by a blasphemer!* Their son was a ruddy, black-haired bawler, big and strong and lusty of lung. She had left him with a wet nurse and gone farther south—Venice, Ravenna, Pistoia, Rome. Her family, though nominally English, had great influence in Rome, and she had come away from that city the Mother Superior General of this convent—in those days, a moribund community with only four nuns and a cloister in such a state of disrepair that most of it was closed up, and the peasants were carting pieces away for building stone.

"...Cosimo is in my heart as if he were my own true son. All here love him and would that he could stay here always. Of one thing I would write, however, that being his tutor, who is unhappy with us. Might he go back to Italy, for his own good and ours? He knows no truth but that of ancient sages, who, being dead, are somewhat out of this world. He teaches the boy disdain and contempt of good Christians...."

Shriven of the illegitimacy, she undertook restoration of

137

the convent as her penance. It became a place of special resort for daughters who were an embarrassment to their families, for young widows whose brothers needed their dowries, for dowagers and spinsters, for women of wealth who were not wanted at home. They brought money, she gave them learning and rigor. Their families were generous; the Bishop was happy; she was content. One could even raise a boy there; one could see to his education and shape his preferences. One could teach him to be an aristocrat and could lie to him about his parentage.

"...salute you as one who respects and reveres you, seeing in the boy Cosimo the working of the hand of God on both of us...."

Did she hate Johan de Mouers? She could no longer remember. She had set something in motion, and, now that it was going, she had forgotten what it was supposed to do.

Giggling, the boy raced to the corner of the building, ducked under a massive brace and slammed himself against the rough-sawn wall, hands flat at his sides. He breathed fast and hard and his belly was convulsive with repressed giggles, as if he had hiccups.

"I definitely heard that sound!" His tutor's voice was high and nasal and, just now, very full of irritation. "I know who made that sound and I will report you immediately to Sire Johan!"

The unhappy truth was that the tutor had no idea in the world who had made that sound—least of all that it was his beloved pupil. Cosimo made the sound expertly with tongue and throat, an imitation of a bullfrog that was as good as any one might have heard at a gathering of expert yokels. When the tutor heard it, his face got even paler and his eyes popped out and he looked more than ever like the slimy amphibian that had earned him Cosimo's cruel nickname—the Frog. "Brr-r-r-r-r-ack-k-k!"

"I definitely know who is doing that!"

Cosimo held his breath for five seconds. "B-r-r-rack, b-r-r-rack!" He ducked under another brace and dashed along the wall, cutting between the barn and a small shed and pushing open a loose board to pop into the stableyard. The tutor would never follow him there—given much freedom to wander, Cosimo knew routes and hiding places adults could not conceive—and so, safe now, the boy let his giggles become

138

open laughter, and he leaned against a stable door, holding his belly and laughing as hard as he liked.

A big hand fell on his neck.

"Playing a trick on somebody again, boy?"

It was Johan. *Johan the horse,* the boy thought secretly. There was something as sad as a broken old horse's look in Johan's face sometimes. Just now, however, it was an angry, stiff face, and it frightened him.

"I was only laughing."

"Aye, at one of your tricks, I think. You know what I told you I'd do if you went on mocking folk."

"I was only laughing."

The big hand tightened. Cosimo had seen that hand wield a smith's hammer. Shocked and almost sickened by the sight of this wealthy man at a laborer's task, he had mentally sneered and entertained himself with one of his internal conversations with a stupid, menial Johan. Still, he had seen what strength was in that hand and in the muscled, heavily veined arm. That hand could crush his neck; the arm could throw him across the stableyard like a kitten. At the thought of being physically punished, the boy began to shake with outrage.

"I'll ask it one more time, boy: what were you laughing at?"

"I won't be handled so. Be damned to you!"

This man loved him. He knew that by now. Love was a thing he had long ago learned to manipulate. Johan's love was different, however; somehow, he could love and still punish brutally.

The tutor's voice came from the other side of the stableyard fence. "I know who is making that disgusting mockery: I know where you are, and I am going now to report you to Sire Johan!"

Johan held him still until the tutor's steps had passed along the fence. Still angry, Cosimo thought that he was now to be let go; Johan, he knew, despised the tutor. He waited for the man's face to relax, to smile.

"Signor tutor!" Johan called in a terrible voice.

Cosimo began to struggle. *"No!"*

"Signor tutor, come around to the stableyard."

"You old *bastard!"* Cosimo's rage burst beyond his own control. This loss of reason had happened to him before; it was as if another being took over his consciousness. He tried to wrench his neck out of that fearful grip, aiming a kick at

139

Johan's groin as he did it. When he missed and when he could not wriggle free, he wept and screamed; twisting, he bit into the hairy wrist and tasted blood. His fingernails raked the wrist and the hand.

"You old shit-ass! You turd! Cocksucking common rabble son-of-a-whore prick! *Peasant bastard!*"

He looked at Johan's face. It looked imperturbable and sad—a horse, indeed, and one on the way to the boneyard. A wise and resigned old horse. Not surprised at the names, not hurt, not even angry. Sad and solemn.

The boy felt himself lifted and slammed against the stable door. The force was terrible, like the force of the hammer falling on the hot metal; the impact drove the air from his lungs and made his ears ring. Something was tickling his nose. Blood. His nose was broken.

The hand spun him around. He was blubbering and incoherent now, still in his rage, humiliated, physically hurt. The wise old horse eyes studied him while the big hand, which was also bleeding, held him there against the stable door, and then the other big hand smacked hard across his face with a blow that seemed to make his teeth rattle in his jaws. It struck him three times, blows like the clanging of a huge door. Cosimo could not believe that he was being hit with such force. The injustice of it made him physically sick: this man was huge and he was only a boy; the man was a peasant and he was a noble. What had he done that deserved such a beating? *What had he done?*

Then the hand pushed him out into the stableyard and spun him toward the water trough over the way. The boy found himself moving so fast that his numbed feet could not keep up; he was spinning and stumbling, tasting his own blood and the rise of vomit; he spun from shadow into sunlight, his feet tangling—stumbling, turning, slipping in the muddy filth around the trough—and went face-down into a puddle of water and horse piss, and there he began to retch.

And he heard Johan say, as if from far away, "Signor tutor, there is the boy who mocked you. How will you deal with him?"

The tutor stuttered. The man was confused, as if he felt the shame that should have been Cosimo's.

"Signor tutor, how would you deal with any other pupil who mocked you?"

"I—I—I would c-cane him, signore."

"Fetch us a cane! You—stableboy—go cut a switch from yon apple tree. A stout one!"

"But signore—I cannot c-cane—this boy."

"Yes, you can. You *will*."

Two of the stablehands, oafs from the neighboring farms, pulled off his tunic and his shirt. The tutor stepped gingerly through the mud to stand next to him.

Cosimo was shaking and still vomiting, though nothing came up now. What was happening to him was so unbelievable that he had gone into shock.

"Pull down his hose," Johan said. Peasant hands stripped his buttocks and upper thighs.

"Begin, signor tutor."

Johan would not let him wield the switch timidly. It was an apple branch as thick around as a finger, and it bruised what it struck.

When Johan was satisfied, he said to a servant, "Bring them both to me in an hour."

They took him to Dame Matilda to have his injuries tended. She was very grave, and for once she would not speak to him. No laughing now, no wit; she knew what had happened, and perhaps she felt responsible because she had encouraged his mockery with her laughter.

The left side of his face was swollen, and she put a cool, damp cloth on it. The eye was closed. Inside his mouth there were lacerations where he had bitten himself, and there was dried blood in his nose so that it was hard to breathe. His forehead was cut and his nose had a flap of skin torn down just where it had been broken. Matilda lifted the flap and stuck it down on the raw flesh and put spiderwebs on it to stop the bleeding.

He smelled of horse piss and vomit. Dung and mud were smeared from his hair to his knees.

"Go to my husband now."

"I won't. *I won't be told what to do!*"

"Go now. If he has to come for you, it will be worse."

He wanted to resist, but he knew what real pain was now and he wanted no more just then. He went, silent and foul-smelling, behind a servant.

Johan looked at him with the same sad-horse look. "You will live, I guess."

"Kill me! What do you care?" His speech was thick because of the cuts in his mouth and because of a loose tooth. "Lady Alys will hear of this!"

141

"I have already written to her. The tutor will take it to her when he goes."

Cosimo stared. The tutor was from his world, not Johan's; how could Johan send him away? "Tutor not going anywhere without me!"

"He has asked to go, boy. I have given my consent."

"You lie!"

Johan's right hand struck him full on the injured cheek. The boy screamed.

"You *will* learn, boy."

Blood was running from his nose again. Johan's violence seemed so gratuitous that he could make no sense of it, could hardly see the connection between it and his own words. Johan tugged at his lower lip with his thick fingers and looked up at the boy with lowered head. "Your tutor leaves at sunrise. You may send a letter along with him to Lady Alys, if you want."

"I want to see my tutor."

Johan pulled at his lip, then knocked on the wall behind him. A door opened; the tutor glided in. He moved like a demure virgin, with little steps and no movement of his upper body. His face was pale and closed. He looked like a sick man, like one who was dying and who hated the world for it.

"You will *not* go away until I send you away!" Cosimo said shrilly. He tried to control his voice, but it squeaked and threatened to be broken by sobs.

"I go to Italy in the morning. I will not be mocked by a boy."

"But—" Cosimo could not grasp it. "But you are only a *tutor!*"

"Only a tutor?" The man seemed to expand; his outrage was so huge that Cosimo felt as if he were being crowded against the walls.

In a moment of understanding, one of those true revelations that mark the leap from childhood into maturity, he understood what he had never grasped before: *the tutor was a man.* He was an individual, beyond any category that Cosimo could invent for him, beyond the confines of any imagined conversations or the limits of any contemptuous nickname. The revelation made the pain and the humiliation almost worth it, for it was true knowledge of the real world, knowledge of an order entirely different from the knowledge that the tutor gave him.

142

Cosimo grinned around his loose tooth. "Go, then. I don't need you any more."

The tutor hissed at him in Italian, words of venom, words perhaps of hatred, of stored-up resentment. More knowledge! *Even supposed friends cannot be trusted.*

"Go!"

"Enough, enough," Johan said wearily. He waved at the door. "Signor tutor, enough. I will send to you this evening to settle with you."

The tutor looked at them both with open hatred, shrugged, seemed to pull into himself. A moment later, he was gone. Johan looked at Cosimo. "Come here, boy."

He went to the man. Yet another lesson had come home to him: when one is threatened by a force that cannot be matched, one submits the body and keeps the mind free.

"You will not mock your elders any more."

"Very well."

"If you want to be a nobleman, you must be noble. Be a lord, if you must—but be a real one. When we call Almighty God Our Lord, we do not mean a being who is going to mock us. We mean the being who forgives."

"And who punishes us."

"Yes, and who punishes us, that too. But as Our Lord is to us, so a lord is to his people. When you mock a man, you try to make him less than he is. What need has a lord of making lesser men still less than they are?"

"But people laugh *with* me."

"Aye. We all have some of the devil in us. I tell you something, boy—it's the easiest thing in the world to make folk laugh at somebody else's expense. But I think that he's a better man who stays silent, and gets no credit for his wit."

They looked into each other's eyes. Even with Johan's hands holding him up by the shoulders, he swayed a little. The shock of the beating was hitting him in a different way now, almost like drunkenness. He was weak and dizzy, and his vision was blurred.

"Tomorrow, you will go to work with my apprentices. I made a mistake in treating you different. They'll teach you respect—real respect, not lip-service respect, like the kind you're used to. Real fear-of-God respect. Or they'll knock you around, you see? And the journeymen will, too. And you'll start tomorrow morning at sunup, still hurting, and with your mouth mashed just like it is, so that if they hit you, it will hurt that much again. Because you did a great wrong,

143

and now you must pay for it. Now go to bed. Want to say anything?"

"No. Sir."

"Go to bed, then."

He lurched from the room, coveting his new knowledge. His body would do as it was told after that. His mind would be free. *I am myself!* And one day, he would pay back as he had been paid.

CHAPTER FIFTEEN

THE FOX WAS as fertile as a new field, and she dropped three babies in three years. The wonder of it was that two of them were boys. Big, husky boy babies. The first one tore her apart as he made his way between those narrow hips, but she survived and bore again more easily, and then again. At sixteen, she was nursing her third child and the wet nurse was still nursing the second one, and, although they still called her the Fox—the name had stuck, although Cosimo never gave a nickname to anybody after the tutor, at least not out loud—they whispered that she was a female rabbit.

She hardly knew her husband as a person. They lived in her father-in-law's great house and she was a member of her father-in-law's family: she ate with the rest of them, gossiped with her mother-in-law, kept peace between their respective servants, treated the Italian as a slightly peculiar younger brother. Rolf was gone as much as he was home; even when he was in Mouers, he spent little time in the house. He admired their children, but he left them to her—to the process by which he had been raised: mother, church, servants, then a tutor and an apprenticeship in the works. When she was pregnant, he slept in another room, and she knew that he often slept in another house, with another woman. He told her that he had a powerful appetite that had to be satisfied, and she seemed to accept this as she had learned to accept other truths from the world of men. Men were different from women. Men were more important. Men *were* the world.

"Rolf will be home again soon," her mother-in-law said. It was a fiercely stormy afternoon, when to be indoors seemed snug and safe by contrast. They could hear the rain whipping the room's one window and the wind buffeting down the chimney as it blew gouts of smoke back into the room. They were sewing on a new altar cloth for Helic Katrin's Chapel. Katrin had no reality for either of them; she was no longer a woman who had once been married to Johan, but a distant saint.

"Johan had a letter from Hamburg. Rolf was there."

"Yes, he told me." Elsbet the Fox had a childish little voice, and she shaped her words carefully as good girls are supposed to do. She had grown two inches taller since she had come to Mouers, but she still seemed too much a child to have three children.

"Home in a week, Johan thinks. We'll have to make some fuss for him. Though he shouldn't have missed little Willem's saint's day."

Elsbet's face was hidden over the needlework. "He missed the birth, too." She seemed to suggest that the more absences there were, the more they forgave each other.

"When he gets home, you'll be starting on a fourth?"

"That is up to my husband." She rarely called him Rolf. Even to his face, he was "husband."

"You two! You make me so jealous, Elsbet! You and Rolf look at each other, you have a son; Johan and I—" An unusually heavy blow of rain struck the window, and she stopped to listen, as if she feared the window would blow in. "Of course, it's too late for us now."

"Why?" The wide-set fox eyes were blank.

"Well, because! We're *old!* I'm old, anyway. Johan will be middle-aged forever, I suppose; men don't get old the way women do. But I've got old. I'm old inside. And look at me—big as a farmcart, and I don't conceive any more, for all I look like I was put on this earth to have babies! And you, skinny as a rake handle, a good breeze would blow you away."

"You had Friede."

"Yes." Friede was deaf and dumb, and the servants whispered that she was not right in the head.

"You could go to Mainz," Elsbet hurried to say. "There is a miraculous doorway there, they say. You walk through it and conceive."

"Well..."

"A woman at St. Eloi's Fair was selling an elixir, it would make barren women have twins, she said. She said it was

145

the same elixir that the angel gave to Sarah, Abraham's wife,
so she would bear, and she was old—I forget how old, but *old*.
I was carrying Carl then, she came up to me behind the booth
and she asked me if I was in trouble, because I look so young,
I think. She scared me. She smelled. She said she could fix
it if I was in trouble. What did that mean?"

"She meant a sin."

"What sin?"

"Murder." Matilda looked up to see if she had shocked the
Fox, but the gray eyes were looking at her with the same
calm blankness. "A woman who doesn't want her baby can
murder it, they say."

"How?"

"Up inside. They do things up inside."

"What things?"

Matilda shook her head. The loss of an unborn child made
her angry. She clamped her mouth very tight like an old
woman and forced herself to think of other things. Thus she
was surprised when Elsbet said something on the same subject a full minute later. "I don't see why anybody would want
to kill her baby."

"To hide the sin."

"God would see it anyway."

"To hide it from other people, I mean. If a girl isn't married, it's other people she's afraid of."

Elsbet digested that. "She could sell it."

"What?"

"Her baby. If she got into trouble, she could sell the baby
and make money—and she'd need money if she wasn't married, wouldn't she?"

"Elsbet, mothers don't sell their babies!"

"Yes they do. On my father's farms, the serfs sell babies
all the time."

"Elsbet!"

"Oh, it's true. When I heard it first I thought they sold
them for the meat, you know, but it wasn't that. They sold
them because they couldn't feed them and there were other
people who wanted babies so they'd grow up into workers."

Matilda stared. "Elsbet, dear, you should not say such
things."

"Why not?"

"It distresses nice people."

"Yes, that's what my father said. But he said that if they
were that nice, you didn't want to do business with them.
146

He'd tell that about the serfs and their babies, or something like it, to see how they'd act. Do you know who acts the way my father would like?"

Matilda shook her head.

"Cosimo. Yes, truly. *He* said, 'And a good idea, too. Serfs shouldn't marry; they should have children and turn them all over to their lord for upbringing.' My father would like that."

"The idea!"

"Yes, it's quite horrible, isn't it! My father admires horrible ideas. He says that's how a man gets ahead, by being able to live with what's horrible." She paused in her sewing. "It's peculiar, you know—my father and Cosimo are very much alike, for all that my father is very vulgar and proud of it, and Cosimo is such a silly snob. For Cosimo said almost the same thing. He said, 'To be great, you must think what everybody else finds unthinkable. You must allow everything inside your head.' Isn't that peculiar?"

Matilda said nothing. She thought that it would have been better if Elsbet had talked more about her husband and less about Cosimo, but she did not say so.

Cosimo seemed almost a man now—taller than when he had arrived, broad-shouldered, strong. He was good-looking, too, but he paid no attention to the girls who came in his way. From the day of the beating for his mockery of the tutor, he had become quiet and inward; Matilda, once his closest confidante, saw little of him, and when he came into her part of the house it was to play silently with deaf Friede. Cosimo played games with her that nobody else understood. He would be there, utterly quiet, and then Matilda would look up and he would be gone.

"How is Cosimo doing in the works?" she asked Johan several days after her talk with Elsbet.

Johan grinned. "He's a wonder." Even his tone of voice had wonder in it.

"Doing well, you mean?"

"The best I ever had. If he was a real apprentice, I'd mean him for a master artisan. They all say it—apprentices, journeymen, yardmaster—he has a way of looking at a problem, the rest of us are thinking what's wrong, he's already solved it! 'Lift there,' he says. 'That strut's bent there.' And it works! And as for cannons—he knows more of how to send a ball to where it should go than most of my gunners. If only..."

"Yes?"

"Nothing."

"Now, husband. Something is on your mind. Tell me."

"I said it was nothing." Yet, when he tried to change the subject, he said, "Rolf will be back tomorrow," and she knew that he had been thinking of Rolf before. *If only Rolf were like Cosimo,* she thought, *that's what he meant.*

Rolf brought two more contracts for monster cannons with him when he came home. He was full of how he had closed the deals—what he had said, what he had done, how clever he had been—and he bored Johan abominably. Rolf's side of the business bored Johan, if the truth were known; all that activity seemed so much running in place to him; all that resulted was the making of more big guns like others they had made before. The business was static, and Johan was finding it tedious.

"King Sigismund's council sent a letter," Johan said in a gap in his son's recitation. "They don't put it just so, but I think they mean to besiege Karlsbirk in the spring. Sigismund doesn't like the idea of a free city in his realm."

"*If* the Teutonic Knights don't get there first. I was talking to old Biedermaier from Kobenhavn—the father, not the son—and he said the Knights were trying to borrow for a campaign. They've already exhausted the Jews and—"

"I hadn't finished."

"Oh? Oh. Go ahead."

"You're sure you wouldn't be bored, letting somebody else say something?"

"Well, I'm sorry I ever opened my mouth."

"We all are. I think I liked you better as a stuck-up coxcomb than I do as an endless talker, Rolf."

Rolf looked very aggrieved. Matilda looked resigned. Johan was chewing a piece of meat and picking bits of gristle out of his teeth with his knife, all the while staring at his son and then down at the plate in front of him, cutting off pieces and putting them into his mouth with his fingers. He had a bad tooth—several bad teeth, if he were honest with himself—and he was irritated.

"Well, go ahead with what you were saying about Sigismund, Father. I'm sure I didn't mean to bore you. But I must say, I'm able to hold the attention of merchants throughout the Hanse, all right. It's only at home somebody accuses me of being boring. In fact, you know what Arman Fugger said to me when I was in Bremen? We were talking about what business sense is, and he said..."

Johan chewed. His jaws moved like pieces of a ponderous machine, like the slow-grinding wheels that pulverized the sulphur. Next to him, Elsbet was chewing her food and looking at her husband with the same vacant stare she gave to everything; next to her, Cosimo looked at nothing in particular and thought his own thoughts. Johan spat a piece of gristle as big as his thumbnail on the floor. "Shut up, Rolf," he said. His voice sounded like two stones rubbing over each other.

Matilda sighed. "Please, husband—not at table."

"It's my table."

"It's bad for the digestion."

"Rolf is bad for the digestion, that's what's bad for the digestion!"

Rolf stood up. "I don't have to stand for this!"

"Yes, you do." Johan gestured toward Rolf's chair with his knife, the motion made threatening by the glinting edge of the implement. "Sit down and listen."

"You love to humiliate me!"

"Yes, that's true. Sit down." His voice became quieter. "Rolf, sit down, or you'll begin to make me angry!" Rolf sat down. "Now, if you'll listen to me, I'll tell you about the letter from Sigismund's court." He looked at Matilda. "May I do that at my table, or will it be bad for your digestion?"

"You're acting very strangely, husband."

"Sigismund is likely to besiege Karlsbirk come spring. He has eleven crows and a lot of firepots and some ribaldekins we made for him over the years— 'in various stages of repair,' as the letter says, which means they haven't kept them up so well. So, somebody has to go and see to their condition, make the carriages ready to march, and oversee the siege itself. *Now* you may talk. Well, Rolf, who shall it be? You or me?"

"I don't—I'm not at my most useful at a siege."

Johan chuckled. "No, no you're not. Every time a crow goes off, you jump like you'd been goosed with the rammer. No, unless we could find a way of letting you talk the Karlsbirkers to death, you wouldn't be at your most useful at the siege." He looked very satisfied, like a man with a secret. "All right, I'll go. And I'll take Cosimo."

Johan looked around the table. Elsbet went right on eating. Cosimo was frowning into space. Rolf was looking at his father with hatred. Only Matilda tried to smooth things over. "Won't that be nice," she said weakly.

Rolf swallowed hard. "I don't get it."

"What's that?"

"Why will you take *him?*"

"I'll need an assistant."

"But..." Rolf looked at the Italian. "He doesn't know anything."

"He knows everything."

"He's a damned baby."

"He'll be fifteen."

"Damn him, Father, I'll be made to look like a fool if you take him and not me!"

"You'd be no use, you said it yourself."

"But... *it's the place the son of the house takes!*"

"So?"

"What's been going on behind my back? Tell me! I'm out running here and there, making the deals that keep this place going, you're sitting here letting that snot-nosed little Italian bastard make up to you! He's been talking about me behind my back, hasn't he? Sneaking around, that's what he's been doing, mocking, I know his ways—when I'm not here to defend myself, getting at you because you're old and you can't have any more sons! I'm not going to let a little piece of shit like that—"

Johan was on his feet and shouting. Rolf got up too, and, with the table between them like a gaming board, they bellowed at each other. Matilda rose and hurried from the room with her hands over her ears, but Elsbet, who had a good appetite, went on eating and staring at the two men. Cosimo had mottled spots of red high on his cheeks; he watched them, too, with glittering eyes. If the argument ended as most others did, Johan would strike his son hard enough to shut him up, and that would be that. This time, however, things ended differently: Johan took the table by the edge and tipped it toward his son so that he had to scramble back or have his toes crushed by its weight. Knives and metal plates and drinking cups clattered; food and wine spilled across the polished floor. Cosimo sprang back. Elsbet sat there with her hand halfway to her mouth, as if she were waiting for the table to right itself.

"Welcome home," Johan said bitterly in the silence.

"You're crazy. You're crazy, just crazy!" Rolf was looking down at the mess and repeating the same words as if he could not get past their meaning.

"Cosimo goes with me to Karlsbirk as my second! You can go to Hell, or anywhere else they'll have you."

Rolf was still staring at the chaos of the meal, as if it were all their lives lying there, scattered and thrown down. Elsbet looked at Cosimo and jerked her head toward the door to tell him to leave, and he did so, though not so quickly as to suggest that he was afraid of Rolf.

Elsbet stood up. She looked around for a place to put her knife, which had been in her hand when the table was thrown over. There was none, and, with a little shrug, she tossed the knife down with the rest of the ruin.

The sound of the utensil's falling woke Rolf. He looked up at Elsbet as if she were a stranger. "He's crazy," he said.

"He's still your father." To Elsbet, fathers were the final rulers of the world. Sane or mad, they were always in command. She called in a servant and ordered that the room be cleaned, and then she led Rolf off to their own rooms, where he got control of himself again.

"But he *is* crazy," he said. "Taking that little prick with him!"

"Why does it matter?"

"Because he means to bring him into the business, don't you see?" He kept his voice low because he was sure that his father's servants were spies who reported everything.

"He'd only be another artisan. When the business is yours, you can get rid of him."

"I think the old fart means to treat him like a son. I think he's gone peculiar; there's something going on in that head of his. You see how he tipped up that table?"

"Of course I saw it." Her voice was like a cracked cup, but calm. The more excited Rolf got, the calmer she seemed to grow.

"He's mad. Or going that way. He always hated me, but it's getting worse. Don't you think?"

"One day, you'll own everything, and then you'll be the father and it won't matter.

"Ah, what do you know about it? Why do I tell you things?"

Contrary to what Matilda believed, he did tell Elsbet everything. Elsbet never repeated any of it, however, and so it seemed that she was ignorant. She was like an open pit, into which an endless stream of resentment, dreams, bitterness, speculation, hope could be poured, a sinkhole that would take all the words and secrets of his world.

"I told you about little Carl, didn't I?" he said suddenly.

151

"Yes."

"Biedermaier—the son, not the father—has a girl a year younger. He'll betroth her when she's seven. Not bad. A link to the Biedermaiers of Kobenhavn—that's a good connection, Elsbet."

"My father says the Hanse towns are fading."

"Don't quote your father at me! What does he know, anyway? He's like my father, a gunmaker, nothing else. Who runs the business, eh? Your brothers, that's who, not the old man. The Hanse cities will be powerful when he and my father are dead and forgotten. Don't quote your father at me."

A flicker of expression crossed her face and was gone.

"The house of Biedermaier isn't bad at all," he said. "Kings come to them for advice, Elsbet. Kings! The Jews are running off like ants; Biedermaier and the others will pick up their accounts. That's where wealth is—not in guns, but in money. Money makes money!" He nodded, as if somebody else had said it to him and he was agreeing. "I'll marry into some good house in every city in the Hanse, and *then* we'll make money!"

His words began to roam over their future, like fingers feeling over an intricate surface. He drank wine. When he stopped talking for a few seconds, she said, "What do you mean, your father wants to treat Cosimo like a son?"

"Oh, you know. It's a way of speaking. They're always together. Like he's bringing him along. You hear it all over the yard— 'just like a son.' I know what they say. A lot of them would rather it was the Italian shit-ass than me, because they know I'm tough. I know that there's gunmakers all over as good as they are; it's deals and contacts make the business, not what goes on down in the yard. They make me sick."

"Maybe Cosimo's your father's bastard."

"Maybe he is. Lots of people think so. He's had other women."

"Maybe he means to legitimize him. Kings can do that."

"What?"

"Adopt him. He could work it with his friend the Bishop."

"But I'd still be the real son. The oldest. Holy Mother of God, Elsbet, you don't think he'd really do it!"

"Well, if you had one son who was good at making deals and another son who was good in the yard, you'd want them to share the business, wouldn't you?"

"In the name of Jesus, Elsbet, where did you come up with such an idea? Did Matilda say something?"

She shook her head. It was growing dark. There were no lights in the room, and it already seemed like night away from the windows. She began to unbind her girdle. "It's only something I was thinking of. My father says you must be able to look every possibility in the face." She laid the girdle aside and unbound her head and put the ribbons and kerchief aside on a heavy chest. She had let her hair grow since her marriage and wore it in tight coils against her head.

"He wouldn't, though," Rolf was saying as he paced. "But he's getting crazy enough. And just out of hatred, he might do it. My God, Elsbet, *what would I do?*"

She had taken off her bodice, and now her long skirt fell to the floor. Under them she wore a linen gown, which she peeled down her arms and pushed over her hips until she was naked, a white fish swimming in the darkness of the room. "You could have him killed," she said. "One of my brothers knows somebody who does it for hire at Mainz."

"Holy Christ, what an idea!"

"Why not?" She carried the clothes to a press and folded them and put them in it.

"It would be a sin."

"You try to buy him off first. He doesn't like it here. He talks to me. He wants to go back to Italy. You would offer him money, and then, if he would not go away, you would write to the man in Mainz." She lay down. He gulped the last of his wine and moved toward the bed, leaving his clothes behind him like a record of his haste.

The Fox lived snug within the den of her own mind. Only a part of her roved out into the world; the rest stayed slyly in the den. Other women—Matilda, for example—believed that their every thought was the world's business, but Elsbet the Fox knew better.

Mons was a more sophisticated place than this little city where her marriage had brought her. At her father's table, one could see Englishmen, Spaniards, Frenchmen, even once in a while someone as exotic as a Moor. Her father had a real painting on one of his walls, done by an Italian and finer than anything in the mother church of Mouers. Next to that brilliance of line and color, what were the agonized wooden Christs of Germany? Worse yet, what were the stark black-and-red stick figures painted around the walls of St. Katrin's

Chapel, next to the blue-green flesh and the wealth of detail in her father's picture?

The Fox adored her father. *Adored.* His greed, his coarseness, his overwhelming appetites—these were her measure of greatness in men. He had raised her with two ideas: to be a perfect wife with her body, and to think her own thoughts, deep in her mind. So, because he had decreed those things, she tried to live up to them. She knew her wifely responsibility: to bear sons, to lie down when her husband wanted her to, to be wise and amoral if need be in helping him, to keep secrets, speak little, never complain.

To be faithful.

It was permissible for her husband to be unfaithful; it was not permissible for her to be unfaithful. That was very simple to grasp. Not quite so simple to repress some of the urges of her own small body, which was left unsatisfied by Rolf's quick lovemaking, but she managed. If she was unfaithful, it was deep down in the den of her mind, and that was entirely her own business.

Once, Cosimo had come into her rooms just at dusk. He was fourteen; she was eighteen. He had loitered about, saying little; he was often like that. She sensed that this time he had another purpose; she had even sensed what a struggle was going on inside his own mind, for he was very pious and very strict. But she knew that two things made her uncommonly attractive to him: she was Rolf's wife, and, because she lived in the same house and was almost a relative, she represented Sin. Sin must be pulling him like a winch, she knew. The fact of Sin drew the pious. So he hung about her in the near-darkness, and it would have taken only a movement from her, a feather-light touch, a word, to give him permission.

Instead, she had said, "It is time for you to go now."

And he had gone.

She could be adulterous with him in her mind, if such a thing was ever desirable.

At the gunpowder mill down the river, Black Cob and Cosimo leaned their heads together across a trestle table. Between them lay a metal tray with grains of black powder on it—Cob's latest attempt to solve the riddle of the making of corned gunpowder. For four years, he had been able to make small batches, but he had never yet found a process to make it in quantity.

154

The two sat in a shed of hewn logs, beyond whose open entry the dreariness of a spring rainstorm stretched to the dripping horizon. Water ran from the eave in a sheet. A laborer scurried across the open yard, leaped a puddle and vanished, and only a white duck that lived there seemed to find the weather tolerable.

"'Tis a great thing if I've done it this time, Maister Cosimo."

"Yes, if."

Black Cob sighed. "She's a powerful powder, that much I know. The best ever. 'Tis a fattening of the alkahest, I think—so much greater a demon is in the grain."

Cosimo frowned at that. He accepted the theory of demons, for the most learned chemists of the day did so, but as a man of intellect, he doubted that the demons were bigger because the grain was bigger. There might be *more* demons—but then again, demons were perhaps only metaphors for something else. He regretted that his education had not included more of these sciences; indeed, he almost regretted the loss of his tutor, though he rarely thought of the man any more.

"I leave the demons to you, Cob. The questions àre, *alpha,* can you make the same charge again, and *beta,* can it be contained in a normal gun?"

"Ee, well now."

It was an oddity of their relationship that Cob was much more the peasant in both speech and manner with Cosimo than he was with Johan. There was an understanding between the boy and the powdermaker that sprang from the very roots of their lives; quite simply, both believed that Cob was a peasant and Cosimo was an aristocrat. It made life between them very easy. It had the sometimes comical side effect of making Cob talk and gesture like a yokel, but neither seemed to care.

"Ee, now, as for your *alpha* there, well, that's always my hard place, ain't it? But I can try. And I think maybe this time I found me the secret, Maister Cos."

"Which is what?"

Cob hesitated. He glanced around, lowered his voice, turned his head away from the open side of the shed. *"Nun's piss."*

"No!"

"Oooo, aye! Got me an arrangement with yon convent of Garnheim, costs me a bit, but I'm taking every ounce of nunnish water they pass."

155

"What, to mix with the gunpowder?"

"Not mixing, Maister Cos, not mixing—*anointing*, that's the secret, eh? Coom to me in a dream, or almost a dream, for was in my head when I woke up one day—Cob, I says, wet down yon gunpowder with spirits of brandy to make her wet, but add holy water so your demons don't take fire. Well, I thought on that and thought on it, and I saw that the way to pacify yon demons and not dilute the alkahest was with nun's piss. I could have kicked meself fer not seeing it sooner, fer I've known of the character of that demon since ever I mixed me first mortarful for Brother Michael, yon daft old monk that first put me in the way of this science."

"And so you thought of nun's urine."

"Yah, well, after some trials. Tried lamb's piss, they being sweet creatures and the earthly emblem of Our Lord, but the gathering of it, believe me, is more trouble than you'd want. So I went lookin' fer other such, and settled on yon nuns. Which do make sense, fer who be more holy than nuns, eh?"

"I'm surprised you didn't try the Bishop."

"Oh, I did! But he sent me back only a little phial with his blessing, and between you and me, 'twas very strong water, and yellow as buttercups. Still, 'twasn't the purity that worried me, but the quantity. How much can one Bishop pass, eh?"

"Well, so you went to the nuns. And my question *beta*, Cob?"

"Ah, that *beta!*" Cob scratched his head as every peasant in the empire learned to do when trying to suggest deep thought. "Gunfounding ain't my craft, so I don't know how the tubes is made so as not to bust from this charge. But I tell you, I think that if they use yon powder in the usual amounts, they'll bust every tube in Christendom."

"Now, Cob—"

"Ye don't believe? Coom."

Pulling back a soiled canvas in the rear of the shed, he revealed a pile of scrap metal. A small cannon barrel lay on the pile. An old gun that had seen much service, it should still have been serviceable, having been cast by Johan himself, but there was a gaping split down the side that was big enough for Cosimo to put a finger into.

"What say to that, Maister Cosmo?"

"It's an old gun."

"Nyah! I done the same with two new ones, and was so ashamed I dunked 'em under yon duck pond to hide 'em from

Maister Johan. I swear on Holy St. Katrin, that powder'll split any gun made."

"Well, we could make the barrels heavier."

"Ooo, aye, and have what? A little gun as heavy as a big one, and got so much metal in her she costs like a great gun. And think of what the monster guns would be like, think of Mouers Bett using my new powder."

"Yes...well..." Cosimo stood negligently, one index finger at his lips, the elbow of that arm resting on the other palm at his waist, his legs cocked negligently. "Still, in a *very* little gun, it wouldn't matter."

"Eh?"

"It's in the nature of gunmaking. The tubes on hand-cannons are already stronger than they need to be. You can be a careless fool and triple-load one of Johan's hand-cannons and it will still be safe."

"Would yon handgun shoot straighter with more force behind the ball, then?"

"It might. It just might."

He shifted his position and stood now with folded arms. Unlike the others in the yards, he did not wear livery or any badge, but dressed like a gentleman's son in pink hose of sharlach cloth, so elastic that the hose fit like skin, and a very tight brown jacket, belted at the hips. His hair fell to his shoulders from a leather band.

"Have you any hand-cannons here, Cob?"

"Aye, one or two. Keep 'em for the testing."

"Bring them out to the try-field, Cob, and enough of your powder for half a dozen shots."

"In the rain, Maister Cos? It's comin' down like curses."

"You said it would shoot damp."

"Aye, damp, but soaked wet, no! Well, you can shoot out the door of the try-house, I guess."

The handguns had changed little in the years since the battle of Garnheim. On some, the wooden staff was shorter, and such guns could be fired by one man, with the staff held under his arm and not grounded. Others had been built into axes and maces so that the gunner had another weapon when his one shot was fired.

Cosimo's handling of the weapons was unorthodox. He held the staff well up in his armpit so that his face could be put close to the barrel, a practice avoided by more cautious shooters; with his left hand holding the hot wire and his right closed over the staff just below its junction with the tube, he could sight along the top of the barrel and bring the priming charge and the hot wire together to fire. With his head bent and one eye closed, however, he had no depth perception, and he had to find the touchhole by putting the wire on the barrel and then bringing it down toward his eye—"stroking the cat," he called it.

There was no doubt that he was the best shot in Mouers. On his good days, he could put two balls out of three in a three-foot circle at thirty yards—incredible shooting!

At his sixth shot, the boy roared with pain. Cob grabbed for the hand that wanted to clutch the injured eye, bent it away from the face, knowing that he could only hurt himself worse that way.

"My eye—Cob, my eye—"

"Eee, I know, Maister Cos—sit down, now—no, no, git your hand from your face—sit!"

He forced the boy down on a stool. Water from a downspout was poured over his face to flush it, and then Cob sponged it clean and found the burned place when the boy winced.

"It blew through the touchhole. Right into my eye."

There was nothing boyish about him now. He was like an old soldier. And, like a soldier, he still held the weapon. "What do you see, Cob?"

"Three bits of black in the eye. Stone from the grinder that's got into the powder, I speculate. Eye burned at the lids, and all your eyebrow and lashes gone—the girls'll weep, ye had such lovely lashes! Now, close other eye and tell, can ye see me?"

"Light and dark. Ah! it burns. Like looking underwater, that's all."

"Well. Shall I fetch yon surgeon from Mouers, maister?"

"What would you do if it was anybody else?"

"Fix you myself."

"Then do it. Do it, man!"

Cob led him back to the shed and into his own room, where he kept a set of needles and knives and lint for bleeding. The boy allowed himself to be led along and gave no further sound about the pain.

An hour later, he wore a rather rakish bandage that covered the injured eye. Cob had picked out the black bits with a needle and covered the burns with goose fat. Cosimo insisted on going back to the try-house, where he examined the guns he had been firing and the targets that he had shot.

"It's a hellish gunpowder, Cob. The guns shoot flat now;

158

you don't have to lob the ball so that you can't sight the thing." He picked up one of the hand-cannons. "If the touch weren't right in the middle of the top, we could put a little fence behind it so that it wouldn't blow back into the eye, couldn't we? But we can't do it, because if there were a fence there, we couldn't sight down the tube. Ergo, we move the touchhole. But where, eh? Anywhere else, and the powder will fall out. Well, that will bear some thinking on."

He carried the lightest of the hand-cannons out of the shed. "I go tomorrow to join Johan in King Sigismund's train. Send three kegs of the new gunpowder after me. We make for Karlsbirk."

It was a little city on the eastern fringe of the empire, in an area that was perpetually in dispute and always being marched over by someone's army. The Teutonic Knights, thrusting eastward when their godly works had turned to earthly wealth, had claimed, conquered, and lost it; the Slavs had held it; Poles, Saxons and Livonians had all struggled for it. Now the city was like a man who has survived the plague, seemingly stronger for the experience—and the richer, for it is he who has first claim on his dead neighbors' goods. Little Karlsbirk was a thriving free city, a beehive in an otherwise barren land. It was like a miniature of a city, with a small river to the Baltic, a Cistercian monastery, a colony of Jews driven eastward to its hospitality. Like the man who has escaped the plague, Karlsbirk was not so fussy as its fellows farther west.

To the east of the little city lay the river, to the north a desolate plain and the Baltic; southward, low hills rose gently toward the uplift of the great central plateau. Only to the west was there a hill overlooking the city—not a mountain, but a good, high hill. It provided a prospect of the city, and there Sigismund established his camp for the siege of Karlsbirk.

Pioneers and two companies of mercenaries had come first, driving ahead of them a mob of serfs to dig fortifications. The Karlsbirkers, who had been besieged before, had withdrawn within their walls and taken in the peasants from the neighborhood, stripping the fields. In an orgy of final gleanings, both attackers and attacked swept the land between the hill and the city clean of everything edible and burnable. The mercenaries and the Karlsbirkers exchanged sallies of almost dancelike formality. Eleven deaths were scored, none of any importance, except to the dead. When the earthworks were completed, word was sent back to Sigismund's court, and the main body of the army set out.

Most of the fighting men were mercenaries. Sigismund paid well. Archers, crossbowmen and pikemen moved over the countryside four and six abreast in a snake train of movement; at the head of each group was a company in Sigismund's colors, followed by the mercenary bands in their wild and barbaric finery, each decked out in a habit of its own inventing. Hard, tough, capable, amoral—they were men of the time. Most of them looked strangely old; they were the survivors, who had passed through danger and come out at the other side.

After each mercenary company, its women and servants and carts came next, its pigs and cattle, its barking dogs and geese and chickens in wooden cages—for this was an army going to a siege, not one going to take the field against a mobile opponent. This was a job, after all, that could be made to last all summer; a soldier would want his creature comforts. One captain even brought his own huntsman in his train, complete with horn and ax and staghounds, thus suggesting his own confidence in the length of the siege.

Johan and his cannon and the Company of St. Barbara were in the middle of the army. There were more than three hundred pieces of ordnance in all, not counting the handcannons; half of them were of Johan's manufacture, the rest pieces bought all over Europe, a third of them oddments picked up for this siege. Of the twenty-two great guns, Johan had made fourteen, three of them that winter—the best guns in the world. Decorated as elaborately as pieces of armor, they were gorgeous objects, shined to a warm, deep brilliance and carried on flat pallets of oak behind teams of oxen. Johan preferred the sledlike pallets because of the absence of roads. Brass, leather and colored ribbons bedecked the oxen; the cannons themselves were hung with colors and bells as if they, too, were living beings, perhaps demons to be pacified with gifts.

Ribaldekins in calibers from half an inch to one and seveneighths inches were hauled on wheeled carriages by horses. Smaller firepots, mortars and bombards followed, and then the oddities that Johan had accepted simply to placate Sigismund's Master of Wardrobe—bombards with removable breeches, wretched things that leaked gas and lost their explosive force; several curiosities made with a large central barrel and many small ones surrounding it, hooped, wood-cased, mounted crazily against recoil blocks of sixteen-inch-thick oak. "None of them worth a fart and every one more a menace to me than the enemy," Johan growled.

Next came the fifty St. Barbarans with their hand-cannons, splendid in tabards of black and red; then eight carts loaded with salpetre, sulphur and charcoal in barrels; after them, six carts of rounded stones, sized for the weapons in the train, and the tools for rounding more (and, if the siege was a long one, he would build a waterwheel on the river and grind cannonballs there); and last his journeymen and laborers and hangers-on, their women and their possessions. The parade of ordnance took up a good part of the army's length, and people came out of houses and rode out from towns to see it as it passed.

Johan ranged up and down the column. Hans Bighead was cursing an outcropping of stone that had grounded the great guns.

"Damned sleds won't go over, master!"

"You need wheels."

"Well, it's got to be the wheels, then. Oh, shit, here goes two days! All right, haul them sleds to the side and let the army pass!" He began to bellow at the oxen and the drivers.

Johan found Josef, the yardmaster, in the train and sent him forward with the wheels. Johan's pride demanded that he arrive at the siege site in the same position he had occupied throughout; therefore, he and all his men would have to work all night, getting the great guns back into the line. If not, he would simply give encouragement to all those military experts (some of them in positions to give or withhold money) who thought that ordnance was nothing more than noisemakers.

"Rider coomin', maister."

"Where?"

"West and south, see 'im?"

"Yah, now I see him." He cursed his fading eyesight. Now he could make out the distant rider, who was coming along the next ridge so that he was silhouetted.

"One of ours?"

"Not wearing your colors, maister. But I do think it be Maister Cosimo, from his seat on yon horse."

"I'll ride a little toward him."

"Aye, he'll see you better that way."

The rider turned down off the ridge and became a blur in

the green smear of fields, but, as Johan closed, he could make out the deep brown of cloak and hood, then the buttery yellow of his coat and his red hose.

"Well, boy."

"Sir."

"You catch us at a bad time. What word from home?" He was trying to hide his pride in the boy. Cosimo looked like a lord's son: he wore the deerskin *lederner* of a knight, its stamped decorations in martial motifs, gold rosettes over the breast from which a dagger hung by his right side. *Already a man,* Johan thought. *Old enough to die.* The army was filled with boys of fifteen whom somebody thought old enough to die. "What in Hell happened to your eye?"

"Little accident at the try-field. Nothing serious."

"Shooting with your eye kissing the touchhole again! How many times have I told you not to do that?"

Cosimo shrugged, looked away. It was his studied carelessness that angered Johan.

"And don't be so damn-all high and mighty about it, my little lordship! When I tell you a thing, I—" He turned on his servant. "What're you eavesdropping about? Get out!" The servant tried to back his mule away. When it would not move fast enough, he jumped down and dragged the animal toward the train. "You could have lost an eye!" Johan roared.

"But I didn't."

"But you could have!"

"But I didn't!"

Johan wanted to slap him. *Moment ago, I was ready to boo-hoo, thinking of him being old enough to be killed, now I want to hit him!* He sat back in the saddle. "All right, what news from Mouers?"

"Dame Matilda sends her greetings and prayers for your success. I have letters. I left little Friede well. Dame Elsbet has two cousins visiting from Mons. Corpus Christi Guild voted not to play 'Abraham and Isaac' this year unless we return in time to do it. Black Cob is at work on his dream of corned gunpowder again; this time, he seems to have something—if the nuns of Garnheim stay thirsty enough. I'll explain that later. I went through the bellhouse before I left, and it looks to me as if the cope for Mickle Meg..."

They rode down to the wagons. Johan's heart was like a bubble in his chest, light and big. For all his anger over the boy's injured eye—and what was that anger, but a father's love?—he was proud that at fifteen Cosimo could make this journey alone and bring with him the understanding of an adult.

It was twelve more days' travel to Karlsbirk. Another segment of the army met them there—horsemen and infantry hired out of Silesia, one company made up of Magyars with high cheekbones and almost slanted eyes. Gathered at last before Karlsbirk, the army was a Babel of languages and a turmoil of colors, a flower garden gone wild. Cosimo's clothes seemed subdued next to those of the mercenaries, who were affecting the style that was coming in from France and the Low Countries: hose with legs of different colors, jackets with sleeves of different lengths, different-colored linings.

"If that's the fashion, I'll go naked," Johan complained. "Everything's going to the devil."

They sent pioneers down to trench toward the Karlsbirk wall and to draw fire. Johan counted six cannons of size along the walls, but no monster guns.

"That Frenchman, Robert de Rennes, was supposed to have sold them a sixteen-footer five years ago. Where is it?"

He let the Karlsbirk guns bang away for two days, and then he had the forward decoys removed. Nobody had been hurt; one wild ball had ricocheted off a rock face and injured two oxen that were tethered two hundred yards up the hill. Some of the mercenaries cheered derisively and went to work butchering the oxen.

Sigismund, content to devote his summer to this amusing pastime of taking an isolated city, commanded that all things should be done well and carefully. Johan was content; he had a contract that paid by the day. To his disgust, the King had brought siege machines along as well as cannons, and his own work was complicated by the erection of these enormous contraptions. Johan's people went about putting up an observation tower and found, as usual, that there was not enough timber in the neighborhood, even when several of the local houses were pulled down.

He sent for the timber, and waited.

It rained for nine days in a row. Gunpowder could not be mixed and guns could not be fired.

It was too muddy for four days after that to bring the guns into position.

The siege machines, assembled where they would be used, went into action. For all the good they did, in his view, they could have been left in Prague. They did lob twenty-pound rocks over the city wall, where they undoubtedly wrecked several houses and frightened the citizenry. From a military viewpoint, however, they did nothing to make the city easier to take. Even the mercenaries were disillusioned by them, and every shot by biffa or ballista was greeted with insults.

"Wonderful! You almost hit Karlsbirk that time!"

"What a shot! I swear to God, if they had aimed, they'd have come near something."

"Shoot it all the way over the city next time; maybe the wind will knock the wall down!"

His observation tower, when finished, would be two-thirds of the way from Sigismund's hilltop to the wall. From it he could sight all his guns, using a system of flags to signal.

"Ribaldekins around the camp itself and our own works; they're bound to make sallies. Mortars in quite close; we'll need forward earthworks and a communication trench back for each lot. Bombards on each of the three gates." They had a map of the city, supplied by a spy; it showed the locations of an armory, private houses being used as mercenary barracks (Karlsbirk had hired mercenaries, too, although the only thing attractive about serving in a city under siege was the high pay) and the squares where groups could be assembled for counterattacks.

"Aim the great guns at the two gates where the squares are. We'll pound them with the mortars so they won't dare gather there, then knock down the gates with the crows. If the weather ever turns."

One day, the clouds broke up, and by afternoon they were scudding away under a blue sky. Next day it was windy and bright and the earth began to dry out. Johan went up into the half-finished observation tower to look about him. He ordered his great guns loaded; at the same time, the crows began to fire from the Karlsbirk walls. They gave all their attention to the siege machines, so it appeared that they were doing some damage inside. In twenty-three shots, the Karlsbirkers missed every time; then they sent a ball smashing through the biggest biffa. The huge arm hung out of line; broken timbers stuck out like bones. The machinists got oxen and began to drag it back out of range; the Karlsbirk guns belched again and again, and then the crew in its haste tried to drag the machine through an uneven place and it tipped, toppled, and fell to a crazy angle with the terrain. Two men were crushed. The rest ran around the thing and then withdrew to the hillside to look at it for several hours, as if by watching it they might make it move. It was out of action for good, however, the first real casualty of the siege; there it stuck for the next months, slowly reduced as the cooks' helpers found it a ready supply of firewood.

"If I could put out the weight those slingers do, I'd have the whole city in pieces by now," Johan said. The siege machines were still lobbing quantities of rock over the walls, ignoring their wrecked fellow. Word came from a spy inside that they had managed to hit the cathedral.

"God will be pleased," Cosimo murmured.

The cannons banged away; the biffas lobbed their rocks. The Karlsbirk mercenaries launched an attack against a battery of mortars, were repelled by the foot troops there, and turned aside to cut into the workmen around one of the siege machines, almost taking it. Sigismund sent reinforcements; for an hour, bowmen and foot soldiers bled and died around the machine.

"Why do they want it?" Cosimo asked.

"It vexes them. Siege machines *look* terrifying, whatever damage they do. It must be unsettling, having rocks falling out of the sky day and night."

"But they haven't hit the walls."

Johan moved four small guns down to the mortar battery and had them loaded with chain and broken crockery, in case the attack turned back that way. The Karlsbirk mercenaries withdrew, however, leaving the siege machine in place but afire from flaming arrows. A line of buckets was formed from a rain-swollen ditch, and the flames were put out.

Sigismund was delighted. No doubt it had looked like a real war to him, sitting atop his hill. He sent down word that the cannons should be more active than they had been.

"Active! I'd give him active!" Johan glared at Sigismund's messenger. "Doesn't he know it's been raining?"

He put Cosimo in command of a battery of bombards and told him to keep the Karlsbirk wall guns under fire.

Cosimo looked at him skeptically. "Command?"

"You're not a boy any more."

Cosimo remembered still the bitter lessons of the beating in the stableyard and the humiliations that followed among the apprentices. "I thought it was humility I was to learn, not command."

"D'you want to do it, or not?"

The temptation to say that he had been too much humbled was very great, but the temptation to command was greater. "Yes!"

"Don't make a fool of me; go about it slow, and remember what you've learned."

Cosimo started for the ladder that led down from the tower. "Would you have put Rolf in command of a battery at fifteen?"

"I wouldn't put Rolf in command of a battery now."

Cosimo grinned—a very straightforward, young man's grin.

Fourteen of the bombards were new. They were rather like oversized hand-cannons on swivel mounts, their long wooden stocks allowing them to be easily trained in horizontal arcs. Under the barrel, a pivot let them be raised or lowered. They fired balls of three-inch diameter, but their shortness and the often loose fit of the projectiles made them inaccurate.

It was work that Cosimo could like, however: guns that could be sighted like hand-cannons, and gunners who could be directed by voice and not with flags.

"You're to command, Master Cosimo?" The head gunner was one of Johan's journeymen.

"I am."

"Very good, I'm sure." The man exchanged a look with another journeyman.

Cosimo wore the deerskin *lederner* over chain mail, a gift from Johan for the siege. The gold chains swung gaily from the gold rosettes. His cloak and hood had been cast aside so that he could wear a light steel sallet on his head; even this he took off, however, so that he could see and hear better. A servant hovered near him, too terrified of Johan's anger to leave him, yet almost terrified enough of the guns to run away.

"Load your pieces!"

They had buried their powder kegs as protection from sparks and burning wadding. Gunners' assistants dipped long ladles into the kegs and spilled the contents back until the gunners judged the amount to be right; then boys replaced the wood covers and pulled a damp cowskin over them. The ladles were turned down the barrels, which were elevated for loading. Dried moss was tamped in; the stone shot was let roll down on top of the moss, and more moss was tamped in. The gunners waited with hot irons, ready to fire.

"Depress that gun."

"What, master?"

"Depress that gun; you'll go right over the wall."

"Peterkin shoots high, Master Cos."

"I'll be the judge of that. Depress the weapon."

The head gunner took Cosimo aside. "The gunners don't like to be pressed," he said quietly.

Cosimo knew the man—had learned to cast bronze from him, in fact. "You told me once, when I could cast better than you, you'd stop deviling me. Remember?"

"Aye."

"When they can shoot better than I can, I'll stop pressing them."

They fired a round, and he went to the first gun and made a mark on the barrel and another even with it on the oak quadrant that rose vertically above it.

"Marks ain't necessary wi' Foul Fowlke," the gunner said angrily.

"How will you aim at the same height again?"

"Grain of yon piece of wood, maister, just a finger's breadth from touchhole. Then it's a matter of eye and judgment, like."

Yes, making a mystery out of nothing, Cosimo thought. He made himself smile at the gunner, even made himself touch the man on the shoulder. "Well, now *I* have a mark to see it by, eh?" The guns were reloaded and Foul Fowlke was brought to the same aim, although whether it was by using the gunner's method or his own, Cosimo could not tell.

The wall gun at which they were aiming returned their fire.

"I think we tickled 'em," the head gunner said. The shot crashed into the hillside behind them.

"Fools," Cosimo muttered. He scored the quadrant plate of each gun and explained how he wanted the aiming done. In the dirt at the foot of each carriage, he scribed a crude arc and marked off its segments. "Now, when we find the aim, you can return to it after loading."

"We a'ready do it."

"How?"

"By eye."

"Yes, but you all have different eyes. Now we'll do it by *my* eye."

They fired off another salvo, and the cannon on the walls spat smoke and a twenty-foot spurt of flame, and a shot came whistling toward them, to crash down thirty yards short and fling bits of rock and dirt over them. The stone split on impact and a small piece zinged through the air to their left, while the rest of it rolled unevenly toward a trench where some mercenaries lounged.

Cosimo's servant was terrified. "You, go fetch a barrel of beer for the gunners," he said. The man left with such happy haste that the gunners roared.

"And hurry back!" Cosimo shouted after him; they laughed again.

He talked to them as he talked to Black Cob—lord to peasant. They would get along. "Three crowns to every gun that hits within a man's height of that wall gun! And aim them my way!"

The guns pounded.

"You're not costing me a groat," Cosimo shouted at them. "What sort of gunners are you? Who's going to win some of that money?"

Down the line they went again, with a hit from the third gun and a hit from the eighth. On the third round, he had four close shots to pay for. The crew of the wall gun was now being sprayed with rock from the wall and menaced by ricochets. He doubted that there had been any real hits, but if such shooting could be kept up, the crew would find it difficult to get off well-aimed shots.

"Fire!"

The little cannons began their sequence. The Karlsbirk gun roared, and the shot passed almost at head-height over them, close enough to one of the bombards so that the crew threw itself on the ground.

"Jesu!"

"And St. Barbara!"

"Fire!"

Then it was load and fire and cool the guns, and load and fire again. The entire siege narrowed to the fifth of a mile of fields between the wall gun and his battery. Along the wall to the west, a second crow had been brought to bear on them and began to fire. Around the bombards, the smoke was often too thick to see to fire, and the crews coughed and spat and fired by the marks without seeing their target.

"Fire!"

He heard a shot whistle near him in the smoke and never turned to see where it had struck. His throat burned and his injured eye was watering.

"Drink, Maister Cos?"

"What?"

"Beer for the smoke!"

Their target had not fired in four of their rounds.

"Bombards gettin' too hot, maister."

"We'll rest, then. Swab with water."

The far cannon on the Karlsbirk wall fired, and he heard it as if it were a sound from underwater. He was temporarily half-deaf. He waited for the shot to pass overhead and was astounded when the end of his battery behaved as if it were on springs. The shot carried off two of the bombards as if they were men whose feet had been kicked from under them. The stone ball skipped over the mercenaries' trench and crashed into their cookfires behind, and voices began to scream.

Cosimo was shouting. "What damage—what damage?"

"Spitting Pol and the Pardoner gone!"

"Injuries?"

"Nothing to speak of, two hit wi' splinters, is all." They had been gathered by the beer barrel instead of at the guns. Not so lucky were two of the mercenary cooks, who were moaning now; he heard Christ begged for mercy by a breaking voice.

"Load up!"

"Bombards ain't hardly cool."

"Load up! Two marks higher on the muzzle."

"To shoot at what, Maister Cos?"

"Any damned thing we hit in there!" He was like a child who has been denied what he wants and is in a tantrum.

"Fire!"

A rider galloped across his line of fire and came to a halt in front of him so abruptly that the animal, a big draft horse with hooves like kegs, almost fell.

"Stop that shootin' at once, you madman!" It was Hans Bighead.

"Don't you dare to speak to me like that!"

"I dare speak to you any way I like, you crazy little fool! Maister Johan says, cut that shooting at once! Now, will you stop it?"

If he had tried to speak, he would have shown how close to tears he was. *How dare he!* He paced away from the horse and back. "Cool the guns." He glared up at Hans Bighead, who looked calmly down on him.

"You don't scare me one bit, little man," Hans Bighead said. "Though if looks could fry, I'd be cooked, hey?"

He rode slowly away. To Cosimo's surprise, the gun crews

were as resentful of the order as he was, and he found himself
cheered by their support.

"Let us do things our way, we'd show them."

"What was we doin' was so terrible?"

"Teach 'em a lesson, what we was doing; why'd they stop
us?"

Cosimo studied the activity on the Karlsbirk wall and
judged that the gun that had been their principal target was
being worked on. He could see a small tripod crane and a
dozen men gathered around the weapon.

"How soon can we shoot?"

"Time it'd take to eat an apple."

"Take aim at the gunport again, then."

The far cannon fired once at them, missed, and shifted its
aim to a battery of mortars that were lofting stones over the
south gate. When the bombards began to fire again, however,
and immediately achieved the accuracy they had before, the
other crow was brought back to bear on them. Cosimo and
his gunners cheered, for they watched their shots topple the
crane on the wall and scatter the figures there. A flicker of
flame showed above the wall, and then smoke and debris rose
from an explosion as a keg of powder went up.

A ball from the far gun landed close behind them, so close
that Cosimo could feel the concussion; the spattering of dirt
and bits of flint had a cruel force.

"Move the guns! Up the hill a hundred yards—we're done
for the day."

When they pulled back, the mercenaries who were there
as their protection from ground assault pulled back as well.
The footmen made more noise than the bombards, for they
had all the tools of battle hung about them—knives, swords,
water bottles, extra clothes, helms, oddments of armor,
shields. Two of them had live chickens, one a lark in a cage.
Everything rattled and jingled.

The captain came across to Cosimo, a lopsided grin on his
battered face.

"I'll give it to you, little cock—you put a cork in their
bottle."

He wanted to flare up at the "little cock." Instead, he said
stiffly, "They shot well."

"Aye. Maybe tomorrow, we'll be some good to you." He
made a face. "It's a dull siege, so far. You gave us a little
change, at least."

"You don't have gunners in your company?"

"Nyah! What for?"

"Handgunners, I mean."

"Roman candles for a saint's day! Like the devil in a play with a squib up his ass."

"One day, every company in the empire will have a squad of handgunners."

"Yah, and the sky will rain down chickens cooked in beer, too! Stick to your craft, little cock; you're Hell's own gunner, but you're a poor prophet." The captain bellowed at his underofficers and the company clanked uphill.

There was color and flash enough there to last a man a lifetime, he thought, if that was all one wanted; there was purpose and strength in them. He understood why a king would want to play at sieges. He glanced up the hill toward the splendid marquees and the pavilions that marked Sigismund's headquarters. *But not to play at it. To war in earnest.*

There were princes of the church who wore armor and generaled armies. That would be more to his taste—the intellectual challenge of the church, the glitter of war.

It started to drizzle. He saw that tampions were put in the bombards' muzzles and the powder was covered, then canvas was thrown over each gun and its equipment.

"Comin' back tomorrow, Maister Cos?" the head gunner said.

"If Master Johan sends me."

"The men are rare pleased by today."

"Good. I'm glad of it. Tell them I'll have the money for their prizes sent down at once."

"Will you share more of the beer with us, then?"

"Oh—no, I promised Master Johan—I must—" In confusion, he hurried away from them. He knew how to behave with such men in the hurly-burly of the battle, but afterward he could not be at ease with them.

He was sharing a tent with a boorish squire to one of Sigismund's knights. They had fought once already because Cosimo had called him "fellow" and told him he had the manners of an oaf, and after they had rolled on the grass and almost upset their tent, the other youth had challenged him to fight with weapons. "Name the weapon, you whoreson!"

"Hand-cannons," Cosimo had said urbanely.

"Those ain't a knight's arms!"

"Then don't take a knight's grand ways to me until you're ready to face one. *Fellow.*"

It had ended with their shaking hands when a slightly

older squire had come by and called them both fools. Cosimo could still not like his tentmate, however, and he avoided him when he could.

Now he bathed like a soldier in his salletful of water—hot water, at any rate, and brought by a servant—and combed his hair and brushed the mud off his clothes. The other squire came in and watched him, hardly able to hide his envy that Cosimo had actually been in a battle.

"Heard you went hunting birds today!" he said with horrible false joviality. "Heard you shot a crow!"

"What did you hear?"

"Did you really command them firepots?"

"They aren't called firepots; they're bombards."

"You *commanded* them?"

"Yes. What of it?"

A gush of boyish questions followed: had he been afraid, how had he given commands, was it all luck? "I heard them saying that Captain Gratten of the Thornforst Foot said it was the best day's work with small guns he'd ever seen."

"Who said so?"

"My ritter was talking to a lady. He says it's cruel ungodly what war is since the Devil give gunpowder to the monks. He says it's all the fault of the universities."

"I'm sure he does. Got a brain just about as big as you have." He studied himself in the tiny mirror that Matilda had given him. He found that he was proud that he had washed like a soldier. He lived like a soldier, too; even the uncouth squire had more luxuries than he. He began to change his clothes and thought of the splendor of the Thornforst mercenaries' dress. Still, he would look like a soldier— blue *schlat* hose with rawhide soles and a short, belted *warre* of wool, exactly what fighting men wore under their chain armor and as their leisure dress by itself.

"You could eat with me and the squires, if you like," his tentmate said. It was a sizable gesture.

"Many thanks, but I have to see my master."

"Who d'you call master?"

"Johan de Mouers, the gunmaker."

"I thought he was your father."

"The Devil he is! My father is a great lord."

"Lord of what?"

Cosimo studied himself in the mirror again. "Of the Church. All my family are in the Church."

Johan was at table in his own tent. He lived well in camp,

almost as well as at home. Not for him the privations of the soldier; instead, he wanted the merchant's display of wealth. It was comfortable, and it was good for business. Even senior officers were glad of a place of luxury to come to. Johan had a large tent for himself, one for his servants and one for his possessions, as well as space for ten horses and two wagons.

"Sit, my boy. Eat."

The small table was flanked by two oak benches. The tent itself had been hung with tapestries that showed scenes from the Old Testament; another made a screen between his sleeping quarters and the front. On the floor were two bearskins, cushions, other furs.

Johan smiled. "You did well today." He was eating a baked chicken with his fingers.

"Thank you." Cosimo could not help beaming. "I ask your forgiveness for the other."

Johan waved a greasy hand. "Forgotten."

"I thought you would be angry."

"Everybody has the right to do it once—get angry, do something like that. Proves you care about your task."

A thrill of pleasure shot down Cosimo's spine; even with all his confusion of feeling toward Johan, he was not immune to his praise. He sat, as much to relieve his weak knees as because he meant to eat. The greasy hands reached across and clutched his shoulders. "I'm *proud* of you." Suddenly, Johan was very busy ordering food; minutes later, when Cosimo was eating and they were both sipping wine, Johan said casually, "His majesty is sending you a small gift, I hear."

"Me?"

"'A token,' the Seneschal told me." Johan winked, and they both got a little drunk, and then Cosimo got quite drunk and had to be helped back to his tent by a servant, where he woke at first light with a bursting head. He lay awake, suffering his headache and thinking of Johan: which was he now, the hated commoner of five years before, or the good companion who was initiating him into this glorious domain of soldiering?

CHAPTER SIXTEEN

IT WAS A WONDERFUL SIEGE. To a fifteen-year-old, however, it seemed stagnant.

"Nothing is happening," Cosimo complained. "We could go on like this all year." He was with Johan and two mercenary captains and the Procurer of Weapons for Sigismund's Seneschal, in Johan's tent.

"They'll get sick of it," the captain of the Lower Blackmarsh foot said. "That's what a siege is like, young man—the attackers are patient, and the besieged get sick of it."

"They'll have to do something soon," Johan said.

"Why?"

"Because we're hurting them."

"How do we know that?"

The Procurer of Weapons grunted. He was a grossly fat man who was a great womanizer, Cosimo had been told, as well as a great soldier. It was hard to believe that he was either. "Spies inside the walls. They're losing people every day. And now there's sickness."

"Plague?" one of the captains said with a scowl.

"No, no—some kind of shits. With a fever."

"Oh, well, that's all right. But we'll have to be careful."

"Maybe they'll be over it by the time we go in. Anyway, your men are tough; they've lived through everything else."

"It's the women they'll have to watch out for. Bound to get close to them, eh?

"Not if Sigismund has his way. His majesty's talking about a 'Christian victory.'"

"What the Devil does that mean?"

"It means no fucking." The fat man put his chin down on his other chins and looked at each of them. "His majesty wants to impress Rome with his piety so that they'll legitimize his claim to that swamp he wants beyond the Oder."

"Yah, let him have it! My men won't want those starved twots inside the walls, anyway. Christ, they've got a tent whorehouse behind every camp already—the farmgirls have been pouring in here from as far away as the stinking Baltic."

Cosimo tried to listen and say little. One sarcastic remark from Johan, and a word from a mercenary officer, had shown him that his opinions were not welcome; one must earn the right to speak in such company, and that right was earned with experience. Now, a little drowsy from wine and summer heat, he listened. He had complained of the siege's length, but he was happy in this place.

In July, the Karlsbirkers started shooting the monster gun that Johan had been looking for. Nobody knew why they had waited, unless it was some sense that the gun was their last resort. It was sited on an inner wall of the city; its roar was like distant thunder, heard long after the lightning's flash has faded. Discernibly louder than any other gun, it was awesome in the same ungainly way as the siege machines. In its first day of shooting, it put four balls between the trenches and Sigismund's hilltop tents—longer shots than any other cannon had made.

"Well," Johan said sourly, "now they know it shoots." He tried elevating two of his own biggest guns to hit it, but the range was too great.

"If we could load them with Black Cob's corned powder, we could put a ball right down its throat!" Cosimo argued.

"Aye, if we could. But I fear it'll blow the tubes, and I've got no guns to waste."

The monster roared again, and shot fell on the suburbs of the camp, reaching as far up the hill as the observation tower. Two horses were maimed, and a communication trench was filled with the dirt thrown up by the ball.

Cosimo was down with his batteries, directing fire against the walls, when the monster spoke and another shot whizzed over the fields. There was a distinctly different sound when it hit, the sort of sound an ax might make on a hollow tree.

"What in Hell?" a gunner said.

"Couldn't see nothing."

"Hit something, all right. Sounded like a drum."

"Maybe they put it up the pud of that big whore behind the Thornforsts."

"Shit, she wouldn't thump, she'd splash."

Cosimo went back to sighting in a bombard. Twenty minutes later, when a yardman came down the line of bombards and touched his arm, he had forgotten the shot.

"Coom, Maister Cosimo,"

"What the Devil? How dare you!"

"Maister's hurt, then. Coom on!"

"Master?"

"Johan." The man had a horsy face and large eyes that turned down instead of up at the outside corners. "Maister be hurt."

"Holy Mother, how?"

"Yon cannon hit his tower. Coom."

Cosimo grabbed the head gunner. "Take charge. Keep up the fire on that wall gun; when you have to cool, put the Pike Battery to work." He followed the yardman back along the communication trench, no longer even noticing the slimy clay underfoot, the walls of wickerwork, the turnouts. There were piles of offal and garbage; most of them had been covered over with straw that animals had pulled away again, so that there was a mess underfoot of rotting straw and mud and filth. The trench was a dirty, unlovely place, yet he no longer even noticed it.

They had put Johan on his back on his oak dining table. The rugs and the pillows had been kicked out of the way to make room, and now he was surrounded by mercenaries and journeymen and apprentices and two men with white batons whom Cosimo recognized as part of Sigismund's court.

"Surgeon's with him," a journeyman whispered.

"That'll finish him for sure," said a cynical mercenary.

Cosimo moved through the fringe of the crowd. "Move away, if you please." Heads turned. "Move away, I say!" One of the courtiers looked astonished, but Cosimo pushed forward relentlessly. "Clear this tent. Use your heads, men—in the name of God, give them light and air!" He shoved the commoners, snarled at the mercenaries, was barely polite to the courtiers. Once inside the tent, he dropped the flaps.

"Are you the surgeon?" he said to the man who remained.

"Who the Devil are you to ask?"

"I am—I am Cosimo, his—assistant."

"Ah, yes. Well, I need light; you can't shut the flaps like that." The surgeon raised one flap and scolded a man who had been trying to peep in under it. "Well, look at him, young man; he won't bite you."

Johan's upper clothes had been cut from his body. Part of his shirt was still on because it was stuck to his wounds and was bright red with blood. His right shoulder looked as if it had been attached wrong; below it, the arm was obviously broken. Bruises were already showing color there, and the skin was scraped in a long red smudge. Dried and drying blood clung to his face despite attempts to wash it. A flap of skin had been ripped away above his right eye, all the way back into the hair, and it had been put down again and pulled into place by tying the hairs together.

"Is he dead?"

"Oh, no. Stunned, of course." The surgeon seemed unconcerned. He was one of Sigismund's physicians. *If he knows no more of war than his lord does, this may be his first wound.*

"You have seen a wound like this before, have you?"

The surgeon's face turned dark, "I see wounds like this at every tournament. Have you ever seen a man who's been hit with an ax?"

"And they live?"

"As often as not."

The tent flap was thrown back and the captain of the Thornforst mercenaries pushed in, clapped a powerful hand on Cosimo's shoulder, and told the surgeon that he was a quack. "I'll get my barber," he said. The surgeon protested; they wrangled, and the tent began to fill again. The captain kept his hold on Cosimo's shoulder, and, spitting in the direction of the surgeon, he said, "There's the horror of war, boy. Better a sword in your gut than a doctor at your side!"

In the midst of the hubbub, Johan's eyes fluttered open. Bright-red blood made little bubbles in the nostrils when he exhaled, and the sound of the air going in and out was like the sound of the bellows in the forge when it was heard from far away.

"Say something to him," the captain commanded.

"What should I say?"

"Anything! He wants to know if he's alive or dead, is all."

His tongue stuck in his mouth. What could you say to a man you had been taught to hate, and for whom you had come to feel a confused, torrential mix of emotions?

"You're going to be all right. This is Cosimo. You're in your tent. Can you hear me? Master Johan? I'm putting my hand on yours; if you can hear me, squeeze once for yes. Master Johan?" He looked helplessly at the mercenary. "He won't squeeze my hand."

"Never mind; look at his eyes." The soldier looked down at the stricken man. "Hey, Master Johan!" he bellowed. "We're all right here on earth; it isn't Hell yet!" He lowered his voice. "It's the first thing I'd want to know."

The ball had broken through a corner of the tower below

where Johan stood, and, in the collapse that followed, he had taken the weight of an eight-by-eight-inch beam on his head and right shoulder. He was a big man, but he was flesh; he had a broken skull, a dislocated shoulder and a broken arm, three broken ribs. The surgeons could not know it, but he had a little trickle of blood in his brain, too, and a weakening of the small vessels there that would never mend.

Sigismund's Procurer of Weapons sent down a litter to bear the gunmaker up to his majesty's own dressing tent, where the surgeons could be more available to give conflicting opinions on his wounds. Cosimo was ordered to move into Johan's tent and be prepared to take charge of all ordnance.

"But I can't!"

"Of course you can. It's the chance of a lifetime, boy." The Thornforst captain was very practical.

"But I don't know anything."

"I thought you knew everything."

"Don't make jokes at me, please." Cosimo looked miserable. "The men won't obey me. Hans Bighead will *never* obey me."

The captain rested one buttock on Johan's table, where, five hours before, the gunmaker had lain bleeding. "I'll tell you what. I'll send six men-at-arms to you. A bodyguard. Anybody won't do as you say, he answers to them."

"No, that's not it. It's respect."

"And while they're with you, you can teach them to shoot those little Roman candles. Yes, they intrigue me, cock. I've watched your men shoot. You teach my six to shoot, I'll back you against anybody who won't obey."

Cosimo seemed not to have been listening. "I always tell myself that if only I could do what I want, I could show Johan how to do things. Now I have to do what I want. And I'm frightened."

And, as if the wounding of Johan were a signal, the pace of the siege quickened. Summer was ending, and perhaps it was simply that nobody wanted to go on sitting through the rains of autumn. The gunmaker's injuries stabilized; the surgeons sniffed his urine and explored his injuries with their crusty instruments and said he was a very lucky man to have them there.

One of the physicians called on Cosimo in Johan's tent. He stood with monkish hands joined, disapproving of everything he saw.

"Master Johan will be returning to his tent tomorrow," he said with obvious disapproval.

The youth looked up, said nothing. His face was creased with a worried man's frown, and it was clear that the physician's visit was an interruption.

"We wanted to send Master Johan home. Master Johan will not go home. Therefore, we wash our hands of him and return him to you. We have told his majesty so."

Cosimo mumbled something and sent the man on his way. He had the presence of mind to set the servants to preparing for Johan's return, and then he sat again and put his head in his hands. That day, he had made a mistake—the kind of mistake that cannot be made anybody else's fault, the kind of mistake that is humiliating and that brings guilt. It made him sick when he thought of it.

He had tried to be everywhere, running everything. The mercenary captain had tried to tell him that he would get more done by delegating work; he had snapped back that he needed no advice, thank you; and when the man had called him "little cock" one more time, he had said, coldly and foolishly, "And I'll thank you not to call me by that vulgar name!"

Then he had gone to the earthworks to oversee the moving of two great guns. It was a task that Johan would have left to Josef or Hans Bighead, but he wanted it done correctly. He and Josef and Hans had all given orders at once, and the laborers, confused and angered, had lost control of a gun, and it had broken loose from its carriage and broken a man's leg and rolled down into a gully, where it would lie while they lost two days' firing. The men were made sullen by the injury to one of their fellows. Worse—far worse, for Cosimo—he was called to the Seneschal's tent and reprimanded in front of several lords, he who had been the darling of the siege for weeks.

He stumbled back down the hill, white with shame and rage at himself, and he called Josef and Hans Bighead to him under a scrubby little tree.

"I take responsibility for the gun and the peasant's leg. It was my fault." This was something he had to do, he knew; he had seen Johan do it. The master stands between the scolding lord and his underlings. Then he did something that he did not have to do; he said, "Tell me what I did wrong."

The two commoners looked at each other suspiciously. They were both angry, angry as mature men grow angry.

179

They would not be easily pacified; they would not change their minds as children might.

"You done everything wrong," Hans growled. Josef murmured something less harsh.

"What did you not do wrong?" Hans demanded. "So, since you ask me, I'll tell you. You're a vain little popinjay trying to do a man's job and doing it all wrong! You confused the men, running in and lording it over Josef and me with your crazy orders. All right, that's one thing. The other is, you make Josef and me look bad before the men."

Cosimo waited. "Go ahead."

"I'm done."

"No, you're not. You're still angry. Say it all!"

"All right then, I will! You're young, you don't know shit about men yet, and there's lots about guns you don't know of yet, for all you think you do! Master Johan, he'd have said, 'Hans, Josef, move them guns down to the pioneers and mind you don't muck it up, or I'll have both your asses for supper!' And then he'd have gone off somewhere more important and left it to us, instead of screaming orders at every man in the gang and mixing up a lot of common peasants that can't put their one foot in front of the other without stopping to think is it walkin' forward or back they meant to do!"

Cosimo swallowed, and his voice shook. "Do you want me to resign from my place?"

Josef spoke up. "Nah, Maister Cos, that's not the point. Hans is that mad, he's said things he shouldn't. Nah, don't resign; what good would it do? Just give us your orders and leave us to stand or fall."

It was a bitter moment for him. "Very well." He felt now that he almost had to ask their permission to do anything. "Can you start pulling that gun out tonight?" He did not add that he had been told by a furious Seneschal that if the gun was not in position by morning, he would be called before his majesty.

"We already started," Josef said. "It'll be out before sunup."

Cosimo nodded; his head moved jerkily. "You know where it goes, then. Prepare it for firing when it's in place."

He walked away from them. His knees were weak and his head ached. He had been in charge of things for six days, and he was drawn very tight.

Johan was brought back to the tent that evening. He slept, worn out by the trip by litter down the hill. Cosimo was glad

180

not to face him; he went out and found his old tentmate and spent two hours with him, drinking with three other squires. Cosimo had expected their mockery because of the gun, but they had not heard of it. The Seneschal had made it a quiet humiliation.

The others decided to go to the whores, and he left them, hearing their laughter. He went farther up the hill and joined several idle knights who hovered about the fringes of the court, and he got drunk and tried to be brilliant on the subject of tactics, and then he was back in Johan's tent, he was not sure how, and he stumbled into his bed and fell into a troubled, vinous sleep.

He woke thirsty and tormented. The watch passed fifty yards away, calling, "Two hours till morning. Praise God." Farther away, the cry was taken up by another watchman, and the dogs began to bark.

"You awake, boy?" Johan's voice was hoarse.

"Yes."

"Sit with me."

He went outside and urinated in the ditch and got himself water from the wood tun. Pale light spilled under the partition from Johan's lamp.

"Drink too much, boy?"

"Yes." Cosimo felt drained, like a moth sucked dry by a spider. "And I talked too much again."

"Aye, you're full of yourself, as they say."

"How do you feel?"

"I hurt, what else? Pain in my head like the Devil's own claw is hooked in there. But better than in the gut. You take a sword or a knife in the gut, the pain can drive you mad, they say. Sit down by me, boy."

He moved to the pile of feather mattresses and slowly let himself down beside them.

"I got something to say to you, Cosimo."

"Yes?" He feared that he was about to be scolded for the day's mistake.

"I love you, boy." One of the big hands felt over the bed-clothes like a crab. "Cosimo, I'm your father."

The hand touched him, and he drew away. "Like a father to me, yes."

"No, boy—I'm your father."

"My father is in Italy! My father is a—." Telling that old story again seemed pointless.

Johan seemed not to care what he had said. He went on

181

talking. "I've worked it all out. I mean to adopt you. Then you'll be my son in the eyes of God and the law."

Cosimo started to get up but found that he was dizzy, and he rolled into a half-prone position, his weight on his right forearm. "I mean to have a lord's name. You know all of it; I've told you before."

Johan grunted. "Then I'll buy us a title. I worked that out, too. Sigismund will sell me one after this siege. Or Wenceslas will—didn't he sell his own title of Duke of Milan to the Visconti?"

"You don't *buy* blood titles!"

"Of course you do. How do you think folk get such things?" Johan sounded old and querulous. He seemed almost simpleminded to Cosimo.

"Blood right is given by God," he said. He sat up, his dizziness forgotten. "Men are a great chain, suspended from the mind of God—king, lord, knight, freeman, serf. From the beginning of time until Doomsday."

"And the Visconti? Did God make the Visconti Duke of Milan, or did he buy the title from Wenceslas?"

"Wenceslas broke God's law by selling his title."

"And the Graf of Grozforst—*his* father owned half the houses in Bremen and lent the money for Wladislaw the Seventh to march on Poland, for which Wladislaw made him graf. Was that God's law?"

"We live in dreadful times!" Cosimo said bitterly. "These are signs of the decay of things!"

Johan made a little gurgling sound. He was chuckling. "I see. Real nobility trace their blood right back to Adam and Eve; Cain was the first Duke of Milan, eh? Or was it Abel? Well, these are bad times, I agree. Bad, bad. The worst of times, they say. Heaven will crack and God's trumpet will be heard, yes, I believe that. Maybe I will live to hear it; if not, I will leap from my grave when it blows. But I can make you a lord's son before it happens, boy. I can buy you any title you fancy." His business sense made him add, "Within good sense."

He wanted to tell Cosimo who his mother was, but the youth escaped him and ran out of the tent and slept under one of the wagons, where he groaned and dreamed of monsters. Awake, he stumbled about the camp and guzzled water and made himself presentable in time for a meeting at the Procurer of Armaments' tent, where he sat straight and unsmiling and silent while the others decided to assault the Karlsbirk gates. It was time to end things.

He called Josef to him. "Have you built a war wagon, Josef?"

"Twice, Master Cos. Once at—"

"I don't care where. We'll require two. Two crows in one. The other for support—one crow loaded with chain and room for footmen. They'll be from the Thornforst Company, so discuss it with their captain."

"Yes, Master Cos."

"Send Hans up to me. We're going to move the mortars."

"Yes, Master Cos."

He stayed away from the tent. It was reported to him that Johan slept most of the time and was very quiet.

The war wagons were ready three days later. Constructed of layers of green oak, they were ponderous movable houses that were to be pushed from within by their occupants. Gun ports in the front would allow them to fire in a very limited field. One was intended to be pushed right to the gates, where it would fire point-blank, hoping to knock the gate down. The other would be used to defend the first.

The war wagons were pulled into position during the night. When the sun was well up, the men went into them— Hans Bighead and two gun crews in one, Josef and one crew in the other. Men from the Thornforst foot sheltered in the rear part of each wagon and behind them, safe from arrows or crossbow bolts. Horsemen waited out of range, with archers and three more companies of foot in reserve.

Cosimo stood with the handgunners of St. Barbara between the war wagons and the horsemen. In a half circle around the entire attacking group, bombards and mortars stood in new positions, with ribaldekins every twenty yards to defend them.

For two hours, as the wagons creaked painfully forward, the mortars fired stones toward the gate and the open square that was supposed to lie behind it, trying to frustrate a counterattack. Bombards kept up a heavy fire on the walls. Three of the big wall guns replied; after an hour, one fell silent.

"Got her," a handgunner exulted.

Not likely, Cosimo thought. He sent word to the observation tower that the walls should be watched where the gun had stopped firing. Forty minutes later, word came back that it looked as if the gun was being moved. He sent another messenger to the Seneschal to warn him that a great gun might be moved into position behind the gate.

The mercenaries strained at the rear of the wagons. The wheels seemed to catch at every rock and hummock as if they had hooks. As they had drawn closer to the walls, crossbow quarrels had fallen on them; now the clumsy structures had bolts sticking from them like porcupine quills.

"Just like two square cockleburrs," an officer of horse said to him. There was nothing to do but watch the clumsy machines inch forward; while they watched, officers moved from place to place, gossiping idly, nervously. The wait was like the siege itself in little.

The mortars pounded. The wagons drew nearer to the gate, near enough for a man to have tossed a rock from the walls and hit them. Then the one with two guns moved in closer, seeming to shudder, to stop and sniff the air. The other held off to the side. Fire arrows came down from the walls, but the green wood refused to catch.

"Move up!" Cosimo led the handgunners forward at a trot until they were just out of crossbow range, a point easily found by the first quarrels sticking out of the parched grass.

There was danger now that one of his own mortars would fire short and hit one of the wagons; it would be a freak shot, but such things could happen. There had already been many hits outside the walls, and the ground there was pocked and heaved with little craters.

"Move the ribaldekins to flank now."

The little many-tubed carriages were run toward the sides of the attacking force to bear on the gate.

There was activity around the wagons, then unexplained waiting. Silence. Then a wriggling forward as the wagon reached the road that led from the gate and, on that smoother surface, lurched ahead another ten yards. Then silence again, and a stillness like death. A summer sky like glass, and under it men like toys. Two mercenaries carried off another who had been hit by an arrow. Even the defenders on the walls seemed to be waiting.

Smoke belched from the war wagon. The sound reached them as a double drumbeat, with the sound of a scream rising over it. *What happened?* Cosimo chewed the inside of his lower lip, reviewing what could have caused that scream. *Gun broke loose, most likely. Could kill ten men in there.*

Were the gates still standing?

Cosimo checked the buckle of his sallet for the tenth time.

The chain mail pulled like an insistent hand. Where it touched bare skin, it was hot.

What is happening in that wagon?

There was an explosion from his left, and he turned to see a puff of dark smoke wisping away from the observation tower. It was a signal shot. A flagman was waving a red cloth as big as a bedsheet. *Assault coming.*

The Karlsbirkers were trying to catch the two wagons in a pincer, one toe of the claw coming from the assaulted gate, one coming around the wall from the east. Horsemen were already pounding into view from the east; around him, Cosimo heard the clatter and jingle of soldiers readying themselves, like the sound of a forest waking.

"Handgunners forward!"

At a good run now, he led them within the range of the crossbows. A bolt seemed to grow magically out of the ground in front of him; behind him, somebody cried out, but he kept on running. Cosimo knew where he was taking them—a slight mound just to the left of the war wagons' heavy tracks. He could feel the slope under his legs now—twenty more yards—ten—

"Poise your handguns!"

The ensign bearer of St. Barbara's Brotherhood was beside him on top of the knoll. Downslope, the enemy horse were moving right under the city wall toward the wagons. To the right, the gates were opening and footmen were tumbling out. The pincers were closing.

"Plant and aim!"

He had the hand-cannon that had been modified for him. The touchhole on top of the barrel had been welded closed and a small pan had been welded on the left side, where a new hole was drilled. A fence of sheet brass rose behind the pan to protect his eyes and face, so that he could put his eye low and sight along the barrel without risk of injury. He held the short staff under his arm as he had in the try-field back in Mouers.

"Fire!"

The massed hand-cannons sent a volley into the horsemen, too late to catch the leaders, but in time to strike the middle and rear.

"Reload!"

Second gunners were running up with new charges of Black Cob's corned powder; carried in small sacks tied with

185

drawstrings, they could be quickly dumped down the barrels.
A ball from the second gunner's shoulder bag followed.

"Fires forward!"

Charcoal fires were brought up in iron pans, wires already
heated among the coals. Used wires were thrust in and new
ones taken out in gloved hands.

"Poise your handguns!"

He could hear the rapid-fire popping of the ribaldekins,
and the low thud of one of the crows. There was a melee
around the war wagons now, and the horsemen were coming
up from behind him to join in, while pikemen trotted across
to take a position between the fighting and the artillery. To
Cosimo's right, two companies of foot were moving up at a
run; another cannon sounded, and then, in almost as good
order as they had ridden in, the enemy horse were crossing
back from his right to his left, leaving the fight.

"Aim!"

The lead horseman turned and began a sweep toward the
knoll. He passed within thirty yards of the oncoming horse
of Sigismund's army, but they were bent on joining the melee
by the gate, even of forcing their way in if they could.

On the backslope of the knoll, a dozen more hand-cannons
waited. They were loaded with scrap metal and small stones,
double-charged; they could do nothing at a distance, but
swept a wide arc close in.

"Bring up those defense guns!" he was screaming. "Get
them into position, in God's name—fire, you oafs—fire!"

He saw horses and men go down, and then more were
coming on through the black smoke.

"Reload! Reload!"

His line broke. Horsemen were riding through the gaps;
the St. Barbara's banner was down and trampled. Something
struck his sallet and he spun around and almost fell; when
he straightened, the line of handgunners was gone and he
was standing on top of the knoll with half a dozen others.
One of the defense guns was next to him, held by a middle-
aged man who was staring with scared eyes at a boy who had
lost an arm.

"Fire! Fire, you sod!"

The man was shaking. He still held the hot wire in his
left hand; in the right, the gun, unfired, hung at his side from
an arm gone numb. Cosimo saw a horseman swing back toward the knoll and head up toward them, swinging a mace
above his head. He pushed the shocked gunner aside so
186

roughly that the man fell; taking his weapon, he planted the trail and leaned back against it as if it were a pike. He meant that if the horseman rode him down, he would have to take his mount over that obstacle.

The horse was laboring a little; it had been ridden hard. Sweat ran down its shining coat. The rider leaned a little out of the saddle, standing in his stirrups to help his swing. The powder had fallen out of the hand-cannon's touchhole, and Cosimo pushed the wire into the hole as if he were stabbing it; deep in the charge, the gunpowder took fire and the tube spewed fire and smoke and scrap iron at the rider and his horse.

The animal was more frightened than hurt. It reared away from the hideous noise and the stab of flame, and the rider kept his seat with difficulty, his mace swinging useless as he tried to stay in the saddle. Plunging, bucking now against the pain of its wounds, the animal turned aside, and Cosimo ran in and swung the brass gun by its wooden stock and caught the beast's left rear leg just at the knee. The horse screamed and its leg buckled and it came down almost on its back, the rider spilling on the ground like laundry.

Cosimo's arms quivered from the blow. He smelled sulphur and sweat and the rank odor of the horse. The rider was trying to stand, trying to extricate one foot from a stirrup, impeded by the thrashing animal's frenzy, and Cosimo took the hand-cannon by the stock again and struck the rider across his visored face, and he went down and lay there. The horse was still trying to rise, dragging itself forward with three legs, and the rider's foot came free of the stirrup and the animal crawled on its belly until somebody slashed its throat.

"St. Barbara! St. Barbara!"

"Form up—form up—"

Cosimo wiped blood from his face. "That ritter on the ground is mine!"

"Form up!"

Thirty-seven of his handgunners could stand. Many of the second gunners had run away and had been caught by the horsemen.

"Count off! Loaded or empty?"

"Kirkhoff—powder, no ball."

"Tek of St. Marc's, empty, sir!"

The second gunners began to dribble in. He tongue-lashed them, distributed their powder charges and made them stand

187

apart from the ones who had held. He sent four men back to the earthworks with the man he had killed and his harness.

He marched the living back to their old position, guns loaded, wounds bandaged, banner flying. Sigismund's cavalry were already back and cooling their horses; footmen were running in under a desultory rain of arrows. As he neared the earthworks, he heard one of the big guns, and then another. The war wagons were pounding the gate again.

"All secure down there." It was the Thornforst captain. "They took a blooding and went home."

"The wagons?"

"They can fire. The big man's dead. Near took his head off with an ax, one of the horsemen."

"Hans Bighead?"

"Big fellow. They're bringing the bodies in." The captain looked very fierce and unsmiling. "You did well out there."

"Some of my people ran."

"Some people always run. That's war out there, boy."

He sent a messenger to the wagons, wondering if he should go himself, then deciding that it would be exactly the wrong thing to do. Word came back that they needed a gunner, and he sent one from the bombards. Two hours later, they breached the gate and the wagons could withdraw.

The nobleman who commanded the assault sent his peasants through first, remembering the message about the gun that had been moved from the walls. It got off one shot of chain and rocks and cleared a path that closed up with screaming, pushing men who were driven on by those behind. The mercenaries drove them on, then cut through them to reach the mercenaries of the other side; they cleaned out the square behind the gate, and the taking of Karlsbirk had begun.

It took three days of fighting through the streets to end it. Then the Mayor and the aldermen came out the west gate under a flag of truce, free men who had governed a free city, giving up at last to the power of monarchy.

"I do not honor the flags of rebels," Sigismund said. The Mayor and the aldermen were hanged and their heads were put up over the gates. Then the army went in and looted the city. Sigismund's "Christian victory" was limited to the protection of churches and monastic houses.

Even before the city fell, Cosimo was inside the walls claiming the prizes that were the gunners' by right of their contract. "Guns and bells are ours," he told Josef. "You know what to do. Most of their ordnance is junk, but we can melt it down for the metal. You might look it over and see if it's worthwhile to build a foundry here to melt it down—or find one in the city." He looked over a wall opposite that had crumbled under the mortar fire. "We did well, didn't we?"

To his disappointment, the lead from the roofs belonged to the Bishop of Muhldorf and Mouers, although he had never come near the siege. It seemed that he had blessed Sigismund's prospects. Lead was a valuable commodity.

The victors rioted through the city. They took everything, and then abandoned half of what they had taken. It became necessary to have protection against his own allies, and he hired the Thornforsters to protect his people as they worked. A second wave of looters went through, and a third—cooks and servants and peasants, then serfs and hangers-on and women. Men staggered away from Karlsbirk laden down with plates and pots and women's dresses; some dressed in fantastic motley of the clothes they had stolen, androgynous, multicolored, otherworldly.

"Is Hell like this, do you suppose?" he said to Josef. It was sundown. Fires were burning in one part of the city. Looters were fighting in the tiny square below them. A woman's naked body spilled from a doorway, dead and bloating.

"Hell is always worse, my pastor says. Worse than anything you could think of."

"I could never have thought of this. Not if I hadn't been here." He looked down into the square with disgust. "Dear God, what a sorry creature man is!"

The smoke of the burning city had a sour smell, like old leaves and musty cellars.

"King means to let her burn," Josef said.

"Yes, all but the churches. I suppose he thinks that God can be bribed that way." The Karlsbirkers had been allowed to take refuge in their churches, and now they were encouraged to protect them against the fire. That way, if a church burned, it was their fault and not Sigismund's.

"It was a nice little city, looks like," Josef said. "Won't be, day after tomorrow."

"Making an example of it. He should have asked us, if he'd really meant to level it. They'll rebuild it and here it will be until Doomsday, despite his fires and his rapes and his looters. If he'd asked us to use gunpowder, we could have made another Carthage of the place!"

CHAPTER SEVENTEEN

THE FOX WAS PREGNANT AGAIN. She was already uncomfortable with it. She shifted her weight from haunch to haunch. The swelling that would be her fourth child rode like a ball on her lap.

"Hot," she said. She shifted her weight again. She felt cranky because one of her teeth ached. Pregnancy was making her lose her teeth before she was twenty, and she had been proud of her small, white teeth.

"Hot as Hell will be," Rolf said. He was swollen, and his face looked like a pudding. He had been drinking all night.

"You're in fine shape," she said.

"Hot as Hell itself will be."

"Oh, you and your Hell." She sucked on the tooth, and pain shot up through her cheek and seemed to touch the floor of her brain. "Maybe in Hell, it will be men who are pregnant." She put a finger into her mouth to press on the tooth, and the pain was remarkable, a sensation as rare as orgasm.

Rolf had a new awareness of Hell. Mouers had been overrun by friars that summer. They preached a strange medley of forgiveness and hellfire, and it was impossible to walk through the city without hearing one of them rant. He hated them and their Hell.

"I feel as if I'm dying," he said.

"You're still drunk."

He had gone to Köln to escape the friars and had found more of them there. The terror with which they filled him had the curious effect of making him more corrupt, rather than less; he had never been drunk so often, nor had he spent so many nights—and days now—visiting places where they promised new variations on the old sins he loved.

"I should confess," he said.

"You confessed at Corpus Christi."

"Well, I've sinned since Corpus Christi!"

"My father said a man should confess once a year. To do

190

it oftener than that was showy." Her father was sick in Mons and was probably dying, if she could read the correct meaning into her brothers' letters. She wanted to ask to visit him before he died, but now she was pregnant, and how could she take that journey and endanger another son? Above everything, she was loyal to her father's idea of the perfect wife. She looked at Rolf's pouched face without any sense of irony or any sense of disappointment.

She shared Rolf's concerns, as a perfect wife should. "The Italian will come back a hero. You've heard?"

"Yes—yes!" He buried his face in his hands.

This was a new Rolf for her. She was still too young to understand that he would go through many stages, as she would, too; she would have several husbands, all of them named Rolf, all of them inhabiting that same body. She did not much care to deal with the one who was sitting with her today, because it was so hard to get his attention.

"The Italian was a hero at the siege. Rolf, listen to me. I hear he was favored by King Sigismund himself—given gifts. He ran the guns when your father was hurt. Now I have a message from your father's clerk that he is writing to Cosimo's sponsor, the woman in Italy, to say he is adopting Cosimo."

"What?"

She sucked on her bad tooth. She looked like a wise and cynical child, for all her pregnant belly. She nodded. "Adopting him. Making him his son."

"Well, what of it? I'd still be the oldest."

"I think you know better than that."

"I don't know—I don't know...."

"We talked of it before. Buy him off or get rid of him."

"I don't know. I can't think, these damned friars have me so mixed up with their Hell."

"Hell is going to have us all, Rolf. Cosimo is in the here and now."

"Maybe I could confess to the Bishop. What do you think? He's a sensible man."

"Husband, in the name of your sainted mother, listen! Confess to anybody you like. We must do something about Cosimo!"

After some seconds of staring dumbly at her, he wriggled himself erect in his chair and shook himself like a dog that has just come out of water. His puffy face was dreadful in its

191

despair, but he was thinking again and he was thinking of what she had said. "We could lose a lot," he said.

"We could lose everything. What happens to your plans for the children if Cosimo is adopted, eh? Who will want to marry your sons if half the house is Cosimo's?"

Rolf puffed out his sweaty cheeks. "I'll buy him off. Just in case, get in touch with your brother about—you know, the other solution. You understand."

"When?"

"At once."

They said nothing more, and, after three minutes, he got up and dragged himself to the door. "I'm going to write to the Bishop," he said. "I can't stand all this Hell business."

He left her sucking on her tooth.

The breeze swept in from the Adriatic over hot fields already harvested. The air smelled dry and dusty and had an unnamable tinge of the sea. The Mother Superior stood by her window with the boy's letter hanging so loosely in her hand that it moved in the breeze. She stood that way for a long time. If she saw the comings and goings on the road below her, the activity in the fields where peasants raked up the wheat straw and bundled it, she gave no sign. She sighed heavily three times.

She looked down at the letter again. "He has told me he is my father, either a monstrous lie or a truth so bitter I cannot put it into my mind. Yet I have had intimations of it before, and of course I know the gossip among the clods, that I am his son, but this is the natural conclusion of simple minds, because he favors me. Now tell me, I beg you, lady, what is the truth of this matter, that I may know what to do; for I know not what feeling I have for him any longer, so much time have I spent with him.

"Seeing him bleeding in the tent, I prayed that he would die. Not for any bad reason, but because he suffered and I suffered, too. I would be rid of this confusion, and it seemed it would be a blessing if God took him and relieved me of this burden. Yet he lives, and improves daily, and I know I must confront this matter again with him. Therefore, I pray you again, tell me the truth...."

She sighed again. After more minutes of looking at that landscape, she turned to her tall writing desk and took up her pen to write. For one instant, tears glistened in her eyes, and then were gone.

* * *

Matilda could not have done a more thorough housecleaning if she had been able to lift the house by its roof and shake it. Windows were thrown open, floors scrubbed, bedding washed and hung out and beaten. Not since its building had the house seen such activity or been so clean.

Cosimo rode in on the horse that King Sigismund had given him and greeted her in the courtyard with a new formality. Matilda knew the forms and ceremonies better than he, and when they were done, she hugged him and dragged him away to her rooms to talk about Johan and about his triumphs. She thought he had grown; she thought he had turned grave. She thought he was very grown-up.

"And how is my husband?"

"Well—and not so well. He finds walking very tiring. You must not be surprised that he looks a little different."

"Different how?"

"Why, he looks like a sick man. And—there is some trouble with his left side—the left side of his face. It is—stiff, maybe from the wound."

Her joy at seeing Cosimo was sobered. "Is that why you came on ahead? To warn me?"

"No, no, no, not to warn you."

"Did he ask you to?"

"No, no. I came on ahead with the servants." He did not say how happy he had been to come ahead, to get away from Johan.

"Well, tell me the truth. Is he dying?"

"No, no, lady! But he is not well yet. And you will find he looks different."

Indeed, the left side of Johan's face had an unwonted blankness to it. His smile hardly touched the left side of his mouth; when he talked, the words did not form well on that side.

"Well," she said firmly, "I will thank God for his life and pray he get better. Come to chapel with me."

Cosimo wandered through the familiar house like a stranger. The summer had separated him from it; even Elsbet seemed strange to him. Friede, Johan's deaf child, was the only one who seemed the same, and he found that he could still spend hours playing silent games with her. *I am somebody different from the one who left here,* he thought. He found that he was waiting, but he did not know what he was waiting for. Johan came home and was carried to his room;

looking gaunt and worn, he appeared on his wife's arm for an hour or two each day. The left side of his face seemed a little better, but he was very subdued. Cosimo avoided him.

Then, two things happened to him on the same day, and the waiting was over.

A letter came from Ravenna. It was short, harsh. "To believe the bellfounder is to tell me I have lied. Have I lied? Can you think in your heart that I have lied? Can you think in your heart that you are the son of a common artisan? I will not bend to try to persuade you. A noble mind is required by noble birth: decide for yourself what you are."

And a servant came to his door.

"Fellow?"

"Maister Rolf be coomin' to talk to you, I was to tell you."

"What, here?"

"Aye, he be coomin' now."

Cosimo hid the letter.

"Let him come in." He had missed the excitement of the camp; some of that pleasant tension came back to him now as he faced a man he disliked. He had noticed Rolf when he had first ridden home—the very picture of a glutted burgher, he had thought, red-faced and thick-necked. He would be fat in ten years. *Overfed stay-at-home,* he had thought.

Rolf looked now as if he had been weeping. Something had made his eyes red, at any rate. "So!" Rolf said with what was meant to sound like heartiness. He wanted a note that would suggest authority and possession of place. "Back from your first skirmish, eh?"

"As you see."

"I hear you did very well for the house. I'm grateful."

"Thank you."

Cosimo did not look like a boy any longer. And he was dressed like a noble. It was one thing for Rolf to flaunt the sumptuary laws and wear furs and velvets and own eight changes of clothes in defiance of the code, but it was quite another for this youth to wear the gifts of a king.

"I am personally grateful, I mean. My father can be difficult, I know. I remember when I was a boy, what it was like. So I am grateful." He cleared his throat. "Quite grateful. I will have a purse of money sent to you, to show that I am grateful."

"Please send it to Hans Bighead's widow."

He was studying Rolf and thinking, *This is what a son of Johan looks like. Vulgar, thick, overdressed.*

194

"You're very easy with money, I must say," Rolf said.

"I've had more than enough gifts—from King Sigismund and others. But I thank you for the gesture. Now, as I haven't been home long, I have letters—"

"I am not done!" Rolf sounded belligerent.

"Ah, yes?"

"I have business with you. Other business. Important business."

Some reply seemed to be called for. "Well?"

"Oh, 'Well'—is that what we say? 'Well.' I don't like to say this, but your tone is very arrogant. I don't like to spoil your hero's return, but I have to say that."

"You spoil nothing."

"In fact, you talk like a snotty brat."

"Yes, that would be your opinion."

"That is the truth! You ought to learn better. People get the wrong idea, if you talk to them like that. As an older man, I can say that to you."

"Was that the business you had with me?"

Rolf squinted at him. Cosimo stared back, unable to hide the sneer that showed his contempt for Johan's son.

"I'd like to make it my business to teach you some manners!"

"One cannot teach what one does not understand. What is your business, Rolf?"

"It's a waste of breath trying to be pleasant to you! You're nothing but a foundling, you came begging around here, took my father in. Well, you don't take me in! I know what you are, boy. You got to my father with your wheedling, but you don't get to me. I'm not fooled!"

"Was *that* your business?"

"Yes, my business is this business of you and my father!" Rolf sounded almost hysterical. Cosimo studied him coolly, as if he were an object on display at a market. "You and my father!" Rolf cried, enraged by the boy's calm.

"Yes?"

"He's not going to make you his son, you understand me? Never!"

Cosimo realized that he had come to exactly the same conclusion, but he did not tell Rolf that. On the contrary, he seemed to resist the idea. There was still some of the old Cosimo in him—a mocking child who sat in a corner of his consciousness, kicking his heels and playing jokes.

195

"Now, I suppose this crazy plan of his to adopt you started with you, but it's not going to happen."

"Ah?"

"No." Rolf hitched up his hose. "I know your kind and I know what your kind want, so let's cut through the shit you've got ready and let's get right down to business here. I'll give you a choice, Cosimo: get out of Mouers and stay out, or I'll have you put out. Is that clear enough?"

"You mean, you don't want your father to declare me his son, and so you're threatening me."

Rolf thrust his jaw forward. "That's right."

"But that's not intelligent of you, Rolf. I could tell him, and he would dislike you more than he already does—for he does dislike you."

Rolf's laugh was a bark. "Do it! You wouldn't last the night."

"But then he'd know. Would *you* last the night?"

"I'll risk it!"

"Then let's send for him." Cosimo made a move as if to call for a servant.

Rolf heaved himself toward the slender figure and blocked his way to the door. "I'm telling you I can have you killed!"

There was a sound like a whisper, a sound like a rat in a corner, a sound like a woman's dress moved quickly by a hand, and the blade of the dagger that King Sigismund had given him was pressed into the thickening flesh of Rolf's throat. "Don't ever touch me again."

Rolf's eyes looked to the side and down. He stepped back. "Italian bastard."

"I could have a guard from St. Barbara's Brotherhood to go with me everywhere, you fool. They'd do it for me now, don't you understand that? You know what they call you? 'Rolf the Carp.' Like the fish, Rolf. Carp get big and fat and are good for nothing, except to eat sometimes. Which of us do you think they would protect, the one who stood with them at Karlsbirk, or the one who stayed at home getting fat? You disgust me. You do. You're contemptible. And you could no more have me killed than you could kill his holiness at Rome." The words had come out in a sudden, hot rush. Cosimo's shoulders were shivering. He sat down again and pushed his back against the chair to disguise his tension. "Mother of God, how I despise you! Pah! I hate being in the same room with you. But no matter. Let us be practical and come to terms. What is it worth to you?"

"What? What, for you to go away?"

"Just so."

"Me, pay for such a thing?"

"Oh, come, Rolf—Jacob gave Esau a mess of pottage for his birthright; surely I would have something coming. What would my mess of pottage be? A round figure—come."

"You little snake, I'll see you dead before I'll pay you."

"I wonder how you ever get business done, Rolf. You bore us all with your endless stories of how wonderful you are, but I find you stupid beyond all belief. Now, the time to bargain has arrived—hasn't it? You've threatened; I've threatened. We've made it clear how much we hate each other. We've laid out the facts: your father dislikes you; he loves me. Rolf, your whole *life* is threatened! In such a perilous situation, Rolf, the angels themselves would make an offer!"

A crafty look came into Rolf's face. "How much?"

Cosimo was playing a role. If he despised Rolf at that moment, he despised himself, as well. Still, he made his voice taunting and light. "Fifty thousand nobiles Florentine."

"I haven't got that kind of money!"

"We brought back twice that much from Karlsbirk!"

"Well, I don't have it!"

"I'm sure you know how to steal it. I don't understand these burgherish things, accounting and all that stupidity, but I know that you do. Or you can cheat your clients out of it, or whip it out of your peasants. You moneymen know all about those things."

"I might be able to raise twenty thousand."

"Fifty thousand. Bargaining is vulgar."

"Don't keep saying that word to me! I could buy and sell you a hundred times; you've nothing but what my father gives you!" Rolf looked as if he might throw the idea of bargaining away and rush at Cosimo. Breathing heavily, he circled the chair for several feet, his eyes on Cosimo. The crafty look returned. "Maybe I could take a note on a house in Bergen."

"Payable in Venice. Find the wretched money where you can, burgher, but pay it in Venice—in Florentine gold." Cosimo's smile was evil, old, hateful. "Then sink back into the softness of your life, Rolf—your women, your gluttony, your business! And forget me."

"I won't forget you, bastard."

"Well, I will forget you. Unless you try to trick me, and

then be very careful! Well, do we have a bargain, we two vulgar businessmen? Have we bought and sold the old man's dreams? Wonderful! What a priceless pair we are, you and I. Well, you may go—go! And tell the servant I want privacy; I have letters to write. And Rolf—understand that if it were anybody else, I would want much, much more money, but because it's you, I've sold myself cheap. You see, I could bear to be Johan's son—but your brother, never!"

Rolf chewed on his beard and contained his hatred and went away, and from then on, Cosimo was seen to go armed and always in the company of two or three of the St. Barbarans, but this was put down to his wanting to flaunt a little his reputation from the siege. When he and Rolf met, as when the family ate together, nothing was said between them.

Johan seemed stronger, but he was quiet. He seemed to have set his heart on a celebration to mark the victory at Karlsbirk, which was a triumph for the house both in reputation and in wealth, and he set a day for the gunworks to be opened to the town. St. Eloi's and St. Barbara's guilds were to come in procession. The aldermen would make speeches; the guns captured at Karlsbirk would be on display before they were melted down. The great bell of Mouers would ring.

He announced to Matilda that he would make Cosimo's adoption public at the celebration.

"What does Cosimo say?" she asked.

"Cosimo will do as I tell him."

"But what does he say?"

"He says nothing; he is very quiet since the battle. Your first battle is a very deep experience."

The night before the feast, Rolf came to Cosimo's rooms. He gave him a paper and waited while the youth read it.

"Acceptable?"

"Exactly what I got down in the wallow to bargain for."

"Then I want you gone before the feast."

"Well—but I will see Johan first."

"No! Write him a letter. I will give it to him myself."

"I ought to face him," Cosimo said, but he said it timidly. He had been trying to think how he would do it.

"Write him a letter. Make it easier for both of you."

"Well—come back in an hour."

"And you'll leave before the feast!"

"At first light. Or in the dark—it's best to do slimy things in the dark, eh, Rolf?"

The letter that he wrote was almost good enough to keep a heart from breaking, for it was graceful and young and almost honest. It had no malice, no hatred. It expressed sorrow. It asked to be forgiven. It did not mention Rolf or the money.

Rolf came back, and the two looked at each other with detestation, and Cosimo handed over the letter and closed his door, and Rolf went away to his mistress's house, where he broke the seal and read the letter and then burned it. His was the smile of the man who has had the last word, after all.

Next day, Johan walked through the upper floors of his almost deserted house. Even the servants were outdoors for the feast. Johan was smiling, the smile a little crooked because of the slight paralysis that still remained. The sound of the great bell of Mouers made him smile; the memory of the Karlsbirk triumph made him smile; his recovery made him smile. Most of all, he smiled because he was going to find Cosimo, who was to be his son. He would take Cosimo down to the yards and show him off to everybody, and when the right moment came, he would tell them that this was not only a feast of victory but also one of new fatherhood. Like Abraham when God accepted the sacrifice of the lamb and his son was given back to him, he was happy.

He had an almost imperceptible limp now. His left foot dragged slightly, and the sound of his footsteps contained the slight hesitation of that limp. A slight tingling numbness persisted in his left arm, as well. He would always have the scar that ran from his right eyebrow back through his gray hair, but most men had scars. It would fade. The scar was a badge of victory.

"Cosimo!"

His voice echoed down the corridor.

"Cosimo!"

The door was closed. Johan pushed it open without knocking; was it not his house?

A chair, a bed, a long chest.

"Boy, where are you?"

The long chest was empty except for lint and specks of black dirt. Under the bed, where his saddlebags and his gifts from Karlsbirk should have been, there was only slightly dusty space.

"Cosimo!"

"He's gone, Father."

Rolf looked haggard and worn and nervous. He had not slept all night. He was dressed richly for the feast, but he looked like a sick man.

"Where is my son?"

"He is gone. One of the servants saw him ride out the East Gate this morning. He thought nothing of it, he said; the boy was dressed rough, he said, so he thought he was going to hunt. But he had a pack mule, he said, and that was strange. The man said—"

"Why didn't you tell me?" Johan's voice was terrible.

Rolf stepped back from the contorted, purple face.

"Father, you look—"

"Why didn't somebody tell me?"

"I just heard it myself. Nobody thought anything about it. They thought he was going—"

Johan pushed his son out of the doorway with a blow that made the timbers of the house groan. Almost at a run, he swept down the corridor. His left shoulder struck a beam and he recoiled from it and rushed on like a pain-maddened animal that has been hit by the hunter. He called the boy's name as he ran, called it twice before he turned the corner and passed from Rolf's sight. He would be just at the top of the steep stairs that wound down through the rear of the house.

Rolf heard the first thud as Johan leaped for the landing, spurning the steps between—and then the old man cried out, and there was a crack and clatter of breaking glass, a scream from outside and then, after a deadly silence, the sound of his body hitting the unyielding stone of the courtyard. Rolf ran to the corner, to the top of the stair, where he could look down and see where his father had plunged through, to fall to the stones among the feasting crowd.

The Fox tended him as she would have tended her own father. His helplessness was their bond. She could understand the sounds that came from the half-paralyzed tongue better than Matilda could. She was not frightened of the face that was half alive and half dead, nor was she offended by the drool that slithered from the dead corner of the mouth. If it had been her own father, she would have tended him so.

Rolf lurked in the doorway for a few seconds each day and then went away. He had much to torment himself with now, and the pleasures of Mouers could not distract him; he needed a carnival of excess. After some weeks, he went away to the

Baltic and hunted for his pleasures there, doing business when he had the time.

Cosimo Tedesco arrived in Venice three weeks after he had left Mouers. A lay brother of the Premonstratensians accompanied him, sent to the borders of Germany to meet him by Alys, Mother Superior of the convent at Vis'Adriatico. The lay brother was supposed to take him straight to Ravenna, but Cosimo insisted upon the Venetian side trip. He was very stubborn, and nothing the brother could do would stop him.

To go from Mouers to Venice was to go from the world of the cold Northern merchants to the warm world of the golden traders, to travel from industry to magic. Venice sent her ships across the Mediterranean, and eastward her traders went to Aleppo and Alexandria, and west and north to Brugge and Flanders. Venice wed the seas and raped what was left of the old empire of Byzantium. Venice was the West's idea of worldly riches, next to which the chilly cities of Germany and the Hanseatic League looked plain and naive.

The Arieto Bank had built a new palace twenty strides from the quais, as if to symbolize the marriage of Venetian money and Venetian ships. Cosimo followed the directions of a passerby to the elaborate front door, and then he let himself be led up an airy staircase to a chamber where one of the four brothers held his court. Slim, handsome now, beautifully dressed, Cosimo belonged in such a setting, and the second-oldest of the Arieti smiled at him.

It was the greater cause for sadness to both of them, therefore, that the Banco Fratelli Arieto could not answer the call for funds that was given in the young man's letter of credit.

"I am desolated, *cavaliere*." The banker spread his long hands; his luxurious lips pouted. "But the cancellation came on ahead of you by post rider."

"The House of Johan de Mouers canceled a letter of credit?"

The banker shrugged. The movement made his golden surcoat creep over his shoulders subtly, as if it were a skin he was shedding to appear in one still more brilliant. "It is most unusual. Naturally, you will want to report this to their bank in Bergen—"

"No. No, I will not do it that way."

"It is most unusual."

"In fact, I was not surprised." He took back the letter and

folded it carefully and put it into a slim pouch. "I will be grateful if it can be kept quiet."

"Very generous of you, *cavaliere*." Arieto cast a jaded eye at his tiled ceiling and sighed. "So many men would seek revenge."

"And so will I, signore. But at another time."

Arieto watched him descend the staircase and leave the house, and then, from a balcony, he watched him join the lay brother and move out of sight. He initiated discreet inquiries and found enough to interest him. The young man's patroness intended him for the University of Padua and the Church. Good enough—quite good enough. Decisive young men of charm and good looks were always worth watching, and when they had letters of credit for fifty thousand nobiles—even letters of credit canceled by an unethical merchant—well, churchmen of that sort were always good investments.

CHAPTER EIGHTEEN

MORS:

> Death am I, and with my hook
> Mankind I take, and kill him utterly.
> To Hell go all that feel my crook,
> Nor spare I any, but take all with me.
> > For king and priest and clerk,
> > I take him everyone;
> > No merchant great nor prince of realm
> > Can 'scape when I set on.
> I cut, I hook, I hack and chop,
> None 'scape me it to tell;
> When Death sets on with hook to reap,
> All flesh be crop, all flesh be fell.
> > Nor monk nor bishop flies away.
> > All to Hell must go.
> > I lead, I drive, I taketh all—
> > To Death's hook none says no!

In the shade of a pavilion, merchants sat in a comfortable row. If the actor's dire message distressed them, they showed no sign.

"What a fine old man he is!"

"Handles that hook quite well this year. Better than last. Not much sign of his affliction, eh?"

"You ought to be proud of him, Rolf. A fine old man."

Rolf de Mouers was not at all convinced that the spectacle of his father playing Death in the play of Herod was something to be praised. He remembered without joy the old performances of the Abraham play, when he had been made to lie on the wooden altar and look up at the knife. That had been bad enough. Now there was this.

"Did you help him, Rolf?"

"My wife did."

"Quite good. Really! One hardly notices the priest reading the words. Pity he can't speak the words himself. Though he makes himself understood well enough, I hear."

"My wife can make out what he says," Rolf mumbled. "He's her pet."

"Wonderful. Really quite wonderful. He's the last of that great old generation, eh? Wonderful."

At that moment, a voice bellowed over the priest's reading of the words of Death. Rolf flinched, but hid his embarrassment behind a hand, his head lowered. The voice was his father's, the tone that of a halfwit or a deaf man who has no idea what sound he makes—too loud, improperly pitched, without inflection. *"Mors!"* he cried. He seemed to have some idea that he was underlining the priest's message. *"Mors!"* The Latin word for "death" fascinated his father, Rolf knew, for it was enough like the name of his city to seem a pun, an emblem. Johan de Mors, he styled himself now.

> Now I swing my hook at Herod!
> He sees me not, none never do.
> No heed kings take of Death's approach,
> Nor of this blade that others slew.

That blade was raised now in his father's wasted arms like a banner. Shaped like a peasant's agricultural pruning hook, it was the universal and cruel symbol of Death's power, and an ironic one in its bitter reminder of the equality of death. Rolf flinched again and looked aside covertly at his fellow merchants in the pavilion. Did they seem more somber? It was with the brush hook that the peasants of Bohemia had pulled armed knights from the saddle, and old Dik, still the leader of the Garnheim Manor peasants, had planted a brush hook at the corner of his fields like a defiant mockery of the wealthy burghers in the city.

"I can't say I like this stuff about Death being equal for all," Rolf's neighbor whispered. "Sounds like more heresy."

"We've been hearing it since we were kids."

"But why do they have to make such a point of it? Just encourages the troublemakers."

"The priest wrote it."

"There be many heretic priests these days."

He wondered if it was so depressing to him because his own, mad father was playing the role of Death. Old Johan made Death doubly frightening because he had become a figure of fear. A whole generation of Mouers children had grown up fearing the mad old man whose demented half-face glared at them from the sculpted great doorway of his house in Johanstraza. He was always there, expounding on the symbolism of the carvings in words that they could not quite understand because of his half-dead tongue.

"I say it's not heresy, it's tedium." Rolf stood up. "I can't listen to such stuff."

He caught his wife's eyes as he moved crabwise down the row of aldermen, but he glanced away from her and rejected her look of appeal. When he reached the end of the row, he was puffing, and he paused to take a breath and then moved quickly down the wooden steps and out of the pavilion, into the open space behind it and so into one of the smaller streets that trickled away from Grozplaatz. There were other voices behind him now—Herod's, and the soldiers at revel after the Massacre of the Innocents.

He saw a girl at the corner. In from the country, no doubt, in to see the sights and have herself some fun. She surprised him a little by pushing away from the wall and saying with an insincere smile, "Have some fun, master?"

She was not more than fifteen. That was a surprise. He had thought she was simply an innocent. Maybe there weren't any more of those.

"What kind of fun?"

"Lick your cod for a florin."

Her youth was all she would ever have. In a few years,

she would be a plain woman; now, there was still a touch of childhood on her.

"Behind the wall over there." The Dean of Chapter's House was a ruin now. The old Bishop that had been his father's friend had stayed there once, it was said, but he had not visited Mouers for years before his death. And now there was no Bishop at all, for the diocese was heretical, some said, and there was a tug-of-war over the office.

Rolf worked hard to blot all that out. The girl was kneeling in front of him. Bent a little forward, he let his loose coat fall open around her. She seemed to know what she was doing, all right. He wished she knew a little less; it would have excited him more if it had been her first time. Still, it was something.

He could not keep his mind off its daily work. A new bishop. *There* was a problem. Rolf had been a member of a delegation to the Archbishop at Prague, pleading for a bishop. But all they thought of in Prague was the university and the heresies of Huss; the spiritual thirst of a free city was of no interest. So they had come home, damned for their failure, damned for their sins, damned...

He tried to blot it out. *Think of her mouth. Think of her being a child. Lips open, tongue busy—*

His father's bellow came to him over the rooftops, a mad cry of God's hunting dogs. *"Mors! Mors!"*

"Shit!" He struck the girl and yanked at his hose. "You're no good at it."

Johan's broken body lay between his mind and the world like the walls of a prison. He tried to tell things to people and they could not understand him, and then he raged at them. God's hand was very heavy on him, and he no more understood God's action than the people understood him. But perhaps he was not supposed to understand. The defect was in himself, not in God.

Every day he went up to the mother church and prayed in the Chapel of Helic Katrin, who had been his wife so very long ago, and then he went into the churchyard and knelt on the bronze slab that covered Matilda, his second wife. He prayed for their souls and for his own, and he prayed for release from the remnant of his body and from this burden of incomprehensibility that had been laid on him. In His own time, God would lift the burden.

He used to go to the Chapel of Helic Katrin and to Matilda's grave with his afflicted daughter, Friede. *What happened to Friede?* Ah, yes. *Rolf helped her into a convent.* But he could never remember her going away. She had been sent to a convent in Sweden, that was it. He had heard Rolf tell it so often that he almost remembered it, and yet there were no pictures in his head of Friede's going away. He always had to remind himself what had happened to her.

Well, Rolf had probably done what he thought was right. Rolf tried to do right. In his own way.

At least Rolf had a good wife. She talked to Johan, took care of him, scolded the servants when they were slow with his clothes or his food. *Not my servants any more. All hers and Rolf's.* It had been Elsbet who had helped him to play Death in the Herod play when he could no longer play Abraham. She was a good woman.

"Ready, Grandfather?"

Johan's answer was a grunt. It was easier to grunt at people. If he tried to speak, they laughed or grew impatient.

"Home, Grandfather?"

He grunted again. The boy was Mark, Rolf's fifth son by Elsbet. Seventeen children she had had for him, nine of them still living. *Five boys!*

"What is it, Grandfather?"

A grunt that became a growl. Like an old dog guarding a dried bone because it is all he has. *This hurt, this is mine, all I have, but mine. No sons now, only Rolf, and look at him! I had a daughter. What happened to her? Oh, yes. The convent.*

There was a friar waiting for him in the tunnel of shade beyond his wonderful doorway. The tunnel waited like the mouth of God; around it, as fresh as the day they were carved, the stone figures of his world climbed through vines and cannons to Death and Death's white beast. The leaves twined; imps grinned; the white beast waited.

"Good day to you, Master Johan! Good day, Mark; run in now, we have God's work to do. Run along. Well, Master Johan, God has given us a handsome day! The play was good? Good. I heard the bell. What will my preachment be today, Master Johan?"

He let the fingers of his good hand play over the carvings. There were Katrin and the baby Rolf; there were his old apprentices and his neighbors and several women he had committed sins with once. *Gone now. All gone.*

The hand touched the figures. The Bishop. Piet, the yardmaster. The Abbess of Garnheim. His lost son, Cosimo. The hand paused. He grunted. The hand smacked the carving insistently.

"What, Sire Johan?"

He smacked the stone. "Co—co-bing. Co—ming! Shoon. Thish boy. Coming shoon."

"What is he, Sire Johan?"

The good eye rolled. "Shun. Son! Son co-ming!"

"The Son of God is coming, indeed! And with him, the cracking open of tombs and the lifting of gravestones and the world's great end! Oh hear, people of Mouers, the wicked city—hear what message God brings you through his afflicted messenger, Sire Johan!" The friar moved into the street and began to harangue the passersby, people heading home from the plays to eat. Many lingered; many hurried on. They knew this place, where somebody was always preaching; the preachments were always Doomsday. That carved doorway was a text for the people of Mouers, and the pious sought it out as eagerly as the guilty avoided it.

Johan felt defeated. He had not meant that the Son of God was coming to the world, but that his own lost son, Cosimo, was coming back to Mouers. He had dreamed it. But now the friar was preaching the Second Coming. Was that how God's message was transmitted?

"Bad times," somebody muttered.

"The worst. The world is dying."

"Aye. Aye. It's the end."

The conviction of imminent doom held pious and impious alike. All time was borrowed time, now. God was sick of His creation, man.

"Who's coming?"

"The Son of God, Lord Jesu, who else?"

"The man said 'my son,' near as I could make it out."

"The son, the son. The old man's son is right here in Mouers, Devil take him. The Son of God, the friar means."

Johan's good eye bulged in his eagerness to get the message right. Nobody understood him.

If it was the last summer the world was to know, it was a good one. Corpus Christi Day gave them brilliant weather for the plays; June brought flowers and the first berries, day after day of sunshine and high, scudding clouds against brilliant blue. Johan and his friars preached on until July, but it was hard to believe that God would bring everything to an end in such beauty.

Summer was the season of campaigns, when armies

207

marched and sieges were held. Mouers had not sent out a siege force since three years after Karlsbirk, and then it had been only St. Barbara's gunners as a gesture of support to King Wenceslas. Now it was the season again, and a few old campaigners sighed and told stories of Karlsbirk and Johan's wounds and the boy, Cosimo, who had disappeared. Boys played at soldier in the gardens, but that was all.

Other armies were marching, however. Armies were good for business; let them march, was the merchants' view. Mouers was a merchants' city. Let sieges flourish!

In Mouers, they heard that there were gatherings of mercenary companies near Prague and Basel, both old and valued customers of the gunworks; good, let them gather. The Emperor's little garrison at Mouers got a new commander; good, he would be buying his supplies from the local merchants, just like his predecessor. The Archbishop was sending out mercenaries, they heard, to punish rebellious peasants on church lands; good, rebellion should be punished.

And then, one morning in the middle of July, a hand-lettered edict appeared on the door of every church in Mouers. The papers had been nailed up during the night and they were thought at first to be the work of devils, especially by those who could not read. The few who could read puzzled them out for the rest, and people were bewildered. For what the bills said was that their city was a sinkhole of sin and heresy, and its priests were false priests and its sacraments were empty ceremonies. And the bills had not been put up by devils, but by soldiers under the orders of the Archbishop.

"Not that again," old men groaned. Old women wept, remembering the last time that their priests had been denied. Friars were everywhere, for it was their season of campaigns, too; they preached all manner of things, most of them openly anti-papal, anti-Rome, anti-episcopal. Men shuddered and looked at each other hopelessly.

Three days later, the new commander of the garrison rode into Grozplaatz with twenty men-at-arms in battle array, rode his horse right up the steps of the mother church and sat there with a sinister-looking young priest standing by, and read to them in a voice that seemed to make the great bell itself tremble. People gathered, thinking he would explain the edict that had come from the Archbishop, but instead he read a broadside that stunned them:

"BE IT KNOWN that for many years past, since at least the reign of His Holiness Gregory the Fourth, and even before that, as examination will reveal, the so-called free city of Mouers has lived in impiety and darkness and its citizens have been damned to Hell. Their priests have not been true priests. Their so-called Bishop was himself an heretic and sinner reviled by God, for he turned his back on His Holiness at Rome and made his place with the kings of the earth.

KNOW then that to save itself and for men and women in it to save their immortal souls, the city of Mouers will submit to examination and inquisition and will, moreover, give up its Mayor and its aldermen at once and put itself under the governance of His Imperial Majesty's commander; and it will dismantle all defenses, including cannons, *ingenia*, firepots, and other such works and give them to the said commander; and it will surrender up its charter to him, to be held until I am satisfied of the cleaning of souls and the eradication of all deviltry and heresy and darkness from the city.

By me,
COSMUS GERMANICUS,
Bishop of Muhldorf and Mouers

"Give up the charter? What's that got to do with our souls?"

"It's all part of the end of things."

"What was that about the old Bishop's being a sinner?"

"I'll see my soul in blackest Hell before I'll give up the guns to yon little soldier-man."

"Examination and inquisition? Holy Katrin's soul, do you know what that means?"

"It's all part of the end of things. Everything's running downhill."

Even as they argued, the soldiers were nailing up the doors of the mother church. No clearer proof of a great change could have been given. For a century, the city had depended upon the uneasy standoff between the Pope and the Emperor, and now those powers seemed to have joined.

"But give up the charter? It'll be the death of the city."

The new commander went to the doors of the other churches and read his proclamation and nailed up the doors, and the people wailed and knelt to pray; some threw dirt on themselves and even hurt themselves beating their foreheads on the ground. Within hours, there were individuals and small groups moving through the streets, mistreating their bodies with whips and goads and filth. Mouers was like a long-closed room that spewed enormities when at last the door was opened.

"Doomed! Doomed! The world is doomed!"

The commander and his men-at-arms and his sneering priest came into Helic Barbara Plaatz before the Church of St. Barbara, and there were the Brotherhood with their hand-cannon and their pans of hot charcoal, just as they had appeared in the fields on every St. Barbara's day and as they had once appeared at Karlsbirk; and when the commander tried to read the letter, they opened fire and killed his horse and three of his men and the priest, and a battle was fought on the church steps and in the church itself, and seventeen men died, fighting with a savagery that would have appalled any professional soldier—but these men were fighting for ideas, and not for money. This was war at its ugliest, war to the soul. Men were knocked down and then stabbed and then hacked with axes and knives when they tried to rise, and when even a mortally wounded man made any sound or moved a limb, he was struck again until he was dead.

From Helic Barbara Plaatz, the remaining St. Barbarans went to the imperial garrison, picking up a hundred more young guildsmen and apprentices as they went, and they killed the rest of the garrison and occupied the little fort and pulled down the Emperor's banner. Next morning, they put the commander's head up over the South gate and hung the priest's body upside down from the wall, and cut off the genitals and fed them to the dogs who lived on rats in the town moat. They pulled down all the papers from the church doors and burned them.

The aldermen met, again and again. "Moderation—we must have moderation!" they groaned. They were all men of business; "moderation" was a word they said they lived by, although mostly what they meant by it was the self-control that other people should exercise. It was already too late for moderation, however. By the time they had got to the point of drafting a letter to the new Bishop protesting his letter, the guildsmen and the St. Barbarans had marched into the Corporation Hall with drawn swords, and they told the Mayor that if he even replied to the Bishop he would be killed.

"But we can make peace!" the Mayor groaned. He was a cordwainer and he was Mayor because it was his turn and his family were all proud of him. He offered to resign and they told him that if he did, they would hang him up next to the priest and cut his balls off while he was still alive and make him watch the dogs eat them.

"Moderation," he begged. "Moderation!"

Rolf sat in on the meetings and said little. Things had gone too far, he knew. Indeed, they had gone too far when the new commander had been appointed; this new Bishop had a plan for Mouers, that much was clear to Rolf, and his plan did not include accepting any pacification. And who was the new Bishop?

"Cosmus Germanicus." Rolf stroked his plump jowls. "Sweet Jesu, can it be the Italian come back to haunt me?"

Next morning, Elsbet came into the room where he was eating. The meal was his supper, for it was still the night before to him. The meetings had gone on and on, accomplishing nothing, until at last he had left in disgust and fought his way home through the turmoil of the streets.

"Could it be the Italian?" he said again.

"Of course it could. He was very ambitious."

"But why didn't we hear anything of it?"

"Maybe because he wanted to shock us. He was always clever."

Elsbet surprised him sometimes, though he thought of her very little. She was like a business partner now, someone unobtrusive who did the accounting or the billing. He was grateful to her for taking care of his father, though he had no idea that she had also taken charge of his father's network of intelligencers, or at least of what was left of it, like the shreds of a spider's web that has been brushed by a careless hand. She received letters now from Rome and Milan and Basel, and even from Brugge and London sometimes, one or two letters from each every year. She knew more than he thought.

"Always clever," she said again. She had only three teeth left in her head now, for all that she was only in her thirties. Children had sucked the teeth right out of her head. She looked old.

211

Elsbet had followed some of Cosimo's career through her correspondents—studies at the University of Padua, membership on the law faculty there, secretary to a cardinal in Venice. Eight summer campaigns as "chaplain" to the army of a papal ally, though her letters said he wore armor and commanded the cannon.

"Surely he wouldn't come back here," Rolf groaned. He guzzled wine and tore off a piece of bread. The bread was stale; had his cook left the house? Everything was falling apart. "He wouldn't come back."

"He would."

"He wouldn't!" He didn't like the idea that his plans would be interrupted. He had the sons he wanted now, and Willem was married into a house in Novgorod, and there were betrothals to Bergen and Bremen, Antwerp and Kobnhavn. "He wouldn't."

"We'll soon know," she said wisely. "It's campaign season."

At first, the army of this new Bishop proved hard to find. There seemed to be three armies on the march that summer, but some of the mercenary bands that were contracted to join them were moving in such large groups that they seemed like armies, too. Rolf reasoned that the new Bishop would be moving north from Italy, but there were no armies coming that way. Maybe he was not coming from Italy—or maybe he was not coming at all.

Then Muhldorf received an ultimatum: submit to episcopal discipline or be punished.

The Mouers aldermen could not help being relieved. "It's Muhldorf!" one crowed. "It was Muhldorf all the time! It's a bigger city—he'll make an example of it." They began to plan how they would bargain with the new Bishop after he had dealt with Muhldorf, by which time the autumn rains would have come and the summer campaigns would be over.

Penitents and flagellants were everywhere in the streets. Johan and his friar were still in their doorway, and many of the wilder ones gathered there. The churches were open, but some of the priests slipped out of the city, and people feared that the sacraments were unholy.

In early August, the Bishop's army appeared at the junction of the Eger and the Elbe. He was closer to Muhldorf than to Mouers, and there was real optimism in the Corporation Hall. On August 9, pioneers and siege cannon appeared along the eastern edge of the Muhldorf leasehold farms.

"It's Muhldorf," the exhausted Mayor sighed. "Thank God, it's Muhldorf!"

On August 14, the Mayor and the aldermen awoke to stare in wonder from the Mouerswand at the army that surrounded them. Ten thousand men ringed their city—two thousand of them the local peasantry, organized by old Dik of Garnheim Manor.

Rolf was not among the merchants who rode out to meet with the new Bishop that day under the marquee that was set up halfway between the army and the city walls. The Guildmaster of St. Eloi's went, however, and when he came back he was grim.

"It's him, all right," he said. "He asked for you."

At sixty, Alys de Monckton was as beautiful as she had been when Johan Bellfounder had struggled with her in the bed of the Garnheim hunting lodge. Rarefied, to be sure, and beautiful in a different way, for she was lined and gray-haired now. Yet there was a wonderful fierceness in her still, that defiance of time that comes from ambition and striving. She had the beauty of the hawk—faintly threatening, faintly rapacious, but lovely.

She had come north from Ravenna like the great lady she was, slowly and with an appropriate train. In Venice, the House of Arieto had entertained her; at the German border, the Cistercian monastery at Shlotz had received her like royalty. She brought five waiting gentlewomen, fifty men-at-arms and all their servants with her.

Now she was installed again at Garnheim Abbey, from whose roof she could see the walls and rooftops of Mouers, with her Bishop's siege laid out between them like a game. His camp was on a nearby hilltop, from which he could oversee his beloved cannons and his army.

It was windy on the Abbey roof. Her ladies held on to the walls or huddled by the chimneys, but she liked the whip of the breeze, which made her cloak snap behind her like wings.

Cosimo's tent was a dark splash of blue among the stripes and patterns of his underlings, with his bishop's banner flying above it. As she watched, the flag came down.

"The Bishop is moving, my lady."

"I see, Anna."

Her women were waiting for her to go in. It amused her to stay up there and prolong their discomfort. They seemed like children to her.

"The Bishop is riding this way, my lady."

"I see him, my dear."

A dozen horsemen were trotting up the valley toward the Abbey gate, the flag showing where he rode. He came to see her every day, but never so early as this, for the sun was hardly over the horizon yet.

"Go down," she said to the women, and they hurried toward the door with relief.

She lingered. The sounds of the camp's waking drifted to her; even its smells carried to her on the breeze. *Ah, to be a man!* She could hear horses, shouts, an ax falling on wood, a barrel rolling over boards, a hammer striking an anvil with the distant *chink* of two coins striking together.

"Will you not come now, my lady?"

"I come, child, I come."

To have come this far caused no great excitement in her. Her breathing was normal, her color unchanged. What she had set in motion so many years before had come farther than she had ever imagined, and had borne the three of them—herself, Cosimo, Johan—along with it like a wheel rolling downhill. She had simply given it its first push.

"My lady?"

"In a moment, child."

It was love, or something like love, that had brought her here. It was not the love of the romances, that stately dance of controlled appetites that was the jewel of her class, but something more basic and irrational. She was still amazed that she had loved him.

Now it was almost over. The flag was almost at her gate. Triumph was almost hers.

"Close the door behind me, my dear. I go down."

Cosimo was waiting in her old anteroom when she got there. The room was slightly shabby, and rather empty, for she had evicted the belongings of the former Abbess like so much trash. That lady had been sent packing the day that the army arrived, and when she had bitterly complained, she had been told to take her woes to the governor of the Cistercians at Clairvaux, eight hundred miles distant. Now Cosimo paced that room like a man in prison.

He wore armor, and over it the *lederner* of a knight. His helm had been left with his horse, but dagger and sword swung from their chains at his side. *Ah, to be a man!*

"Well, my Lord Bishop?"

He came toward her with his hands out as if to keep from falling. "I had a dream. A terrible dream!"

"Dreams are only froth."

"A white beast on a black field. A wood—no, it was stubble, or grain. I don't know. But the beast—terrible! Eyes of fire."

"What sort of beast? The unicorn?"

His heavy brows knotted. The head that had been so slim in boyhood was massive now, and two battle scars along the forehead seemed to be part of the scowl there. "A beast like none on earth." He clutched her hands. "What was it? Why am I so appalled?"

"It is nothing. A bit of food, the weariness of travel—dreams are only chaff."

She led him toward a table where wine and small cakes had been laid out. He would be all right when he was among his cannons, she knew. Still, his dream was a strange one. Johan had dreamed of a white beast the night before the battle at Garnheim. *It is an omen for them. But of what?*

Some of the penitents crept through the streets on bloody hands and knees, leaving trails behind them like snails. Others, whipping themselves and each other, drove their bodies from square to square and church to church. Death crashed out of the sky and broke down houses. Cannon smoke hung over the city like Death's shadow.

Johan wandered the streets with the other lost ones. He carried in his good hand a brush hook like the one he had carried in the play. Some of the penitents followed him. To them, he led them toward Judgment; to himself, he was a seeker after he knew not what. Sometimes he thought he was looking for Cosimo in the flames and the smoke, and sometimes he thought it was his afflicted daughter Friede. Yet again, it was the White Beast that led him on.

"Where is your father?"

"Out with the other lunatics. Take care of the children!"

"You must find him, Rolf! Rolf, listen—you must find him!"

"Where?"

"I don't know, but I won't leave him behind!"

"He's out in the streets! Sweet Jesu, Elsbet, what do you expect of me? I told the servants to keep him in, but they're all scared of him, think he's death or the devil—they let him walk out the front door!"

"The boat is ready, Rolf. *Go find your father!*"

The Fox was strong. He knew her as a bed partner and as a confidante, as a bearer of his children. Now she was showing a new strength. Through the three days of the siege, it had been the Fox who held the household together as the cannon-shot rained in and the fire arrows buzzed over the walls and set roofs afire. Many of the house servants had fled, and the workmen had deserted the yards; the world had turned upside down, but Elsbet had stayed sane and stable. One morning there had been a corpse in the doorway; it had been Elsbet and two servants who had dragged it down to the river on a cart and dumped it in. She had kept most of the servants loyal, although in the next street servants had murdered master and mistress and stripped the house. It was said that Dik had spies and agents among the servants all over the city, but Elsbet's were loyal.

"Get your father," she said.

"The children are all that matter now." His voice was a croak.

"Find him. You owe him everything."

As she scolded him, she was keeping order in a line of children and servants who were carrying possessions down to the dock. There a river cog waited to run the Bishop's blockade. Other merchants were already putting out in barges and sailing scows.

"All right, Elsbet." He was weary of it all. He could hardly raise his voice enough to be heard over the noise of siege. "I'll go look for him."

He shoved against the line of people and hurried through the almost empty house. It looked as if it had been looted—hangings down, clothes scattered, furniture overturned. Elsbet had ruled that only essential articles would go—food, gold, business records. Each child and servant was allowed one bundle of clothes.

The Mouers cannons roared from the walls. *My father's voice.* Little good they seemed now. Cosimo had brought almost two hundred cannons, enough to take a city five times the size of Mouers.

He huddled in the doorway as three penitents passed him. One had a whip with studded ends, with which he was lashing the bare and bloody legs of the other two. They chanted, "Vengeful God, accept our penance; vengeful God, accept our penance; vengeful God..."

"Lunatics," he muttered. Such self-punishment was as

great a sin as the others, he thought. He prayed a different prayer. *Merciful God, spare me.* He lumbered for another doorway. A small cannon-shot hummed overhead and thudded into the next street. *Bombard, about a three-incher. Merciful God, spare me.* Cosimo was using a magic gunpowder, they said. It made the guns hit wherever he wanted. *All nonsense. But he has good gunners. Merciful God, spare me.*

He went as far as the house he had rented for his mistress. The place was deserted. He thought he heard a door close at the back as he came in, and he walked with one hand on his dagger. *Looters.* In the bedroom, the wine cupboard was still locked, and he opened it with his key and drank greedily.

"Te deum laudamus—"

The church in Helic Barbara Plaatz. Was there time to go there and pray? The boat would have to leave soon; if they left after dark, there would be too much risk of going aground on the shoals a mile downstream. *Merciful God . . .*

He had had some idea of going on to the other house he had rented. He was glad for an excuse not to; there was something hidden there he did not want to face. *Leave it to God. He sees all, spares those He wants to spare.* He wondered if he had been gone long enough to convince Elsbet he had looked for his father. His deception weighed on him, made him still wearier. *Merciful Father, lift this burden from me!*

He ran from the house and hurried down the cobbled slope of the street, past the cordwainers' guildhouse—half gutted by fire now, the front black around the burst-out windows—and cut through the outyards of a friend's house. *No sign of life. Gone already.* Behind All Souls' Church *Merciful God* past the churchyard *spare me* turn left *roof knocked in there; Merciful God* cross the street *Is that my father with that pack of fools running after him? Can't be, it must be—*

The wild figure at the head of the mob of penitents veered toward him. Brush hook in hand, wild eye rolling, it was the figure of Death itself; seeing him, it came on at a grotesque run, and behind it came Death's helpers, like a pack of rats. Rolf screamed, and, turning from it, fled toward safety.

"Cast off! cast off!"

"Rolf, where is your father? *Rolf!*"

He carried her aboard like a screaming child. He put her down on her flailing legs and she swayed and fell and then lay there, inert, howling like a dog because he had left his father behind.

He was panting. His heart felt as big as a head in his

chest. He watched with horrible curiosity to see if Death would pursue him here. *Merciful God, was it my father? Could it have been? Oh, spare me!*

The yards slid slowly past as the heavy craft took the current. What Rolf's exhausted vision saw was neither the disappearance of the wonder that his father had built there, nor the end of the city in which he had grown up and lived, but the sloughing off of the horrors that pursued him. *Faster, faster!* It all slipped away behind him, all his sins, all his punishments, Death itself; and he slid past the Mouerswand and into the fields and thanked God that he had left his old life behind. *I will be a better man, I will, I will. . . .*

Johan had searched the streets of the Old City and was now roaming in the New, just outside the wall that had been the limit of the town when he had come there as a boy. No one followed him now; the air was too thick with smoke and there were too many guildsmen and citizens rushing about, pushing civilians out of the way, cursing, dragging guns to the walls. Their desperation was plain. They lacked experience and they lacked leadership; they were fighting back now as a cornered hedgehog would fight. Most of the people had gone to the churches, because they sensed that the city's collapse was close.

Johan limped down alleys and across courtyards as if he were the city's spirit looking for its own past strength. Dodging under low doorways, dragging his bad leg along sewers, he crossed the backyards of the city and came almost to the river's edge. There were craft moving out there in the lavender twilight; there was shouting and an occasional cry.

He knew these docks. He knew the granary and the shed where the grain traders kept their wagons. He knew the wool merchant's house, even from the rear. He could name each house he passed. He went through a hoarding and across a puddled alley and then he was stalking along the side of his own works, and he went through a hole in the fence and came out in the vast emptiness of his yards. Nobody was working—nobody in the grinding house, nobody in the loft, nobody in the lumberyard, and nobody but his beloved copes in the stillness of the bellhouse.

"Piet!"

His voice boomed from the abandoned walls. He could have thought that the world was coming to an end and he had been forgotten there, but for the thud and hum of the cannonballs.

"Hans Bighead! Josef!"

Katrin's window glowed at the rear of the house. The old rush of pride flowed from that window. It was lighted from within as if with the light that flowed from the faces of the saints.

"Katrin!"

He moved quickly through the yard. There were boxes and bundles and piles of clothes dropped there. Had his house been robbed? No matter—he had to find whatever it was he looked for.

Under the bridge and into the house he had built with cannon money; along the paneled, silent corridor and out to the front, through the hall where once thirty merchants from all over the German Baltic world had gathered to bid for his cannons. The front doors of the house stood open, as if to invite the world in.

"Cosimo?"

My doorway. Of course. It was here all the time. There was the history of his world, beginning and end. *Katrin. My Abbess. Piet, Matilda, Cosimo—*

A shot hummed through the evening air, a great bird coming to grasp him in its kindly talons and carry him away. The doorway arched above him, too high for him to reach Death and the White Beast behind him; and then the doorway dissolved and Death tumbled toward him and the bird's talons grasped him by the chest—not kindly, after all, but tight and painful—and he could not breathe. *It must be the end of the world.*

Air like crystal enveloped him, and the world was vivid and wondrous through it. The White Beast came into view. At last he could see it for what it was. He smiled. The beast pawed the ground like a horse and made a sound to him, and Johan of Mouers, bellfounder and master gunmaker, stood up and walked to join it across the rubble of the world that had ended.

CHAPTER NINETEEN

"IS HE DEAD?"

"Since yesterday, anyway. Stiffness gone already."

"Maybe he's the one. Tell the Bishop's man."

"Aye. Getting tired of this, showing every dead old fart we find."

"Yah, tell the Bishop that. Have you hanging up with pegs through your heelbones like them others."

They sought out one of the Bishop's men and told him that another old man's corpse had been found.

"Take him to the big square. They're all laid out there."

"Aye, the big square. That makes sense. It's the farthest away."

Cosimo, Bishop of Muhldorf and Mouers, who would be called the Bloody Bishop when the summer's work was done, paced slowly along the line of corpses in Grozplaatz. His victory was a model of good order, even of austerity. No looting, no rape, not so much as a dog stolen to make stew. Five mercenary companies had occupied the city and held it now in iron discipline, and neither the terrified residents nor the greedy victors dared make trouble.

Cosimo studied each dead old face. He had known three of them, but none was the face he sought. Then he reached the body in russet gown and dark-brown hose. Big of hand and foot, wasted by time, it was the remnant of a powerful man.

"Send for the Abbess of Garnheim."

He turned his back on Johan's corpse and went into the church to pray until she was brought to the city.

Her litter was carried to the square and set down at the church door; a servant told him, and he came out and, taking her by the hand, led her to the bodies. She stepped delicately around the corpses as if they were beds of flowers.

"Yes, it is he."

Her small hand tightened in his. An intake of breath, nothing more.

"Yes, I knew the scar on the forehead. He got it at Karlsbirk."

"I need no proof. I would know him, even after so long."

She knelt beside the dead man and passed one hand over the sunken cheek and smoothed the thin hair over the scarred forehead. "We come such a long way for so little."

"My lady?"

"Why—for all these years, I have said what a lowly man he was, and now—he has dominated my life. The jest is on me."

She rose and turned away; passing the Bishop, she put her left hand on his upper arm to steady herself. He was still in armor. Plaintively, he whispered to her like a frightened child, *"Was he my father?"*

She touched her hand to her forehead—a gesture of forgetfulness, the rousing of memory.

"No."

It was a handsome lie. Once, when he had been an infant, she had dreamed of telling him that he was a commoner's son; now she loved him and she could not do it. "Your father was an Italian nobleman, as I always told you."

She moved back to the litter.

The Bishop glanced again at the serene, dead face. "Bury these in a common grave. Have a chaplain say mass."

His face was as hard as the stones of the mother church. What his soldiers said of him seemed to be true: *His soul walks in armour.*

For three days, he sat in the Corporation Hall and judged the people of Mouers. He bound over many for the Inquisition, condemned some to death, released only three. The entire city was under threat of excommunication.

"The men are very impatient, my lord."

"Tonight. Are we done here?"

"Little matters left. I'll deal with them."

"I will sit until sundown. Send the next one in."

"These are nothing, my lord."

"Send them."

They were trivial, indeed—a man found stealing food, a boy of seven whose parents could not be found. The third matter, however, intrigued him—a woman of twenty, both deaf and mute, with a baby in her arms. Half-starved, half-crazed, she seemed to have come from the very ruins of the city.

"Where did you find her?"

"A house up by the new church, my lord. It belonged to Rolf the gunmaker, they say—one of the ones who have skipped."

He knew very well that Rolf had escaped. It intrigued him that the woman had come from his house.

"One of his women?"

"Not likely. Not much of a looker, eh?" The captain lowered his voice. "Mental, I'd say."

"A deaf-mute, you think."

"Aye. Unless she's faking, and why do that?"

The Bishop's massive head lifted as he studied the woman. To the captain's surprise, he rose from his chair and knelt in front of her and began to put coins on the floor at her feet. The coins formed a pattern, though the captain could not grasp the sense of it. The woman did, however; after some seconds, she made a sound and swiftly bent down. She moved one of the coins. The Bishop moved another; she put a coin in its place.

The Bishop pulled himself upright. "Dear God!"

"My lord."

"I know who she is!" He looked down at the dirty brown hair. "I used to play with her. She is Friede, daughter of the old gunmaker."

"Don't look like any merchant's daughter, my lord. Are you sure? She's been on short rations for weeks, to be as thin as that. And her color, it comes from being kept close, eh?"

"Have a chair brought for her. And food."

It was difficult to pull the woman away from the game on the stone floor. She was smiling until they pulled her up, and then she made harsh, angry sounds. But, seeing Cosimo, she moved to him, sat patiently across from him when he motioned to her. He laid out the same game on the table, and she smiled. He called for pen and ink.

"Can she write, my lord?"

"We'll find out. Her mother could. If not—she and I used to tell each other stories, drawing pictures in the dust. I will find her story out, one way or the other."

An hour later, he knew. It was dark outside by then, long after the time when he said he would leave the city.

"Incest!" He shook his head. "He's a devil! Look at her—he could buy any woman who was for sale from here to Hanse,

222

and he raped his own half sister! A deaf-mute, a pathetic piece of a whole woman, a perpetual child! And we say the fear of Hell is enough to make men obey the law? Idiocy! In some, it simply spurs them on to greater vice, I think. *His own half sister!* Dear God, what has he not done, I wonder?" He studied the emaciated woman and her spindly child. The baby was almost a year old; in all that time, both child and mother had been locked up in Rolf's house. A glint of dreadful mischief showed in Cosimo's face, like the mockery of the boyhood self. "What would she do to revenge herself, do you think?"

He drew more pictures. She was slow to understand, for the concept of revenge is not an easy one to communicate; but when she understood, ink splashed across the table and she howled.

"Good. Good! Sometimes God means for us to take charge of these things for Him. Well, I have a plan—a plan for Friede and her brother Rolf. Kind for kind." His rough hand caressed her filthy head. "Trust me, Friede. Trust me."

"Her child's a boy, nameless, unbaptized. Well, I will name him. And christen him, too, oh, yes! And in the chapel of his grandfather's first wife, the Helic Katrin. Tonight, Captain, we will have a christening! We will call him Lazarus, for he is the old man reborn—Johan's grandson by his daughter and his son, the man himself brought back to life!" The Bishop laughed; the sound was strange enough to cause the captain to study him intently. "The last christening in Mouers, Captain! An event fit for nighttime, don't you think?"

He rose and took the woman by the hand. "Turn the free companies loose in an hour. The other soldiers at dawn, the peasants at sunset tomorrow. At sunrise day after tomorrow, begin setting powder charges." He walked carefully the length of the Corporation Hall, the wretched woman dragging by his side—son and daughter of Johan moving down the hall the man himself had built, while from its walls the Bishop's curious laugh sounded.

The fugitives from Mouers moved north and west. The river took them partway; when they seemed safe from the Bishop's army, they went overland toward Flanders and the Baltic states that had always welcomed them. The escape by water had been kind to some, fatal to others; almost at the whim of the peasants who lined the shores, boats passed through or were destroyed. When their mood was right, they had merely hooted and waved and done such things as raising their shirts and exposing their bare behinds. Other times, they rowed out in small craft and boarded the escaping boats, murdering everyone on board.

Rolf and Elsbet had moved downstream in a flotilla, protected somewhat by the numbers of craft that moved together. Those nearest the banks had suffered most, and there was some scrambling and bumping as they tried to seize the middle of the current. Arrows and stones fell on the boats; one of Rolf's servants fell with a quarrel in his gut. On they had floated, borne by the current and hurried by the sweeps, at which men of wealth and wives with soft hands and even children labored—on past the Garnheim Manor fields, on past the fulling mill and the fishweirs, on past the Ford of Three Oaks, where peasants tried to stop them in the near-darkness by wading out, and the heavy craft had floated on, their momentum too great to be stopped in such a way. People had died there on both sides; Rolf had done great work with a handgun, killing two peasants and frightening the rest, for they had never faced a gun before.

On they had glided in the darkness, down past the ruin of the gunpowder mills, blown up on the first day of the siege; down through the black arches of the Stone Bridge, where mercenaries loyal to nobody had exacted a toll before letting them pass on—on, on, between willow-bordered banks where Rolf had fished with Johan as a boy, on through farms and manors and villages too far from Mouers to be familiar in the darkness; on through the uneasy quiet of a countryside racked by war, on to the morning and sunlight and the sight of mounted soldiers cantering along a road, of farms burning, of a landscape like a dream in which little figures killed each other at a distance.

Rolf did not feel safe until they had passed Dresden, and even then he feared to appear in public, because Cosimo would have spies out. He pushed them on to the Baltic, traveling now by road like people of their proper class, Rolf and Elsbet and the children in new clothes, Rolf and his sons on horses and Elsbet in a litter. They hurried on to Lubeck, where he began to feel safe.

Rolf believed that the family fortune—his fortune, now—had been reduced by half. He spent the nights in strange inns and the houses of business allies, poring over business records. He had money out in many places; that would still come in, he hoped. The firm was owed money by three cities and eleven other establishments. That could be collected. The works were gone, as were the powder mill and the great house on Johanstraza, stores of copper and iron, three great guns in the warehouse, all of the bell molds and the cannon molds and the drawings for every gun and bell the house had ever poured. Nonetheless, Rolf insisted upon seeing these losses as only temporary.

"Indemnity," he murmured. It was late at night and he had worked by a stinking lamp while Elsbet watched him from the damp, chill bed. "I'll demand indemnity."

"All he has to do is declare you a heretic. Then he'll be awarded everything."

"I'll go to the Pope, if I have to. I have connections in Rome. Believe me, the Pope knows enough to listen to men like me! The Church can't survive without men like me."

She said nothing. Her calculations produced different results from his. She believed that they would have a tenth of what had been, on paper, theirs. Her father had pounded a business maxim into her head: old debts are always old debts, old credits are dust.

Rolf was a dreamer, she found. When it came to money, he was a dreamer.

He installed his family in the finest inn in Lubeck. They took the entire inn, except for two rooms that were already occupied by eleven pilgrims going by ship to Spain. "It's important to look well off," Rolf said. He put the children on one floor, Elsbet and himself and their personal servants and his clerks and his accountant on another. "They know me in Lubeck," he said.

He told Elsbet that he was going to Gdansik, then to Stockholm and Kobenhavn and on to Bergen. He would demand the money that the firm was owed and he would beg for extensions of their debts. "I'll be gone for two months. Write to your brother Dirk at Antwerp; you can live with him until I find a new city for us to locate."

"Dirk is a fool. I don't like his wife."

"Your father liked Dirk well enough to give him half the cannon works!"

"Yes, and now he has run that into ruin and is making cannon carriages instead of cannons; if my father were alive, he'd whip him! Dirk is a fool." Her gray eyes looked blankly past him, through the rain-streaked window, over the wet, gray street and into some unknown distance. "I don't like Antwerp," she said vaguely.

"What's wrong with Antwerp? Your whole family is in Antwerp."

"That's what I don't like about it."

"Elsbet!" Rolf got red. Until then, he had been calm; indeed, he had been calmer than she had seen him for years. She would almost have said that he sweated less, ever since they left Mouers. And now, instead of shouting in a rage, he mastered himself and said quietly, "Elsbet, I want to know the family is safe in Antwerp."

"And have my brothers and their snippy wives lord it over me because we've lost the gunworks? I will go to Hamburg, to my sister Ursula."

"But Ursula's married to a very common fuller!"

"Well, she's no poorer than I am now. I've already written to her."

Rolf might have objected; however, he was thinking again that it was she who had got the family safely out of Mouers. Maybe it was best to let her have her way until all this was over. She was showing a new strength, and perhaps it was she who was meant to get his sons through their homelessness.

Rolf took four servants and a clerk and took a ship for Gdansik. "Two months—no longer. I'll send letters by the Fuggers' courier. They're dependable."

Elsbet did not go down to see him off; such a thing would have been unseemly. They all bade him goodbye in the courtyard of the inn, almost formally. Nobody wept, for he had always been going off somewhere, even when they lived in Mouers. They did not like public displays of emotion, anyway.

Elsbet spent four more days in Lubeck. First, she paid a lawyer to come and sit with her for three of those days while she went over many matters that she understood far better than any man would have given her credit for. She dismissed the family accountant and two of the clerks; the family chaplain had already slipped away, probably fearing that an accusation of heresy would be made against the family and would rub off on him by association.

At the end of four days, she paid the lawyer and sent him on his way, and then she went sadly among the household servants, giving each a gift and a year's money, keeping only her own two personal maids and the baby's nurse and two male servants to act as grooms, bodyguards, and men-of-all-work.

This time, everybody cried.

"Why, Mama?" her little daughter Bette wailed. "Why must Tante Griet go away?"

"Because we are poor now."

"But Tante Griet will live with us for nothing!"

"Yes, but she will eat food and wear clothes, and one day she will be too old to work, and then we will have to take care of her and get nothing back. The world is a very hard place, little one—weep, weep, it's the only good answer now."

Mark, who was eleven, was incensed. "My father will hear of this!" he threatened. He somehow thought it made him seem older to sound like a prig.

"Of course he will," Elsbet said sadly. "He will be angry with me, won't he!"

"My grandfather will hear of it!"

Elsbet shook her head. Old Johan had been a favorite of the boy's, and it had been Mark who accompanied him to the play of Herod, Mark who had often waited in the tunnel-like shade of the great doorway while Johan and his friar harangued the passersby. "Your grandfather is dead, child. I told you that."

"He is not!"

"Mark, he is."

"You didn't see him die!"

"No—but I know he is dead, as well as I know anything."

"Grandfather will be furious at you for letting all the good servants go and keeping those two lazy good-for-nothing men."

"In Heaven they don't get furious. Anyway, if he knew how poor we are, he would say I did the right thing."

"We are not poor! Not, not not! Father says we are rich!"

"I know—I know." She sighed.

She rode on a horse now instead of in a litter, with her five-year-old daughter Anna in front of her on the saddle, and Elsbet hardly bigger than a child herself; she led them out of Lubeck in a procession that looked, as the priggish Mark said bitterly, "like a pilgrimage of beggars." He and Bette were particularly humiliated by the small number of servants, and he was clearly afraid that they would meet somebody they had known when they were rich. There were only the five servants and the clerk now, for a family of Elsbet and seven children.

"We could go to my Uncle Dirk at Antwerp and live like decent people!" Mark whined.

"We could sell our souls, too, but we aren't going to."

227

To her older children's disgust, she attached them to a group of half a dozen mercenaries of the very lowest kind, with whom she displayed an affinity that was really outrageously flirtatious, for she laughed with them and told jokes that were distinctly off-color and recounted tales of "my father, the great Johan de Mouers." The mercenaries were hardly better than scavengers, but they were protection on the road (although they were as bad as any brigands the little procession might have met), and when they finally reached the market cross near Hamburg and had to take a different road, they seemed truly sorry to let Elsbet go.

"See you at another war sometime, my lady!" one of them bellowed.

"Or one of our guns—and don't let it be the wrong end!"

They laughed, and a reference was made to balls and rammers that seemed to be part of a continuing joke among them, and then they rode off, leaving Mark and Bette crimson with shame at their mother's suddenly vulgar behavior.

"I wish my father were here!" Mark hissed to Elsbet some minutes later.

"So do I," the Fox said equably. "But as he isn't, we must take whatever protection comes the cheapest."

"I wouldn't say that that was cheap," the boy said bitterly. She said nothing. He refused to let it go, however, and he said, "I don't think that the family name and your reputation as my father's wife are *cheap* things to bargain away to every ragtag group of soldiers on the road!"

She considered that. "Maybe. But they're cheaper than pain and death." The gray eyes looked ahead with the same great calm, and the boy, enraged by her impassivity, rode next to her in silence.

Rolf de Mouers spent only a week in Gdansik, but he was more successful than he had hoped in getting money that was owed him. The news of the fall of Mouers was everywhere by then, and his creditors were astonished to find him alive and eager for business, and so they granted him extensions they might otherwise have denied.

"To Stockholm, Master Rolf?"

"Bremen next, then Stockholm. I've changed my plans."

"Shall I write to your dame, Master Rolf?"

"Send her copies of the new contracts and tell her I can be reached at Bremen through the Hospitalers. Use the old code."

228

Rolf trusted his clerk. The man was years older than he, almost old enough to be his father, and he was one of those people who seem to have no existence—no reality, no dreams—beyond their work. An expressionless man without remarkable features, he had a face that Rolf would have had difficulty describing, although he had been seeing it for years. No hint of a confidence had ever escaped him to a competitor, and Rolf assumed that nothing on earth was of sufficient value to the man to tempt him to deception.

"I am going to the cathedral," Rolf said now.

"The letters will be ready when you return."

When Rolf was gone, the clerk scribbled a message and gave it to a stranger who was lurking in the courtyard. Rolf should have remembered that every man has his price—and his clerk's price for passing on news of where Rolf went next was an indulgence of his sins, given him by the Bishop of Muhldorf and Mouers.

Rolf prayed daily in his mother's name. He had confessed and had been shriven. The new man who had seemed to emerge as they slipped down the river from Mouers was still there, a penitent and grateful man, a grave sinner seeking redemption. Death had come very close to him at Mouers, and now he was resolved to die a better man than he had been. Besides, he had left his crazy father and his half-sister Friede to die at Mouers, and without those two—his burden and his crime—he could breathe free and start over.

Rolf was such a new and changed man that his old business associates were confused, and several who had hired women for his visit were bewildered when he did not use them.

Shipping was disturbed by storms at the change of seasons, and he had to stay on at Gdansik when his business was done, until he found a captain willing to brave the seas for higher pay. The craft, a clinker-built old cog of twenty-two feet, wallowed through the waves from the time it cleared the port, and after it turned the Hel and headed into the open Baltic, it was on its ends for five days. The servants and the clerk were sick, but Rolf took it with the healthy calm of a man whose soul was cleansed. He reached Bremen looking fit and even thinner, and even the captain marveled that he had survived the trip so well.

"Won't you rest today, master?" the clerk said; he was still green of face and wobbly on his legs.

"Rest is for the night—and my debts haven't rested since the day I left Mouers, alas! Send to the Fuggers and the

229

Hospitalers and to the Arieto Brothers; tell each one I'm here in Bremen and will call—'Rolf de Mouers, son of Johan the Gunfounder of Mouers, greets you with respect and honor,' and so forth; you know the style. Ah, and go yourself to the guildhall and remind them that they are two years overdue on payment for three great guns and so many hundred-weights of powder—look it up in the ledger—and you are instructed to wait for payment or a message. Also, the Abbey of the White Friars want an extension on their debt for three crows, but they're not to have it; *don't* go to the Abbot, but go to the prebend of the Abbey Church of Our Lady; he handles all that. And don't be too polite with him; he's very shifty."

"Am I to say you will call?"

"No, I think not. Let slip that I'm in Bremen, and if they seem as if they're not going to pay, tell them I will be along to visit with my lawyer. Eh?"

He prayed at a small church and then called on a creditor, who was not eager to extend the time of indebtedness but would listen to reason. He made three other calls and then, toward the end of the afternoon, moved resolutely to the Foreigners' Quai and the house of the Arieto Brothers. He had put it off until last because he did not like doing business with the Arieti, since he had, long ago, canceled a letter of credit that he had given to that devil Cosimo. Still, they were always courteous—now, for example, servants bowed when they heard his name, and the majordomo led him through a crowded anteroom, clearing his way with a sideways movement that allowed the man to bow and walk at the same time. Beyond the antechamber, the youngest of the Arieti waited for him—bearded, slightly overweight, elegant with an opulence that seemed, to German taste, almost Moorish.

"Signor Rolf!"

"Master Alessandro."

"What good news it was when we learned you had escaped your poor city. And so tragic about your poor father; believe me, my heart was touched when I heard. He was an old friend of the firm."

"Bad news travels fastest, they say."

"Ah, we have our intelligencers, you know; all news travels fast. And your honored wife?" Arieto led the conversation through graceful little loops and whorls that enclosed family, acquaintances, politics. Sweet wine was brought. Rolf went to business and asked for forgiveness on the interest for the

230

loss of two ships, lost last year in the Channel with paid-for loads of tin, iron and sulphur.

Alessandro put the fingertips of his two hands together, like a child making a church with his fingers. "I believe we might make some arrangement," he said carefully. "The interest, of course, is not ours, but those Jews from whom we borrow—"

"Of course, of course."

"There would be the matter of collateral."

"We had already put a block of houses in Bremen on the shipment."

"I know. But I am thinking of what my brother Gabrielle would say. He is our cautious one!" Alessandro grinned and showed slightly yellow teeth. "It is a bad time, I am sorry to say—all these wars, this heresy! The Jews seem almost Christian in their restraint, but the Hospitalers are the Devil!" He pursed his lips. "At any rate, we can cover our own need for cash if we postpone—not cancel, I fear, but postpone—a payment and the interest. But, naturally, the rate will be high. Perhaps thirty percent. In effect, we would be lending the money to you—not cheap these days." His tilted head suggested that of a very large and attentive bird. "Further collateral would be the first thing in Gabrielle's mind, I fear."

Rolf pretended surprise. He, too, could touch his fingertips together and squint and seem to sigh over the sordid facts of business. In fact, he, like Alessandro, loved this sort of thing—although he did regret his father's death because it denied him that small-minded bogey man—in Alessandro's case, Gabrielle—who could be called up to explain any hard dealing. He fenced a bit over the matter of collateral and said, "With my Mouers properties, ah, in litigation—"

"At best," said Alessandro.

"We are very hopeful."

"My intelligence says that the city was leveled. With gunpowder."

Rolf had not heard that; he masked his dismay. "There are always reparations. I am very hopeful. But with the Mouers holdings out of consideration for now, my assets are limited. Let me be frank—they're limited! I have a small gunpowder mill—well, half of it, actually, owned jointly with the den Hoecks in Flanders—"

"No, no, no joint properties."

"The countinghouse in Novgorod, but—"

231

Alessandro was very casual. "What about the warehouses here in Bremen?"

"What about them?" Rolf was smiling inwardly; he had led the Italian exactly where he wanted him to come.

"We have a client who is looking for dockage and warehouse space. I cannot say too much about it—confidentiality is very important—but if you would consider putting the property up as collateral, well—something of advantage to all three of us might—you know—"

Ownership of the small dock and the warehouses had been Rolf's idea and one that his father had scoffed at until their yearly statements began to show considerable profit from it. In a busy port, dock space could always be rented out when one's own ships were not in; since much of their trade went through Bremen, ownership of warehouses caused a great saving.

"I couldn't give it up entirely," Rolf said cautiously. This much was true; he had five guns and a quantity of metals stored there now.

"No, no! But perhaps..." Alessandro described an airy, birdlike flight with one hand. Was it an Italian's description of a business deal taking wing? "Would you go so far as to meet with our client?"

"Of course."

Alessandro lowered his voice. "Could it possibly be this evening? I am having a few of the foreign community to my house to hear my consort—my brothers sent me three new musicians as a surprise gift—and I am sure you will think me a barbarian to ask you there to discuss business under such circumstances, but, you see... with other people there, who would know that you and my client had come to meet?"

"Delighted, of course."

"How very helpful you are! You always give me cause to realize why you and your late father were always among our favorite clients."

Rolf had never been inside the Arieto house, which was quite separate from the business building. It looked quite German on the outside, with the usual courtyard where his horse was taken by a groom and where two linkboys with torches saw him up a steep flight of exterior steps. Inside, however, it was all Venice: gold gleamed conspicuously from sconces, and floors of black and white marble squares glowed underfoot. The very number of candles was like a statement of the firm's wealth—and there were servants everywhere,

232

several of them dark and turbaned, and one, who had high cheekbones and strange eyes, in a fur cap of a sort that Rolf had never before seen.

"From Tibet," Alessandro murmured. Despite himself, Rolf was impressed. *Where is Tibet?*

The consort of music played harmonies that were strange to him, too. Several melodies seemed to wind about each other like climbing vines, the sound richer and more complex than any he had heard before. Like other Northerners, Rolf found the Venetians fascinating and surprising. Being in the home of one was faintly like doing business with the Devil—if the Devil were a nobleman.

"Signor Rolf de Mouers, the Lady Magdalena d'Este of Milan." Alessandro squeezed his upper arm. "This revered lady is the client of whom I spoke."

She might have been as young as sixteen or as old as twenty. Fair-haired for a Southerner, she had features so perfect that he almost gasped, eyebrows and hairline plucked to make her forehead high, her nose long and narrow and as aristocratic as a Caesar's. That face held him so long that he knew he seemed rude, staring at it, yet she was absolutely quiet. If the statement of the face was silent, however, the body was a shout of sensuality, the more so because of a gown more revealing than any that a good German lady would have dared to wear. Both sleeves and sides were slashed to reveal bare skin, yet her pose suggested chastity itself. Beautiful, then, and young, she mixed purity and physicality in a breathtaking fashion.

Alessandro Arieto was talking—dockage, three-way business deals, percentages. Rolf wanted to laugh out loud. How could any man imagine that such a creature as this cared for such things? He wanted to touch her, to smell her. He imagined her nude; unless her dress was padded, she must be glorious. Her shoulders were narrow and just slightly rounded, her hips large; he could imagine the slope from the pouting belly, the fair hair below it....Dock rental, port tax, haulage—was Alessandro mad, or was he blind?

"It desolates me, but now I must see to my other guests. May I leave you together? Confidentiality, you understand, is paramount. Through that door, you will find a little private chamber—my servant will show you, yes. Any agreement that you two could reach would be a joy to my brothers—details to be worked out later...."

He sat with her in a tiny room lighted with six candles.

From floor to ceiling, the walls were covered with scrolls of pale blue and red, through which ran gold leaf. It was like a page from a book, something labored over by a master illuminator.

"If I could possess your docks, Signor Rolf, my hopes—"

"Madonna, must we talk of docks? I will *give* you a dock!"

Eyes, large and sad and young, raised to his. "What have I done wrong?"

"Nothing—nothing! But it seems cruel, to waste your sweet breath on such heavy words."

She looked down. She had tried to be businesslike, but it was difficult, she told him, for she was only a woman. Ah, how well he understood. Did he, truly? Yes, truly. It was all so very hard for her—a woman alone, bereft. Bereft? Widowed after only a month, left with the affairs of a large business. Could he understand? Oh, yes, madonna, yes—

Dare I touch her? Dear God, to put my hand between those legs! Another voice told him something cautionary, but he would not listen. *I will make my peace with God tomorrow. Tomorrow, I will confess....*

"I must go, Signor Rolf. Perhaps we can talk more tomorrow."

"No, madonna!"

"No? Alas, and I—I depended on you."

"I meant only that I did not want you to go yet."

"Oh, how kind you are. But my head is splitting. I know we must talk more, but—but perhaps you could accompany me!"

"I should be enchanted, madonna."

"Signor Arieto showed me a private way out of the house, so I would not be seen. My own house is not far. I have servants. They could come for your horse if you care to walk beside my litter."

Walking beside the swaying litter, he saw his shadow like a monstrous shape in the flare of the torches. His hand touched hers on the padded bar. His knees went weak with expectation. The hand was warm and soft, and when he left his hand in contact with it, one finger wound itself around one of his like a tendril.

In her own house, she proved to be passionate and naive. Uninitiated as she seemed to be, she was yet as uninhibited as a dream.

"Are we sinning?" she asked innocently.

"Only a little."

"Then we should give ourselves a little penance."

"What penance?"

She giggled.

"What penance? You are an imp! Tell me."

"In Milan, there is a famous lady who has herself whipped for penance, they say. She has her women whip each other, too, on the nether parts, you know, and she watches them and grows lubricious."

There were small pine branches laid in a fireplace. The small twigs snapped on her plump buttocks, which grew pink under the whipping. Aroused anew, he plunged into her as she lay belly down over a stool. "Gently, gently—oh, Sweet Mother of God, not there—! Oh, *Amore—che grandezza—*"

She unwound ribbons from her hair. "I will make you my slave."

"I am your slave already." The room was a smear of light and blackness. He had been drinking wine all night. *Is it dawn?* He felt his speech slur, and he did not care.

"I am going to tie my slave to my bed so he will never leave me. I will bind him and then force him—*force* him to submit—to such sweet torment—of my mouth on his...But he will find out."

She was tying his wrists with the ribbons. He found it an exciting idea, to be bound with such fragile ropes. Wrists, ankles. Her glorious body was a blur against the candles.

"Such sweet torment, my darling! Only a moment more."

The candles blew sideways in a gust of wind, and he was aware of movement. There seemed to be someone else in the room. *Two women now? Who? Brought in somebody else—*

He recognized Friede with astonishment. The surprise of it numbed him—Friede should have been dead in the ruin of Mouers. Then he began to struggle against the ribbons, which were not so fragile as he had thought.

Friede had a knife.

She cut off his penis at the root and stuffed it into his astonished, screaming mouth, and the voluptuous whore who had called herself Signora d'Este and a man tied his mouth shut over its terrible meal, and his screams became the weird cries of a mute.

Friede cut off his scrotum and forced it into his rectum. She slashed his arms and legs and then slipped the knife into his abdomen and between his ribs in many places so that he would live for a while, and at last she put it into his heart and twisted it until he was dead.

Four days later, the body was found in a farmyard dungheap fifteen miles outside of Bremen. It had a bit of doggerel scribbled on a parchment tied around its neck:

Rolf of Mouers was my name,
A great man did I be.
Of women had I many a one,
Now women have had me.

The news of Rolf's death reached Elsbet by the courier of the Arieto Brothers. A representative of that house came with the messenger and expressed shock, sorrow and outrage.

"Is it my husband, absolutely?" she said.

"Beyond question, Dame Elsbet. His own clerk identified him, as did my master, Alessandro Arieto, who had been with him that very week. My master has posted a reward. Your revered husband had been a guest at his house; we feel so—so—*responsible,* lady!"

"We have no home now," she said as if she had not heard him. "I would ask that he be buried at Bremen."

"Of course! If we could make the arrangements, we—"

"Please do." The Fox had a little frown but did not otherwise show any feeling. "I would like him to be buried as a Christian. There might be some objection to that, since we were cried against by the Bishop of Muhldorf and Mouers. If that happens, I will offer money to whatever parish would bury him."

"Madame!" The man held up a gloved and ringed hand. "Please! Arieto Brothers will arrange that the Bishop of Bremen himself say a funeral mass."

She accepted his further outpouring of sympathy and grief; the loss might have been his, not hers, he was so eloquent. When he was gone, she summoned one of her remaining servants.

"Send for a priest," she said. "Then bring my children to me. I have something to tell them."

Weeks later, a young deaf-mute went to work as a lay sister at the Abbey of Garnheim. The other women thought that she was simpleminded. She died there seven years later of cancer, an overworked drudge who never smiled, never refused any task, never hinted at her secrets. The Abbess of Garnheim had no contact with her. The Abbess herself outlived the newcomer by another three years and died, shriven and at peace, in her bed in the tower room with the view she loved over the ruins of the city of Mouers.

The Bishop of Muhldorf and Mouers stayed in his diocese all the rest of that first summer, impressing his charges with the seriousness of his intentions for them. Muhldorf, studying the example of the city of Mouers, confessed its errors and gave up its charter to him and the Emperor's representatives. The Bishop then visited the religious houses in the diocese and swung back toward Mouers in late September despite the onset of the autumn rains. The peasants continued to be restless in the area, and there were free companies of mercenaries terrorizing the country. Cosimo swept through it and scoured it clean, hanging Dik of the Manor Farm and ten others and driving the mercenaries into neighboring, and more complaisant, lands. Then he went home to Italy and never visited Germany again.

He grew almost middle-aged. Often he was seen with the boy he called Lazaro, whom many supposed to be his bastard child. Bishop Cosimo became an odd mixture of father, mother and Socratic tutor to the child, taking him on many of his travels and even carrying him into battle on his saddle. By the age of five, the boy had seen a cavalry melee from its midst; by six, he had stood in a battery of cannons at a siege. His education mixed the ethics of Aristotle with the ideas of Marsilius of Padua and the military tactics of the Bishop of Muhldorf and Mouers. At seven, he owned and shot his own hand-cannon, one made with a very short staff so that it could be held against the chest in the new way. At nine, he had his own horse and his own armor, and he went on a summer campaign like a precocious Caesar.

When he was ten, the boy lived with the Bishop at Rome for the winter. Cosimo had become a moody man by then, one sometimes dangerous to others and to himself, full of black moods and sudden shifts. The boy Lazaro was alone in being able to approach him in any state; he played David to the man's Saul, appeasing some madness that had mastered his reason. Lazaro would not see him for days at a time, and then Cosimo would appear in their apartment, ashen-faced, weary, explosively unstable.

"Oh, to go to war, little one! Oh, that God and his holiness made winter wars!"

"We could have a new crusade!"

"We could—we could! Shall we do that?"

"Yes! Can I ride my horse next to yours again?"

"Yes, yes, yes! We'll ride together, boy! Maybe God will smile and we'll be killed together!" Cosimo laughed in the way that the boy knew and disliked, the laugh of a stranger. Then Cosimo talked wildly of the politics of Rome and of all his enemies, of wars and the coming end of the world, and at last he wound down and the boy sang to him and he slept.

Cosimo wanted to be Pope. He had sat at the Council of Constance as an observer and a critic for half a year and had come away in disgust; his letters to certain great men of both the world and the Church on that subject had made him known. Now, Gregory the Twelfth had resigned and there was no Pope and Rome wondered who the new Pope would be. The "will of the people of Rome" was not a joke in that selection, and Cosimo had been courting that will with his military fame and his cultivation of certain citizens. Yet the will of the throne of France was not a joke, either, and he had set himself directly opposite to France. It was that stage in the selection when everybody had a candidate, and no churchman of Cosimo's eminence could be ruled out.

He had received unexpected support from the Bishop of Naples. The offer surprised him, for he thought the Bishop of Naples wanted to be Pope himself. "Next time," the Bishop said when they met secretly. That seemed to mean that he expected to outlive Cosimo, but then nobody supposes he will die soon.

Papal politics required stamina. There were dozens of deals to be made, dozens of secrets to be kept. It was not at all surprising that there were many meetings at night.

"Why must you go out now?" the boy demanded. "It is past midnight."

Cosimo wiped his hands down his exhausted face. "Picking a Pope is one of the deeds of darkness, my boy. There are others, as you will learn when you are older." He had received an invitation to a meeting; it carried the Bishop of Naples' seal. "Order out my bodyguard," he told his servant.

He looked down on the child, who had fallen asleep again. He touched the hair, which was the color of Johan's.

"The palace of the Bishop of Naples," he commanded.

The wind howled down between the buildings; in the decay of the Forum, dogs howled back at it. Cosimo walked with two torchmen and two handgunners ahead of him and two more behind, for Rome at night was as dangerous as a country road. They had only half a mile to walk, but he wrapped himself tight in his cloak and shivered in the wet wind before they had gone fifty yards.

Rounding the bulk of the Castel Sant'Angelo, he lost sight of his torches for an instant. The torches behind him cast his long shadow over the stones. Suddenly he heard over the wind the sound of hissing steam, and he knew without thinking that the torches up ahead had been doused in water. He backed against the wall and turned to look behind him, but the torches there were black, too, and the sound of their hissing reached him. *They had casks of water ready. Dear God, I am about to die.*

"Gunners! Gunners!" It was the cry of the battlefield. It sailed down the Roman wind like a pennon cut loose from its standard, and it found no answer but the receding sound of running feet.

He drew his daggers and waited to be killed. He was not afraid. Enraged that all his effort should come to this, but not afraid.

In the darkness, hands found his arms and then his throat, slashed it. His hamstrings were cut. His anger and his ambition and his passion to be great flowed out over the stones and were washed away, down into the Tiber and to the sea. His last thought was of the boy and of Johan, the two merging; the last words to bubble to his lips were, *Forgive me.*

An hour later, a young man entered the private apartment of the Bishop of Naples. "It is done," he said nervously.

"Break up his household."

"There is a boy there."

"Had he made arrangements?"

"The boy was to be educated and placed in the Church."

The Bishop of Naples shook his head. "Bury him. Not literally, my son. Put him away somewhere—somewhere far off. Apprentice him. I don't want Cosimo's bastard showing up in the Church in ten years to trouble my old age."

"It is done, eminence."

The Bishop was a glum old cynic, and he had actually rather admired Cosimo, for all that he had seen him as a rival. "What about the body?"

"They're burying it in the Forum."

"A mass has been said?"

"As you instructed, eminence."

"Good. Go now." Alone, he stared at the manuscript he had been reading, and then laughed. "It was the right thing to do. No man who trusted me is fit to be Pope."

CHAPTER TWENTY

SHE WAS THE AXLE on which the family turned. For three generations, she was its conscience and the center of its awareness. She was the iron link between a past whose history she made them learn and a future of which she alone seemed confident.

The boy named Mark grew up and became a gunmaker because she demanded it of him, although he would rather have been the trader his father had meant him to be. She held off her own rapacious brothers from gobbling him up, and she held off their creditors and their competitors until he was old enough to manage the business himself. Mark was the best of her sons, she knew, for all his bitterness and his black moods; the others wanted to be rich without working. Willem, already married in Novgorod when Rolf died, faded away from them, writing a letter back every year or two until one year there was no letter and they learned that he had died childless there. Carl married into a bank in Bergen and was swallowed up by it, though he and the banker's daughter he had married parted after only a year. Another son recoiled from Rolf's death into the priesthood, and the other left home at eighteen and moved from place to place, a wanderer without a calling. Her daughters moved away, as she knew they must—one into a convent, one into early death, two into marriages whose progeny ran out in another generation.

Mark married and had three sons and a daughter; one of the sons died of typhus when he was fifteen. Father and sons cordially disliked each other, perhaps because Mark was an unhappy man who raised them in unhappiness; yet they stayed together in the small gunworks he had put together because Elsbet—old Elsbet now—drove them to it. She was still their spirit and their axletree, though it seemed that as she got older and tougher, the descendants of Rolf got weaker and less vital, men who went on with their daily lives out of inertia rather than out of a passion to live. When Mark died, she picked the new head of the family and told him she was leaving him her dowry, the dowry that her father had cannily caused to revert to her if Rolf died before her. It had been her dowry that carried them through the poverty-stricken years after Rolf's death, and it was always her dowry that hung over them like a golden cloud.

She told all of them about the Father. In her head, there was a joining of Johan and her own father, crude old den Hoeck, and although she could keep them separate in her mind's eye, to all the others they became a single figure, a man more talented, more gifted with the hammer, stronger, wiser, tougher than they would ever be, a Titan whose guns were always perfect and whose every mold had poured without cracking.

"Well, there's one for the Father," Mark would say morosely when he made a good gun barrel.

"Aye, tell that to the Father," was what they said when they were disgusted or when they doubted something.

She settled them in Brugge, the City of Bridges, before Mark was old enough to decide for himself. She paid a bribe to the Mayor and a bribe to St. Eloi's Guild and another to the Founders' Guild, and it was part of her written arrangement with them that her family would make only "small engines fit to be fired by one man alone," and no cannons. She apprenticed Mark to a smith, and when he started his own shop, he worked mostly in iron, although now and then he founded a small weapon in brass or alloy if a customer wanted such a thing.

She never told them about the White Beast. Johan had told her of his dream and of the beast carved in stone over his doorway, but she kept that to herself. If the beast was seen again, she would take it as a sign.

The Fox held them together, and she waited. Through two insipid generations she waited, growing old, frail, lonely. She outlived her sons, outlived most of her sons' sons, lived to see some of their sons as men grown and turning downhill toward middle age. She was a hundred years old, and by that time her descendants had been making handguns in Brugge for sixty years. She was getting ready to die and she was still waiting, and she was afraid to die because she feared that the White Beast and the Father and the last remnant of the glory that had begun in Mouers would die with her.

Mark died at forty-five, victim of influenza. Of his sons,

only Piet stayed in Brugge. Hans went to Antwerp to work in another gunmaker's shop and died there, an alcoholic whose wife could stand him no longer and ran off with a tinker five years before he died; Friedrich went to sea at fifteen, came home at sixteen, and died there of typhus within two months. If Piet had hoped to have help from his brothers in living up to Elsbet's impossible demands, he was disappointed.

Piet married twice and lived to be fifty and dropped over at the forge on a hot summer morning, red-faced and already dying when he mumbled, "Take care of old Elsbet." His sons Jacob and Abraham were there to watch him die, and they were stupefied, because it had never occurred to them that their father would die before them and leave them to carry the burden of Elsbet's ambitions. Jacob was "not quite right," it was said; he wound up in the Cistercian house at Damme as an attendant on the brothers, a seemingly contented prisoner of the place who gave no sign of unease until he hanged himself one night.

Abraham was shrewd but short-sighted; he took his father's death as a ticket to freedom and ran off, to come back two years later like the prodigal son that he was, but to find that there was no fatted calf because the family was too poor. Now he worked the forge with help from a pleasant but rather stupid giant from the den Hoeck side of the family.

Piet had no other sons, and he had two daughters. One was Margit, flat-faced, merry and silly, who got pregnant before she got married and chased the man all the way to Maasdam, where he got on a boat for England and she became a whore, leaving the child on the steps of a church.

And Piet's other daughter was Trude.

"Trude is the best of the lot," old Elsbet would say sharply. Everything about her was sharp now, as if she had been filed down by time. Her bones showed and her skin was like a dried leaf, a network of fine wrinkles and blue veins. The bones in her nose pushed against her thin skin as if they might break through. Her face was a beautiful, foxlike skull covered with white silk, and her hair was thin and fine and pure white, like milkweed fluff.

"Trude is a good, good girl."

"Yah, but what's to become of her?" Trude's stepmother was a bit of a whiner, a big woman whom Piet had married from a kind of animal sympathy, for neither of them ever said much and they were both sighers and whiners and weep-

242

ers. She was sure she had been in a decline since his death and she was waiting for her own, she said, although she was ten years younger than her dead husband and had the solid look of a cow on grass. "What's to become of poor Trude, with no father and one brother a halfwit and the other a no-good?"

"She's the best of the lot. The Father would have liked her."

"Oh, you and that Father! Mother Elsbet, men must've been wonders a hundred years ago!"

Elsbet still had eyes that snapped and sparkled, eyes that showed her emotions, now that she was old and no longer had to pretend. In a way, she was the youngest of them, and like a girl she let her feelings show now. Her eyes were full of contempt, but there was pity there, too, as if she were an empress looking at a donkey with a bad foot. Sara understood the look, and she turned away, flushed, and began to knead bread. "If Trude finds herself the right husband, I'll promise her my dowry for her wedding portion."

Sara's face became crafty. "Yah, that dowry got more lives than a cat. It was Piet's, I thought, till he died." She punched the dough. "Your dowry is like that Margit's virginity; it comes up new every month."

"Trude will have my dowry if she marries right."

"How much?" Sara loomed over the frail body. "How much have you got, old woman?"

"More than you can imagine—and less than you hope for." Elsbet shook her head in sudden disgust. She was thinking how far down she had come—she, who had been the daughter of the richest man in Mons, daughter-in-law of the great Johan—to be in this little house, arguing like a peasant with a plump fool.

Outside the open door, beyond the henyard and the muddy gravel with its green mounds of goose droppings, past a wood-pile and a rundown little shed filled with charcoal, the ram-shackle building that housed the forge stood in a little field of high grass. It seemed all additions and afterthoughts, an unplanned building whose history was obvious. The original building had been a shed hardly bigger than a three-hole outhouse; off to one side of it now was a small storehouse for raw metals, and above it two rooms for apprentices, of which only one was needed now; in the other direction was the forge itself and the huge bellows, a pile of scrap and a wall covered with tools, and beyond it another addition of a lean-to shape for whitesmithing and the big grinding wheel that was driven by a half-collapsed windmill. There was also a room in the building where the den Hoeck cousin lived by himself, and there were empty rooms that had been needed in the more prosperous days of Mark's and Piet's management.

The pounding of hammers came from the forge, three of them falling in regular order with the heaviest blow coming first—*chink*, chink-chink; *chink*, chink-chink—as the man who led the barrelmaking gave the first stroke. That man should have been Abraham, last in the male line from Johan, but it was the journeyman cousin named Derek.

"It's finished, Derek. Let's rest."

"Nay, see the dints down that face, Master Abe; got to do her once more."

"Nyah, you're like God building the world, Derek; let be who's to notice?"

"Anybody with two good eyes." The journeyman put the barrel back into the fire to heat and gave the master a reproachful look.

Handguns had changed since Johan's day. Many were built now out of strips of iron wrapped around a mandrel and hammer-welded. Derek's barrels were octagonal or half-octagonal and half-round, the finished shapes coming from the grinding wheel. More noticeable was the way the barrel ended opposite the muzzle; there was no longer a hole into which the butt shaft fit, but an extension called a tang for attachment to a wooden stock. Guns were fired from the shoulder now, not from under the arm or even from the chest and the stock curved down from the tang and ended in a huge, clublike concavity into which the shoulder fit. And most important of all, guns had locks: Cosimo's crude pan had been moved from the left side to the right, and a gun-maker in Genoa had devised an S-shaped holder for a piece of burning cord called slow-match, so that when the shooter wanted to fire he moved the bottom half of the S, and it, being pivoted in the middle, dropped the burning slow-match into the pan of powder. There were even "snapping locks" now—that is, spring-driven slow-match holders that snapped the glowing cord into the pan at the touch of a tiller.

The locks were called "match locks," from the burning cord, and the best ones were made in Italy or in the part of Germany around Nuremberg. The guns themselves were no longer called hand-cannons—only somebody as old as old Elsbet called them that—but were mostly called "hook-guns" after the shape of the match holder, though the commonest name in most languages was the German, which became *hakbus* and *harkboos* and various other words more or less like it. Derek called it a harkboos.

"That's eight harkboos barrels, ain't it?"

"I guess. Twelve of the damned things to go. Yah, we'll never finish in time, Derek! Now, if we use the two old barrels that my father left—"

"Now, master, you know as well as me them barrels was bursted and reworked by an apprentice for the practice. Suppose they burst again, then where's the profit? Back they'd come on you, them and all the others, and there goes a contract for twenty harkbooses."

"Sometimes, Derek, you have to trust in Our Lord. I'll just have a look at those barrels."

"Ah, master—!" Derek blew out his breath in exasperation. When he saw the one apprentice grinning at the master's laziness, however, he cuffed the boy and set him to working the bellows at double speed. This apprentice was an irrepressible rebel, one of those perpetual adolescents who neither know nor care when they behave badly. He accepted his punishment without complaint and pumped himself into a sweat, and he was still pulling down the long oak lever and panting when he began grinning and jerking his head toward the open doors of the forgehouse.

"Well, what now, you puppy?"

The apprentice grinned and gave the bellows a terrific pull. He paused and leaned on the handle and whistled shrilly by pulling his lower lip against his teeth.

Derek looked out the doorway. There was Trude, blushing because of the whistle. At sixteen, she was old enough to marry and old enough to be whistled at, but she had had no real offers. For one thing, she was a big girl, as tall as many men and as broad-shouldered, yet she had the small head of the Fox and looked almost freakish because of it. Her face was pretty, if anybody bothered to look at it, and she had good hair and good teeth and big hands and feet. She looked as if she would make a good farm wife.

"You whistle again, pup," Derek growled, "and I'll beat you with both hands." She was his master's daughter and so deserving of respect, no matter what her father was like. It was supposed that Derek might have ideas about her himself, but Derek was a placid man who "thought he might marry when he was older," although he was already twenty-seven. It was all too risky in a world that was running pell-mell to

Doomsday. Most things, in fact, were too risky for Derek, and that was why he would always be a journeyman and not master of his own shop.

Still, he liked being with Trude.

"Morning, Trude."

"Yah, Derek."

"Pay that yapper no mind, Trude. He's a layabout; don't know why your father keeps him."

"Oh, because he can't get anybody else." Trude had an unnerving honesty, and that trait was not one that men were looking for in wives just then.

"Didn't see you here, Trude, till yon yapper started his whistling. Do something for you, can we?"

"I brought down a pitcher of cider for you." She made no move to hand the pitcher to him, however, but let it dangle from one big hand, which was crossed over her aproned belly. In truth, she was paying a great deal more attention to Sint Salvator Church over the way than she was to Derek. "But in truth, I come down here to watch the Italians," she said with the same dreadful honesty.

"Oh, at Sint Salvator's." Derek folded his arms and regarded the church. He might have been appraising its value, so carefully did he look at it. After much meditation, he said cautiously, "I hear they be painting a wall inside."

"A mural of the Pentecost."

"Aye." Derek looked judiciously at the church again. "They be from Italy," he said after some seconds.

"Firenze."

"Italy, I heard."

"Firenze's in Italy."

"Ah!" He spread his legs a little wider to get his whole body comfortable. "That's interesting to know, the name of a place in Italy." He frowned. "Of course, I know another place there. Called Genoa, where the gunlocks come from. This Firenze is near Genoa, is it?"

"I don't know. But they sailed from Genoa to get here to Brugge, so I suppose it ain't that far."

"Ah!" Staring at the church, he frowned terribly and began to nod his head. "Aye—aye—! There's still another place in Italy I know. Venice! That's in Italy, ain't it? *And Rome!* Well, it's wonderful what you know without suspecting it." He continued to shake his head. "Italy must be a big place, to have so many places in it."

There was movement next to him, and the apprentice's young voice, made soft, said slyly, "Morning, lovely."

Trude glanced at him without malice. "Good morning."

"Who you calling lovely, you layabout? Get back to that bellows!"

"I was only going to ask if her Italian had come out and waved at her yet this morning, is all."

"Well, divil a gunmaker you'll ever be, with your mind on Italians and your mouth full of 'lovelies'! Get back to the bellows!"

"But the barrel's ready."

"Well, keep it ready. Go pump till your arms fall off, if I tell you to!" Derek's lifted hand was threat enough. It was unfortunately true; this lazy, irresponsible jokester was the only apprentice Trude's brother could keep—like teaching like. "I better go see might he for once know what he's yammering about," Derek said to Trude. "Good morning, Trude."

"Morning, Derek."

Derek made a show of thinking the barrel was at the wrong heat for welding, although it was, indeed, ready. After some seconds, he pulled the iron out and began to hammer its irregularities, with the apprentice holding the mandrel in oxskin gloves; and while he hammered and turned, Derek turned and hammered in his mind the thing that the boy had said about Trude and an Italian. Italians were bad, was Derek's view of it; mostly they were bad because they were not from Flanders. They were thought little of in Brugge, which had its own painters, of whom it was very proud; that a church in the City of Bridges should commission a mural of the Pentecost all the way down in Italy made some people quite unhappy. Derek finished the barrel and put it aside to cool, not tempering it in a cool bath but letting it come to air temperature slowly to keep the iron soft, so that it would flex with the explosion of the gunpowder and not crack from being too brittle.

He paused in the deep shadow where he had gone to wrestle more scrap iron from the pile, and, standing close to the apprentice, he muttered, "Now what's this about Mistress Trude and some painting Italian?"

"One of them yonder."

"Well, I know where they are!"

"She talks to one of them a lot."

"And how would you know that?"

"Well, I got eyes."

247

"Yah, and you use them when you ought to be working you no-good!"

Derek made it his business to pass the big doors often and the third time he did it he saw Trude in the middle of the road, talking to a thin young man who was certainly not a local. On his next trip past the doors, he saw them there still; Trude looked more excited than he had ever seen her laughing and blushing, and the young man was drinking from the cider pitcher that was supposed to be for the forge workers. "An *Italian!*" he said with disgust.

It was his duty as a journeyman to tell his master, even so poor a master as Abraham. Abraham had no sense of duty, but he passed the information on to old Elsbet as a way of getting rid of it. Abraham felt good, for he had concluded that the two old barrels could be used to satisfy the contract for twenty harkbooses, after all, and that left him with only ten more barrels to make. Then he could go to stocking the weapons, which he did not mind, for he liked working with wood—the smell of it, the feel of a good sharp drawknife, the curl of shavings. He was not so pleased that Derek had used the news about Trude to give him a little lecture about being head of the family, and he had told the giant journeyman so. Derek sulked.

Abraham did not want to be the head of the family. He did not want the burden of Elsbet's tales of the Father; he did not even want her mysterious dowry, if that was the price for being head. The thought of supporting Sara and Trude and old Elsbet until his dying day made him physically sick. Worse yet, there was the temptation represented by his proximity to Sara, who was a big, tempting woman that he had had some very evil thoughts about. She had had some thoughts, too, he knew—he could see it in her shy smile, in the swing of her hips when she passed and in her hints of being in the house alone when everybody else was gone. Sara was his stepmother, and such thoughts were the next worst thing to incest, and incest was a sin—one more burden on his already weary soul. It all made him groan.

"Afternoon, Sara—Trude."

"Abraham!" Sara smiled and her hips twitched; her floury right hand went to the lacing between her big breasts. *Nice to have a squeeze of those, dear God forgive me for that thought; the world is full of nice squeezes, but this one's so close, forgive me!*

"Eaten your dinner, Abraham?"

248

"Oh, yah, ate my fill, thanks. Brought my own, Sara, as always. Where's Granny Elsbet?"

"It's terrible hot, Abraham, won't you sit?"

The kitchen, despite its being a half-cellar that was reached by steps down one side from the rest of the house, was the hottest place he had been in all day, hotter than the forge. It was baking day, and the brick oven radiated heat into the room as if it meant to turn the whole place into an oven. *Hell will be like that, if I go on thinking what I'm thinking.* "I've got to see Granny."

"She's laid herself down upstairs. Sleeping. Won't you sit to wait for her, Abraham?"

"No, I can't—got to talk to her now, thanks, Sara. Trude, you're keeping well, I hope. Help your stepmother and be a good girl."

He ran up the tiled steps. Seeing Trude, he had a horrible idea—suppose she got pregnant? *Suppose she was pregnant already?* The whole thing was in his head like an ache: The Italian would run off, Trude would be unmarriageable, he would have to raise the child and take care of all these women into the bargain, the responsibility would draw him and Sara closer, she would get her hooks into him, and then—

"Grandmother!"

Fully dressed, she was like a doll that a child had left on the big bed. He could have picked her up with one hand. It touched him that she was so tiny and so old and that she cared still about what happened in this difficult world. He was man enough to know that age was a burden to her and that she kept herself alive because he was unfit to head the family.

"Grandmother?"

Her eyes opened with a flutter. They stared at the ceiling. Her toothless mouth had been open in her sleep, the skin curled down over the gums without any appearance of lips. "What?" she said. "Is it Mark?"

"It's Abraham, Grandmama. I have to talk to you."

Her eyes focused and swung to look at him and she grunted. "Uh, it's you." She pulled herself up on one elbow and told him to put a pillow behind her. "I was dreaming," she said. "I was dreaming about your grandfather when he was a little boy. We were riding from Lubeck to Hamburg because our city of Mouers was on fire. It was all so clear!"

"I have to talk to you, Grandmama."

"There were soldiers. Mark was carrying a hand-cannon.

249

The old kind, you know. But there was no butt shaft, only the hole."

"Grandmama—"

"Quiet! Mark wanted to shoot, but the soldiers said no. 'That's all right,' one of them said, 'the butt shaft is coming.' Wasn't that a funny thing to have a dream about? What do I care for hand-cannons and butt shafts any more? But it seemed very important in my dream. It seemed to make everybody unhappy. 'The butt shaft is coming.'" Her lips became visible as purple-brown lines, pursed forward over her toothless gums. Her eyes, gray and huge, stared at Abraham. "Well, what now?"

Twenty minutes later, Abraham came out of the room, much relieved of one of his burdens. Passing by the kitchen, he put his head in at the top of the open stair and shouted, "Trude! Grandmama wants to see you!"

Trude wiped her hands on her apron and then took off the apron and draped it on a hook and came up past him. He flattened himself against the wall, catching her smell as she passed. *Something sweet, dried flowers, bread, whiff of sweat, woman.* He looked down into the kitchen and felt his knees weaken. Sara was turning hot loaves over to cool; from the top of the stair, he could see her profound cleavage and, when she turned, the swing of her skirt and her petticoats over her big rump. It was all too much. It was always the same—he got caught off guard. He pulled the door closed behind him and went down the stairs.

Next morning early, the old woman announced that she was going to Sint Salvator Church. The change in the day's routine vexed Sara, who seemed preoccupied, anyway. "Oh, go on," she said to Trude, who would have to go along with the old woman. "Go on and get her out of the way." When they left, Sara was looking out the yard door at the ramshackle forge buildings the way Trude had looked at the church.

Old Elsbet walked with a stick. She was bent over like a fishhook. She did not limp, but she moved very slowly. When she sat down, she clasped her hands over the top of the stick in a way that made her seem solidly planted and immovable. After she had prayed and crossed herself with holy water, she had Trude lead her along a side aisle to a place that smelled of dampness and of new plaster and of something sour that she could not name. There old Elsbet sat down on

250

a box that was covered with a paint-stained cloth, and she planted her stick and waited.

"Point him out."

"Yes, Grandmama." Trude was very nervous.

When her thin young Italian came whistling along the aisle with a bucket of plaster on his shoulder, he started to grin at her, but she gave him some signal—perhaps it was only her own seriousness—and he saw the old woman and became serious.

"That one," Trude said. Her voice trembled.

"He's skinny."

"He's very strong, though." They watched the young man swing the bucket of plaster down next to one of the master artists. Two of them were directing the plastering in preparation for painting a fresco in tempera; while the plasterers worked, another artist laid out a cartoon taken from the work of the *ultissimo*, the master of masters. In the cool shadow of the chapel, two assistants were working from pots and sacks of dry color, mixing up the day's paint. The *ultissimo* himself, a bushy-haired, hulking Italian with a fierce beard and a scowl, moved from one group to another, never satisfied with what he found in any of them.

"Does he speak our languages?"

"No, Grandmama."

"How do you two talk?"

"We—I don't know."

"Huh. Fetch me the priest of this place. Who is priest now?"

"Father Stanislas Boercken is here."

"I never heard of him. Fetch him anyway, and pray he not be a fool."

Father Stanislas came, short and only a little plump. "Can you talk to that Italian?" Elsbet said, pointing her cane at the master of masters.

"He understands slow Latin, Goodwoman."

"Bring him here."

Whether the priest would have dared to interrupt an Italian master for a younger woman was a question, but for old Elsbet, he never hesitated. The artist's eyes grew tiny with rage; he waved his arms and shouted, Italian exploding from his mouth like gunshots. Sitll, he came to her. Standing in front of her, he spat out Italian with such passion that tiny flecks of spittle shot from his mouth like sparks.

"What does he say?"

251

"I think he says that he does not like the interruption. The plaster is setting."

She swung the cane at the master artist. "You!" The man glowered at her. *"Parla tedesco?"* The accent was all wrong— she had not spoken Italian in sixty-five years—but the words were clear.

He put his hands on his hips and nodded his head rapidly. "Aha!" he said. "Aha!" He pointed his finger at old Elsbet and shook it rapidly in the air. He looked at the priest and at Trude like a man who knows that he has been tricked. "Eh? Eh?" He laughed bitterly.

Elsbet shook her head as he launched a new barrage of Italian. "No, no. *No parlo italiano!* Is he crazy, do you think? *Tedesco—tedesco—parla—parlo—*oh, shit! Talk Latin to him, father."

"What am I to say?"

"Say that one of his young men has compromised my great-granddaughter."

The master artist shifted instantly from anger to caution. The response was so smooth that she assumed he had met the situation before.

"He wants to know exactly what has happened."

"Tell him I am too gentle a lady to instruct him in such a subject."

"He wants to know what you expect of him."

"I expect him to come to my house for dinner."

"He is astonished."

"Tell him I want him and the boy who is bothering my great-granddaughter, no others. Ask him if he likes goose."

"He adores goose."

"Geese are fat in summer. Oh, well. Tell him we make good beer—such I have come down to, I talk of making beer like a housewife—and he can drink beer. If he must have wine, he must bring his own."

"He adores beer."

"He lies. Oh, well. Tell him his plaster is getting dry."

From the grating that screened the chapel's entrance, the *maestro* turned back and blew her a kiss; his whole manner had changed. A smile illuminated his face as if he were a man in love.

Trude was shaking. "He never asked which of his men it is," she said miserably.

"Do you think he doesn't already know? Goose, it's you we ought to cook for dinner. Take me home!"

Father Stanislas went with them to the church porch. Leaving, she dropped a groat into the poor box. With the condescension of a queen, she said, "You have a very nice church here, father. I will come again." A thought struck her. "I will come back and you can hear my confession. Eh? What an experience for you—the sins of a hundred-year-old woman!" She laughed and laughed and bent over her stick and went home.

Next day, and the day after, and the day after that, she was with Trude when the girl met with her Italian. She had not forbidden the meetings, to Trude's amazement; she even managed to do a little rough translating as the Italian words she had learned from Cosimo so very long ago came back to her. Her gray eyes followed their faces and their eyes. On the third day, the young man stayed a long time with them, and then the bearded *maestro* stormed out of the church and sent him inside and Trude fled, weeping. The Italian master took out a bit of red stuff and began to sketch old Elsbet as he tried to slow his Italian enough to talk with her.

"You are very beautiful, madonna. Understand me? Eh? *Bellissima?* I don't know the word in this wretched tongue." His hand worked without his ever glancing at the paper. *"La bellezza del tempo, lo crede?"*

He crouched before her on his knees. He was a man with no concern for forms, and he could crouch in a public road at the feet of an old woman and touch her face with his paint-stained hands and whisper *"Che bellezza! Che bellezza!"*

She licked her thin, purple lips. Her mouth opened as if she were trying to make way for words that would not come, until she was able to stammer, *"Molti anni—fa—"*

"Yes, yes, many years ago—yes?"

"Molti anni, fa, a—io—a—amico italiano. Giovane."

"A young Italian friend. A lover? *Amore?"*

"Giovane." She held out her gnarled hand at the level of a small child's head. *"Piccolo."*

"Aha, a little boy. And he taught you your Italian. What was his name? *Nome?"*

She started to speak, but then, with a motion of her hand, she seemed to push it all away. She returned to Flemish. "It was all too long ago. Everybody is dead. Understand, my beautiful man? All, all dead but me. *Morte,* eh?"

"Ah, si, morte. Eh!" He kissed her. When he got back to the chapel, the plaster was almost too dry to paint, but he scolded nobody. He seemed bemused.

*   *   *

They set a table up under the willow tree, where the cool air from the canal could blow over them and keep the insects off. The Italians came early and the *maestro* brought wine, after all—bottles and bottles of it, as if he thought there would be a dozen other guests. Abraham greeted him with the formality of a man whose sister had been compromised; the Italian responded with cautious gravity, as befits a man in a ticklish situation. Abraham had surprised everyone by speaking a rather pure Venetian dialect. He was a rolling stone who had come to rest in Venice for a while, it seemed.

"My name," the Italian master said in a very heavily accented Flemish, learned expressly for the occasion, "is—Bernardo Dorati." Derek and the apprentice grinned at his awkwardness, but when the apprentice began to hee-haw, Derek dug him with an elbow big enough to knock down a wall. Sara blushed, for Dorati had discovered her even while he was speaking, and his look was a very frank one.

"I—no speak—your tongue but—. Drink wine!" He gave a great shout of laughter and then looked at them as if in a rage.

Sara and Trude brought out small cakes, then cheeses and the breads from the week's baking, as well as egg bread and sweet bread made for the day. Old Elsbet sat in an armchair brought out of the house and looked them all over without saying anything. To her, it looked like a peasant wedding, yet she bore it silently; she had lived with peasants so long there was nothing more to be said. The food was devoured, the wine and beer drunk; people went to sleep under the willow tree, sprawled like farmers in haying time.

When the goose was produced and eaten, when Dorati had sung them two Italian songs to the young Italian suitor's lute, when Abraham was lying asleep in a field of grass and Sara had vanished into the house with Dorati only steps behind her, when Derek and the apprentice had taken the trestles back to the shed, the young Italian came slowly toward Elsbet. He had his sketch paper in his hand. Perhaps he hoped Elsbet was asleep so that he could go back to Trude, who was lying sadly under the willow.

"Signora?"

"Eh? Oh, come—*viene*." She knew now that his name was Francisco. She knew little else, and that is why she had told Trude to send him to her. He bowed very prettily to her, then

254

stood there, smiling a little, not so very ill at ease. "Signora, I want to ask—for I may, ah—make love to Trude."

The gray eyes never wavered. "'Pay suit to her,' I suppose you mean. Well. And if I say no?"

"Trude and I—already so much—close, eh?"

"Yes, too close, maybe, that's what I'm worried about. But if I say no, will you go away and not see her again?"

"Yes. I am a man of honor. Like my father."

"Who is your father?"

"In Brescia, he is a man of—of—solidness."

"Substance."

"Oh? Much respected. If he thought his son did not show respect to Trude, he beats me."

"Is he a painter?"

"Oh, no!" The young man laughed gaily. "He is gunmaker, like your Abraham."

The gray eyes narrowed. "A *good* gunmaker?"

"Oh, yes."

"Better than Abraham?"

"Oh, well—is not polite for me to speak."

"I want to know—is he better than Abraham?"

"Much better, signora." The young man looked apologetic. "He makes guns for the Duke di Milano, for great men in Venezia, Firenze..."

"How is he called?"

"He is Pietro di Brescia, but everybody call him Lazarino, little Lazaro, after his father."

"So you are Francisco Lazarino, eh? Why are you a painter?"

"I am not good enough to be painter, signora. Dorati says so. I am put to Dorati for two years to learn better the drawing so that—then—I, what do you say? I make the decoration of the guns. My brother Eddo, he will be a gunmaker, I will be the—the—"

"Engraver?"

"Yes, engraver! And to put scrolls on the wood, and pictures on the metal, and all that. And to plan the shapes of the beautiful guns for noblemen."

The old woman's eyes quickened. With an effort, she pulled herself up in the huge chair, her fingers like claws on the ends of the chairarms. *Can you make guns, Francisco?*

"Oh, yes." Now, he was not sheepish, but quite boastful. "Better than Abraham." He offered her the sketchbook, which

was made of sheets of very heavy paper bound with string
"I brought here my, ah, plans, drawings—"

"Designs."

"Yes!"

The pages were covered with drawings in red and black
crayon, rendered with an attention to detail. Many of them
were merely life sketches; many showed Dorati's commands
and corrections. Some, however, were almost doodles—scrolls
and cartouches, designs for the plate of a gunlock, scenes of
hunting that were clearly related to the gun. Page after page
turned without comment from her; suddenly, her hand came
down on one as the paw of a cat comes down on a wriggling
mouse.

"What is that?"

"Oh, is—idea. Yes? Like the gun, for the *arquebus*, but
new."

"Is it a gunlock?"

"Maybe. I don't know." Her shrewd old eyes had fastened
on a drawing that any gunmaker would have recognized as
a lockplate, seen from above and inside. At first glance, it
seemed not to be markedly different from the more advanced
locks coming out of Genoa—long and narrow, it had the same
sort of serpentine cock, made to swing toward the shooter in
firing—but examination showed it to be curiously different:
it had no slow-match, and there was a bizarre circular machine at the lock's middle.

"What is this?" she said almost angrily. "What is this?"

The young man looked helpless. He glanced toward Trud
for relief, but she was asleep. "In some places, signora, the
monastici—"

"Monks."

"Monks, they carry for making fires an engine, it has iron
and—*piriti*, I know not the word—like a stone—to scratch it
and make little, ah, fires, little—"

"Sparks?"

He had turned to another page, where there was a drawing
of the very fire-starter he was describing. It had a filelike
piece that rubbed over a chunk of pyrites. She looked at the
drawing of the gunlock, then at that of the fire-starter. She
shrugged and put the sketchbook away. "I am too old," she
said. "New things make my head ache."

"It is only idea," Francisco said sadly. "My brother Eddi
and I, we talked about it. I made the drawing here in Brugge.
For—thinking more clearly."

But she had forgotten about the imaginary lock already. She was looking far away, and her thin skin was wrinkled between her brows in a painful frown. "I want Trude to marry," she said as if to herself. "She is the best of them. But he must marry somebody to carry on what was started." She looked up at him. "Make me a gun. If it is a good gun, you can pay court to Trude."

"But—signora—I have not the tools, the, the—"

"Use our tools."

"But, signora—"

"Make me a good gun! Then you can *marry* Trude."

The young man moaned. He was nineteen. He had not looked at the reality of Trude, although when the old woman mentioned marriage, it seemed to him that that was what he had always meant. His father would be angry, for he meant to marry his son to an iron importer's daughter in Genoa; besides, he would think Abraham's gunworks a pathetic joke. Still, love is love, and to be young is to be courageous. "I love Trude, signora!"

"Then make me a gun."

"But—but— *oh, maladetto! Oh, che brutezza di—!*" He held his hands in front of him as if he cradled a globe there, the world of all his hopes. "All right, I will try! Oh, Trude—Trude!" He began to talk very fast in a mixture of Flemish and Italian; the gist of what he said very excitedly was that it was one thing to make a gun in his father's shop with the help of Eddo and two journeymen and six apprentices and half a dozen laborers, and another to make one here where the men would be more hindrance than help. Old Elsbet was not impressed by his complaints. She fell asleep.

Sara had just had intercourse with the bearded, fierce Dorati, her second man in a week, after an abstinence of four years. She was reeling with the wonder of it. Dorati was very pleased; when she put her clothes back on, he grabbed one of her ample buttocks and then began to undress her again. "Hey, hey," she kept saying. Finally she pushed him off and laced herself up very tight, making him laugh at her with delight. He followed her outside and leered at her as she got more beer and set out apples and pastries. Abraham shambled in from the grass and got quite drunk. It was a Sunday afternoon to remember, what with one thing and another.

For two weeks, things went on very quietly. Francisco was allowed to see Trude for fifteen minutes each day in Elsbet's presence. In the evenings, he could be heard working at the

forge. Abraham stayed away from Sara, who was gone from
the house much of the time anyway. Elsbet, noting the
woman's changed behavior, finally called Dorati to her, along
with Father Stanislas Boercken as translator.

"Messire Dorati," she said from her bed, "what are you
doing with my dead grandson's wife?"

"He says he doesn't know which one is your dead grandson's wife."

"The fat one!"

"He says he—um, the word is odd—he loves her with his
eyes."

"Eyes, indeed! It's his great cod he loves her with. Ask
him if she's been climbing out her window every night to be
with him until dawn. Tell him I already know the answer."

"He says yes."

"Huh!" Elsbet stared at Dorati. She was supposed to have
forgotten what sex was like, that coal carried between the
legs. "Ask him what he means to do about her."

The priest blew out his unshaven cheeks in dismay. "He
has a wife in Fiesole, he says. I told him he is a great sinner."

"I don't care about his sin, that's between him and you
and the Almighty. What does he mean to do about Sara?
She's a big, stupid cow—does he mean to break her heart?"

The priest and the artist whispered together as if they
were in the confessional. "He says he likes to have her near
him. He paints her picture, he says: I believe when he does
so, she is—unclothed."

"Will he support her?"

"Goodwoman Elsbet! You suggest an enormity! God does
not want these two continuing their sin."

"Neither do I. But if he wants to paint her naked and she
likes it, will he support her? Forget the sin part for now,
father; anyway, he can't paint and sin at the same time. Can
he?"

The two men conferred again. The priest flashed a grin
and then suppressed it; he glanced at Elsbet, and she guessed
that they were talking about her. "Well?" she demanded.
"What does the Italian say?"

"He says he wishes you were younger, and he would run
off with you and forget Sara."

"Ah, but I would not go! What about Sara?"

"He is only a man, goodwoman—weak, tempted. Sara is
a woman of good years; she must take some of the responsibility."

"How?" The little body came upright on the bed. "How dare he bring his big, beautiful face around here and say such a thing! He's a devil! Tell him I said that—a devil!" When she had calmed, she said, "Sara is a cow, and he means well, but he is careless. Tell him he can paint her all he wants, and he can sin all he wants—for me, only for me, I don't speak for God—but when he leaves, *she must marry somebody!* And the only somebody around here is my grandson Abraham. So, my handsome Italian *maestro* must see to it—and that includes paying for the dispensation so that Abraham can marry his father's second wife—what a tangle! When you think what idiots they are, you wonder why they bother. Ah, well. But you tell him, father—if Sara doesn't marry, I will send after him to Fiesole and have him excommunicated by the Bishop himself. And tell him that I know where Fiesole is!"

Dorati was unhappy, but he saw the wisdom of it; and anyway, he loved the old woman and he accepted her rather cynical terms. That done, Elsbet lowered her voice to that of a conspirator and said, "What about Francisco and Trude?"

"They are *not* sinning together, he thinks."

"Good. And the gun?"

"The boy works. He works so hard he is not getting enough sleep."

"Good! Maybe he will be too tired to sin with Trude. Now, how much longer will the *maestro's* fresco take?"

"Three weeks."

"Three weeks? Time enough—the Father could have made a cannon in three weeks, much less a little handgun. Good." She sank back. "Let me sleep now. Go away."

She was still waiting. Sometimes she thought she had been waiting for a miracle, but now she was weary and she was willing to die, and she gave up on the miracle and waited for Francisco to prove himself worthy. She watched Johan's and her father's dreams weaken and weaken from generation generation, trickling away through Rolf and Mark and Piet and Abraham, and now their ideal of a great gunhouse was nothing more than a few sheds under the trees of a city in Flanders. Trude was the Father's last hope. Not a miracle, but a hope. Better than nothing.

Francisco came to see her each day after her meeting with Dorati; no doubt the artist had told him to go. The boy looked hollow-eyed and years older, but he filled pages of his sketchbook with drawings of her—her veined hands, her finely

259

drawn old face. Dorati may have talked to him about th
beauty that surpasses time, too.

She told him all her stories of the Father. All except th
White Beast. She told him about hand-cannon and the sieg
of Karlsbirk and the ruin of Mouers.

"And my gun? How is my gun coming, Francisco?"

"Oh—well—"

"You have had almost four weeks. Anybody can make
plain gun in four weeks!"

"Is not a plain gun, Donna Elsbet." He looked bereft. "
decide to make the gun in my drawing."

She had forgotten it. Reminded, she was angry at th
audacity of what he had done. "But it won't work? *And the
you will lose Elsbet!*"

"Pardon, signora—forgive me, please, forgive. For this—
for you—I could not make just *a gun.*"

A little gleam of new hope flared up in her. His audacit
infuriated her—but was that not precisely what had mad
the Father great?

The making of the gun had become for Francisco what
quest had once been for armored knights. The barrel and th
stock could give him no trouble, but when he had come t
the decision to create his imagined lock in steel and brass
he had had to put his brain to its perfection as he never ha
in his life. When he saw how much more difficult it was tha
he had dreamed, he accepted Derek's offer of help. Derek wa
slow, but he was very steady, and he knew metal. They mad
a superb barrel together, a lighter and shorter one than an
that Derek had made before; then they made a lockplate o
thick brass that he would engrave later, and then he too
the time to make a model of his lock in wood to see how we
it would work. He had drawn the part that would functio
the way the stone in the fire-lighter did as a matchlock ser
pentine, but in the model that part became angular an
heavy in cross section and it no longer looked at all like
snake.

Derek played with the wooden lock like a child with a toy
"It's like a chicken pecking, Master Francis." Derek had go
over his suspicion of Italians when he found that they coul
make better guns than Abraham could. "Like a hen eatin
grain."

"A mighty thick hen."

"Well, a cock then. Peck!" He laughed. "Peck!" He pulle
the wooden piece back a third time and it broke just at th

pivot. He was humiliated, but Francisco was glad to learn where the weakness was.

They forged the serpentine—now called "yon cock" by Derek, and so called by Francisco for lack of a better name—out of hard iron, and a trigger and a piece for it to bear on, and then Francisco showed Derek how to forge and temper springs. They cut and filed and polished until all the pieces were made—and then Francisco tried to assemble his lock, and when it was almost together, pieces flew off and disappeared in the sawdust at their feet. Retrieved and forced into place at last, they bound, and the lock would not function.

The heart of the lock was a spinning circle of serrated steel that was meant to rotate against the pyrites clamped in the jaws of the serpentine-cock. But it was all too complex: the wheel had to be chain-driven, and the chain had to be pulled by a spring whose power was very nicely tuned. There were simply too many parts, Francisco believed. To an eye accustomed to the matchlock, it seemed impossibly busy—everything happened at once, the cock descending as the wheel began to spin, the little cover over the priming pan (meant to keep the powder in and the rain out) opening just in time to admit the sparks—all of it needing to be timed to a nicety and all of it set going by the single pull of a finger. In actuality, it never worked; either the cock swung down too soon and struck the pan cover, or the wheel spun and bound before the cock could lower the pyrites to it, or the cock did not come down far enough, or it came down before the wheel ever spun. Or the chain would slip its mooring and would snap.

"It won't work!" Francisco stood alone by the workbench with the parts assembled into a frozen mass of metal. "It won't work! To Hell with it!" He picked up the lock and threw it with all his force, and it struck the wall and bounded out into the late sunlight and hit the cobbled paving, to break into its many parts—springs flying, cock ringing across the stones, the wheel and its drive chain falling into a clatter of rubble. "To Hell with it!" He wanted to add *And to Hell with Trude,* but he knew guiltily that the fault was entirely his own, not hers.

It was almost evening, the only time that Dorati would give him to work on the gun. The barrel waited on the bench, beautiful in its simplicity, half-round, half-octagon, needing only the work of the engraving tool to show its full beauty. The stock, roughed out, lay nearby. It cried out for a lock, but the idea now of putting a matchlock into the recess of fended him. He had designed it to use the bulge of the whee housing of his new lock, and the line would be spoiled; a well, he had made the stock short, shorter than any match lock, perhaps dangerously short for the shooter's eye to com so near the smoldering cord. No, to put the matchlock int such a gun was repugnant—better to admit the failure an give up his quest.

He did not come that evening to sit with Trude and th old woman. When no message came, Trude sat by hersel "Go to bed," the old woman said when the sun was only hal a disc on the horizon.

"When it's dark, Grandmama." She sat on until the star were out. Elsbet lighted a candle and called her in.

Lunn, the apprentice, slept over the storage barn. He ha a room to himself, but the place was filthy and rat-smellin, and cobwebbed, and he was too lazy to clean it. His few clothe were scattered over the dusty floor like rags, and a dirty cu and plate with moldy crumbs sat under the bed.

Lunn had dreams of Trude's coming to his room at night Trude had never given him any reason for such dreams, bu adolescence has its own erotic logic, and it seemed to hin likely that she might come wriggling up the ladder to hin naked but for her shift, grateful for his skinny lust. In truth he was generous in his fantasies, for he included Sara an a woman he saw in church and several others whom he mad up in his head. They made the room quite a busy and bearabl place.

After midnight that night, he was still awake. The su baked the wood-shingled roof by day and the boards held th heat in their airless grasp by night. Yet in winter it woul be many degrees below freezing there.

He heard a sound like metal striking stone. *Trude,* h thought. Maybe she had thrown a pebble against the buildin to wake him. The thought that one of his fantasies was com ing true made him sick with anticipation. It also frightene him a little.

He rolled over when the sound came again. He saw gleam of light coming through the cracks between the board of the wall. It seemed to move. He raised his naked uppe body and put his eye to the widest crack and tried to loo down. There was a long, hooked shadow moving over th barnyard cobbles like a stain.

Ghoulies! he thought. His heart pounded. In his village

veryone believed in ghoulies. Ghoulies lived in the ruins
f old churches and stole dead children from their graves and
ut gold in the places of the corpses. If caught in the act, they
urned into women and tried to rip out men's throats with
oglike teeth.

There was an oath down below. This ghoulie spoke Italian.

Murderers, maybe, he thought. Lunn had fantasies on sub-
ects other than sex. *Or robbers. The Italians are robbing the
enhouse!* Lunn had a peasant's set of values and a peasant's
tore of suspicion.

He crept across the loft floor and down the ladder, naked
nd barefoot. He made ready to shout for help, seeing himself
lready as a hero who would be rewarded, perhaps with
noney, and certainly with Trude.

"Maladetto," he heard a voice mutter. Lunn's hand closed
ver the handle of a shovel; it would do well enough in the
ark for a weapon. He thought of its edge coming down on
ne robber's head. Another step forward—and he put his foot
n a piece of broken crockery and yelped. "Sweet Jesu Son
f God Almighty!"

"Nome de Dio! Chi e?"

"Keep off—I got a gun here—I can kill—"

"Shut your loud mouth. Is that Lunn? Shut up, peasant!"

"Shut up, yourself! Oh, my fuckin' foot—stand still, Ital-
ano, or I'll gut you like a bunny—oh, shit—"

"Eh, be silent, Lunn, it's Francisco. Hold up your foot—
ool—eh, blood—" Francisco had raised his lantern. He was
aughing, having an essentially positive view of the world;
) see a naked and rather starved-looking adolescent stand-
ng on one foot was comical to him. Seeing the blood, however,
e became more serious and made the apprentice sit down,
nd he got water from the farmyard well and bathed it and
andaged it in his own sash. Then Lunn, who had meant to
e the hero of thwarted robbery, helped him search the cob-
led yard for the remaining pieces of his gunlock.

"Why'd you ever throw the cursed thing away, then, hey?"

"I was disgust. *Pazzo,* eh?"

"What you want it for now, then?"

"I have a dream. In my dream, the gunlock works. You
ell nobody, yes—I look a great fool if my dream lies. It will
e our secret. I *am* a great fool, but better if nobody knows
ut me."

Lunn did not understand about quests and love. He was
onvinced that Francisco and Trude must already be doing

263

everything that he wished that he were, and so the onl
explanation he could find for the Italian's behavior was tha
he somehow figured to make lots of money from his gur
Winning a girl's hand with it was unimaginable.

Eight days later, Francisco laid an awkward bundle o
Elsbet's lap. His smile was beatific, grand; Trude, who ha
sat for nights waiting for him, looked woebegone and hope
less.

"Well?" the old woman said.

"It is very—hard?—no, rough—*rough,* signora." He looke
at Trude. *"But it works!"*

"Show me."

He unwrapped the cloth, his fingers so delicate that h
might have been lifting leaves away to reveal a flower.

It was a very peculiar-looking gun. It was only thirt
inches long, a miniature among guns. Where the matchloc
harkbooses were long and bulky in the stock, it was rathe
short and very slender, ending not in a wide-curved butt t
accommodate the shoulder, but in a ball of beautifully figure
walnut that was seemingly held by four bands of brass wir
like the fine wires of a birdcage. It seemed fragile in the stoc
and in the barrel, but the lock was so massive that it seeme
almost monstrous. The clean simplicity of the snappin
matchlock had been replaced by a bulbous lockplate an
hodgepodge of exposed springs and parts.

"This is a gun?" she said.

"The first of its kind, madonna. Next time, I do better."

"And it shoots?"

He moved the cock back and forth for her; he wound u
the wheel, for which he needed a quite separate part, a smal
wrench that he had in his pocket; he pulled the trigger an
the wheel spun and the cock pressed its load of pyrites dow
and sparks jumped. "For long a time, I tried to make it to
good," the young man said rapidly, winding it up again. "To
much doing everything, so I find I have to leave things fo
the hand to do, fewer parts, easier putting together—the par
cover, he's by the hand; the cock going back, he's by the hanc
But the wheel, it works—see, madonna?—so *fast!"*

He charged the pan with powder and fired it and a puf
of acrid smoke blew out as soon as the trigger was pulled. I
was faster than any matchlock ever imagined.

She made him take it outdoors where she could watcl
from her window. He had already proofed the barrel in th
forgehouse, and now he loaded and fired it four times for he

without misfiring, and then he came and leaned in her window like a gallant leaning in to enjoy the admiration of his lady.

"Well, signora?"

"It is good. I believe you are a gunmaker."

"It is a little graceless, and I will do better next time, but it is a real gun. And I will engrave it so beautifully!"

"Trude will thank God for your hard work."

"Ha, as for that, madonna, we must thank the white beast."

A clawlike hand closed over two of his fingers and their nails bit into his flesh. He was too astonished to complain.

"*What white beast?*"

"In my dream, signora."

"What dream? *What dream?*"

Her terrible earnestness frightened him. She was a fading old woman no longer. She could have been a devil, so intent was she on piercing to his soul.

"One night—madonna, are you well? yes?—one night, the lock did never work, I said, 'No good,' and I threw it away and—madonna, my hand—to the fields I went, to, ah, walk and so on, you know; I slept, I dream—this dream, it was—good—a good thing, pleasing—I am hunting, I have this very gun, comes now a white beast walking—walking, walking before me, I am glad, I am very happy, I raise the gun and I see it is this gun *but it works*, and I see all at once how it works, so simple!—and the white beast, he stops and waits for me, but I cannot kill him. How to explain this thing? It is—as if—the beast and the gun—they are the same, or—I cannot explain—"

"What kind of beast was it?"

"White—like a great horse, or a stag—I could not draw it, yet I know it was so beautiful!"

"Yes—*yes!*"

His eyes had been focused far away. He seemed to come to now, recovering from his dream. "You know this beast, madonna?"

"No, I have never seen it. But I knew—someone—who did. *Who was your father?*"

"Lazarino, son of Lazaro. That is all."

"And he? Who was he?"

"A man. From—I don't know, he talked of Rome— stories of being a boy, going to battle with a great man of the church,

265

he said—but I thought they were only stories. Signora, my hand is bleeding—"

"Marry Trude." She reached up and touched his face as if he were her lover. "Marry Trude. It is meant to be."

They were married five months later in Sint Salvator Church. The family Lazarino were resistant at first, but they gave permission when a letter came from the Fugger Bank in Brugge, assuring them that the bride's portion would exceed fifty thousand nobiles Florentine. The amount was hard to believe, but the source was unimpeachable.

Francisco was released from the rest of his term with Dorati, who sent a painting of the Holy Family as his wedding gift. From the groom's father and his relatives came gifts worthy of a wealthy merchant—carved chests, linens, gold cups, glasses from Venice, two bolts of silk damask. The gifts outshone the little house in Brugge, but Elsbet insisted that they be shown there. They had come by sea and by land, as goods and riches had been coming to Brugge for two centuries.

It was part of the marriage contract that the couple would live in Brugge and that the groom would take the old name of the bride's family, "to wit, Mouers or de Mouers or der Mouers as they are called, also Moors and *Mors* as is sometimes seen on their weapons of old, and by this name shall their children and their children's children be called, and Francisco will call himself the same and be Lazarino no longer." Nobody had put the word *mors* on a barrel since Mark had died, and he had done it out of bitter memory of his grandfather's part in the Herod play, putting the Latin word for "death" down as an ironic pun on the family past. Whether Francisco saw the pun, or whether his ignorance of German and Flemish made him naive, he took to himself the name of Mors, and so it appeared thereafter on his beautiful guns—the first of which was the one he had made for Elsbet, now engraved with a scene of a lone hunter facing a strange magical beast.

The painter Dorati went away as he had said he would, and Abraham, looking sad but resigned, married Sara as he was supposed to do. Dorati left behind him a record of his presence and of his part in their lives; in the crowd behind the Apostles in his fresco of the Pentecost they could all be seen, as if the event had happened right there in Brugge that very year. Elsbet was there, gazing toward Heaven with clear gray eyes, beautiful now even to those who were not artists; Trude and Sara and Abraham were there, and even Derek and Lunn the apprentice, who had just run out of the door of the forgehouse to see such a sight, a hammer still in his hand. And there was Francisco, too. He seemed only that instant to have lifted his eyes from the curious object in his hands—a gun, too short and slender to be a matchlock, its butt short and bulb-ended, its lock oversized and awkward and clumsy, as the first thing of any kind must be.

A month after his wedding, Francisco Mors went to the Fuggers' bank to claim his wife's bridal portion. Old Elsbet was still alive, but fading now, a light going out; she had written out a paper giving him title to the famous dowry that had carried the family through three generations. He expected a sum of money that would let him build a proper shop for the making of good guns.

The Fuggers gathered. They fussed, They consulted books. They took him to their inner chambers and gave him dinner, and they sent for two lawyers and an accountant, and when a stunned Francisco emerged, he knew only that he was a very, very rich man. The famous dowry was a hard reality, multiplied by interest, added to by shrewd investment, left like a fertile field to reproduce itself and grow and nurture. Elsbet had not waited for him idly.

CHAPTER TWENTY-ONE

FROM GERMANY, like the ghost of war that the family had long before tried to escape, the unrest of heresy came hunting, and, after it, the chaos that came to be called the Reformation. What had happened to Karlsbirk and Mouers became the fate of cities from the Rhine to the Oder and beyond; what had happened to Jan Huss and those rebels who had acted in his name now happened to hundreds of thousands. War, rapacious and insatiable, tramped across Europe, taking as its excuse now not the accidents of boundary and language but the quirk of religious belief. So-called Protestants lived

next door to men who called themselves Catholics, and they
killed each other; cousins fought, then brothers; cities fought
each other; duchies and baronies attacked each other; kings
fought against kings, and men and women and children died
and died and died. The ones who were left looked in stupor
at a landscape made numb by war. Men said it was the end
of the world; they prayed that it was the end of the world,
but it went on, and on, and on.

It was a good time for gunmakers. It was a good time for
mercenary soldiers, for they were in great demand—until
they were killed—and the pay was good—until they lost a
leg or an eye or a head. Europe was stirred around as if with
a stick; in the mix, Italian mercenaries wound up fighting
on the Baltic; Swiss were spun into Swabia; Bavarians tumbled into Denmark; all of them were whirled and buffeted
and dashed across the land in senseless motion; and when it
seemed that the wars might end at last, the mercenaries went
on the march for the sheer deviltry of it and stirred things
up again. These were the Landsknechts, the superb fighting
men whose allegiance was not to any monarch, but to war
itself. Homeless, their camps were their territory; whatever
they hungered for, they ate; what they conquered, they conquered for others.

Guns changed. The *arquebus*—hakenbuch, harkboos, ark-
bus—remained the principal weapon of military gunners.
The matchlock was still the mechanism; it was cheap, efficient and deadly enough for its purpose. The Landsknechts
wore cartridge bandoliers, on which individual charges could
be hung in containers. Corned gunpowder became common,
although not for cannon. Firearms were still at the mercy of
the weather, and on wet days men killed each other with
things they could hold in their hands.

Where there was peace—those islands in the stream of
war—men shot birds and game with matchlock guns. They
shot ducks on the water and they shot deer that were driven
into pens by servants. They occasionally shot bears that were
cornered by dogs. Kings and landed noblemen began to see
the wisdom of limiting the use of guns for such purposes, for
not only did they permit a greater slaughter, but they also
accustomed common men to the use of weapons that were
cheap and far easier to learn the use of than the longbow.
Laws were passed, but they might as well have tried to outlaw
the broom.

In Brugge, Francisco Mors made better guns than Abraham or Piet ever had. He built more guns like the one he had made for old Elsbet, too. His father and his brother Eddo saw the possibilities of that crude wheel-lock, as it was called, at once; within a generation, the fine wheel-lock pistols coming out of Brescia were the best in the world, and not to be equaled until a few began to come out of Germany.

For Francisco, the making of guns was not a matter of the perfection of the parts but one of perfection of line and decoration. More artist than technician, he engraved and chiseled fine weapons as no one in the Low Countries of his time. Before he was forty, the King of France owned a pistolet by Francisco Mors, engraved, blued, inlaid with gold, with a stock of select walnut inset with ivory scenes of a subject that was almost a Mors trademark, the pursuit of a white stag through a forest of sheer magic. The Duke of Burgundy, who kept his court at Brugge, owned several Mors guns and gave a half-sized hunting wheel-lock to his son Jehan when the boy was nine. When the burgesses of a German city wanted to present a gift to the mercenary captain who annually collected tribute from them, they chose a Mors wheel-lock long gun.

Thus, as Francisco and Trude grew older, the world demanded guns—war guns, peace guns, beautiful guns, plain and deadly guns. Somebody discovered that slightly spiraled grooves on the inside of a barrel would make a gun shoot straighter and harder, and a few rifles were made, but they were brutally expensive and too slow to load for military use. Rich men wanted wheel-locks because they were clean and lovely things, capable of being made small and light enough to carry on the belt or the saddle, but they were expensive and quirky, and when dirt or the grit from the pyrites got into their works, they were useless.

Francisco made the dying gunworks a place of importance. He kept Derek as a journeyman and Abraham as nominal yardmaster, but Abraham got as weary of authority as he did of Sara's scolding and he went away again. Lunn the apprentice was turned out after six months for laziness; he became a tapboy in a tavern. Two Brescians were brought in to make locks, and other journeymen and apprentices came as the reputation of the house grew. Francisco remained the artist who finished the guns, and he demanded perfection, a noble ideal in any craft but one that does not make a man rich. It was good that he had Elsbet's dowry, for his superb weapons lost money for him all of his life.

Francisco sent his son Thaddeus to Brescia to study lock
making when the boy was fifteen, just in time to get him ou
of Brugge before the Vatican threatened the city with ex
communication for holding King Maximilian as its hostag
there. The town burgesses—of whom Francisco was by the
one—defied the threat, and the Pope sent an army. Maxi
milian made concessions and the burgesses gave him up, an
then he reneged on his promises, and the men of Brugge wer
embittered. Theirs had been a great city—trading partne
of Venice, famed for its beauty, seat of the Hanse wool stapl
and the Fugger financial empire, home of master craftsmer
of all trades.

Within a dozen years, Brugge fell from its place. The trad
ers of the Hanseatic League moved their headquarters, leav
ing only clerks in Oosterlinge-Plaats; the court of the Duke
of Burgundy pulled out of the Cour des Princes and left thei
palaces to the wind; the Fuggers withdrew to Antwerp. Per
haps worst of all, the Zwyn silted up, and Brugge had to face
a reality in which ships from the sea could not sail up to its
docks.

Francisco's and Trude's was a happy family, itself an is
land of peace in the turmoil of generations. Loving, close, the
liked each other's company more than that of anybody else
Until their three boys were grown, their house was the center
of their lives. Francisco taught them his ideals and tried to
teach them his art, but none of his sons was an artist. Perhaps
they were too happy or too placid; perhaps the times were
wrong. Weeping as he did it, Francisco sent his sons off to
expand their knowledge of the trade in other houses, and
then he encouraged them to settle away from Brugge, which
was not a place any more where so many craftsmen could
find trade. Thaddeus went to Dordrecht, Matthew to Ghent
young Marcus to England, where he meant only to spend a
year and where he fell in love and married and decided to
stay. Trude's and Francisco's daughter Pia was widowed at
twenty and entered the Ursuline convent and died there, a
very old woman; Hulde married a painter from Memling's
studio and spent the rest of her life wondering what he was
doing on the trips he made to accept commissions. Still, she
had five children.

The borders of the empire were pushing closer to Brugge
too. Fear of that old repression still lingered, even after Els
bet's death. When Francisco and Trude died and were buried
in the cemetery of Sint Salvator, only Hulde was left i

Brugge; her son Klaus became a painter like his father, and a wanderer, too, and one day he wandered off eastward into Germany's wars and was lost, except for three paintings in a church in Lubeck that were thought almost intolerable for the reality of their scenes of the Crucifixion. Hulde's daughter Matilda had only one eye after a childhood accident, and she married a farmer from beyond Damme; when she produced no children and the land produced no crops, they settled into a bitter life on the edge of the salt marshes that lasted until a troop of Protestant mercenaries came through on their way to the wars and killed the husband for his horse and drowned Matilda in the silty Zwyn.

Thaddeus was making pistols almost as fine as his father's, lavishly engraved and chiseled, but without that touch of genius that separates greatness from excellence. He used the name Mors on his pistols, with a skull below it; the name without the skull appeared on the long guns of Matthew of Ghent, and, because he made long arms in quantity for military use, he became the more famous of the brothers. He produced a rifle now and then, but they were not as good as German rifles; he was best at plain, rather old-fashioned harkbooses or their oversized cousin, the caliver, a gun five feet long that had to be fired from a forked stand like a small cannon. Matthew de Ghent had five journeymen and eleven *manoeuvres* and four apprentices, and he made good, plain guns in great quantity. He had no sons and no daughters, and when he died of blood poisoning at forty-three after a barrel exploded, he left a wife still young and rich enough to remarry within two years. And thus, although the name Mors continued to be stamped on some guns, they were not his, and in time the men who bought them knew the difference, for the quality declined as his widow put the business out to farm to anybody who would rent it and meet her price.

Marcus learned English and stayed in London to work for His Majesty Henry the Seventh and then for his successor, Henry the Eighth, King of England and Ireland and, after his staunch defense of the Church against the impieties of Martin Luther, Defender of the Faith. The young King was a great connoisseur of weapons of all kinds, often the more odd the better, and he delighted in the breech-loading little guns that Marcus set in the center of battle shields for him. Marcus was called "his maj^ties gonner" in the rolls, and several "gonnes de fer, de latten &c." were of his making; he kept a forge and a foundry within the walls of the Tower of

London itself. In the wardrobe accounts of those years, he was listed variously as Maccus Mars, Marks Marris, Mark Morris, Morrice, Morse and Mors, depending on the taste for spelling of the clerk. His sons preferred the spelling Morse, but again, clerks of churches and public records spelled the name in several ways: the one who became secretary to Cranmer was called Ralph Morrice, while his brother William was imprisoned for heresy but released under Queen Mary; Christopher was knighted and became master of ordnance as Sir Christopher Morris; two later descendants of Marcus became Jesuits, and one was hanged at Tyburn; but, almost certainly, none of them was the satirist who called himself Roderigo Mors and who was banished by Queen Elizabeth.

There were in England wandering tinkers and country blacksmiths and itinerant gun-menders named Morse and Morrice, too, and they trickled in latter years from Marcus's line; and a manufacturer of fishhooks recommended by Walton in the third edition of *The Compleat Angler* was a Morse of that line; and, although they did not use the death's-head mark or the name Mors on the things they made, they did, as the family liked to say, "run to metal."

Jan Mors of Dordrecht, son of Thaddeus, was as prolific as Rolf had been, but the very opposite in his stiff chastity outside marriage. Married three times, he sired seven sons and six daughters; four of each sex lived to be adults, and every one of them suffered from their father's grudging and narrow-minded pietism. He was a Puritan before there were Puritans; he demanded of the world a moral rigor that would have done credit to a band of hermits in a desert but was too much for ordinary men and women. With the whip of his morality, he drove his children from him as if they were hungry dogs who had invaded his chaste house in the night—Piet and Koop to Amsterdam, Grete to the arms of a strolling actor, Jan to sea, Maria and Trude to marriage beds before they were fifteen, Jaclyn to the Protestant commune in Leiden, and Karl, then only eleven, to a rootless delinquency that washed him up on the shores of war when he was fourteen. From cook's helper to a Landsknecht company, he advanced to common soldier, to sergeant, to provost, captain, aide-de-camp to a king and at last to himself—Karl-Friedrich Mors, whose company carried his death's-head banner eastward through Prussia and Silesia and down to the Eger and the Elbe as if he were seeking out the grave of old Johan to meet with him on death's ground. Death was his profession, orture and maiming his avocations; like certain other soldiers to the east, he acquired a reputation for impaling his enemies on stakes. He was a sadist and a sometime sodomist, one who took both men and women with utter casualness and pursued sensuality with only one emotion—anger.

A Protestant because his father was a Catholic, Karl was hated by the papal forces, whose chaplains went further and declared him a witch or a creature of the devil. When he was twenty-seven, they surrounded him outside Lutzen and took him alive, although he killed eleven before he was captured. He was tried in the presence of the Bishop of Magdeburg, disemboweled while still living, and burned at the stake. The story that, after the burning, his sooty skull rolled down the street and bit the Bishop's mistress in the left buttock is pure fabrication, although the accounts of his singing a filthy mercenary marching song while he burned are quite true.

Of all that bitter pietist Jan's children, only Piet and Koop made guns after they left their father. They set up a meager shop in Amsterdam on borrowed money, for Jan had kept all of what was left of Elsbet's majestic dowry, and he finally left it to the Church for the endowment of a glorious colored window in his perpetual memory—which lasted only until the Protestants ran through the city, smashing everything in which they could detect a trace of Romishness. Piet and Koop tried to reproduce the elegant wheel-locks that their grandfather and great-grandfather had made, but they had no way to acquire the skills. Their father was still making guns and still using the name and the death's-head mark, and he went to court to forbid his sons from using either.

The two brothers, impoverished, disinherited, cut off, split from each other over the same madness that had split the world. Koop remained a Catholic; Piet broke away.

Koop Mors took ship for Scotland, because there was a market for gunmakers there, and too many of them already in Amsterdam. It was said that they made strong liquor there, too, and he valued that. At the head of the Firth of Forth, he found the little city of Stirling, the seat of the King of Scotland for part of each year. Where there was a king, there were little nobles; where there were little nobles, there was killing. Koop settled in Stirling.

Koop married, drank *usquebaugh*, built plain guns, and died of an alcoholic insult to the brain when he was forty-one, having drunk off a quart and a half of whiskey in four hours and fallen down senseless, never to stand again.

273

Koop's wife was only thirty-five and saw no reason to sta
in Stirling, and so she went back to her relatives in Cupar
telling her fifteen-year-old son that he was welcome to com
with her if he wanted, darling, but she was just too tired ou
to go on with it there. The boy, who was as sober and practica
as his father had been wild, stayed in Stirling and made gun
until he was an established, quiet, very serious old man o
nineteen, who wrote three letters a year to his mother's pries
so that he would read them to her, and who decided almos
cold-bloodedly that both he and the business would be bette
off if he had a wife. He wrote to his old Aunt Maria in Hollan
for she, being far older than his father, had taken care o
that renegade as a child; and Aunt Maria sent him her grand
daughter Katrin almost by return boat—or, at least, afte
the shortest possible of delays for the posting of banns an
the arranging of a contract.

Kenn Morse (for so the Scots spelled his name) had littl
but his father's tools and a basic sense of decency to offer hi
second cousin Katrin, but it was enough, because Katrin wa
a woman of wit and practicality, almost a throwback to ol
Elsbet. And they prospered, at least as much as a couple coul
prosper who had little else but honesty and courage and eac
other—and a set of tools, and a basic knowledge of how t
make plain guns, and three wooden chairs, a table, six spoons
two knives, two plates, two real Venetian wineglasses (on
cracked), a washtub, a bed with a broken leg and two slat
missing, and seven pounds three shillings Scottish—and a
old wheel-lock carbine that had come down in the famil
from God knew where, and that had beautiful engraving an
a comically crude old lock and a lengthy inscription in Italian
which they could not read.

"I'll fix the old thing up," Kenn Morse said. "Maybe it'
make a good thing to hang up for a sign."

"It's a funny wedding present," Katrin said in Dutch. Sh
had been married for three days. She had neither friends no
relatives on this side of the North Sea, but she had come wit
her broken furniture and her gun and her wedding clothe
and she had been left on the dock like lost property. "Ou
grandpapa set great store by it, Mama said."

He hefted the gun. "It's an odd one. Still, it will shoot,
suppose."

He never did hang it up for a sign. He repaired it an
fired it, finding it uncommonly accurate and very well-bal
anced. He was tempted to replace the lock with the new
274

invention that had come from Holland and Italy, a device that the Dutch gunmakers called a *shnaaphans,* but some sense of violation kept him from doing it.

"We'll hang it up," he told her. He wanted to reassure her. She seemed so frightened and so alone that he tried to reassure her a great deal. "You can frighten off anybody that comes unwanted," he said. She smiled, and it was he who was reassured.

The old gun helped them to know each other, for it gave them something to share besides their loneliness. It even got them into bed together at last, three weeks after they married, for they talked about the newly repaired gun one balmy evening so much that they sipped too much beer and lost some of their common inhibitions, and with those, their common virginity.

She bore a daughter, whom they named Maria. The child died. A second died a year later. A boy baby lived long enough to be baptized Martin Morse before he, too, was buried. Katrin wanted no more babies. The deaths were her fault, she said, and she went into an ugly depression that made both their lives hellish for two years, and when she became pregnant again she said she would kill herself. Kenn, who loved her now with a stubborn and abiding love, would not allow her to do such a thing. He made her stay in her bed, and he cooked her meals, and when she wept and said she was no good, he held her and kissed her.

"You're my own wife," he said softly. "God sent you to me. You're my own wife, and I'll take care of you."

"I'm no good," she whispered. She sniffled and had to laugh a little. "It was not God sent me, but my grandmother Maria."

"There, that's better, to see a smile." He held her away so that he could look at her. "When I'm sick someday, you'll take care of me, eh? Aye, that's what you'll do. And I take care of you now, and so all's even."

He brought the midwife in a week early and made her live in the house, while he slept in the outhouse that served him for a forge. He worked at his guns and kept to himself, and several times a day he went in and looked at the midwife, and she shook her head and looked grim. And then in the dark hours of a morning long after midnight, he felt his shoulder being shaken, and there was the midwife standing over him, looking grim.

"It's started," she said. "Your baby's on its way."

CHAPTER TWENTY-TWO

IT WAS A SHORT LABOR, made easier still by the measly size of the baby, a tiny thing of only five pounds with the wizened and sour face of an old weasel. Still, it was born alive—and it stayed alive.

"Oh, it sucks so greedy!" she exclaimed when she first nursed it. The words were a cry of glee, not a complaint. On her shapely young breasts, the weasel looked like something the bad fairies had substituted for the big, healthy baby that they should have had.

"He's a bit of a runt," Kenn said carefully. He said it only after she and the midwife had made a joke about it, for fear he would depress her again.

"Aye, but our own—and alive, Kenn, alive!"

They called the weasel Jan, which became John in the parish register. He grew into one of those children who are secretive and moody because they are sickly: pampered by his mother, he was never quite the kind of son his father had assumed he was to have. Kenn had never thought out what the alternatives to a healthy child might be, and in his mind he had always pictured quite conventional scenes of father and son as companions, climbing the hills beyond Stirling and fishing in the streams where farmers let him fish now. And here was the weasel, an unattractive, undersized child who had no interest in fishing and who might be up to anything in his secretiveness.

"What you been doing, Jan?"

"Nothing."

"Can't do *nothing* all the time."

"I can."

He had a narrow, impish face, and he smiled slyly at things that amused nobody else. He had a mean streak, too; his father did not see in it a deeply inquisitive quality that happened to wonder about such things as touching live frogs with a burning twig or sprinkling gunpowder on a kitten. To he boy's credit, he never did any of these things more than once, but once was more than enough for his straightforward father.

"The boy's possessed, I think sometimes."

"He's moody, Kenn. Let him be."

"Moody! He's fair daft!"

"He ain't like other children. Let him be. He's sickly."

"Oh, aye—that's the excuse for everything, ain't it!"

She had no more babies. Kenn thought it was because of some problem with the boy's birth, and blamed him. In fact, she wanted no more children, although she did not tell him that. She asked the midwife how to keep from getting pregnant, but all the woman said was, "Cross your legs." She tried to abstain, but she loved him too much. So, luck and a certain amount of care, and two visits to the witch-woman in the hills above town who knew how to abort a fetus, kept her childless.

The boy helped his father in the gunmaking when he was old to. He could read and write early, and so, whenever there were no more than thirty seconds when he was not needed, he would be writing or reading some black-letter book borrowed from the priest, or staring into a dark corner, his lips working, so that they knew he was telling himself a story, of which his rich imagination seemed to have unlimited store.

"What're you *doing*, Jan?"

"Nothing."

"Y'are, I see your mouth moving, you're storytelling yourself."

"Oh, yes."

"Y're supposed to be working that bellows."

"You said I was to rest."

"Yes, but—! Ah, if you can't do the job y're asked, go to yer bed!"

And the boy would go, without complaint and without any grudge; in bed, he would continue his story. Usually, this was an unending adventure in a place he called Darkland to himself—a place of peculiar people, pygmies and dark-skinned people and giants, of magic and constant peril. In Darkland, he was heroic.

He had first taken the old wheel-lock apart when he was six. Not quite able to put it together correctly, he had kept the two parts left over and had hidden them under his floor. Kenn, finding that the gun would not work, was angry. The boy lied and said he had never touched it. A year later, he

277

took it apart again and put the missing parts in correctly
easily able now to unravel the mystery of the lock. When
Kenn took it down from the wall and found that it worked
he was, to the boy's surprise, angrier than ever.

"Did you do this?"

"No, sir. Do what?"

"You done something to this here old gun!"

"Done what, sir?"

"I ought to lather you one—!"

Whenever he raised his hand, Katrin warned him off, and
like the protective goose who shelters the brood under her
great wings, she put the boy behind her.

"He's turnin' into a mama's boy, Katrin. For his own good
give over a little!"

"He ain't strong."

"Katrin, he won't be strong as long as you protect him.
Let him take his lumps like the rest of us."

"He's sickly. Let him be."

Jan could take the wheel-lock apart and reassemble it
faster than Kenn could. With tools stolen from his father's
bench, he filed the parts down and made it work faster and
better—almost too much so, for the trigger was fined down
to a hair-touch. The change was noted by his father.

"Did you do this now, Jan?"

"No, sir. Do what?"

"By God, you little devil—!"

"Mama!"

"Let him go, Katrin! I'm going to lambaste his ass from
here to Leithwater! Look what he's done."

"I didn't! Mama!"

"All right, you lying little sneak! Keep it! It was your
mother's and mine for our wedding, and damned little enough
we got, but it's yours now, for you've wrecked it with your
lying and your meddling in other people's possessions! You
little devil!"

Yet the boy could delight his father—enchant him, almost.
He had a fey imagination that could invent stories about
anything, and an antic sense of humor that saw anomalous
meanings in serious scenes.

"You know what yon saint is saying?" he said of a particularly lurid depiction of a saint stuck full of arrows and
gazing heavenward with longing. "He sees a bird the painter
didn't show, and he's saying, 'Go ahead—everybody else
does.'"

At eleven, the boy walked a curving path between dislike and delight in his father's heart. Neither of them was very happy. Kenn Morse worked fourteen hours a day, six days a week, and he worried every hour of every day about money. His son lived much of his life in Darkland and felt rather distant from both father and mother, not because of their lack of love for him, but because of his own oddity. He believed that he was different from them. He lacked their strength, their robustness, their willingness to go at life directly.

"I think he's meant for the church," Katrin said. "He could go to that choir school in France that Father Dungess told me of. He's got a fine little voice for singing."

"Maybe, maybe." Kenn rubbed his jaw. "But you know, he's going to be a good craftsman, for all his dreaming. If only he was more of a—more of a *boy*."

While the court were at Stirling, the wilder Scots of the Highlands came down and paid their homage in almost barbaric ceremony. Some of them were true nobles, wealthy, with courts of their own; others were hardly more than tribal chiefs, with followers but one level above the shaggy sheep that grazed the hills. They informed the boy's idea of Darkland, for they were wild and mysterious people, violent and narrow-minded; they became his villains, the models for his ghouls and harpies. Yet they prized good guns, especially good pistols with the new *shnaaphans* lock, which combined the efficiency of the wheel-lock with the cheapness of the matchlock. Crude as the early *shnaaphans* were—called snaphaunces in Scotland—they were functional: the cock swung away from the shooter and struck a piece of steel on a pivoted arm, the flint in the cock's jaws sending a rain of sparks down into the pan of powder that waited below. The problem that had so vexed Francisco a century and a quarter before had been long since solved on the wheel-lock, and the improvement was carried over to the snaphaunce, so that the cover on the powder pan was swung out of the way by the same force that activated the cock. The lock even had a double safety factor: the steel could be swung all the way forward, putting it far out of reach of the cock so that no spark could be struck, and the cock itself could be left in the forward position, inert. It was an efficient lock without the many moving parts and the quirks of the wheel-lock. On the pistols that the rough Highlanders came to prefer in pairs, it was part of a deadly little weapon.

279

Kenn Morse made his pistols with long, quite straight, very flat stocks, with a fishtail flare at the butt below the hand. Some of these he decorated with brass; others were left plain, to be sold more cheaply. The pistols had no trigger guards, the safety of the lock itself being trusted to prevent accidental firings. Above the trigger, the stocks were given clean, angular lines, so that many of his pistols were as severe as the climate in which they were carried. At the breech of each barrel, he put *Mors* and the death's-head; on the little fence that blocked the outward side of the pan, he put the date of manufacture. The wild Highlanders came to him out of preference, and then stood uneasily in his shop, long-haired men with restless eyes who looked as if they would have to get into the outdoors soon or die.

"How much for yon gun?" more than one of them asked, seeing the ancient wheel-lock over the fireplace.

"You must ask my son; it's his."

The boy would look up slyly and would say, "What is it worth to you, sir?"

"How much you askin'?"

"I've got a man coming up from Leith to look at it, special, on Saturday. He's offered me three pounds ten," the boy lied.

"So much as that!"

Once one of the savages offered him four pounds for it.

"Alas, sir, I couldn't take it."

"Why not?" The man glared madly. Like all the others he smelled, but more rankly because it had been raining, and his woolens gave off a rich mix of garbage and unwashed underclothes.

"It wouldn't be half enough, sir."

"But yon fella from Leith-side's only givin' three pound ten."

"He offered it, sir. I ain't taking it."

"Arr! Ye shit-faced whelp, y'ought t'be thrashed one!"

Then Kenn gave the enraged savage a drink and he bought a matchlock musket and two snaphaunce pistols, which he stuck into his broad rawhide belt; he walked off in the rain, his wife trudging behind him with the musket and their bundle of food and a stool they had bought somewhere. He turned and swore at her and she moved faster without complaint.

"I wouldn't be a woman for ready money," the boy said softly.

"Whyever not?" his mother said. "Men work so hard!"

280

He gave her his cunning smile. "'I wouldn't want to be a skillet,' the egg said when she saw the pan go on the fire. 'And I wouldn't want to be an egg,' the skillet said when he saw the man eat his breakfast."

"You do talk strange, Jan."

Typhus visited Edinburgh that winter that he was eleven. Katrin waited with dread for it to reach Stirling, but it seemed to swerve and miss them. There were deaths at Leith and then at Perth and Scone, and some said it was the plague again. She lived through January and February in terror that her son would die, but in February, when it abated everywhere, she began to be easier. At the end of that month, Kenn Mors complained of a feeling of weakness and lethargy, and she was frightened.

"God, I think it's got me," he said. He had developed a severe headache, and his fever was rising. "You been fearing for the boy, and—it's me, Katrin—it's me!"

He breathed in shallow gasps and his fever climbed and he became delirious. She did a remarkable thing: to protect her son, she moved her husband outdoors. She remembered what he had said about her tending him if he was ever sick, and she wept to do it—wept and wept, right through the appearance of the typhus rash, and the crisis, and his death. Her son's survival gave her a fierce, guilty joy, and she knew that she loved him more than she had her husband.

To her surprise, the boy wanted to keep the gunshop going, for there were a dozen finished pistols in it and a dozen more needing work. She believed that he was too young and too weak, so she promised him that he could have the tools and the business when he was older, and she brought in a powerful journeyman named Campbell to run things for a year or two.

"Know about guns, ma'am? Wasn't I apprentice to McNab at Kinross for six years?" He grinned at Jan. "That lad has a bright look to him, if I may say so, ma'am. A fine, canny boy, I can see."

Campbell moved into the loft over the forge. For six weeks, he seemed to work well, and he was an easy man to have near. His guns were more than a little crude, the boy thought, and he could not make locks at all, but the weapons were serviceable.

"What you starin' at, my lad?"

"Only wondering when you mean to finish that gun, Mr. Campbell."

281

"Oh, it's finished, lad."

"Oh." The boy kept his face blank. "I guess I couldn't see it, compared to one of my dad's."

The bench for filing and making screws and other small parts was inside the house, where Kenn had always kept it. After some weeks, Campbell seemed to find Jan an annoyance there, and more and more he sent him off on errands when he was working in the house.

Jan was confused, and he was suspicious.

"D'you like Mr. Campbell, Mama?"

"Don't you?"

"Well, as the mouse said when asked about the cat, 'As eats go, it's a fine cat.'"

Then he came back from one of the many errands to find the house door locked and the curtains drawn. There were sounds inside and he knew his mother was in there, and he ran from the door to the window, screaming to be let in; he pounded on the door and kicked it with as much strength as his puny legs could manage. After ten minutes, the door was flung open and Campbell jerked him inside.

"Ye're noisy, for a little rat," Campbell snarled.

Katrin was sitting in a straight chair by the fire. Jan knew at once that something had happened; her cap was askew on her tumbled hair; her face looked frightened; and Campbell's hands, for all his strength, were trembling. Had it been a rape? He would ask himself that for the rest of his life, when he understood precisely what rape was and what sort of man was capable of it. Or was it some erotic pull between the Scotsman and his mother? He never knew, but after that day, Darkland got darker, and what happened there was more violent.

"Go blow up the fire in the forge," Campbell said, giving the boy a hard push, as if to prove that he could do such a thing.

Campbell moved into the bedroom with Katrin; Jan, of his own volition, moved out to the loft. He hated what he heard in the house. He hated the bruises he saw on his mother's arms and face. He had bruises of his own, too.

Campbell was as savage as any smelly brute from the farthest reaches of the mountains. Women were property to him; children were chattels. A blow was better than a word. He had a veneer of manners, acquired in his years in Kinross and on the coast, but under it he was violent and primitive. The three of them survived together for eleven months, a strange, sad trio who compounded one another's miseries. Even Campbell was miserable, Jan knew, for he was a dour man who had no real way of being happy, at best. Jan withdrew even further into his fantasy. His mother found it hard to meet his eyes, and more and more she moved through the house like a shadow, quiet, moving aside for either of the others, flinching at every quick movement as if she anticipated a blow. Something held her to Campbell, however, and only years later did he understand that it might be guilt and the chance to punish herself. When she felt the first languors of typhus, she seemed simply quieter than usual, and even when the restlessness of the fever reached her, she went about the house cleaning and picking up after Campbell as if nothing were different. When she knew what it was, she made Jan stay away from her, but she kept close to Campbell. She hoped she could contaminate him, at the least.

In a week, she was gone. Campbell pulled the boy into the room to see her, but he hardly recognized the mottled corpse in the dirty bed. Still, he knew his mother was dead, and he crept up to the loft and cried until he slept.

There was a dreary funeral; the priest and three neighbors looked at him in a grim way that was meant to express grief, and that was that. There were too many people dying to lavish sympathy on a child people had not liked. Anyway, Campbell had told them he would take care of the boy.

"Oney you an me now, rat," Campbell said to him. The house stank of him. There were dirty clothes on the stair, filthy dishes on the hearth. "Pack up the tools."

"Whatever for?"

"We're moving, you and me. Taking my business inland."

"It isn't your business. It's my dad's!"

"Dead, isn't he? I don't see him working at the forge, do I? Pack up the tools."

"I don't have to do what you say, you greasy lout!"

Campbell swung and the boy dodged back. Campbell sat in his chair, staring narrow-eyed. "Come over here and get what you missed."

"I won't."

"Don't make me get up and come to you with it, lad. You know how I hate to be moved. Now come here and get it." He had done this trick before, both with Jan and Katrin. His was the fascination of the snake for its victim.

"You're not my dad! You're nobody! Get out of our house!"

"Come *here,* boy."

But the rat has a peculiar kind of courage. "You go fuck yourself up your great smelly asshole, Mr. Campbell."

Campbell caught him before he could wrestle the outer door open. He beat the boy on the shoulders with a stick from the fire and then beat him on the legs, and when Jan doubled over with the pain in his bruised shins, he took off his belt and whipped his back until it bled. Campbell was panting when he finished.

"Now, I'll tell you, shitface," Campbell said between gasps. "I'll tell you what else I'll do if you don't mind me. I'll box yer ears with my two hands, and I can make you deaf in both ears. Then I'll take yer arms over my knee and I'll break them like two sticks of wood, one by one. And I'll do it, by God!"

The boy was weeping as he never had in his life. He tried to nod that he understood.

"Go pack up them tools now. We're moving off to my part of the country, where there's honest people."

Campbell went out to the forgehouse. The boy dragged himself to his feet and made himself walk to the fireplace, using a broom as a crutch because his legs wanted to buckle. He had pissed himself during the beating, he found; he hated the smell and the filth of it. He hated Campbell for making him do it. He took down the ancient wheel-lock that was his and he dragged himself to the filing bench and found the box of gunpowder that was kept for testing locks, and he charged and primed the old gun, putting in a ball from a dish of odd loads of all sizes that was always there, for as long as he could remember. Then he hid the wheel-lock that Francisco had made for Elsbet. Behind the door seemed a safe place.

He put the files and wrests and the tiny engraving tools and hammers into lightly oiled cloths and rolled them up, tucking the ends under to make neat bundles. He sniveled. His chest erupted with a sob and fell quiet. He saw his face in the wavy glass of the window: he was cut on the cheekbone; his left eye was almost closed, and there was a swollen bruise on his right temple.

He rolled up the wood chisels, half a dozen to each cloth, and the piles of tight cloth grew higher. When he was done, he put all the rolls into a rucksack, which was heavy for his thin shoulders, and which held the future in it—a future and a fortune for a man who knew how to use those tools.

"You done packing like I told you, shitface?"

"Yes, sir, Mr. Campbell."

"Then get out. We leave when the sun is up."

"Yes, sir."

He walked to the door. He feared that it would creak when he moved it to find the gun, but it was as quiet as if the hinges were greased. His hand closed over the slender barrel.

Campbell had sat down by the fire with his back to Jan.

"Mr. Campbell, sir?"

"What now?"

He relished the look on the man's face when he turned around. It almost made the pain go away, if only for a few seconds. They stared at each other, and then he pulled the trigger, and the face was hidden by the quick, black smoke—and then there it was again, with a hole where the nose had been and blood spurting over the floor. Campbell's hands came up to his face as he toppled backward over his chair and crashed against the floor. He twitched there like an epileptic for almost a minute, dying grudgingly. The boy watched, as he had once watched the burned frog and the kitten with the gunpowder. He could smell Campbell's excrement, forced from his body by the shock.

He reloaded the wheel-lock and limped to the body and poked it; assured that it was dead, he did not fear to search it for money, and he found almost a pound in a purse, and four more in silver tied around the neck. He had eleven shillings of his own hidden in the loft wall, and he thought that his mother had kept a hoard in the pantry, but it took him thirty minutes to find it. It was a remarkable lot of coins, big and small, pennies to guilders, Dutch, Scottish, English, even French and German—a fortune for a boy to start off in the world with.

He put the rucksack on his skinny shoulder and wrapped the old wheel-lock in an oiled cloth and went out and hid both gun and rucksack behind the garden wall, and then he found the bundles of finished guns and gun parts that Campbell had been packing up in the forgehouse, and these he took out into the dark field that led toward the hills, and he scattered several of the poor guns that Campbell had made over the field, and he hid the rest and went home again.

He looked around the only home he had ever known. It had a corpse in it now, and a huge amount of blood all over things. His own face was battered, as a boy's might be if he had been surprised by robbers.

"You rotten son of a bitch," he whispered to the corpse.

And then he went out to the priest's and told him about

285

the horrible robbery at his house in which poor, good Mr Campbell had been killed and he had been beaten himself and had only just come to. He was very good at stories.

CHAPTER TWENTY-THREE

THE TWO MEN'S LAUGHTER rattled out the open windows and bounded down the narrow streets, on whose bricks the rain had left shining puddles as if a housewife had only then finished washing the pavement. Inside the narrow house, the men leaned back from a heavy table and smacked their full bellies and told each other that it had been a good meal, a splendid meal. The serving girl cleared away their dishes and they chatted on without noticing her. She was fat and a little slovenly, and she had nothing about her that was pretty—the kind of girl a wife would hire so her husband would not be tempted.

"So," the rougher of the two men said after a silence. He had old skin and a face that looked as if it had been left out too long in bad weather. "So." His left hand slapped the edge of the table lightly. Both men were feeling the wine they had drunk. "And Edward?"

"Moved to Utrecht. Everybody's moved someplace; there's too damned many of us in Amsterdam. Abraham's in Gravelines still, trying to make a living out of whitesmithing. Hendrick's gone to -'s Hertogenbosch."

"Too many Moorses, or too many gunmakers?"

"Both!" They laughed. The smoother of the two men looked somber. "I wish they were close by, of course. A man wants his family around after a certain age, eh? But truly, the competition here in Amsterdam—I swear to Heaven, I think everybody makes guns these days."

"But I can't get the guns I need."

"It's not the guns you need, it's the way you need them—eh?"

The smooth man, who had the potbelly of a sedentary and was about forty, leaned his chair forward with his forearms on the table. He tapped a finger close to the other man's folded hands. "I can furnish you guns enough—but not without telling the guild and their high mightinesses. But you say you got to have them in secret. Hey?"

The rough man shrugged. He was used to secrets and to double dealing. "Sometimes their high mightinesses are better off not knowing things."

"Isn't it exactly what I've often said, my friend! But they make the laws—you and I obey them, hey?"

"On the Mauritius River, their high mightinesses have very little to say."

"Ah!" The city man expressed genuine interest, for he had never been anywhere. "Tell me about that place."

"It's very wild. But a good harbor." The rough man was a sailor. He had some of that inward quality that sailors and woodsmen share, an ability to bear loneliness and a desire for space. "It's like Sweden, some of it."

"I've never been to Sweden. And the savages?"

"They're savages, right enough. Go about mostly naked, kill animals with stones and clubs. Smell like a privy, some of them."

"And their women?"

"Well—" The sailor made a face. Then he smiled. "They get better looking as the summer goes on." The two men laughed. When they had quieted, the sailor tapped the table and said, "So," two or three times and fell silent. And then, unasked, he began to talk about that land on the far side of the world, where he had just spent a summer.

"I swear, it could be a paradise, Arnolt. There are mighty forests that come right down to the water, with trees in them, my God! We built a little bark when the *Tiger* burned, I swear we found every timber we needed but some of the ribs, already formed and waiting to be cut—there are so *many* of them! The savages came down to meet us when we sailed in, they have these coracles made of bark—ingenious! Without iron, mind you—not even brass; a bit of raw copper they have now and then by way of ornament—and they'd devised ways to make stems with a right-angle bend! They're not stupid, for all they're savages.

"And that river! Jesu, Arnolt, it's like a sweetwater ocean. *Huge!* Even up where we put the fort, it's big. Salmon in it, sturgeon so thick you could walk on them in their season. It could be a paradise, I don't mind saying. For the right man.

"And furs! Jesu, I've seen furs on those savages any king
287

would give his right nut to own. The savages say they take the animals in the winter when they're sleeping, instead o using traps; well, that's probably a story. Who cares? They make cloaks of them, the furs sewn together very cleverly with sinew, they wear them with the fur in for warmth, and that fur takes on a luster from the grease of their bodies— It's gold, Arnolt. Gold!"

Arnolt Moors tapped the table again, eager now for busi ness. "And you say they want guns—*already?*"

The hard-featured seaman grunted. "Want? They'll trade a mountain for a gun. They see one, they have to have it. They're not stupid, Arnolt. I could have traded fifty hark booses, easy—and for such furs!" He shook his shaggy head His blunt fingers played with the empty wineglass. "A par adise," he muttered to himself.

"Better than Africa?"

"Bah, Africa! Africa is like Amsterdam; *everybody's* there There's thirty forts scattered down the Gold Coast; when was down to Ankobra, all I heard was what the Portugee were doing and what could be had at Sekondi! Anyway, that's slave business down there; I want no more of that." He waved his hand. "To sail with a load of slaves, a man has to be either deaf or hard. I ain't either, whatever you may think of me. I don't ever want to hear one of them songs again— like hurt dogs howling, day after bleeding day." He poured himself wine like a man who thinks he needs drink. "I'll run guns past their high mightinesses any day before I'll sai with slaves." He grinned. "If I can persuade a friend to sel me the guns."

Arnolt Moors held up his hands helplessly. "There are laws!"

"What laws? You'll sell a gun to any Landsknecht that comes buying so he can go off and kill women and kids."

"But the law allows me to do that."

"Well, it shouldn't." The sailor twirled the wine. "So." He drank. "So, maybe I must become a Landsknecht for a little while. Or hire one to front for me."

"Such things are done," Arnolt Moors said slowly. "But there would have to be a real Landsknecht, which means a payment."

"But you could let me have the guns on credit? Twenty good *shnaaphans* long guns, my friend—"

"*Shnaaphans!* For savages? Plain old matchlock muskets are good enough!"

"But they're not." The sailor grinned. "I told you, they're not stupid. They know the difference already, Arnolt. They don't want to walk about their forest with a lighted slow-match glowing and stinking. They want the *shnaaphans*. They don't know how it works and they don't know how to fix it if it breaks, but they want it. Twenty of them, eh, Arnolt? I will turn them into such furs! And as an investment—I'll multiply your cost by ten *at least*, Arnolt—maybe by twenty."

The homely housemaid put her head in. "There's a boy outside, master," she said. She spoke as if all hope had long since vanished from her world.

"I don't want a boy; send him away."

"He says he's family, master." She looked utterly bewildered. "I don't know how I'm supposed to know who's family and who ain't."

Arnolt looked at his guest. "Could be Edward's son, I suppose, but what'd he be doing all this way from Utrecht?" He scowled at the maid. "Well, put him in the shop, you numskull." She disappeared.

"I suppose I'll have to see to this," Arnolt said. "Have some more wine and I'll be back."

"Need to stretch my legs anyway," the other said. "My God, I ate too much! Who does the cooking, that ugly piece who was just in here?"

"Nyah, she's only the maid."

"At all, uh, friendly, is she? You know what I mean."

"Who'd care, with a face like that?"

"Ah, they're the best kind, my friend. With the lights out, as they say....Maybe I'll go out the back when I leave."

In the room that served as showroom and repair shop for customers' guns, a frightened, undersized, thin boy waited. Despite his obvious fragility, however, he had a contradictory air of cocky independence that both adults found unnerving.

"Well?" Arnolt Moors said. "What lies are you telling my maid, boy, saying you're family?"

"Please, sir, I am." He spoke with a slight accent, which the sailor placed first. "Scots are you, boy?"

"Yes, sir, Herr Moors."

The sailor laughed. "I ain't Moors, boy; I'm Kleynties. That's Herr Moors in the chair."

Arnolt put his feet up on a stool. "And who the hell are you supposed to be then, boy?"

"I'm Jan Morse, sir, from Stirling. Kenn Morse's son. My mother is—was—Great Aunt Maria's granddaughter."

The feet came down from the stool, and Arnolt looked at Kleynties and then at the boy. "Jesu, I knew I had a cousin in Scotland, but—. You don't look family, boy!"

"No, sir."

"Where's your father?"

"Dead, sir."

"And your mother?"

"Dead, too, sir."

Arnolt exchanged a disgusted look with Kleynties. "How'd you get here, then?"

"Ship, sir. From Leith."

"Must have taken money."

"My mother gave me money before she died, sir, and said I was to use it to come to my good Uncle Arnolt in Amsterdam." The boy could lie with a wide-eyed innocence that was absolutely convincing. "Didn't you get Father Bethune's letter?"

"What letter?"

"Why, the one he wrote the day my mother died. Commending me to your care, sir. Surely you got it?"

"Devil a letter I've had from any priest! I suppose you can't prove you're a Morse, eh?"

Jan held out the ancient wheel-lock. Arnolt swayed back from it a little, almost as if he knew that it was a weapon that had just done a murder. "What's that?"

"It's family, sir. My dad give it me. It's an old Mors gun, see the mark?"

But Arnolt did not look at it. "How come your da to give it to a runt like you?"

"He had it for his wedding. He give it me because he loved me better than all the world, and when he died, he said, 'Jan, my lovely boy, take down the old gun that means so much to me; it's yours.'"

Arnolt turned to Kleynties and spoke as if the boy were not there. "They been making guns in this family for so long nobody remembers when they began, but the boy could have any old piece we made a hundred years ago." He turned to the boy and took the wheel-lock. He ran a finger over the worn engraving and the *Mors* mark. "Well, and if you were Kenn Morse's son, what of it?"

"I hoped I'd work for wages, sir."

"I don't need more apprentices. How old are you?"

"Sixteen, sir."

"Liar, you ain't fourteen. What d'you think I'd do with a boy not old enough to apprentice? You meant to lay about and play the young gent, I suppose."

Jan Morse wrapped up his wheel-lock carbine in the oily cloth. His lower lip seemed to tremble for an instant; he curled it tight against his teeth and bit down with his upper lip. He tied the strings of his bundle and hoisted it over his shoulder by a long loop of cord.

"What are you doing now, boy?"

"I'll be going, sir."

"Going where?"

"Why—." The look of craftiness and damn-all independence came into his face again. "If you got no use for me, then I guess where I go ain't your business, sir."

"Why, you drowned rat—!" Arnolt started forward, and the boy dodged nimbly to the door; Kleynties, holding his friend back, pushed him into his chair and put himself between Moors and the boy.

"Now, lad, now—I ain't going to hurt you, just you stand there—and you, Arnolt, let me ask you to sit there and be silent. Now easy, boy, you look like a hedgehog caught between the garden and his holt. Now—how old are you? *Truth?*"

"Thirteen. And a bit."

"No da, no ma, no money. Right?"

"Got a bit of money."

"Now, the way I make it, you're a sharp little bugger who's been seeing some hard times, am I right? Been learning some lessons and learning them quick, and now you just learned another, namely, don't go to relatives when you're down and out. Oh, sit still, Arnolt; you ain't the first man I known to turn somebody's child away from his door. Now, boy—do you know guns?"

"Know them how, sir?"

"Well enough to shoot one."

"Oh, aye. I can shoot a gun well enough."

"Think you could kill a man if you had to?"

There was no hesitation. "I could."

"It's easier said than done—put any Netherlander farmer's son behind a caliver and put a man at the other end and he turns to jelly. Can you fix guns, boy?"

"What, do gunsmithing?" The boy became contemptuous. "I can fix any gun!"

291

"Fix a wheel-lock?" Arnolt Moors said suspiciously.

"Oh, yes." He was elaborately offhand. "My da turned all the wheel-locks over to me. 'Jan, my loved boy,' he'd say 'you're a wonder for knowing such difficult machines, so I'll just leave all the—'"

"All right, all right," Kleynties said. "Can you make a gun?"

"Why—" The small eyes studied Kleynties's face. "Well no, I can't. I haven't the strength of arm to forge barrels. But I can make plain locks well enough! And I stocked lots of guns, plain ones, though neither my da nor me was what you'd call a stockmaker."

Arnolt asked two or three close questions to find how far his knowledge really went. He wanted to see the boy's tools. He put the boy at a bench by a window and had him start to inlet a new lock into the recess of an old stock. Fifteen minutes later, he nodded at Kleynties.

"Not so bad," he said grudgingly. "He's learned it some place, all right."

"Arnolt—." Kleynties began, and then stopped as if he did not want to be overheard. Drawing the other man out into the tiled corridor, he said in a hoarse mumble, "Could that boy assemble guns, do you think?"

"Yah, sure. Yah, good enough."

"Could he make the stocks?"

"I suppose so. What're you getting to?"

"I could ship gun parts to New Netherland lots easier than I could ship whole guns—hide them all over the ship, if I had to. And if they could be stocked after they got there, why it'd just be all so much easier."

Arnolt Moor pushed out his lower lip. "What, take that little jack-pike with you?"

Kleynties shrugged. Where else does he have to go? he seemed to say.

"Well." Arnolt Moors scratched his beard. "I wouldn't want it spread about that I'd turned him away and that he went to New Netherland and something bad happened. You'd have to take care of him."

Kleynties stared at him with hard eyes that had not flinched from far more cynical scenes than this one. He patted Moors's shoulder and turned back to the shop; coming in silently, he caught the boy bent over a table in the far corner of the room.

"You damned little fool," he murmured. His hand closed

ver both of the boy's and took out the objects that were
here—a snaphaunce lock, four hand-cut screws, a trigger
guard. "Bit of a thief, are we?"

"I was only looking!"

"Yah, with your fingers. Go sit, before Arnolt comes in
and has you packed off to the jail."

He pushed the boy down on the hard stool where he had
been working. Kleynties leaned his right haunch on the
workbench and loomed over the small body, arms folded, face
scowling. "How'd you like to sail up the River Mauritius,
boy?"

"I don't know where that is, sir. Is it Africa?"

"It's America! All the way over the ocean." Kleynties
stared hard at him and then reached some decision and began
to talk as if to an adult. "There's money in it, see? Trading
guns to savages. One summer of it, and you can come back
here with money in your breeches."

"Rich?"

"It'd take three voyages to be rich." Kleynties lowered his
voice. "The guns would be mine, but I'd give you a cut for
assembling and stocking them over there. Their high mightinesses—that's the Estates General, for we got no king here—
don't like guns as a general rule. We'd have to take them
along privately. So you'd work for a wage on ship, and take
it in beads and knives and such stuff as their high mightinesses put their blessing on, and you trade all those for fur.
And I trade the guns on the sly for more fur, and give you
a cut, and we come back here in autumn and we're well off."

"What if the ship sinks?"

"Why, then, we sink with it—so what have we lost?"

Jan Morse laughed. The idea seemed to amuse him might-
ly.

"Well, how about it, Jan?"

"I'll do it, sir."

"You ain't scared?"

"Yes, sir, I'm scared, but I been scared before. Lots."

CHAPTER TWENTY-FOUR

THE *PEARL* SLIPPED into the mouth of the broad river in a summer downpour like an errant husband returning late with his shoulders hunched against the weather. Gray sail luffed lightly as she came around in the skimpy breeze and taking the tide, moved into the maze of bays and the moving sheet of fresh water that Henry Hudson had found six years before.

"Soundings!" the captain bellowed. "Give me soundings! Why in Hell ain't I getting soundings?"

Hands hurried the wet rope aboard. "Eleven fadom!"

"Bottom?"

"Sand and black mud, sir!"

The captain growled. They had lain off the entrance all night, waiting for light and tide to take them in; three days before, they had made their landfall to the north. The same gray haze of coast had presented itself to them all those three days—days of rain and mist, with the sound of surf on sand beaches like distant guns.

"A hand more off the wind."

"Aye, sir."

In the waist, Jan Morse stood by two falconets that had fallen under his charge since he had been named second gunner. An iron pan loaded with burning charcoal was at his feet in a box of sand. The canvas waist-cloth, which had kept the 'midships from the waves in the open sea, had been taken down and stowed the night before, and he was able to watch now the wonder of this wild haven, one hand on the rail, the hissing sound of the bow in his ears as it cut through the whorled water of a flowing tide.

Kleynties came forward with the coiled lead line. "Like what you see, youngster?"

"It's rare," he said. "Rare." He was thinking, *It's Darkland.*

Traders or gunners or sailors, they had all been mariners on the crossing and would be until they reached the for

priver. The bark carried thirty-six men, six more than its
usual complement because there were soldiers of the New
Netherlands Company aboard.

"Sandpunt!" a lookout shouted. Hands pointed west where
low, sandy point jutted out. Many of the ship's company
had made this landfall before; the captain had not, and he
used their knowledge to guide him in.

Two hours later, they saw small craft put out from the
eastern shore.

"Savages!" Jan cried excitedly. He reached for his firing
irons.

"Easy, Rat!" the first gunner called from the other rail.
They're Manahatties—they're tame. Or they was last August."

They hove to and dropped an anchor, partly because the
captain wanted some respite from the tension of sailing in
close in unknown waters. He would allow none of the Indians
on board, however, and they stood off in their canoes under
the muzzles of the falconets and three arquebuses to a side,
held by the soldiers.

"Why, they dress just like us!" Jan exclaimed. It was true:
many of the Indians wore sea-gowns of bright blue or red,
hooded just like his own. His words were met with the first
gunner's laughter.

"Yah, where d'you think they get such stuff, Rat? From
us, last summer, is where! Shit, they'll give thee a sable cloak
for that slop-jacket y're wearing. Give thee a dark girl, too,
if you're old enough to have your balls in order."

Buckets were let down the side, and the Indians put in
oysters and a huge crayfish of a kind that Jan had never
seen. The sailors threw them in a pile on the deck.

"What're them?" the captain called.

"Lobsters, captain!"

"What d'you do with them?"'

"Boil 'em, captain!"

"All right, take one or two for every man down to the
cookroom, tell him to start boiling. I'm so tired of salt maggots
I could puke! Boatswain, let's take the wind! Up anchor!"

Jan and the gunner took their turn at the crude windlass
that raised the thick anchor cable. Fore and main courses
unfurled over their heads; aft, the lateen-rigged mizzen was
cropped to give them maneuverability as the wind changed.
For a mile, the Indians paddled alongside in their light bark

boats, and then abruptly gave up and let the ship hiss uprive
without them.

They anchored well out from shore for the night, with
double watch posted and lanterns hung over the sides. A
dawn, the tide was ebbing and they waited for the flow; th
weather broke and clouds scudded with a wind that ripple
the water like a field of grass. At midmorning, the sun cam
through full and Jan could see the mountains that ros
steeply from the western bank, higher and steeper than an
he had ever seen. Kleynties had told him over and over tha
the place could be a paradise for the right man, but to Ja
it looked, with its impenetrable tangle of forest that cam
right down to the water's edge, like Darkland with its magi
thickets. *Have to be a wild man to live here,* he thought. *C
a magician.* Wild men to him would be like the uncout
Highlanders who came down to Stirling, rank-smelling an
violent. Still, Kleynties was not such a man, and he spok
of paradise.

"Don't look like no land of milk and honey," a sailor a
the rail said. "What I say is, if it's so wonderful, how com
them savages is so glad to get the shit we trade them? If
was so wonderful, they'd want nothing, would they?"

"Maybe they ain't the right men for it," Jan said, but h
said it so softly nobody heard.

On up the river they sailed, meeting more canoes and the
a shallop under sail from Fort Nassau, sent down to mee
them. Word of their coming had sped up the river throug
an Indian network; by the time they reached the tiny for
a hundred Indians were already gathered on the bank t
trade. The fort itself was a disappointment—worse than tha
it was so insignificant that Jan was frightened, seeing a
those aliens on the bank. There was merely a log buildin
surrounded by a crude stockade and a ditch, the whole of i
set on a swampy little island out of the main course of th
river. A rough dock jutted out, but the captain anchored ou
in the river and they began the tedious business of movin
themselves and their cargo to the fort by longboat.

Jan found now that he was a privileged member of th
company, for he was made carpenter's mate because he kne
tools, and with the ship's carpenter and two seamen he wa
excused from work onboard and was sent ashore with th
disassembled pieces of the pinnace, which had been brough
over in the hold. As the Indians looked on, gabbling amon
themselves, often laughing at what they did not understand

hey rebuilt the ways on which, two years before, a craft alled the *Unrest* had been built, and then put together a rude cradle and assembled the numbered pieces.

In three days, the cables were cut and the boat slid side-ays into the water, to bob there to the satisfaction of both arpenters and Indians, who had been sure that the incomrehensible Europeans were sinking their new craft when hey let it go down the ways.

Shallow-drafted, the pinnace was eighteen feet long, half-ecked, with a single mast and sweeps. With it, the expeition would explore and trade upstream and down to the nouth, putting into smaller waters along the way.

"Weary, youngster?"

"Weary enough. Been pounding an oakum sledge two days gether."

"Carpenter says you're a fair workman. That's praise. It'll ll seem worth it when you're back in Amsterdam."

They were under the shadow of the stockade. Jan lowered is voice. "What of our guns?"

"Still on board. We'll wait until captain takes yon pinnace ut."

"What if he takes us with him?"

"You, yes—me, I'm to be second in command of the fort hen he's gone. The commander'll be Lents, the head of the oldiers came over with us. He's already paid off." Kleynties yed him shrewdly, hesitating, it seemed, to ask another uestion. "Getting to you yet, is it, boy?" he said finally.

"What's that?"

"The strangeness of it. All that emptiness out there."

"I like it."

Within its tangle of dark beard, the cynical old mouth urned down, then up in a grin. "Christ, you're a rum kid." here was no malice in the words, and even a certain adiration.

The captain took the pinnace on a three-week journey that vent down to the island where the Manahatties had met hem, then eastward into a huge saltwater bay upon whose outh shore they touched whenever friendly savages apeared. Jan went as crew and gunner, with nine other men. he *Unrest* and the *Fortune* had both been before them, but he trading was good and there was still much of the vast ay to map. They went north and east to its meeting with he ocean, then back along the north shore. Jan manned the ingle stern gun, a swivel that could be brought quickly to

bear to either side or the rear; next to him always was th
old wheel-lock.

One morning on the north shore, their camp was attacke
and they had to scramble into the pinnace and push it in
deep water through the gently sloping sand while stone
tipped arrows fell among them. A mob of savages swept int
their camp so fast that they left two wounded Hollanders o
the beach. The captain stood in the waist and shook his fi
at the scene and then ordered the stern swivel fired, and, t
Jan's young ears, the howls of glee from his shipmate
sounded every bit as fierce as those of the Indians. The littl
gun flung small shot and scrap into the mob, and Jan followe
with a shot from the wheel-lock. The Indians fled, leavin
three of their own to bleed on the sand, and the captain pu
the pinnace around and went back ashore, and they kille
the three Indians and cut the feet off one of them and skinne
them for a pair of slippers for him.

"Covered yourself with glory in a scrape, I hear," Kleyr
ties said when they were back at Fort Nassau.

"Yes."

"Captain gave you an extra eighth, I hear."

"Yes."

"Not too pleased, for a boy wanted to get rich."

"There's not much glory in shooting naked folk with
falconet."

"Captain says there is."

"We were off safe in the boat—what'd he think they'd do
swim out and shoot us with stone arrows?"

"They had to be taught a lesson."

"What lesson? What's the lesson in a cannon turned o
men with no more armor than a bit of rag around their ball
and a clamshell on their chests?"

"Jan—listen to me, Jan." The blunt fingers twisted int
his hair and pulled his head upward. "Here's the lesson. I
this work, you don't get rich without killing. Mind you lear
that, and learn it well. When I asked back in Amsterdan
could you shoot a man, and you said yes, I thought you wa
shitting me, for what'd you know of shooting men then? Bu
now you done it, and you done it well. And believe me, boy
it's better killing men to get rich than it is making slaves c
them."

He relaxed his painful grip. Jan kept looking at him. H
was growing up quickly, but he still had his mysterious
298

hild's stare. "You said this place was a paradise," he said
itterly.

"Could be a paradise. And maybe will be, one day—when
here are farms and white men living on it. But not now."

"Maybe it's a paradise for the savages."

"Well, maybe. But what do savages know of paradise, eh?
And who would want to live like one?"

Kleynties looked at the distant shore, where the lush pro-
usion of trees blended into the hot green of cattails and water
rass. Two herons stood like thin stumps among the green
hoots, and, as he looked, a fish jumped high and silver.
Maybe in your time, it will be a paradise," Kleynties said.
I'm too old."

Near the place where they had assembled the pinnace,
here was a log shed where most of the trading was done.
The carpenter and Jan and several others made it bigger and
added a wall to close the shed in and make a proper building
of it, and then they put up a stockade because so many river
ndians were coming now that they pushed into the shed and
nterfered with business. Kleynties and the others doing the
rading used uncut alcohol—*aqua vitae*—brought in kegs
rom Holland, which they mixed with river water and honey,
ubricating the trades with it. Many of the Indians left the
ost too drunk to walk straight. After some weeks, their
wives began to show up with them, and the wives would not
drink. They sat with their men and murmured to them and
ven struck the cup from their hands if they drank so much
hat they made poor bargains.

When he finished his work on the stockade, Jan went back
o the shipway and helped the carpenter fashion a longboat,
maller than the pinnace but big enough to carry five men
and a small gun. The old carpenter told him how to find
uitable trees in the forest, preferably oaks with curves in
he branches and the knees that matched the plans brought
ver from Holland; they would go into the forest and spend
he day looking up tree after tree, estimating, measuring,
an climbing them often to get the precise bend of an upper
ranch. In this way, Jan penetrated several miles into the
woods, the old wheel-lock always on his shoulder.

They dug a sawpit near the new stockade and cut the
green oak into boards and stem and sternpieces; the green
wood was a torment to saw, but it was all they had, and the
ld carpenter laid the extra wood aside to season "for the

next old shithead that has to build a boat in this godforsake: desert."

The old man pointed out other trees than the oak and ha one or two cut and brought in—native chestnut and mapl and walnut. Some of it he pronounced "not bad wood, for desert."

Knowing now that the Indians would not trouble him, Ja: went into the woods by himself. Upriver or down, he migh be treated differently, but close to the post, the whites wer untouchable, at least while the trading lasted; he walked th spongy forest floor, poking into its mysteries, savoring it dark places and its secret holes. Once he met two bears; the rose on their hind legs and stared at him, and he aimed th wheel-lock with shaking hands, not quite daring to shoo because there were two of them and he would have only th one shot.

Holy God, protect me—

The bears dropped to all fours and ambled away, and h sat down where he was, shuddering, jelly-kneed, as if he ha met a spirit.

He shot a fawn still in the spotted hide and missed marten, and when he had killed enough to satisfy a boyisl blood-hunger, he stopped killing and simply watched th birds and animals.

"What in Hell do you find out there?" Kleynties asked.

"Nothing. Everything." A look came into his face tha Kleynties would have recognized if he had ever sat in th Stirling forge and watched the dreamer in the shadow: "Paradise," he said slyly.

"You're daft."

"I found a tree, at least. Big enough to stock the guns."

"Now you're thinking, boy! But a whole bloody tree?"

"To get the length, yes. It's already dead, but sound; there' enough straight wood to make stocks for all eight." They ha brought twelve guns disassembled but with stocks, and eigh more unstocked. He had assembled nine of the twelve al ready, working nights in the trading post.

"Not that green oak, is it?"

"Nah, the tree the Mahicans get the sweet sap from. don't know their word."

"Talking to them now, are you?"

"Trying to. They're always underfoot when I'm workin; at the shipway, wanting to trade for my ax or my drawknife.

"Good, boy. Learn their tongue. I know a little of it, but ids learn quicker. It'll make you a better trader."

The *Fortune* arrived from Amsterdam, off-loaded its trade oods and another complement of six soldiers and sailed with he furs they had acquired so far. The pinnace and the new ongboat set out together to explore to the south, for a Ma- ican had told them of another river that rose in the land of heir bitter enemies to the west, the Maaquas, and flowed outh into a bay as large as an ocean, passing through the ands of the Mingoes and the Delawars on the way. The in- ormant had been bribed with a brass kettle and a red shirt; aost of the Mahicans would say nothing of any other peoples n any side.

"They want it all to themselves," Kleynties said with rudging admiration. "See, the Mahicans are traders, too; hey want to be the middlemen and keep us from ever getting nland to the other tribes. And at the same time, the red •astards're dealing with the French while they deal with us!"

"The French! Where?"

"Up north someplace. They say 'beyond the mountains,' ike it's off the edge of the world, but it's my guess it ain't ll that far. One of them showed me a piece of French silver, nd another one said something about 'when the French at- acked the Maaquas.' I even had one of their chiefs—they're ll chiefs when they're drunk, you know—tell me yesterday hat he could get a better price for his furs from his 'French riends.' His wife shut him up right quick, but he said it, all ight." Kleynties's face took on the same faraway look as vhen he had looked over the river and talked about being ld. "God, there's lots of the bastards out there, boy! And hey'd pay! Christ, how they'd pay! Twice what the Mahicans o, I'll bet."

"What would they give for guns, if they're the Mahicans' nemies?"

Kleynties stared at him and made a wicked little grin. Christ, boy, for guns they'd make *us* chiefs."

The *Goodheart,* a tiny *vlieboot* of twenty-five tons, an- hored and off-loaded and departed; two weeks later, the *Strength* and the *Pride of Netherland* came up together and hen stayed for three weeks. There was more carpentry to be one then, but the time was almost festive—news from Am- terdam, new faces, novices to be mocked and taught the vays of this new world. Jan was able to swagger a little, hough in his private rambles through the woods he thought the swaggering was childish. Some of the newcomers, seeing him actually conversing with two Mahicans, asked him if he had lived there all his life.

Half a dozen Mahican women set themselves up as whores, conducting their business from four lean-tos a hundred feet from the trading post.

"Got your end wet yet, infant?" a sailor asked him, nodding up toward the lean-tos. "Close your eyes and hold your nose, you'd think you was fucking a woman."

"Yah, you probably pretend it's a sheep and think you're at home," Jan said. The whores embarrassed him; the fact of the prostitution blighted the whole world of the forest. The sailors stayed only five or ten minutes behind the hanging of the lean-tos; if they took longer, one of the Indian men would pull the hanging aside and start to shout. The women went about almost naked, even fully so, most often drunk. There were fights, and Kleynties sent two of the soldiers out from the trading post, and once he sent Jan across to the island in a canoe to get six more from the fort.

After three weeks, the two ships sailed and the river was quiet, the crossings of three pinnaces and a dozen smaller boats ended. The *Pearl* was making ready to go home. It was late August, and there were already cool nights. Kleynties told him to hurry with the gunstocks. They began to see the same old faces among the Indians at the post, and now they looked mostly for alcohol and would trade anything to get it—carved native pieces, personal possessions, even the European goods they had acquired two months before. A week after the *Strength* and the *Pride of Netherland* sailed, three of the whores went away, and they pulled down the lean-tos. Jan worked fiercely at their destruction, irrationally pleased to see them go. Still, the patterns of that traffic remained on the ground, in the weeds and the cuttings in the woods, a sorry history of the traffic there. Later, he would understand that his bitterness came from innate understanding of the terrible process that made civilized man miserable: confronted with the chance of paradise, he knows only how to turn it into Hell.

They cut new spars for the *Pearl,* and pulled the longboat and the pinnace up inside the island stockade and battened them for winter. The captain announced that he would be ready to sail in a week. Jan and the carpenter made double thick shutters for the trading post, both window and door 'he Mahicans thinned to a mere trickle. The trading year ⱱas over.

"Lents has fucked us," Kleynties said. "He's told me flat ⱱut, he won't allow any more trading of guns to the Mahicans, ꞁe bastard! I told him it was his own throat he was cutting ꞁecause he was going to lose money, and he says, 'It'll be my ꞁhroat they're cutting this winter if they get twenty guns.' Ξver since he had to send the soldiers over to stop the fight, ꞁe's afraid of them."

"Well, he's the one who has to spend the winter here," Jan ꞅaid. "We can take them back to Amsterdam, I suppose." He ꞁhought of all the work he had put into the stocks.

"Like Hell! There's no money in those guns in Amsterdam, ⱱoy! No, I'm going to trade those guns here, and I'm going ꞅo trade them high. Very high!"

"Lents can stop you—or make trouble with their high ꞁightinesses, can't he?"

"Not if I trade them to savages that can't get at his little ꞁort, he won't. Not when he sees how I do it. You sit tight at ꞁhe trading post, boy, and shine those guns up nice and bright. ꞁf anybody asks where I am, tell them I've gone down the ꞁiver to sell the Queen."

Kleynties kept his own woman at the post. She was a Ϻahican captive from far west of the river; Kleynties had ꞁought her for a double string of Venetian beads and two ꞁxes. He had given her the ironic name the Queen, because, ꞅaptive or not, she had the manner of one.

Next dawn, Kleynties and the Queen were gone. Jan ⱱorked alone in the post until last light failed, and then he ⱱorked by the spitting light of pitch-pine torches. Twice ꞁhere was knocking at the barred door—diehard Mahicans, ꞁoping for alcohol. He did not answer.

Next evening after sunset, a canoe poked out of a side ꞁhannel near Fort Nassau and hissed through the water grass ꞅo a landing by the post. Jan recognized Kleynties, even at ꞁ distance. The Queen was not with him.

"Where is she?" he asked when they were close enough to ꞅalk. After all of Kleynties's complaints about slaving, his ꞁreatment of the woman seemed paradoxical.

"Not here."

"Where?"

"Too many questions, boy. A long tongue gets cut off the ꞁuickest."

"You sold her!" Jan said angrily.

Kleynties grunted. "As a matter of fact, I set her free. That was her price."

Jan looked at him in confusion.

"For taking me to the Maaqua country, numskull! The Queen called herself an Onayta, whatever they are, but she knew all about the Maaquas and how to find them. That's where I've been."

"Last night?"

Kleynties nodded. "It's a hell of a haul through the woods. Twenty miles, anyway. Part of it by canoe."

"Did you trade the guns?"

"I think I did. They're to bring the furs."

"Here?"

Kleynties laughed. He was worn out, and his laughter sounded ragged. "Not so easy as that, little one! We're going back in there—in an hour. Get together enough food for three days. Three people. What's the matter?"

"I—I'm frightened."

"That's wise. You may get killed."

CHAPTER TWENTY-FIVE

FIRST DAYLIGHT MADE a confusion of strange shapes in the early fog. Neither darkness nor light, it turned the forest around them into a place of trickery, where trees and rocks were not what they seemed to be. They stumbled under their awkward loads, and Jan was frightened by what seemed to be enormous bears and menacing, half-human creatures. Then birds began to sing; a stream splashed down next to them and a breeze made sounds like quiet breathing in the treetops. The woods became one enormous being, mysterious in the uncertain light, breathing slowly as they climbed its breast.

They came up a glen that had been cut by a stream. The Queen was in the lead; then came Kleynties, then Jan, and last a man from the *Pearl* named Mindaerts. Each man carried three muskets and ten pounds of gunpowder. Jan carried

ree guns and his own bundle; the Queen had lead balls,
ars, molds, iron knives and eight axes.

She had waited for them where they beached and hid the
anoe. The Mahicans would have killed her if they had found
er there, but she had waited. The Mahicans might kill them
ll if they found them, especially if they understood that they
ere crossing to the Maaquas with guns. There were not
nore than twenty guns in all of the Mahican territory. Any-
ody who put nine in the hands of the Maaquas would have
o be an enemy.

"What does 'Maaqua' mean?" he said to the Queen in his
alting Mahican when they stopped.

"'Men who eat men,'" she said. *Cannibals*. Jan made a
ace at Kleynties.

"It's only a word, boy. The Mahicans call them that to
nake them seem bad."

"What do they call themselves?"

"Flint People."

Well, that's not so bad, then.

They met the first Maaqua at midmorning. The meeting
hould have made Jan feel better, because it meant that they
ere out of the Mahican country, but it did not. He kept
ninking of cannibals.

Two Maaquas materialized out of the woods and stood in
ie Queen's way—big-shouldered, short men with powerful
nests and arms. They had faces like the Queen's—round and
eavy-cheeked, with a big lower jaw that made the head
eem to taper toward the top. They did not look much dif-
erent from the Mahicans to him, but he thought that they
ooked nervous.

The two men signaled them to follow.

"Where are they taking us?" Kleynties said to the Queen.

"Meeting place."

"I want to trade and get out of here."

"They know. They are afraid, because of the Mahicans."

They went through open woods now, where the humus
as thick and soft as a carpet. Rotted mats of last year's
eaves lay against the roots of trees and under rocks; fallen
rees, like the columns of collapsed buildings, lay across their
ath, gray as ghosts with lichen. Wherever light could pen-
trate, green had shot up.

After an hour of walking, they came down a hillside to a
mall, clear pond. Two more Maaquas waited there. Between

them was a mound—furs. Kleynties grinned over his shou
der.

"I should have brought ten gallons of *aqua vit'*, not jus
a flask! I could probably have their whole damned territory

But when they stood in front of the two Maaquas an
Kleynties greeted them, the trading did not go forward. In
stead, a great many savages—Jan counted thirty, and h
knew there were more in the woods—came around them s
that they were surrounded. The Maaquas were armed wit
arrows and spears and heavy clubs with round rocks boun
into their shafts.

"Shit," Kleynties said softly. "Shit, shit, shit!"

"Holy Mother of God," Mindaerts moaned. Kleynties ha
assured him there was no danger.

Kleynties and the Queen jabbered too fast for Jan to fo
low. Kleynties kept pointing at the heap of furs. He wante
to trade and get out.

One of the Maaquas pulled off the bearskin that covere
the mound. Under it was a pile of stones.

"They tricked me." Kleynties was incredulous. "The fuck
ers tricked me!" The Maaquas had not understood him, bu
some of them were laughing. The Maaquas had a rathe
raucous sense of humor, Jan decided.

"Oh, Jesu," Mindaerts said. "Oh, sweet Jesu." Mindaert
had been saying that off and on for some time.

"What do they want?" Jan whispered.

"They want us to come to their village. The crafty ba
tards!"

Kleynties was carrying two pistols and a sword, and Min
daerts had a pistol and a boarding ax. Jan carried the whee
lock. He looked at all the men around them. "We'd better d
what they want."

"I do believe you're right, boy."

"Oh, sweet Jesu."

"Shut up, Mindaerts."

The Maaquas wanted to carry the guns, but they hel
tight to them. Jan felt the wheel-lock being tugged away; h
scuffled with the man and wrestled it back. The Maaqua
laughed.

"Maybe they think they're going to get everything for fre
anyway."

"Maybe they do."

He had thought that the village would be just over th

ext ridge, but it was not, nor was it over the next, nor the
ext.

"The *Pearl*," Jan muttered. "The *Pearl* will leave without
s if we aren't back."

"Don't you think I know that, boy?"

"Oh, Mother of God!" Mindaerts had come along because
leynties had promised him that he would make enough
oney so he would never have to return to New Netherland.
lindaerts hated New Netherland.

When, at sundown, Jan saw the Maaqua village at a dis-
ance, it seemed to dance for him like a swarm of gnats, so
izzy was he with fatigue. There was a smudge of smoke in
ie sky, and, under it, a palisade that danced on the horizon
r him.

"It smells like the *Pearl*," he said. The *Pearl's* main deck,
ter five weeks at sea, had been a horrendous mixture of
weating men, piss, garbage, vomit, and fumes from the bilge,
ito which everything ran and where it rotted. A trick of the
reeze had brought the village smell to them in all the same
ulness; seconds later, it changed, and he could smell wood-
noke and pine.

"Maybe they mean to stink us to death," Kleynties mut-
red.

The village was palisaded with head-high stakes, through
hich smaller branches had been woven to make a strong,
asketlike fence. *But it would never stand up to a ball,* Jan
iought. There was a gate like a sally port, and people tum-
ed out of it now like children pouring out of a school. Round,
g-jawed faces poked close; fingers touched, jabbed, probed.
he muskets, the wheel-lock, his bundle—everything was
igged and explored. They were rough people.

Three old men came toward them; the crowd parted. Old
ands were laid on their chests, just where their hearts were.
he old men talked to each other. When they got to Min-
ierts, they snarled.

"He is afraid," the Queen explained.

"How do they know?"

"They feel the heartbeat."

Kleynties gripped her wrist. "Tell them to start trading."

"No trade until tomorrow."

"I want to get out of this!"

"Not until tomorrow. Nothing until tomorrow, they say."

They were taken to a small building close to the palisade.
he other buildings in the village were much larger, as long

as forty feet long, double-walled of bark, with doors at the ends. Theirs was only half that size, but there was a fir burning in a pit in the middle and there were shelves alon the walls for sleeping, and some of the Maaquas' hides an clothing, as if people had moved out to make room for then *Then maybe they don't mean to kill us,* Jan thought, seein this hospitality. The Queen gave him food that he was almo too weary to eat, although he had not eaten since mornin Kleynties offered his flask. "Drink," Kleynties said stoicall "I haven't got enough to get a whole village drunk, so wh waste a drop on them?"

He fell asleep by the fire, woke to crawl to one of th shelves, and was almost asleep when the Queen bent ove him. "You want a girl?" she said.

"What for?" he said stupidly.

"Lot of girls here. They never saw a white boy before."

But he was already asleep again.

He woke thinking he was at sea. There was the sam dislocation, the same lost sense of balance. When he saw th Queen bending over the firepit, he began to remember: *Ne Netherland...Fort Nassau....* The village.

The Queen, instead of turning to look at him, dropped he head forward and looked at him upside down. "Hungry?"

He nodded. "Where's Kleynties?"

"Trading."

Another body was huddled on a shelf across the hous "Mindaerts?" he whispered. She bobbed her head and he up a finger for quiet. The house was very dark, because ther were no windows; through the smokehole, he could see th it was a gray day. She gave him a wooden bowl of the sam food he had eaten the night before—a mush of squash an something else, a handful of seedy berries.

"Will you stay here now?" he asked her as he ate. The foo was bland and saltless, but he was hungry.

"I go home." She pointed with a piece of firewood: west.

"Will you miss Kleynties?"

She laughed. "He was good to me."

"But will you miss him? Like a wife?" He did not kno the word for love.

The laughter stopped. "He bought me. Now I have boug myself."

He continued to eat. He was no longer frightened, but h felt a great exhilaration, instead, and he got up, still eatin

nd went to the door and back, unable to be still. "Will they
ill us?"

"They want guns too much."

"They can kill us and take the guns."

"They want more guns—next year, the year after. They
re not stupid. They know there are other Netherlanders
ver the salt lake. Why would they kill you and become the
etherlanders' enemies?"

"I saw iron knives on some of them yesterday. Not our
nives, though—I know our knives, Where do they get
em?"

She pointed to the south. "Up from the Suskehannas.
ther white men down there."

"Yes, the English."

He thought about that as he ate the tasteless mush. There
ere the English, down on their strip of coast, and up above
meplace were the French, and here were the Maaquas,
ceiving goods miles and miles away. Paradise must already
e crisscrossed with trading routes. That fact depressed him
little. Did the English have Indian whores? And the
rench? Would they all push paradise back and back, until
went out like a candle or fell off the edge of the world?

A gun went off outside. Jan and the Queen stared and
indaerts sat up, and Jan put down his bowl and grabbed
e wheel-lock and ran to the door, expecting to see Kleynties
ying to hold off the village with an empty weapon. Instead,
ere was Kleynties with a smoking musket in his hands,
inting thirty yards away at a dead dog at the foot of the
alisade. He had shot it for a demonstration.

"He could have shot a log," Jan murmured. "Why did he
ave to kill a dog?"

The Queen's hands were on his shoulders, pulling him
ack against her. He could feel her warmth, her firm belly
ainst his back. "It is only a dog. There are many dogs.
tter a dog than a man." She turned him to face her. "I am
ing home now."

"What about Kleynties?"

"Kleynties and I are done." She touched his face with her
ngertips and slipped out the hide-hung doorway. Her going
ft him suddenly lonely.

He fashioned a new strap for the wheel-lock from a piece
 deerhide, and, with the weapon slung over his right shoul-
r muzzle down, he went out to join Kleynties. There were
ty Maaqua men around him, at least, and almost as many

women. Beyond the crowd, men lounged against trees an
in the lee of the longhouses, and still farther away, a line
women and children were bringing firewood in from th
woods far beyond the wall. It was an active place, more activ
than a Scots or Dutch village—dogs barked, children ran i
and out of the crowd like butterflies darting among flower
old people gossiped.

"Morning, youngster." Kleynties was reloading.

"What's happening?"

"I think I've pulled it out of the fire, boy. Shoot that whee
lock while I load another musket, will you?"

"I won't part with it."

"I know. I only mean to lead them a little by the nos
That's how I'm getting us out of here—by promising the
lots more wonderful guns like that one that are waiting f
them over the ocean."

Jan put a big squash up on a stump and blew it apart, an
the crowd shrieked and pounded their hands on the hard dir
Maaquas made a good audience. What they liked, they love

"How soon do we leave, Kleynties?"

"Tomorrow."

"Tomorrow?"

"Yah. The best I could do. Load for me."

The trading began that afternoon. As the piles of fur
grew, Jan wondered how they would get them all back
Fort Nassau. There were dressed furs and furs made in
robes—beaver, marten, river otter, bear, deerskins with th
hair on and without. Furs were heavy, and even an oaf li
Mindaerts would have trouble making it through the woo
with more than eighty pounds on his back.

"Kleynties, how will we get all this back?"

"I have an arrangement."

"What?"

"Tell you later."

Kleynties had begun with the iron knives and a dozen b
strings of beads. Then he went to the guns. It was hard
tell whether the village had pooled its furs or whether a fe
were doing the bargaining for everybody; at least, there wa
no competitive bidding. The Maaquas had traded before.

There were more furs than Jan had ever seen at one trad
Mindaerts stared glassy-eyed at the piles. Kleynties had bee
right: he was getting better than twice what he had got f
a gun at Fort Nassau. Twenty-five times the Amsterda
value.

After the guns, he traded gunpowder, one pound at a time. Then he traded flints for the snaphaunces, getting two pelts per flint by telling the Maaquas that the flints were magic and not like any flint in their country. After that, lead balls. Then he was down to chunks of lead and four brass molds to make lead balls. Then there was nothing left.

"Want to trade that old wheel-lock, youngster? They're mad to have guns."

"No."

"You can buy a dozen with the furs they'll give you for "

"No. I'll never trade it."

Kleynties and four Maaqua women tied the furs into bun-les for carrying. The Maaqua men giggled and touched their guns. The belly laughter was gone, and now there was the nervous response to magic.

"Who's carrying all them furs?" Mindaerts said.

"They will." Kleynties nodded at the men with the guns. "An escort through the Mahican country."

"Let's go, then."

"No—tomorrow."

"The *Pearl* will sail!"

"Tomorrow is the best I could do, Mindaerts. Just shut your mouth and sleep."

Jan wandered through the village, as separate from the Maaquas as he had ever been from the people of Darkland, that dream place. Yet he was not unhappy here. The exhil-aration of the morning remained, compounded of the aware-ness of danger and the sense of newness, of promise. His skin tickled with it.

A small group of young men and women followed him. Children followed him, too, gaping much more openly than the others at his strangeness—clothes, skin, hair. What was not strange about him? He laughed. *That's what I am—a stranger. I've always been a stranger.*

There were four girls a little older than he, and two husky adolescent boys, almost men. There were dogs following him, too, but the dogs got interested in other dogs and in the doors of the houses and they left him, and their places were taken by more dogs. Jan laughed again when he turned and saw his wild entourage; seeing him laugh, they laughed, too. He stopped and tried to ask for water; one of the girls understood and brought it to him. She smelled of smoke, he found—not at all like the bilge of the *Pearl*. They could all communicate

311

with him, after a fashion, for they shared a few Mahic[
words. When he walked on, they walked closer to him, th
next to him, out of the village and near the place whe
Kleynties was teaching the men to shoot, past the vast cor
fields that surrounded the village, past paths to the dista
woods and the cloud-shrouded hills.

At the western prospect, he stopped. The sun was a whi
eye in the gray clouds near the horizon.

"Onayta?" Jan said, pointing toward the west. It was t
word the Queen had used for her people. "Onayta?"

Yes, yes—yes—

"Other? Other who?"

A jumble of names: *Gwayugwaya, Onundaaka, Sono
tuarana.*

"How far? Far?"

They looked at each other in bewilderment. *Five days?*

"No, no—how far—the west? How far does it go?"

One youth threw out his hand boldly. His words we
unintelligible, but the gesture was expansive, palm dow
the arm swung wide. *Far, far.* He pointed up into the sk
then west again. *Forever.*

It was a breath-taking idea. *The land that goes on foreve*
The boy who had sat cross-legged in the forge in Stirli
would have liked such a land. His eyes met the young Ma
qua's. There was an exchange, even understanding. Mutu
awe. *Forever.*

When he went outside their house into the dark that nig
to urinate, Kleynties slipped out, too, and stood next to hi
The trader pulled down his worn breeches and pretended
go through the motions at the palisade. "We leave at fir
light," he murmured.

Jan was mystified by the behavior. "All right."

"Mindaerts won't be going."

"What? Why? But he's the one who's scared of them!"

"Mindaerts won't be going! Don't ask questions."

They faced each other as they laced their breeches. "Do
he know?"

"You think I'm daft?"

"How will you get him to stay?"

"I've got another flask. He'll be drunk."

"But—why?"

Kleynties gave a lace a vicious tug. "The Maaquas insi
that one man stay with them. That way, they figure, we
come back to them. We're big medicine, boy—magician
312

hey figure they got to keep a magician to bring the magic ack." He wiped his hands on his already dirty doublet. "He'll ven have the honor of leading them on a raid against the Iahicans."

"Mindaerts?"

Kleynties shrugged. Their breaths were making thin visps of steam in the night air. "The French sent a war party gainst them with a couple of whites, and they want to return he favor. Now they've got the medicine. Guns are *big* med- cine. You're medicine."

"Me?"

"Yah, it's something about the wheel-lock. You're the only ne to have a different kind of gun. That makes you medi- ine." Kleynties started back for the house. "Not a word to ur friend, remember."

"But—" Jan hurried to catch up. "Mindaerts won't last the vinter here."

"Maybe not."

"He's too—too *Amsterdammer!*"

"That's his problem. I told you, boy, you don't make money vithout killing somebody. Better Mindaerts than you or me. Anyway, he's a big piece of man; he'll take a lot of killing."

Mindaerts was already wrapped in his blanket. He turned is head, his big cow eyes filled with fear and longing for ome. Jan realized how young Mindaerts was—twenty, per- aps—and he could not look at him.

"Mindaerts, my friend!" Kleynties said cheerily. "Have ome more *aqua vit'* to celebrate our getting out of this hell- ole. No point in carrying it home, hey?"

Jan wrapped himself in his blanket and lay down. The undles of furs, tied for transport, were ranged along the far all. In the shadow, they seemed to make a single shape, a ng, black box—*a dark canoe, a coffin, a low house....*

He slept. It grew cold. The blanket was not enough. He ied to wrap it more warmly; sleeping and half-waking, he noved restlessly on the bench, muttering, dreaming, clutch- g himself in the cold. Mindaerts was in his dreams, begging or his life; then Mindaerts had metamorphosed into Camp- ell and Jan was going through the frightening experience gain of murdering him, calling the man's name, lifting the un—

He tried to pull the blanket tight at his neck and then ınk into anguished dreams again. The young Maaqua with ıe expressive gesture was there, his eyes mysterious and

313

huge, eyes that held a secret and a promise. Then Camp
bell's eyes, wide with the fear of death; Mindaerts, th
Maaqua—

He woke. There was no wind blowing down the smokehole
The fire had gone out and Kleynties and Mindaerts had fin
ished their drinking; their breathing was quiet and deep. Th
house was in half-light and he thought it was dawn; silve
light flowed under the curtain at the doorway. With his blan
ket wrapped around him, he went out, pausing only to slin
the wheel-lock over his shoulder.

In the night, winter had come. The world was white an
silver with snow, and as silent as deafness. He was not cold
only exhilarated as he had been that morning, seeing tha
silent wildness, that chill paradise.

And then there was movement near the palisade. An an
imal was crossing his line of vision. Huge. Antlers like
tree. A white beast—from the snow, he thought. It move
with the slowness and grace of an animal that has no ene
mies. *I could shoot it,* he thought. He thought of the animal
he had shot in the woods near the river, and of those he ha
not shot when killing had had no point. The white beas
passed in front of him and turned its great head to stare a
him with wide, knowing eyes, and then it walked carefull
across the snow to disappear into the village. *Going to th
west.* He knew the direction—knew, too, that the beast woul
go on over the paths through the fields, into the forest, th
shadowed hills. *Forever.*

He tried to follow it but could not find a track, and h
found his way back to the house with difficulty and went in
cold now to the bone, shivering as he lay down again, as h
pulled the blanket close at his neck, trying to get warm.

Kleynties shook him awake. "Not a sound."

It was dark. There was no fire. Silent figures were already
moving the furs outside.

Jan pushed his way through them. It was like the mornin
when they had entered the Mahican country, years ago, i
seemed—shapes emerging from monochrome and fog.
warm breeze blew over his face.

"Where's the snow?"

"Snow! You had too much *aqua vit',* boy."

"But there was snow!"

Kleynties said something to one of the Maaquas. The ma
laughed. "No snow. Lend a hand, boy."

He carried a small bundle of furs to the gate. It would b

314

n onerous weight before they reached the river. There were
x Maaquas already there.

Jan walked down the route the white beast had taken. No
now, no tracks.

But it had happened!

Daylight made the houses distinct now. People were mov-
ng. The smell of newly kindled fires reached him. Somebody
oughed.

"I had—a dream. A strange dream, Kleynties!"

"Tell me on board the *Pearl*. Let's go, boy."

More Maaquas gathered around them. The youth was
here, the one he had dreamed about. Impulsively, Jan said,
Dream," in Mahican. He tapped his chest. "Dream." Interest
uickened in the dark eyes. "Dream," he said again. The
outh repeated a word to people around him and they looked
t Jan with interest. Indians believed in dreams, he knew.
had been a joke at the post that when one of them paid a
upidly high price for something, he had dreamed of it, for
reams were supposed to express the demands of the spirit.

"Animal—white—west...."

Behind him, the Maaquas began to lift their bundles.
leynties stooped and picked one up by its deerhide straps
nd began to put himself into them as if he were putting on
garment. "Get a move on, boy! I'm moving out!"

"I'm not going."

"Holy Mother of Christ, what now!"

"Take Mindaerts."

"Mary's Mother's milk! Are you insane?"

They were standing fifteen feet apart. The Maaquas
atched them. "I got nothing to go back to, Kleynties. What
m I in Amsterdam? Sell my furs for me, send me back the
oney in guns and powder in the spring."

"Jesus, you're bewitched—I hear they got witches here.
his ain't no time to play jokes, boy!"

"Go! Leave me—I *want* to stay, don't you understand me?"

Jan broke and ran to the house and shook the drunken
indaerts awake. Stumbling, shambling, Mindaerts crashed
ut through the doorway and pushed the Maaquas aside in
is haste to get a bundle of furs and be gone. He tossed it on
s back and glared at the village.

"Let's get out of this pesthole!" he bellowed.

Kleynties was whispering with several of the men. They
oked at Jan.

315

"Tell them that I had a dream. Tell them that my dream says I must stay here."

Kleynties talked quickly. The men nodded, still looking at Jan. Seconds later, Kleynties broke away, glanced at the sky, then at the boy. "You damned little fool," he said. That was his farewell.

"Next year!" Jan called after him. The trader's back was already turned to him. Mindaerts was hurrying out the gate at a drunken trot, not even understanding that Jan was staying behind.

"Next year, Kleynties!"

But Kleynties was going through the gate.

The six men with the loads of fur swung out the gate after him along the trail eastward through the fields, going at a trot toward the sunrise and the *Pearl* and what Jan himself should have wanted. He watched them go. And then the trail was empty; those who had followed them trickled back; the dogs fell silent.

An old man stood in front of him. He touched Jan's chest above the heart. "Come," he said in Mahican. "Come tell us your dream."

The young Maaqua was there, and three of the girls from the day before. He had no doubts. He turned back into the village, borne along now on the excitement of a new life.

The wheel-lock carbine hung at his side like a friend, sign from the past that pointed him toward the future.

About the Author

enneth M. Cameron was born in upper New York state,
here he still lives on the farm where he spent his boyhood.
various times, he has been a Naval air intelligence officer,
lightning-rod installer, a university professor, and a play-
right. He writes extensively about the theater and about
hing as well as about guns; since 1973 he has published
x novels, including the highly praised historical comedy,
ur Jo. He is addicted to work, fly-fishing and running, al-
ough not necessarily in that order.

NEW FROM POPULAR LIBRARY

NEW FROM FAWCETT CREST

THRILLS * CHILLS * MYSTERY
from FAWCETT BOOKS

☐	THE GLOW	24333	$2.
	by Brooks Stanwood		
☐	THAT MAN GULL	04637	$1.
	by Anthony Stuart		
☐	THE GREEN RIPPER	14340	$2.
	by John D. MacDonald		
☐	MURDER IN THREE ACTS	03188	$1.
	by Agatha Christie		
☐	NINE O'CLOCK TIDE	04527	$1.
	by Mignon G. Eberhart		
☐	DEAD LOW TIDE	14166	$1.
	by John D. MacDonald		
☐	DEATH OF AN EXPERT WITNESS	04301	$2.
	by P. D. James		
☐	PRELUDE TO TERROR	24034	$2.
	by Helen MacInnes		
☐	AN UNSUITABLE JOB FOR A WOMAN	00297	$2.
	by P. D. James		
☐	FINAL CUT	14372	$1.
	by Max Perry		
☐	FALLING STAR	24347	$1.
	by Lillian O'Donnell		
☐	A CLUTCH OF VIPERS	04632	$1.
	by Jack S. Scott		

Buy them at your local bookstore or use this handy coupon for ordering.

COLUMBIA BOOK SERVICE (a CBS Publications Co.)
32275 Mally Road, P.O. Box FB, Madison Heights, MI 48071

Please send me the books I have checked above. Orders for less than
books must include 75¢ for the first book and 25¢ for each additior
book to cover postage and handling. Orders for 5 books or more posta
is FREE. Send check or money order only.

Cost $_____ Name _____

Sales tax*_____ Address _____

Postage_____ City _____

Total $_____ State _____ Zip _____

* *The government requires us to collect sales tax in all states except A
DE, MT, NH and OR.*

This offer expires 1 December 81